AN OTTER CREEK PRESS
BOOK

PRAISE FOR THE MAGIC BICYCLE

"It brings back all the allure of E.T. Hill creates and nurtures a likable character, young Danny Chase, because he's real . . . .A story to dream with."
—*The Book Reader*

"This book had a good pace and the storyline was never boring. Overall, I liked it, because it dealt with an issue of changing past events or leaving the present as it is. Also, it's about how a new kid can beat the meanest of bully's, while making the best of friends. *The Magic Bicycle* is definitely a thumbs up kinda book and one I would say, 'parents, buy for your kids!'"
—*Mercury Register*

"Readers will identify with Danny, sympathize with his moral dilemma, and enjoy watching him wrestle with the tough choices that come with his magic bicycle powers."
—*Booklist* (American Library Association)

"Danny, 13, and his talking cat travel from Texas through time and space on a magical shape-changing bicycle given to him by an alien that he rescued.His quest is to consult famous thinkers (Socrates, Franklin, Einstein) and others about the wisdom of time travel and changing the past."
—*School Library Journal*

"*The Magic Bicycle* may not be an instant classic, but it is a bit deeper and more thought-provoking than many of the young adult titles being published today."
—Science Fiction SF Site

Invasion of the Shadow Daggers

The parade of footsteps grew louder, calling forth images of a condemned prisoner ascending the steps of an execution tower to be hanged. "Be a cat! And keep quiet!" Danny pushed the alien, Krindee, inside his bedroom closet.

As Danny moved away, a bluish, shimmering glow spilled under the door from inside the closet. The weird light crept toward the bedroom door, threatening to radiate out into the hall.

Murg sat back and watched. "Relax, Danny. Imitate me. Be cool, calm, and collected."

Danny took three deep breaths, then eased open the door.

His father reached for the knob, then stepped back. Captain Chase's black hair lay wildly tousled, giving him a deranged look. Upholstery marks creased and dented his chiseled features. Sleep clung to his dark eyes.

"Danny, this is Colonel Hawker and his associates. They're with a special division of the Air Force."

A pretty, raven-haired woman and a pair of stern men in dark suits, crafted from the fabric of black holes, waited impatiently. A menacing air surrounded the trio, black hawks ready to dive upon unsuspecting prey.

"Shad. . .Black-Ops?" Danny asked, biting his tongue to keep from calling them Shadow Daggers—a term his father used when talking about the Shadow Box Projects and 'cloak and dagger' agents of the U. S. Government. Danny swallowed heavily as his heart sank.

CHASING TIME

THE MAGIC BICYCLE 2

A MYSTERY

by

William Hill

OTTER CREEK PRESS, INC.
FLORIDA

CHASING TIME

BY

William Hill

Copyright © 1999 by William Hill

ISBN: 1-890611-03-4 SC
       1-890611-06-9 HC

Library of Congress Card Number: 98-091705

Retail Price: $14.95 SC
                $22.95 HC

All inquiries should be addressed to:

Otter Creek Press, Inc.
3154 Nautilus Road
Middleburg, FL 32068
1-(904)264-0465 or 1-800-378-8163
e-mail otterpress@aol.com http://www.otterpress.com

Cover Art by Harold Paulsen and Terry Pasquini
First Printing 1999

DEDICATED

To my sister, Lynne, who very early recognized the writer hidden behind the limited vocabulary and poor grammar. Whether she liked the genre or not, she was one of the first to encourage me and edit my fantastic tales.

TITLES BY WILLIAM HILL

Fiction for the Young in Spirit
The Magic Bicycle
The Magic Bicycle 2 -Chasing Time

Young Adult:
The Vampire Hunters

Fiction:
Dawn of the Vampire
Vampire's Kiss
California Ghosting
*Hunting Spirit Bear**
*The Wizard Sword**
*Dragons Counsel**

*forthcoming

NOTE ON BABE RUTH

As with the other historical figures that Danny and Murg encountered on their time travels, the Babe is depicted fictionally. I researched the Big Bambino, just as I did Einstein, Franklin, Wells, Joan of Arc, Shakespeare, Socrates, Plato and Aristotle, attempting to bring them to life as if this story actually occurred. My biggest fear was that someone would say, that's not what they would do or say. That's totally out of character!

Shakespeare rehearsed and performed at The Globe Theatre. Joan of Arc trekked through enemy lines and a dark wintry forest on her way to the King of France. But the Sultan of Swat did not play his first game as a Red Sox at Boston's Fenway Park. The Wizard of Wham played his first game and hit his first home run in Forbes Field in Pittsburgh against the Pirates. As writers often do, I enacted my literary license to alter events—change time—so that the Babe, who is so intricately linked with Red Sox and Yankee lore, played his first game in Fenway against the Yankees. If fate were a writer, history might have unfolded differently.

ACKNOWLEDGEMENTS

Thanks to the following folks who helped me and improved Chasing Time. They edited. They picked. They suggested good improvements: Dub, Kat and Ellen Hill, Lynne and Evan Crankshaw, Jean Augello, Jon Thatcher, Susan Spencer, and Patti Elder.

NOTE TO READERS

Fonts are a complete assortment of type in one size and style. In the coming chapters, we use a few different fonts and styles to enhance your reading pleasure. Here's a guide.

Times: Used as the baseline text.

CAPITALIZATION: FOR YELLING AND LOUDNESS

Italics: To emphasize a word, highlight the title of a book, or a non-word, such as BOOM!

Caslon Open Face: To show mind-to-mind speech, also known as telepathy.

PROLOGUE

Past Failing

"SPIKE! STOP! YOU'RE MAKING A MISTAKE!" Danny yelled. The red-headed youth captained his magic Spacelander bicycle—'Kalyde II'—and two feline companions on a chase through the rainbowed time tunnel.

"Spike can't hear you." From the padded book carrier atop the rear wheel, Danny's calico cat, Murg, projected her thoughts, sending them directly into Danny's mind. "And he doesn't care. He's intent on leaving you far, far behind."

"SPIKE! SPIKE! LISTEN TO ME . . . ." The piercing wail of the winds swept away Danny's words. "I guess you're right," Danny thought back.

Ahead, the huge bully, Spike, also rode a magic bicycle. His monster bike appeared alive, a scuttling black insect with a blue-shelled nose like a cowcatcher. Spike put on a burst of speed, racing farther ahead on the rainbow.

The time tunnel's colors continued to fade, growing worn and ragged. Larger and deeper potholes filled the pathway. Worried eyes peered from the jagged tears lining the tunnel walls. Each hole vented chilling winds that ripped at the riders.

Danny's red Spacelander shuddered, shaking with every rut and bump. Kalyde II struck a chunk of fallen wall, careened airborne, then landed cockeyed. Swerving wildly and hitting more debris, the magic bicycle rattled as if ready to fly apart.

"THE TIME PASSAGE IS GETTING WORSE BY THE MINUTE!" White-knuckled, Danny held on for dear life as the bike's vibrations sapped his strength. His left foot slipped off the pedal. An untied shoelace dangled perilously, threatening to get caught in the chain.

"I have a bad feeling about this." Murg's green eyes bounced as her claws dug deeper into the padded carrier.

"If it's the last thing I do, we're going to get back the star metal he stole." Danny focused on the rear tire of the monster bike and visualized pulling the bikes together, wheel to wheel, steel irresistibly drawn to a magnet.

Glancing over his shoulder, Spike saw him coming closer. "YOU'RE NEVER GETTING THIS BACK!" Below a protruding brow, his expression was grim, close-set eyes narrowed with determination.

"SPIKE THIS IS WRONG! THE STAR METAL WON'T SOLVE YOUR PROBLEMS!" Danny yelled over the howling winds.

"WRONG, CHUMP! SOON, I'll BE RICH! RICH AND FAMOUS!" Spike's monster bike hit a chuckhole. The strap on his backpack slipped. A baseball tumbled out, bouncing away.

As Danny steered closer, drafting Spike's bike, the winds lessened. The monster bike's rear wheel suddenly met Kalyde II's front wheel. Rubber melting to rubber and spokes merging, the two tires became one, creating a strange, three-wheeled tandem.

"GOT HIM! If at first you don't succeed . . . ."

"Danny, we've tried this before. Think of something else!"

Spike suddenly whirled, swinging a baseball bat. The blow drove apart the magic bicycles. The Spacelander swerved sideways, hit a rainbow rut, then skidded out of control across the tattered time bridge, sliding toward a tear in the wall.

"Look out!" Murg began.

Like a giant, jagged mouth, a dark breach swallowed the magic bicycle. Kalyde II, Danny and his feline companions fell head over wheels, spinning into a bottomless darkness.

ONE

The Headbangers And Starborn Visitors

With the wind tugging at his baseball cap, fourteen-year-old Danny Chase smiled over his shoulder. "Gretchen! Imagine us on the beach!"

"I can see us there already!" Her blue eyes sparkling, Gretchen laughed delightfully. Her ponytail streamed behind her like a trailing halo. "I love riding Kalyde II!"

The magic tandem, named after an alien, streaked ahead, a bright crimson blur rocketing down the alpine road. Along the hilly route, the center line blinked. Telephone poles appeared to shrink into the tall posts of a long brown fence.

A loud caterwaul sounded from Danny's left. Racing neck and neck with them, Murg, the calico cat, his sister Sarah, and star-born friend Kah-laye-dee rode the other magic bicycle. The second gift from "Kalyde" was sky blue with white trimmings.

"We're going to win!" Sarah's brown eyes narrowed. Billowing in the wind, her hair fluttered like a red-gold cape, streaming toward the alien sitting in the back seat.

"You work too hard, friend Daw-nee." Kah-laye-dee sat relaxed with his saucer-like eyes almost closed. His hands were tucked behind his overly large head and below his wind-slicked blue mohawk. With his shirt off, the skinny Cor-ror-o'lan seemed to be cast from living metal.

On a padded book carrier atop the rear wheel, the calico cat leaned around the shiny alien. The winds rushed through her Halloween-colored fur. With her eyes closed, Murg seemed nonchalantly excited and indulgently satisfied.

A school of rainbow butterflies seemed to abruptly surround the racers, colors swirling along in their wake. Then the air quaked and thundered mightily. With a brilliant flash of white light and the roar of a thousand lions charging, the bicycles and their riders disappeared.

When the wind returned, the cyclists blew through the thick clouds and onto the rainbow bridge. Wheel to wheel, the tandems raced up the dazzling skyway, never more than an inch in front or behind the other. They crested the peak, then plummeted down the rainbow's arc, heading for the white sun below. Still tied tire to tire, the tandems sped through the gate of light.

Sand sprayed as the racers appeared on a beach. Just ahead waited a gray and white house sitting atop stilts. Standing at the base of the steps, Danny's mom and dad waved at them.

Something hit Danny on the shoulder. He sure missed Mom and Sarah. Had they only died six months ago? It seemed like just last week. The hole in his heart still ached, though less agonizingly; at least now Danny didn't feel like he wanted to curl up and die.

Again, something tapped Danny on the shoulder. He glanced to his left.

Jason held a bicycle pump in his hand. "I said, are you having fun?" The very tall boy was Danny's riding buddy and friend, a cyclist hopeful who dressed the part in a yellow jersey and black lycra pants. His helmet mimicked the color of a canary with wings stretched back by the wind. "You zoned out, Mister Speed-demon."

"I was daydreaming," Danny replied.

"Stop the presses. Call a news conference," Murg mentally projected. With all four feet tucked underneath her and eyes closed, the calico rested atop the rear fender on a thickly padded book carrier. "Danny Chase is daydreaming." The calico could speak while in contact with the bicycle; but when others were around, the boy and his sister's cat spoke telepathically—mind to mind.

"That must have been some dream!" Jason laughed. "You were flying! I can barely keep up with you! I'm afraid if I fall behind, I'll never catch up! How can you ride so fast in blue jeans?"

Danny looked around. The pastures along the farm road blurred green, one field blending with the next. He'd let his imagination run away; now the magic bicycle raced just as fast. As they climbed a hill, Danny relaxed; the pair of riders slowed. The world settled into its rightful pace.

"Sweet!" Jason cried. "We were flying! We're ready for the Tour de France!"

"Uh . . . yeah! Quite a tailwind!"

"Without a cloud in the sky."

"This is Texas, remember? Wait a minute and the weather will change." Danny hid his relief. His best friend didn't appear suspicious, never dreaming that Danny rode a magic bicycle powered by his imagination. He found it interesting that Kalyde II could affect another bicycle. What else could Kalyde II do?

"Humans often use accidents instead of planning ahead to discover something." Murg's eyes remained closed as she spoke mind-to-mind. "Too bad you can't take Jason flying."

"Riding fog, you mean. We haven't learn to fly, YET. I hate not being able to share the magic bicycle with Christina and Jason. I wish I could, but . . . ." He sighed. "I told Gretchen and look what happened. Our dads told the U.S. government, and they seized it. If I hadn't changed time . . . . who knows, I might have lost Kalyde II forever." Danny shuddered. "I'm not sure I can ever trust anybody again with our secret."

"Have faith in the people who care for you. They . . . . Hey, I believe I smell company. Odd, this feels very, very familiar."

"*There they are!*" came the cry over a barrage of heavy, pounding metal music.

"IT'S THE HEADBANGERS!" Jason cried. As he and Danny topped the hill, four boys mounted on dirt bikes roared from a copse of trees. Square-faced Spike led the pack, guiding his smoking mini-motorcycle through a hole in the fence. Once clear, each boy put on a black-coughing burst of speed, then ramped onto the road. With a squeal of burning rubber and the thrashing of guitars, the Headbangers raced after Danny and his friend.

"HAUL, MAN!" Jason stood on his pedals, running on the bicycle, driving it faster and faster as though sprinting toward the finish line. Danny joined him, slowly pulling ahead as he urged Kalyde II faster.

Even on old, smoking dirt bikes, the Headbangers gained quickly. The music grew deafening.

Danny looked left and right. Beyond the fences, flat ranch pastures scattered with bushes and large trees provided some shade but no place to hide.

"You know, I have feelings of deja vu. Drier this time. That's nice." Murg cracked open a green eye.

"You are so funny," Danny muttered.

"Except this time you have a friend with you . . . and you're riding a magic bicycle. You can outrace anything you can imagine."

"I can, but Jason can't," Danny replied.

"A difficult choice."

"*HA! HA!* CHASE!" Spike cried over a screaming guitar solo. The large, heavy-set brute appeared to dwarf the small dirt bike, his knees bowed awkwardly wide. Below a protruding brow, his close-set eyes glowed feverishly dark. "This time, you're finally going to get what you deserve!" Spike waved a bat, then spat, sending a green stream squirting. "Right, Reggie?"

Reggie looked gangly with a sickly pallor and deep-set eyes. The pale boy gunned his motorbike. As Reggie surged closer, he brandished a chipped and chewed Louisville Slugger.

"Danny, I'm riding as fast as I can." Jason struggled to keep pace.

I'm not, Danny thought, but he couldn't use the bicycle's full power. He'd either reveal his secret or leave his friend in the dust. Danny refused to desert Jason; but at this speed, they'd never escape their tormentors. All too well Danny recalled being sat upon, punched and having his face ground into the dirt.

"What are you going to do, Danny?" Still appearing relaxed, the calico perused the thugs. "You know, I count at least five tattoos. Why would anyone want a snake on their neck? Is that guy's hair really that color?" Murg nodded to a ape-jawed boy with bright orange hair. "And why wear jewelry? Don't they like the way they look? I abhor wearing a collar."

Danny growled. "I could use some help here. An idea maybe?"

"If cats, like me, gave reasonably intelligent people, like you, answers all the time, they might think cats were smart and you'd stop feeding us and cleaning our litter boxes. Feline civilization would be absolutely ruined. You don't want that to happen, do you?"

The motorbikes and music roared deafeningly. Jason, Danny and Murg found themselves suddenly surrounded by angry boys wielding bats. The orange-haired boy with several pieces of jewelry sticking from his face swung at Jason. He ducked and swerved, running into one of the motorbikes. Sparks flew. Reggie gassed his bike, crowding Jason.

"Headbangers, bang some heads!" Spike swung his bat. Danny dodged the blow.

A blur with claws, Murg slashed, then she rested as if she'd never moved.

"*YEOW!*" Spike cried. He dropped back, cursing the cat.

"I wish Jason rode a magic bicycle, too." Danny could feel Murg's stare bore into his back. "Wait! Don't say anything. I don't need to be hit by a truck."

"Oh no, a hill!" Jason cried.

"Come on, Jason, we can do it! Just like before!" Danny quit working so hard and relaxed. He imagined a magical link connecting the two bicycles, a cannonballing locomotive hauling a caboose. The wind parted, swirling around to catch them from behind in a mighty tail wind.

"Where'd this headwind come from?!" Reggie squawked. "It's slowing us down, but . . . .but not them! I don't believe this!"

"Chase, come back here and face me like a man!" Spike's voice and the discordant music grew weaker and more distant. "This is impossible . . . . Stupid bike!"

Murg turned away from the motorbikes, flicking her tail as if dismissing them. "Well done, my friend. You saved yourself and Jason without giving away our secret. Good thinking."

"Wow-whee!" Jason cried. "We're smokin' them! I love a good swirling Texas wind!"

Danny smiled broadly. Riding the magic bicycle was a blast! "Yee-haw! Thank the winds! They can't catch us!"

The road felt perfectly smooth and nearly flat as they sprinted uphill, the wind hurling them ahead ever faster. Cows and horses seemed to appear and disappear as though images flashed on a screen. Fence posts ran together, a long ladder running east and west.

"Yee-haw!" Jason cried. "We're ready for anybody or anything man! Yeah! We are the Speed-demons! Sounds like a great promotion for a pair of blazing riders!"

"Yee . . . ." Danny began, then stopped in mid cheer. Off to his right, he thought he saw a flash of green—some kind of bright balloon—but it was gone now. Danny shivered. It gave him chills. "Murg, did you . . . ."

"DAW-NEE CHEZ, COME HOME."

Danny straightened. "Kalyde? Murg! Did you hear that?!" Could Kah-laye-dee have returned?!

"Hear what?" Murg asked.

"Nothing. You probably didn't see anything either," Danny replied, dropping from exhilaration to depression. He was just hearing what he wanted to hear—that Kah-laye-dee had returned to Earth.

When they stopped at a traffic light before splitting to go their separate ways home, Danny said, "Jason, I don't understand. Why doesn't Spike give it a rest?"

"Spike doesn't like me because I'm black, and worse, probably because I like you. You're kinda short, freckled and red-headed. Go figure." When the light changed, Jason turned left onto Ranchero Road, heading home. "See you tomorrow!"

"BYE!"

"Murg, where would I be without the magic bicycle? It allows me to escape, go anywhere I want to go. I should have called it 'Freedom'."

"Give yourself some credit, Danny. Your imagination helped you elude Spike and his gang of uncouth youths."

"With a little bit of feline advice," Danny replied.

"Where would man be without us? It's a wonder we are not referred to as man's best friend."

"You don't hunt."

"I bring you birds," the calico disagreed.

"Or fetch."

"Exercise is necessary for a sound mind and a healthy body. Do your own fetching."

They pulled off the road and walked into the trees. Danny looked around, checking for witnesses. "Is it safe?" Danny whispered.

Murg listened as she smelled the breeze, then nodded.

"Good." Danny unlocked his old bicycle from an oak. The bike looked exactly like Kalyde II but wasn't magical. This was his original, everyday ordinary ten-speed two-wheeler, red with black trim and handgrips.

With his hands still on Kalyde II, Danny pictured the magic bicycle shrinking, transforming into a wristwatch. A flash of light washed over him and a squeaking noise, as if something were being crushed, made his ears twitch. When Danny opened his eyes, he held a watch identical to the one he wore. He put that one in his pocket, then attached Kalyde II to his wrist. "I wish I could silence the noise when it changes shape."

"Keep working at it. I think you're smarter about this in your old age, now that you're fourteen." By wearing the magic watch, Danny could still hear Murg's words in his head.

"Yeah, that's me. Fourteen going on forty. I just don't want Kalyde II stolen again."

"DAW-NEE CHEZ COME HOME."

"What was that?" Murg asked, ears perked.

"I told you I heard something! Kalyde's back!" Danny cried. He raced home, skidding to a stop in the garage.

"Don't barge in. Breathe."

After several deep breaths, Danny walked into the house. His dad slept on the couch. A college bowl game played on the TV screen.

Danny snuck upstairs, then rushed into his bedroom. "Kalyde!" he tried to whisper.

Something grabbed him from behind, covering his mouth and eyes. "Surprise!" a voice whispered in his mind. "Keep quiet, we do not wish to awaken your dad. To make a scene, I think is the correct colloquialism."

"I'll be quiet," Danny whispered. He removed the silvery hand; it only had four fingers. "Kalyde?" Even before he turned around, Danny knew the answer.

"No, not Kalyde," a female Cor-ror-o'lan told him. With large lavender eyes the size of saucers, the alien stood a little taller than Danny. Her skin appeared flawless and silvery white, the color of a full moon's splendor. Her magenta hair was similar to half a mohawk but cut sideways, stretching from ear to ear and falling just past her shoulders.

"I hope you're not disappointed. I am Kri-neee-dee. Kah-laye-dee's older sister."

Danny quietly closed the door. "I swear I haven't been traveling time. I've been good! Very good. And I've been very, very careful. Nobody but Gretchen and Murg here know about the magic bicycle."

At first, Kri-neee-dee appeared confused, then a look of understanding dawned across her alien face. "Be calm, Danny Chase. I have not come to take the Xenozilit from you. The star metal bicycle is a gift from Kah-laye-dee to you."

"Then why are you here? Is something wrong with Kalyde?" Danny asked.

"No, certainly not. You worry too much. Why is that?" she asked Murg.

"Time doesn't heal all wounds," Murg replied. "It just dulls the edge."

"Oh. I thought 'Time heals all wounds' was the Terran quote."

"That's a quaint saying, not a quote," Murg replied. "Why are you here?"

"I wish to stay with Danny for a while. Danny, the Corror-o'lan Elders thought it would be wise to learn more about your species, especially since there is some debate and confusion over the value of Terrans."

"No surprise there," Murg agreed.

"Will you help me, Danny? Help us understand you better? Kah-laye-dee said you'd understand. This is very important. I believe a famous human, a United States President named John F. Kennedy said, 'Ask not what your country can do for you, ask what you can do for your country.' In the galactic scheme of things, your country is your world."

Danny stammered, tongue-tied. He was supposed to help them understand people? He didn't even understand people. He wasn't even sure he understood himself some days.

"Danny Chase as a representative of the human race?" Murg mused. "Well, there's an old human saying that no good deed goes unpunished."

TWO

Alien Mission

Danny plopped heavily onto his bed. "You want to stay with me to learn about people?"

"Exactly," Kri-neee-dee replied. "Terrans. Earthlings. Humans."

"As he's getting older," Murg cleaned her tail, "he can occasionally grasp the obvious."

"Kri-neee-dee, instead of using telepathy, can you whisper?" Danny asked. "My head hurts."

"Certainly," Kri-neee-dee whispered. "Kalyde said that you had an unusually vivid imagination that might help me with my mission."

"I wish he could have come along with you," Danny said wistfully.

"The Council of Elders thought him too young for such a mission."

"Kalyde did fine last time."

"Yes, he did; but he had help—your help. Believe me, Kah-laye-dee wanted to be here, but in Terran years, he is barely ten. I have first-contacted races many times. Our ship is one of exploration. My parents are biologists. We discovered Earth quite by accident. Your world is in a remote portion of the galaxy. Reports claimed no intelligent life exists in this sector."

"I'll hold my tongue, since the statement is so obvious that it must be true." Murg yawned.

"Well, due to the attack on our ship by your world's governments," Kri-neee-dee continued, "Cor-ror-o'lans are wary. Can we trust humans? Do you believe in the sanctity of life? Or are you warlike?" She pointed to the superheroes and scenes of fighting depicted upon the comic and fantasy posters lining Danny's wall. "Well, after the attack, of course, many believe the latter."

"But since you befriended Kah-laye-dee, some Cor-ror-o'lans think otherwise. Now some believe your race might have potential. Morals. Ethics. Belief in Life and Light. Your Ralph Waldo Emerson said 'The true test of civilization is not the census, not the size of cities, but the kind of man that the country turns out'. In other words, character is important."

"You have been studying, haven't you?" Murg asked.

Kri-neee-dee nodded. "Yes, I have been cerebral-studying Earth day and night for months. Learning its history through books, newspapers and television."

"What was your favorite show?" Danny asked.

"*My Favorite Martian*," Kri-neee-dee replied with a smile. "As Martin did, I wish to live among you. Meet other Terrans."

"You may be disappointed in humans as a whole, but Danny shows potential." Murg stretched and eased toward a sunbeam.

"What if you *are* disappointed in us?" Danny asked.

"It will affect future contact, if any. I am not the only scout. So we aren't . . ." she grew thoughtful, "putting all our eggs in one basket, as the locals would say. Is that right? Excuse me, are you all right, Danny?"

With his head in his hands, Danny leaned back. "I'm just a little . . . overwhelmed. I'd love to help . . . but what if you get caught? Kah-laye-dee was nearly captured. How would I hide you here?" Danny flashed back, vividly recalling his father and the government agents seizing his bicycle. What if it happened again?! He didn't want anything to happen to his bicycle. Kalyde II was freedom. With it, he could go anywhere! Do anything!

"Easy. Breathe easily and deeply. Pretend you're lying in a sunbeam." Murg rolled onto her back, feet curled askew in the air.

"But Dad might find out!" Danny glanced at the door, expecting it to suddenly fly open. "Kri-neee-dee, I'd loved to help . . . ."

"Call me Krindee."

". . . but if my dad finds out . . . ." Danny glanced toward the door. Did he hear footsteps? He suddenly felt watched.

"How will you disguise yourself?"

"An old trick but tried and true." Krindee smiled at Murg. "I will take the guise of a cat. They have unusual personalities, making it easy to blend in."

"Easy to be a cat. Easy to blend in." Murg's tail snapped this way and that.

Krindee raised her arms. When her hands shone bright blue, she slowly lowered them along her body. The azure light caused the Cor-ror-o'lan to shimmer and ripple. With a surprising abruptness, her form collapsed upon itself, gathering into a smaller figure.

Her nose became pugged. Her ears rose to her forehead, growing devil-like. Fur sprang from her skin to cover her from head to twitching tail. The black and tan Siamese cat's eyes were much smaller and more slanted than Krindee's own, but still purple as though carved from amethyst.

"You look like a cat all right. This should be easy." Danny snuck a glance at Murg. "All cats do is lounge around."

"I beg your pardon. Felines do more than 'lounge'. Our work is extraordinarily important. We are just exceptionally efficient. Krindee, there's more to being a cat than just looking like one. There is an air to cultivate, especially if you wish to portray a Siamese. You must adopt an attitude that you are the best of all The Creator's creatures. Why would anyone wish to be anything else?"

Krindee's eyes slanted more as her smile widened.

"Danny, I don't think your dad would ever realize Krindee wasn't a cat, unless she acted oddly, say like a canine."

"You mean obeying me sometimes?"

"Exactly. Sitting. Fetching. Rolling over. That sort of obey. Frankly, I prefer having options and making choices."

"Murg, I shall need help. Will you be my mentor?" Krindee asked. "This way I can learn about people and cats. To tell the truth, I know less about felines and their history than Terrans. Suzy Becker of your world claimed, 'All I need to know I learned from my cat'."

"A brilliant woman and kindred spirit," Murg replied. "I would be honored to help."

"Eventually, I'd like to appear human."

"Who would you be?" Danny asked.

"Your cousin from somewhere foreign." Krindee waved blue-glowing paws about her Siamese body. Her wavering cat form enlarged, her hair receding before she filled out into a girl. Her features shifted as though made of wax, leaving her very beautiful.

Krindee now stood taller than Danny. Instead of a sideways magenta mohawk, her long red-blond locks splayed across her shoulders. The Cor-ror-o'lans eyes still shone the deepest royal purple; when the light caught them, they sparkled as gemstones.

"How's this?" Krindee wore jeans and a Dallas Cowboys jersey.

"Ok." Danny was thoughtful. "You look familiar."

Murg slightly cracked open a green eye. "In many ways she looks a lot like Christina," Murg told him. "Well, Sarah and Christina combined."

"I pulled the images from your mind," Krindee told Danny.

"Reading another's mind without permission is impolite." Murg suddenly pawed at something invisible in the sunbeam.

"My apologies." Krindee clasped both hands to her chest and bowed slightly. "On Cor-ror-o'lan our hearts and minds are open to each other. Secrets are rare, and trust is commonplace."

"That's okay," Danny replied. "I see Sarah in Gretchen and sometimes Christina. That helps keep her alive in my thoughts."

"I also modeled myself a little after France's Joan of Arc. I was most impressed with her. She accomplished much by the time she was eighteen. Her faith and spirituality held steadfast and positively influenced many others." Krindee noticed Murg's expression. "Is there something wrong with this form?"

"People of both sexes react to you differently based on your appearance." Murg intently watched the descent of golden dust in the sunbeam. "Your beauty will attract attention."

"Then should I be ugly?"

"Either extreme calls attention. Although in truth, it does not matter. We are all but motes of dust, like these in this sunbeam, similar of make and drifting through the universe. "

"Your John Davies said, 'Beauty is but skin deep'."

"But ugly goes right to the bone," Danny replied before he could stop himself.

Murg appeared nonplused, as usual. "Margaret Wolfe Hungerford was credited for writing, 'Beauty is in the eye of the beholder.' That seems more appropriate to me."

"How do you know that?" Danny asked.

"Two cats lived with her."

"I think it would be wise if I posed as a foreigner," Krindee said. "That way, if I act awkwardly, it would not seem so strange. *Comment allez-vous?* That's 'How are you?' in French."

"That will work better," Danny said. "But I'm still not sure."

"This is supremely important," Krindee told him. "Our experiences could be the building blocks of a wonderful and fruitful relationship between my race and yours, Cor-ror-o'lan and Terran. Judgment is pending. You can prove one person makes a difference. Two can make even more. Before Kalyde met you, our initial impression of you was . . . unflattering?"

"Abysmal."

"You sound like you're an alien in disguise," Danny told Murg.

"Who told you?! Maybe he can make a leap beyond the obvious."

Danny rolled his eyes. "Are all cats aliens?"

"Certainly."

"Danny, please help me understand your people. Reading Terran history is enough to scare anyone. All those wars and killing. Voltaire said, 'It is forbidden to kill, therefore all murders are punished unless they kill in large number and to the sound of trumpets'."

"Do you have a quote for everything?" Danny asked. "And who is Voltaire?"

"A French poet and dramatist."

"This could be so cool!" Danny whispered. "There's so much I can show you. I have good friends, so you'll see that . . . that others have potential, too. I really hate keeping secrets; but I owe Kalyde for so much—healing me, giving me the magic bicycle and being my friend. What do you think, Murg? It sounds important."

"It's your choice. You live with the consequences."

"I know."

"Then so long as we're smart about this, it sounds like a good idea. I suspect Krindee will regret this, though; but it's her decision, too. Krindee, I would be honored to teach you about cats. And frankly, I have a plethora of advice about Terrans."

"Thank you! Thank you!" Krindee hugged Danny, then scooped up Murg, who acted indignant. "Shakespeare said, 'Be not afraid of greatness: some are born great, some achieve greatness and some have greatness thrust upon them'."

"Danny, you've just been thrust," Murg thought wryly. "Again."

"Danny!" came his dad's call from downstairs. "Danny! Are you up there?"

"Yes, Dad!" Danny called back.

"There are important people here to see you," his dad called.

"Quick, hide!" Danny whispered as he directed Krindee toward the closet.

"No need to be formal, Captain Chase," a deep-voiced man said. Danny cringed. "We'll go see your son." Hard footsteps, heavy, brisk and measured, ascended the stairs.

THREE

The Shadow Daggers

The parade of footsteps grew louder, calling forth images of a prisoner ascending the steps to be hanged. "Be a cat! And keep quiet!" Danny pushed Krindee inside his closet.

As Danny moved away, a bluish glow spilled under the door. The shimmering light crept toward the bedroom door, threatening to radiate out into the hall. Hoping nobody would see it, Danny tried to block the light.

Murg sat back and watched. "Relax, Danny. Imitate me. Be cool, calm, and collected."

Danny took a deep breath, then opened the door.

His father was reaching for the knob, stopped, then stepped back. Captain Chase's black hair lay wildly tousled, giving him a deranged look. Upholstery marks creased and pockmarked his chiseled features. Sleep still clung to his dark eyes. "Danny, this is Colonel Hawker and his associates. They're with a special division of the Air Force."

A pretty raven-haired woman and a pair of stern men in dark suits crafted from the fabric of black holes waited impatiently. A menacing air surrounded the trio, blackhawks ready to dive upon unsuspecting prey.

"Shad . . . Black-Ops?" Danny asked, biting his tongue before calling them Shadow Daggers—a term his father used when talking about the Shadow Box Projects and 'cloak and dagger' agents of the US government. Danny swallowed heavily, and his heart sank.

"Your son is astute," the woman said, her dark eyes scrutinizing Danny. "Hi, Danny, I am Major Amelia Torque."

"As you know, Major Torque, Danny's met some of your people before," Captain Chase replied. "Is something wrong, son?" His sleepy look gave way to a dark gaze.

"Heck no! Why would you think that?" Danny asked breathlessly.

"Because I know you. You're my son, unless you've switched with an alien again," his father replied.

The tall, dark woman studied her watch. After a moment, Major Torque shook her head. Her look spoke volumes to the broad-shouldered man with immaculately combed gray hair. His granite eyes and inscrutable face matched her stony expression. The stocky black man stared at Danny as if trying to see through a disguise.

"What's wrong, son?" his father asked.

Danny imagined he looked guilty. Secrets seemed to leap from him as though rats abandoning a sinking ship. "Murg, am I broadcasting my guilt?"

"Body language, telepathy, or empathy," Murg replied as she jumped onto the bed. She sauntered across the spread, then leaned against an open box. "Any and all give you away. Now, quiet with the telepathy."

Danny stepped back and motioned to the closet. "You caught me, Dad. I have an alien hiding in my closet, disguised as a cat."

Danny's father stiffly put his hands on his hips. "Danny, that isn't very funny. These people are here on serious business."

"Then you wouldn't believe the aliens left a time machine in the garage?"

"Your son has quite an imagination," the gray-haired man said. His gaze flicked about the room, taking in the crowded bookshelves and the superhero and dragon posters. "Danny, do you mind if we ask you some questions?" Colonel Hawker asked.

"I guess not," Danny said, moving toward the bed. "I'm not going to get in trouble twice for the same thing, am I?"

His father shook his head. "Just answer their questions truthfully, as always."

"That's what got me in trouble last time," Danny thought. *"Whoever said the truth never hurt anybody was a moron."*

"Danny, we'd like you to recount the night you met the alien, Kah-laye-dee," Colonel Hawker said, his eyes not asking but demanding.

"But you know that story," Danny replied. "They even taped it."

"We'd like to hear it again, please," Major Torque said. The nameless man studied the shelves of knickknacks, books and comics. He stopped in front of a movie poster for *The Time Machine.*

As Danny retold his tale, he kept his guard up and an eye on the nameless man. Danny began with being chased by Rocky, Hank and Spike. His recollection of the crash was a bit fuzzy; but his memory of the haunted mansion remained vivid. Colonel Hawker's and the woman's interest heightened when he mentioned the light that drew him to the basement. After falling down the steps, he'd confronted a double of himself. The friendly Cor-ror-o'lan healed him, then they'd exchanged stories.

Again, Danny left out the part about exchanging memories. If they knew, they'd poke and prod him, and he'd never get to go riding again. That would be like being caged. Even worse, they might discover something harmful to the Cor-ror-o'lans.

Was it his imagination, or did the stern woman notice something? Major Torque pretended to be friendly, but Danny knew it was an act to get him to speak freely. The nameless man moved nearer the closet.

Danny glanced away. Despite his fears, he kept talking without missing a beat, recounting Kalyde's flight from the basement. Since he wore Danny Chase's face, the agents had been fooled. Danny didn't mention being able to see through Kalyde's eyes. He finished with hiding in the basement from the searching agents, then getting picked up while walking home.

"How many different shapes do you think these aliens, the Cor-ror-o'lan, can assume?" Major Torque asked pleasantly. "Could they become animals or plants?"

"I don't see why not," Danny replied. "Heck, one could be my desk over there. If so, he should be helping me with my homework. I'll bet they don't have a problem with algebra."

The woman smiled. The wandering agent stopped at the closet to check his watch. A furrow cut his brow as he checked it again, then tapped it.

"Why are you questioning me again? Have they returned?" Danny asked.

"Let's say there's been a lot of falling stars the last few nights," Colonel Hawker replied. "Would you like to see these aliens again?"

"Sure. Kalyde was a lot like me and friendly," Danny replied, then tempered his enthusiasm. "Except I promised my dad that if I saw Kah-laye-dee again, I'd report him."

Fortunately, Danny thought, he wasn't hiding Kah-laye-dee. And he hadn't promised *when* he'd report him. Danny hated twisting promises—essentially lying; but this was so important! The government handled this all wrong!

The Cor-ror-o'lan Elders trusted him; but then so did his father. Dad expected him to keep his word. What should he do? His decision might affect how human and extra-terrestrials interacted. What would his Mom have done? He knew. She would have sheltered Krindee.

"And you keep your promises?" Major Torque asked.

Danny nodded. "Don't you keep yours?"

"Of course. Is there anything you've remembered but didn't tell us before?" Major Torque asked.

Danny thought, nervously trying not to look at the unnamed agent. "Uh . . . Yeah. I think." The man at the closet paused. Major Torque leaned closer. "Durlens."

"Durlens? What are they?"

"I don't remember much except that they're also shapechangers and enemies of the Cor-ror-o'lans," Danny continued, making it up.

"What do they look like?" Colonel Hawker asked.

"I don't know. Kalyde never said. He was afraid some of you might actually be Durlens in disguise," Danny replied. That should keep them thinking. Major Torque and Colonel Hawker exchanged meaningful glances.

Not watching the roving agent was difficult. The nameless man pulled open the closet door. Danny held his breath, hoping the doorbell would ring or lightning would strike the house.

A loud crash sounded from the far side of the bed. Danny whirled around, finding his box on the floor, the contents scattered. Murg walked away saucily, tail flicking as if a disclaimer of blame.

"Oh no!" Danny jumped across the bed.

"What's wrong son?" his father asked.

Danny picked up a shattered frame. "My picture of Sarah and Mom at Hoover Dam. It's ruined!" Danny grabbed a pillow and threw it at Murg, who nimbly dodged out of the room. Danny tried to hold back his tears but failed.

"I'm sorry . . . ." Captain Chase began.

"It's all right," Major Torque replied. "We know what happened. We apologize for stirring up unpleasant memories."

Looking puzzled, the nameless agent stepped from the closet. A look passed between the agent and Colonel Hawker, who finally motioned for them to depart. They left in silence.

Danny's father hugged his son, then took the frame from

his hand. "Danny, we'll find the negative and have another one made."

"What if we can't?!"

"Then we'll have this one repaired. Danny, is this what's wrong?" Captain Chase asked, holding the shattered frame. Danny nodded. "Danny, I miss Sarah and your mother, too, very, very much. If you want . . . ."

"I don't want to see the doctor on base. He doesn't believe me and keeps asking about aliens."

"Then let's talk. How . . . how are you holding up?"

"Better than two months ago. Writing and riding help some. And not being the new kid anymore helps, too. So does having good friends like Murg, Jason, and Christina."

"We need friends and each other," his dad replied. "Are you still talking with Murg?"

"We don't need to talk. We can project our words into each others minds. It's called telepathy."

"I see. You and your imagination."

"How are you holding up?" Danny asked, wiping away a tear and looking his father directly in the eye.

"Like you, better than two months ago."

"Does seeing Ms. Mayfair help?" Danny asked, surprised by his own question.

His father looked startled. "Sometimes yes and sometimes no. When she does something that reminds me of your mother, it makes me both happy and sad. She's a kind and gentle person, very caring, much like your mother. I enjoy her company. I think you would, too, if you'd give her half a chance."

Danny stood quietly for a long time.

"Speaking of Andie, she left a surprise for you. It's downstairs, do you want to see it?" his father asked. "I promise you'll love it. If you don't love it, you can send it back."

"Well, okay." Danny climbed to his feet.

"Follow me," Captain Chase said, heading for the door. "Aliens! I can't believe my son's associated with aliens! They're still talking about it at the base. My son, the ET sympathizer. The teenager who fooled the Shadow Daggers."

"Dad, how come they assume aliens are here to do us harm?" Danny asked.

"Son, we've talked about this before. People fear the unknown. Life's always changing; but people prefer stability to the unknown."

Danny wondered where Krindee was hiding? Was she still in the closet? Or had she slipped out? And where was Murg? She'd intentionally turned over that box. It was a good idea, but the picture . . . .

When they reached the laundry room, they found Murg sniffing the door. "I don't like the smell of this."

"Surprise!" His father opened the door with a sweeping motion.

Danny stepped inside. A large box with an open top sat in front of the washer and dryer. From within came the ticking of a clock and the whining of something small and frightened.

"OH NO!" Murg cried. "ANYTHING BUT THAT!"

FOUR

Micro Spies

Danny peered into the cardboard box. The tiny creature was coal-black except for a white-gold star running between his golden eyes and along his nose. "A puppy! Cool!"

"Definitely not cool. My sanctum has now been thoroughly violated!" Though her face held feline aloofness, Murg's green eyes bulged.

Danny scooped up the puppy and hugged him. A pink tongue shot out, licking Danny. He laughed. "He looks like a retriever. What's his name? Where'd he come from? How old is he? Is he really mine?"

Captain Chase laughed. "One question at a time! Yes, he's really yours. Andie's neighbor's dog had puppies. He's six weeks young. When he grows big enough, he'll be able to run alongside you when you're out riding. He'll be a true companion instead of baggage like Murg."

Murg stared at Captain Chase, then blinked unevenly with slow annoyance. "Dignity prevents me from responding to an opinion voiced in total ignorance."

"And he doesn't have a name," Danny's father continued. "You can name him whatever you like, as long as it isn't Murg Jr." The calico appeared prissy. Captain Chase laughed. "You know, sometimes I'd swear Murg understands English."

"She's smarter than she looks." Danny winked at the calico.

"This is undoubtedly the second worst day of my life," Murg moaned. "I believe I hear the paper truck."

"You'd say anything to escape," Danny thought back, then he also heard the delivery truck.

"Do you think it chases trucks? Or plays in traffic? You know, if something happened to the pup, then Krindee could take its place."

Danny just glared.

After folding papers and stuffing them into his carrier, Danny opened the garage and walked to his bicycle. "At least you could be sorry you broke the picture," Danny said.

"Tipping the box onto the floor was necessary," Murg replied as she darted ahead. "We needed a diversion and being upset helped Krindee escape. The memory you hold of your mother and Sarah are sharper than any photograph."

"Yeah, I guess. You could still be sorry." Danny stopped, thinking something looked different about his red bicycle.

"Why are you just standing there? Is something wrong?" Krindee asked as she snuck out from under the car.

"Oh, there you are. Where have you been?"

"I slipped out the door during all the commotion. Thank you, Murg. Now that I know about their devices, I can alter myself to fool their equipment."

"How?" Danny asked.

"By changing my vibrational pattern. Please, don't worry about me. They won't catch me with their primitive equipment.

I've had more difficult assignments on Gavron and Telekinaes' moon, so believe me when I say I am safe. Danny, what's wrong?"

"I'm not sure. Dad and I built this bicycle from used parts, so I know it from top to bottom; but something's different. I just can't figure out what." Danny knelt next to his bike, then felt around with his hands. "What's this?" He held a red-fleck of paint smaller than a dime.

"So that's what the fourth agent was doing," Murg mentally projected. Danny's look spoke the question. "I saw four people in black suits get in the car."

"Maybe one was the driver."

"He came from the direction of this house."

"He came from the garage. He left as I entered," Krindee projected.

"I think you hold a homing device." Murg nodded toward Danny's hand. "It tracks you, relaying your location."

"Why do you think that?" Danny walked to better light and examined the flat, red device.

"Feline instinct. Actually, my eyes are very good. I see advanced micro-circuitry."

"As do I," Krindee agreed.

"Why would they do this?"

"Imagine. Shadow Daggers were just here. They're interested in aliens. You've met an alien. You helped an alien. They might want to keep tabs on you. This is cheaper than tracking you by satellite or having you followed."

"Why on my bike and not me?" Danny asked.

"You take it just about everywhere you go," Murg replied.

Danny looked at Krindee. "What do you think we should do?"

"Be careful."

"What are you doing?" Murg asked.

Danny continued searching the bicycle. "I thought I was being paranoid, but here's a second one." Danny pulled off another circular red device. "Think I should destroy them? We can't go anywhere fun with these around." The felines remained silent. "Naw, destroying it would announce that we'd found it, wouldn't it? I think I'll ride around with them, then leave them someplace, maybe the mall when I want to go rainbow riding." He put the devices back on his plain ole' two-wheeler.

Murg climbed onto the bicycle. "See anything that appears to be a camera lens or microphone?" Danny shook his head. "Neither do I. Then your plan, as well as talking freely, should be safe."

By the time they'd changed bicycles, stashing the normal one in the trees and transferring tracking devices to Kalyde II, twilight had descended, blanketing the neighborhood with chilling darkness. With a thought, Danny turned on the magic bicycle's headlight. He wished he could just as easily banish the feeling of being watched. He sent a paper spinning. Hitting a garage door on the fly, it *thumped* loudly.

"Ease up. Relax," Murg whispered from the book carrier.

"But I feel watched," Danny replied.

"You're not doing anything out of the ordinary. Just keep delivering papers."

"Let's talk about something more pleasant." In her Siamese form, the Cor-ror-o'lan rode in Danny's backpack, her paws resting on his shoulder. "What are you going to name the puppy?"

"Him!" Murg's sprawled position on the book carrier implied distress. "Must we talk about him! What about me? My life's ruined!"

Danny hit a bump, jostling Murg. She twisted nimbly to grab hold of a padded side rail. "Thank you very much. You are becoming quite the master of silent communications."

Danny laughed and tossed a paper. It landed next to a discarded Christmas tree. "Krindee, I think I'm going to name him Comet."

"Why Comet?" the Siamese asked.

"Since he's black, I thought about Blackie, Shadowrun, Shady, Inky, Ebony, Pitch, or Coalsack . . . ."

"Name him Thesaurus for all I care," Murg moaned. "Or Backpack. He's the color of your backpack."

". . . and he's not all black, but has a glowing white patch, like a nebula. Maybe the star is a sign of a very intelligent dog."

"You can dream," the calico continued.

"Besides, if he's going to keep up with us, he'd better fly like a comet!"

"He's going to ride with us?" Murg spoke, disgust heavy in her voice.

"Sort of," Danny said. "But since he's not a cat, he'll have to run alongside us."

"As is only just and proper." Murg sighed. "I guess you have your mascot now."

"Comet reminds me a little of our pet yogguth, Zap-cidy," Krindee told Danny.

"What's a . . . ."

"Quiet! It's Mrs. Wilson." Murg adjusted her position, returning to her sleeping pose.

"Good evening, Danny," the elderly woman greeted him. "How are you?"

"I'm doing okay, ma'am," Danny replied. "I'm ready for longer days. I prefer delivering papers in daylight."

"At least you have company. You are traveling with quite a crew." She nodded to the calico and the Siamese. "May I pet them?"

"If it's okay with them," Danny replied. "You know how cats are."

"Yes I do. Until last month, I'd had Sylvester for company for almost thirteen years." She sniffled as she reached out to pet Krindee.

"She has a friendly and caring touch," Krindee observed as she stretched languidly. "No act of kindness, no matter how small, is wasted."

"Aesop loved cats," Murg agreed. "If humans loved each other as they often love pets, the world would be a better place."

The calico purred under Mrs. Wilson's touch. Murg stood and stretched, rippling with the caress.

"Danny, did I tell you that the plant I replanted in the pot you gave me is growing like a weed?" she asked. "Thank you very much. A lot of people would have lied about breaking the planter. Well, I've taken up enough of your holiday." She gave him a rolled up ten dollar bill. "I forgot to give it to you for Christmas."

"Thank you! Have a Happy New Year!" Danny told her as he rode off.

"Danny, did she see you break her planter?" Krindee asked. Danny shook his head.

"I see. You replaced it because it was the right thing to do?"

"That and a guilty conscience," Danny replied with a wan smile.

"Ah yes, your H.L. Mencken said that 'Conscience is the inner voice that warns us that someone may be looking'," Krindee quoted.

"Where to now? What else can we do for fun?" Krindee asked. "Riding is *very* enjoyable. The sensation of the wind on my fur feels like I'm brushed by dozens of hands."

"Danny, what's wrong?" Murg asked. Danny shrugged his shoulders. "Things are going your way, my friend! You are wired by the government—a special honor there, received a cash tip, and a new puppy all in the same day. What a momentous day."

"Comet's a bribe," Danny replied morosely. "Andie Mayfair thinks that if she gives me a dog, then I'll think she's all right. Mom II or something."

Murg sighed heavily. "Danny. Danny. Danny. We need to go for a high speed cruise. Blow away your cares. You're your own worst enemy when you set foot on the path of despair."

"So you keep telling me. Some things just don't change, or if they do, they get worse. Men and women in black are watching me, and Spike's still after me. Now he's part of a motorcycle gang. What if they start shooting at me instead of trying to catch me?"

"Danny, you're letting your imagination run amok again," Murg cautioned.

"The strangest thing. I somehow know they're going to resort to guns. Sort of like deja vu but not the same. Weird." Danny grew thoughtful.

"*IF* you're going to let your imagination rampage, let's try flying once more."

"Kah-laye-dee told me the magic bicycle couldn't fly." The Siamese stretched.

"We're still trying. How do you want to do this, Danny?" Murg asked. "Drop, launch or plummet method?"

"Plummeting's the easiest and you don't mind it. As soon as we deliver these last couple of papers, we'll zip over to the mall. We can leave the micro spies on a bike rack."

As they left the gathering of shops behind, Murg stood and stretched. "We're off to Nevada. Long steep hills here comes the Speed-demon."

"You almost sound excited about this." The Siamese cocked her head to examine her fellow feline. "Almost like, dare I say, a dog? I'm sure you and Comet can share the excitement when the puppy gets older."

Murg simply blinked, then looked away, ignoring the alien.

"Krindee, can you see Little Antelope Summit in my thoughts?" Danny asked.

"A desert road running over a snowy mountain?"

That's it, elevation 7433 on Highway 50— The Loneliest Highway. Picture it in your mind. Feel the chill. Smell the crispness of the air."

Danny pedaled faster, letting the rhythm flow. On the drawing board of his mind, he pictured an arid, mountainous land dotted with sage and bitter brush. Most of the bushes and stunted trees grew along a ravine or in the higher elevations where snow nurtured them.

The lay of the land appeared to be one long rollercoaster, ranges of barren mountains jutting between stretches of high desert. The black ribbon of road rolled up and down, over white-dusted summits and along bone-dry plains.

"We . . ."

The air lost its heavy humidity and grew colder as if they'd ridden into a freezer. The sun shone starkly in a merciless sky. The winds swept through the high desert, frigid at high altitude.

". . . are . . ."

Telephones poles whizzed by as though slats along a fence. Colors blurred, green melding with brown, white and yellow. With a thunderous roar, a white light engulfed them. They ripped through the clouds and raced onto the rainbow highway. Its colors dazzled, clear and bright as though poured from amethysts, fire opals and other gemstones. Gaining speed, they plummeted toward a white ball of light sitting on the rainbow. Exhilaration nearly overwhelmed Danny; he loved riding Kalyde II!

". . . there!"

The threesome burst through the bright exit ramp and appeared in Nevada, racing along a mountainous highway. The summit appeared covered with strawberry ice cream, the snow pink from the setting sun. The air smelled crisp and clean and tasted fresh. The sky grew dark, Venus hanging high like a bright silver ball.

When they crested snowy Little Antelope Summit, the riders could see the next valley. The dusty plain spread out wide below with the highway running across it. The black strip traveled to the next set of mountains and beyond for as long as there lay land.

"Starkly beautiful," Krindee said.

"If you like litter boxes with downhill running water." Murg sat perkily, taking in everything, her tail flicking as if checking things off a list.

"It reminds me of Mars long ago, or Galaydus' moon in the Acron Five System."

"How long do Cor-ror-o'lans live?" Danny asked.

"Four to five times your lifespan. What am I supposed to do now?" Krindee asked.

"Think light, like we're a bird," Danny told the Siamese. "They have hollow bones that enable them to fly."

"Wouldn't a ramp help? Something like the Wright brothers used?" Krindee suggested.

"We tried that. That's the launch method." Murg shuddered.

"I'm hoping our combined imaginations can lift us," Danny told her. "We've already ridden atop fog. That isn't much different than clear air. Here we go! Let's have some fun!" Danny pedaled rapidly, putting on a burst of speed to start downhill.

Murg leaned past Danny to catch the rushing wind. Krindee stretched over Danny's shoulder, the wind ruffling her whiskers and making her eyes water. Her tail thudded wildly inside the backpack.

Danny squinted against the wind. It pulled at his cheeks and roared around his ears. "See us fly!"

They raced down the mountain, ripping through the air like a falling star. The bicycle grew lighter and lighter. Sensing a release of gravity, Danny pulled back, trying to lift the front tire. For a moment, Danny thought they cleared the ground, then things felt solid.

"Failed again." Relaxing, Danny let the bicycle slow to normal coasting speed. "I can't help but feel I'm doing this wrong. I know I can do it! I've flown before with my dad in almost everything, even a jet fighter. Do you have any ideas? I *know* Kalyde II can fly."

"If I told you, people would think cats were intelligent, then they . . . ." Krindee began.

Murg guffawed.

Krindee raised her head and cocked it, looking very prissy and superior."Keep trying, Danny. I know you can do it. And I don't think you need us. Just believe you can do it. Confucius said, 'Our greatest glory is not in never falling but in rising every time we fall'."

"I just need the right idea. The Wright idea. Hey, maybe I need to do a little research. Fortify my imagination. Prepare like I did for traveling back in time. Einstein told me that imagination is greater than knowledge. I think he meant that imagination allows us to build on knowledge and go where we haven't gone before."

"Sounds good to me." Murg was balled up once more, eyes closed.

"And if at first you don't succeed, try and try again." That saying rang in Danny's ears. Now why did that sound so familiar? "Besides, it's easy to keep trying when you're having a blast!"

"A blast?" Krindee asked.

"So much fun you feel like you'll explode!" Danny replied. Krindee laughed.

They visualized being back in Texas, riding the gleaming sky highway back to Ft. Worth. They stopped by the mall and removed the two homing devices from the bicycle rack. After Danny reattached them to the magic bicycle, they rode home. "I guess this worked. None of the Shadow Daggers came after us."

As Danny turned onto Oak Ridge Lane, he saw someone riding a bicycle toward his house. The shadowy figure behind the headlight seemed familiar. "Hey, Jason! Over here!"

His friend waved and rode toward him. "Danny! Spike stole my bicycle!"

"Oh no! So that's why you're riding your old bike!"

"Yeah! He and the Headbangers just broke into our garage! They didn't take this one because it was in the storage shed."

"Are you sure it was Spike?"

"No," Jason grumbled. "Nobody saw anything, but they heard sputtering motorbikes. That's why I'm headed to his house right now. If it's there, I'm going to confront him! You coming with me?"

Danny's heart leapt into overdrive. Go looking for the Headbangers? Go looking for trouble? Danny swallowed heavily, then stammered. "S-Sure. What are friends for?"

FIVE

Hammer Fists

As they followed their headlights through neighborhoods of tract homes, Danny juggled second and third thoughts. "Spike probably didn't take your bicycle home. We should call the police or something. Tell somebody." Danny chewed his lip.

"I don't want to give him time to move it! I don't know where the Headbangers hide out! Don't worry, I can protect myself. Spike's bigger, but he's not *that* tough. It's numbers I worry about. I hope Reggie and the others aren't there."

"Well, there's four of us," Danny replied weakly.

Jason roared with laughter, then finally managed, "What I think is crazy, is riding a bicycle with two cats. Isn't one strange enough for you?"

"The Siamese is Krindee, a friend of Murg's," Danny replied.

"They'll protect you from Spike, right?" Jason asked.

"Yeah! Attack cats," Danny replied.

"At least the cats get along. It'd be bad news to be cruising down the road when they started clawing at each other." Jason smirked.

"Cats, unlike humans, are very civilized," Murg replied.

"Man, I hope we don't have to fight at all," Jason said.

"Fight?!" Danny squeaked.

"I'm not afraid," Jason continued. "You have to stand up for what's yours. You know, I think Spike is worse now that he's no longer The Big Man at school."

"I think so, too," Danny agreed. "People ignoring him seems to encourage him."

"He does things to get noticed," Murg thought. "Now that ReggieTuckett has joined him, Spike probably feels there's safety in numbers. Us against the world! A standard and trite gang motto."

"How do you know where Spike lives?" Danny asked.

"One of the guys pointed it out," Jason replied. "He told me to stay away. Far away because of Mr. Pickett, Spike's stepfather. He doesn't like anybody. And he really, *really* doesn't like kids."

"Y. . . you've met him?"

"No, but we probably will in a minute." Jason nodded ahead of them.

"This should be interesting," Krindee thought to Danny.

"If you find the sight of blood interesting," Danny replied by telepathy.

"I see you have a morbid bent to your imagination," Krindee told him.

"Sometimes imaginations are hard to channel," Murg mentally projected.

"Your Mark Twain said you can't depend on your judgment when your imagination is out of focus," Krindee quoted.

They turned onto Whippoorwill Road, moving through another rural sub-division. "We're close," Jason said. He nodded toward a mailbox reading '312 J. Zorran'.

Danny thought of Zorro, the black clad sword-wielding hero.

Jason stopped next to a mailbox reading '316 Pickett' in front of a two-story house. The Pickett place appeared recently painted white with dark green gutters and shutters. The house and yard were immaculately manicured, the lawn squared off and cleanly shaved around trees and bushes as though each blade of grass had been hand-clipped.

Two white pickups sat parked in the driveway. One appeared to be for business, the doors reading, Pickett's Lawn Service. The other vehicle was built for four-wheeling with a roll bar, extra bumpers and additional lights.

Both garage doors rested open, revealing a workshop inside. A single light bulb starkly illuminated the front of the garage, casting heavily draped shadows across all the machines. Beyond the neatly arranged saws and sawhorses stretched a long bench. Above it, at least a hundred tools hung. The sharp edges caught the raw light and flashed as if eager to be used for dismantling and destruction.

A mammoth man stepped from the shadows and walked toward the jigsaw table. He seemed as huge as a bear, but a starving brute, his big bones hugged by gaunt flesh. He set down a board, arranged it, then pulled down his goggles from his square forehead. Above big ears, his hair was cropped short in a military fashion. His face looked angular, his brows protruding, and his jaw lantern-shaped like . . . .

"Frankenstein," Murg thought as an emerald eye peered through slitted lids. "Remember, appearances can be deceiving."

"Something doesn't . . . feel right about him," Krindee projected. "He reminds me of a dark storm waiting to burst and rage."

"Speak of the devil. Come on." Jason walked his bicycle toward the hauntingly illuminated garage. When the saw's roar quieted to a whine, he yelled, "EXCUSE ME, SIR! IS ERNEST HOME?!"

"Who's that?" Danny asked.

"Spike's real name is Ernest Blocker," Jason whispered.

"WHAT?!" The big man lifted up his goggles, squinted at them, and then turned off the saw. Mr. Pickett limped toward them, his shadow lurching in front of him. "What are you doing here?"

"I-I'm l-looking f-for Ernest," Jason replied.

His hammer fists restlessly clenching, Mr. Pickett warily studied them. His left eye drifted off center, eyes moving independently as if Mr. Pickett were of two minds.

Danny shivered; he felt pierced by the odd look.

"Maybe Frankenstein wasn't a bad description," Murg said.

"Neither of ya look like a friend of Ernest's. He doesn't have many 'cause he doesn't play football worth spit." Mr. Pickett coughed, then spat. It landed with a loud, wet splat.

"I see where Spike learned his manners." Murg continued to observe, her gaze hooded, almost appearing sleepy.

"Mark Twain said, 'Good breeding consists in concealing how much we think of ourselves and how little we think of the other person'."

"Krindee, sometimes our silences say more than any volume of words, no matter how learned. A wise man speaketh little."

"Sophocles said a short saying oft contains much wisdom."

"Not if taken out of context," Murg replied.

"Kitties! Please!" Danny thought.

"Why are you looking for Ernest?" Mr. Pickett asked, then breathed on his goggles. He rubbed them on his crisply pressed work shirt. His scarred hands oozed blood from numerous tiny cuts.

"I believe he was involved in stealing my bicycle." Jason's hands clenched white on his bicycle's handlebars.

Mr. Pickett nodded toward him. When he wiped sweat from his cheek he left a dark, bloody streak. "You're riding a bicycle."

"This is my old one."

"Two bicycles. Boy howdy! What's the world coming to?" Mr. Pickett appeared thoughtful, a huge hand rubbing his blocky chin. Then he reached into his pocket and pulled out a package of cigarettes. He tapped one into his big, bony hand, then dug for a match to light it.

"What makes you think Ernest stole your bicycle?" Mr. Pickett's stare flashed hot and demanding, warning them to tell the truth or . . . else.

Jason swallowed, then explained about being chased.

"They didn't catch you?" Mr. Pickett sadly shook his head, then dragged on his cigarette. "That boy can't do anything right, even when he's doing wrong."

Danny shifted nervously from one foot to the next; he didn't like where this was headed. Somehow, when Mr. Pickett appeared thoughtful, he seemed even more dangerous, as if contemplating what would be most destructive.

"Well, I tell you what . . . ." As Mr. Pickett dragged on his cigarette again, the pause gave the sense of thunder building. "What did you say your name was, boy?"

"Jason."

"And you, cat boy?" Mr. Pickett nodded toward Danny.

He swallowed, then managed, "Chase. Danny Chase."

"Another brave one, I see, surrounded by cats. To tell the truth, I don't like cats. They're sneaky, underhanded beasts. Give me a good, obedient dog, I say."

"That preference comes as no surprise." Murg's whiskers twitched. "Hey, this could be a home for Comet."

"I tell you what, boys." Mr. Pickett paused, the tension building as if a landslide waiting to break. "When I see Spike, I'll ask him about your bicycle. Don't worry. I will find out the truth." Mr. Pickett's gaze narrowed, dark slits where his eyes should be. He took a long draw on his cigarette, then exhaled like a dragon, breathing a cloud of gray smoke.

Back in the shadows of the garage, a door opened. "Daddy!" came the yell of a young voice. A crash resounded through the garage.

"Raymond!" Spike's father yelled. "I told you never to come into the garage! Look what you've done!" Mr. Pickett stepped into the shadows. "If you've broken anything!" A wet, fleshy *smack* echoed throughout the garage. A cry followed it. "Now, get back in the house."

"I don't believe he did that!" Krindee mentally gasped, then hissed.

"But Mom said . . . ."

"Don't interrupt me, Raymond!"

Danny winced.

Jason could see better. His eyes widened with shock.

"I am going to do something!" Krindee moved.

Murg snagged the Siamese before she could leave. "I thought you said you were only supposed to watch."

"Your Elie Wiesel said that 'Indifference is the epitome of evil'."

"True, but you have your orders," Murg reminded her. "Leave this to Danny and Jason. Humans like to settle things with their fists or weapons. Now we know why Spike hits people. He thinks it's normal."

"Now, get back inside!" Mr. Pickett's voice slashed low and menacing. "It's dangerous out here."

"Are humans born this way?" Krindee asked. "Or taught this?"

"Do you mean are they a product of their environment? Or of societal pressure? Not to mention chemical imbalances, a lack of money, heredity or past spiritual sins. Take your pick. The debate has raged for centuries."

"But . . . but William Penn said . . . 'Right is right, even if everyone is against it; and wrong is wrong, even if everyone is for it'."

"Reading is fine, but you can only learn so much from books. Didn't you say Cor-ror-o'lans based their decisions on their own experiences instead of others' opinions?" Murg asked.

The Siamese nodded.

The looming figure stepped out of the shadows. Mr. Pickett's face gleamed, a sheen of perspiration glistening on it like a Halloween mask. "About your bicycle . . . ."

Danny tried to say something but couldn't. He wanted to run; but his legs refused to move.

"Yeah . . . uh, it's . . . you know . . . ." Jason stammered.

"I'll find out the truth." Mr. Pickett exhaled a cloud of smoke. "And I have my ways of finding out, don't worry." He smiled, showing teeth chipped and broken. "If Ernest stole your bicycle, he'll bring it back. Oh yes he will." Mr. Pickett smacked a hammer fist into the palm of his other hand. "So if you don't have it back tomorrow, then Ernest didn't steal it. Is that all right with you, boys?"

Jason and Danny quickly nodded.

"And I don't expect to see either of you boys near my house ever again, hear?"

"Yes, sir!" Jason and Danny cried simultaneously.

Under the biting stare of Mr. Pickett, Jason and Danny clambered onto their bicycles, getting away as fast as possible.

"He gave me the creeps," Danny managed.

"That's an understatement," Jason replied. "He scared me witless. I guess there's nothing else I can do tonight. Thanks for coming with me. I would've been scared to talk to him alone. See you tomorrow."

Danny waved and then rode toward 115 Oak Ridge in the darkness, following his headlight homeward. "I am not looking forward to tomorrow."

"Why not?" Krindee asked, speaking aloud now that Jason was gone.

"Spike hates me, but he'll hate me even more after his step-father gets through with him."

SIX

Spike's View

Spike parked his motorbike in the dark woods behind his house, then jumped the fence and walked to the back door. It was shrouded in darkness, the only light coming from his stepfather's room on the second floor.

Spike didn't want to see Ike. He just wanted to sneak in quick, grab his stuff, and leave even faster. The Headbangers might start without him, and he didn't want to miss destroying Jason's bicycle. First a little target practice, then a little fire, followed by the grand finale, a pipe bomb. Spike smiled. It was gonna be fun!

Stepping from the shadows near the back door, Spike's stepfather surprised him. Ike Pickett's eyes narrowed to laser sights as the old man studied him. "You did it, didn't you, Ernest?"

"W... what?" Spike stepped back. He loathed being called Ernest. "W... what are you talking about?"

"You took the black boy's bicycle didn't you?" His stepfather advanced, fists tight and white at his sides as if wild beasts held to heel. "I can tell when you're lying." His nose twitched as if he smelled blood. His smile grew as grim as the Reaper's. "He and the cat boy came to talk to me. Said you stole something. Bad enough you had to steal, but you had to get caught too, didn't you?" His hands came together with a resounding *smack*. When Ike cracked a knuckle it sounded as a gunshot. "And call me, 'sir'."

"It was Reggie . . . ."

"I told you to stay away from that black boy, didn't I?"

"Yes, you did, but . . . ."

"You mean, 'Yes sir, you did.' Ernest, you embarrassed the family name." Lightning quick, his stepfather lashed out.

The first blow rocked Spike; he staggered backwards, pain blossoming from his left ear. The second fist stunned him. Another hit, Spike doubled over, gasping for air. The next blow, Spike crumpled. Fists rose and fell, repeatedly pounding him. Spike saw red, then blackness crept over him, concealing the pain.

Sometime later, Spike awakened inside the house, nose to nose with the monster, his stepfather's face large and twisted. "You're a sissy boy! You won't fight back and can't take a love tap! You are an embarrassment to the Pickett family! Aren't you?"

Spike nodded.

"Aren't you! Say it!" His stepfather reared back, open hand poised and ready.

"Yes! I'm an embarrassment!"

"Sir."

"Yes, sir!"

"That's better. Maybe your feeble mind can learn something after all. You know what you're gonna do?" his stepfather asked.

Spike just stared, mute, not sure he wanted to know.

"Tomorrow, you're gonna return that bicycle. Yes, you are. It better be in the same shape it was when you stole it. We don't need to steal to live. And we certainly don't need to steal from their kind. You hear me boy?" he hissed.

"Yes . . . sir!"

"If I hear otherwise, you'll be very sorry. Even sorrier than you are now." Ike Pickett backed away. After a long, hammering stare, he left the room.

Spike crawled to his feet. How long had he been unconscious? Hurry! If the Headbangers destroyed Jason's bicycle . . . . Spike shuddered. He didn't even want to think of the consequences. Ike might put him six feet under, or worse, make him wish he were dead.

Spike staggered out of the house, then limped across the backyard. Crawling across the fence almost seemed impossible. Cursing Ike Pickett and praying that the Headbangers would wait for him, Spike stumbled to his motorbike, a Honda 150.

Spike crawled aboard, then fired it up. The motorbike coughed black smoke, then died with a metallic death-rattle. Spike twisted the throttle, then kicked the starter again. The motorbike coughed, shuddered twice, then died again, stone cold silent. "NO! Don't do this! Don't do this! STUPID BIKE!" He tried again and again, the bike sputtering, then dying again. "If you die, I die!" With a string of curses and tears running down his face mingling with desperate sweat, Spike tried over and over and over again.

After what seemed hours of trying, the motorbike coughed and caught, starting up with a roar. "Thank you! Thank you! There is a god!" Kicking it into gear, he raced off, bounding through the dark woods. Mindless of the danger, he raced and weaved through the forest, here and there almost grazing a tree. He clipped a branch. The rearview mirror sheared away, tumbling behind. A limb slapped at him, nearly dislodging him.

Go! Faster! He didn't care. Spike hunkered low and gave it more gas, shooting ahead.

Ramping airborne, he sailed out of the woods and into the street. The tires squealed as they spun, then burning rubber, he raced down the road, heading out into the country.

As the minutes passed, he alternately prayed and cursed. This was Jason and Chase's fault. If they hadn't come to see Ike

. . . . Who would've thought they had the guts! And how did Jason know it was the Headbangers! Chase! Somehow Chase had put him up to this!

Barely slowing, Spike turned into a gravel road, sending rocks spraying. He righted the Honda, and flew toward an old, rundown farmhouse. Slivers of light splayed through the cracks, cutting through the darkness and striping a host of oaks and a rickety barn of pick-up sticks. Heavy metal music cut through the night, the drums pounding as if some ancient ritual.

Spike skidded to a stop, hopped off and stumbled up the step. Throwing the door open, Spike staggered inside. A wall was missing, making it a great room with a black wood stove and a large, banged-up table waiting for the next meeting of the Headbangers.

"HEY, WHERE'S . . . . OH NO!" Spike cried over the music, then cursed. He raced through the empty room toward the open back door. "Stupid leg. Slowing me!"

"All right! OPEN FIRE!"

"NO! NOOO!" Spike threw himself through the doorway. "STOP! STOP OR ELSE . . . ."

The three boys turned away from the gleaming bicycle, their guns now trained on Spike. The orange-haired kid called Vargas lowered his gun. Page, the one with the tattoos, pointed his rifle skyward. Reggie Tuckett did not. "Spike! Just in time for the blast and burn." He tapped a can of gasoline with his toe. "What's up? You look . . . beat. What happened to you?"

Spike lowered his head. "The bicycle. I . . . I have to take it back to Jason, undamaged."

Page scratched the snake tattoo along his neck, then trailed his fingers over the writhing serpents along his arms as though they covered bruises. He reached over and turned off the boom box. "What changed your mind?"

"Guys, if . . ." Spike mumbled, thinking this was the hardest thing he'd ever done. ". . . I don't return the bike to Jason in one piece, my stepdad is gonna beat me to death." He pointed to the bruises on his face, already adding yellow and green to the dark purple. Spike pulled off his shirt, revealing more bruising. "Jason and Chase stopped by my house. They told Ike that I stole the bicycle. Ike, I don't know how, but he knows the truth." Reggie spat profanities. "You need to learn to lie better, bud." Vargas ran a hand nervously through his orange hair, then took a long drag on a cigarette.

"I can wait." Page clicked the safety back into place.

"Sure," Reggie finally said, lowering the rifle. "We understand what you're going through, Spike. Don't worry. We'll stick together. I have some ideas. First we'll deal with Jason and Chase, then your stepdad."

SEVEN

The Showdown

Danny awakened dreading the forthcoming hours. When he stepped outside to fold the newspapers, he looked to the sky. Dawn glowed beautifully, pastels painting the three rows of puffy cotton clouds stretched across the horizon. The air was cool and crystal clear with a touch of brittleness.

"What a magnificent morning." Murg breathed deeply. The calico and Krindee, as a Siamese, sat next to the pile of papers.

"For a minute, it makes me forget about Spike, the Headbangers, and the Shadow Daggers." Danny sighed, then began preparing the papers for delivery. "I wish I didn't have to go back to school."

"Ah, the post holiday blues," Murg projected.

After a few minutes of folding, Danny loaded the papers on his bicycle and climbed aboard. Krindee and Murg jumped onto the back, curling around each other on the book carrier.

As Danny pushed off, he looked back at the cats. "Hey,

don't go to sleep! Stay alert! I'm sure Mr. Pickett gave it to Spike, so he'll come after me."

Murg didn't respond. At times like these, the calico claimed she mentally 'surfed' other dimensions.

Danny thought he spotted a motorbike rider hiding behind a car; but it was only a shadow trick.

"How long has Spike been terrorizing you?" Krindee asked.

"From the very first day of school," Danny replied. "It hasn't stopped. But Spike has been more underhanded since I smoked two of his friends in a bicycle race."

"Smoked?"

"You know all this world's history, but you don't know late twentieth century slang?"

"Smoked?" Krindee asked again.

"Burnt. Toasted. Fried. Crisped. Torched. Creamed . . . ." Danny continued.

"A lot of cooking terms."

"You know, whipped, spanked, slaughtered . . . ."

"Violent and cooking verbs."

"Trashed? Beat? Defeated?" Danny asked.

"Oh! You won a contest!" Krindee clapped her paws together.

"That response is unworthy of a feline," Murg thought.

"Won a contest! That's an understatement," Danny replied. "It was the second time Jason and I became friends. Now, because of the race, Hank and Rocky don't bother me anymore. Instead of bullying me, Spike steals stuff, like the story I wrote called *The Alien Bicycle.*"

"What have you done about this Spike?" she asked.

"Been careful. Tried to avoid him." Danny tossed a paper. It skipped across the concrete driveway and nudged the garage door. "It's a little easier now with the magic bicycle. And he doesn't strut around anymore with all the guys jumping at his every word. Back in October, it was 'let's get Chase,' and everybody fell into line. After the race, they quit chasing me. Now the Headbangers have taken up the tradition."

"You haven't done anything to stop Spike? Asked for help?"

"Telling my dad or teachers didn't help. I already changed time once and didn't care for the results," Danny replied. "In the second . . . reality I lost the race. Well, I mean, I didn't defeat Spike like I did the first time we raced. It's not confusing unless you talk about it."

"If you had won the race the second time, do you think Spike would've stopped stalking you?" Krindee asked.

"Probably not." Danny scratched his head under his helmet. "Do you hear that? That's a motorbike." The roar came closer, ripping down the street.

Danny pulled off to the side. A large Harley-Davidson motorcycle thundered past.

"What would stop Spike?" Krindee asked.

"How about if one of us moved? Hey, I know, a Magnum .45. Ka-blam!"

"You don't mean that seriously, do you?" Krindee asked.

"Grim fantasy and wishful thinking." Danny paused at an intersection to let a UPS truck pass through, then proceeded to the the next block. He neared the newly constructed homes at the edge of the area's current development in Red Stone.

"Okay, using your imagination," Krindee proposed. "What do you think would keep him from bothering you?"

"Growing to seven feet and having arms and legs the size of tree trunks?"

Krindee laughed. "Eating spinach like Popeye might work, but again, it's wishful thinking."

"I could strap him to the back of the bicycle and leave him deep in the Amazon jungle with starving cannibal pygmies."

Krindee chuckled again, looking not at all like a Siamese cat.

"No! I've got it! I could carry him to the future where genetic engineers can fix him! Murg, why didn't you suggest that?! Hey, what if some mad scientists clone him?!"

Murg cracked open an eye. "*No* time-travel, remember? Take care of this in the present."

"Yeah, I remember. I'm not so sure my last travels were worth the trouble," Danny replied.

"I'm sure, that with your imagination, you'll think of something. Just as your imagination will take you flying one day," Krindee said.

"I've been thinking about flying. I have to write a major report for Mr. Gordon, so I think I'll do it on the history of aviation. Maybe I'll learn how to fly!"

"And solve your problem with Spike?" Murg asked. Danny frowned.

"Danny, I'd like to go to school and meet your friends. It would help me better understand you and discharge my mission," Krindee said.

"Cats aren't allowed in school." Murg's whiskers twitched. "Not that we need such education. Our knowledge is either passed on or gained through experience."

"How about as a student?" Krindee asked innocently.

"You can't just appear out of the blue and go to class," Murg replied. "Only cats appear and disappear mysteriously without triggering suspicion. Stay home. I'll teach you more about being a cat. After this morning, it's obvious you need work on being indifferent."

"As you are about bicycling and speed?" Krindee asked. Murg ignored her with superior feline disdain.

Eyes alert, Danny was very careful riding to school. The Headbangers weren't waiting for him, and Spike wasn't lurking in the shadows at school, either. Danny was glad, but the day was just beginning.

During a class changeover, Danny saw Spike. His glare was scalding, as if Spike were a boiler building steam to blow sky high. His face looked battered, the flesh around his left eye badly bruised. The weight of his stare and clenched fists promised payback.

Lunch passed peacefully, because Danny spent it in the library. He searched for anything on the history of aviation.

On a whim, Danny picked up a book on birds. It discussed their anatomy and the aerodynamics of flight. He read about gliders—planes that could stay aloft without engines. Ever since flying with his father at age six, Danny had dreamed of having his own wings, going wherever he wanted by flying.

Yes, he'd learn to fly. Definitely. Certainly. Absolutely, positively.

While leaving the library, Danny bumped into the new kid at school carrying an armload of books and a briefcase. Jimmy Chang was skinny with short dark hair, and angular ebony eyes. He wore a Dallas Cowboys jersey with Aikman's number 8 on it.

"Hi, I'm Jimmy Chang. You're in my history class. Are you researching your paper?"

"Yes. My name's Danny Chase. Welcome to school and watch out for Spike." Danny described Spike as a Neanderthal with a protruding brow, beady eyes and a square jaw. "Spike enjoys harassing new kids. I was new last semester."

"I'll try to avoid him."

"You're a Cowboys fan?"

"Yes. I'm a huge sports fan. I know a lot about players and the history of games, especially baseball. Do you like sports?" Jimmy asked.

"Some." Danny didn't want to admit he didn't like sports because he stunk at athletics. "What's your favorite class?"

"Math," Jimmy replied. Danny blanched. Jimmy laughed. "I'm good with numbers. I like English, too, because I hope to speak and write it better one day. I enjoy writing."

"I like writing stories, too, and reading comics."

Jimmy smiled broadly. "So do I! Many great comic-book artists and writers have come from Japan."

They spent the rest of the time talking comics and books. Before they knew it, lunch was over. Danny had to run to Biology, barely making it to class on time.

By the end of the day, Danny grew edgy. He hadn't seen Spike again, or any of the other Headbangers. Maybe they waited for him after school. He kept picturing them with knives, clubs and guns! For some reason, when his imagination ran wild, he saw Spike, Vargas and Page looking like adults.

Danny shuddered, then looked at the clock. It was almost three. The second hand moved stiffly as if chilled to the bone. The minute hand appeared frozen in time, every single minute crawling with glacial slowness towards an hour.

Usually Mr. Gordon was very interesting and thought-provoking, as Murg would say, but today class dragged, every second stretching into minutes. Every hour . . . .

Stop doing this to yourself! Danny screamed silently. You're only making matters worse.

Christina would be waiting for him after school and before practice. She'd be cheering at tomorrow's basketball game.

Danny wasn't quite sure how to thank Christina. She'd rendered several wonderful drawings to go along with his short story, *The Alien Bicycle*. He'd spent the lonely holidays polishing his tale, a work of fiction based on his real life adventure.

Christina was right; not only was it fun to write about Kah-laye-dee and Kalyde II, but good for him to relive things and ponder events. He saw things more clearly now, as if from a distance.

The class bell rang, signaling the end of the school day. Leaping to his feet, Danny no longer felt drained.

"Remember, your topics are due by Friday!" came Mr. Gordon's call as Danny raced for the door, then wove his way through the masses to the main lobby.

Christina leaned against the wall near the announcement board, searching the crowd while talking with Cynthia. Danny waved. Smiling, Christina waved back.

He'd met her through Jason, after beating him in the first race (which was in a different time) and after helping Jason in the second race (this time) when they'd crashed while sprinting toward the finish. Christina had approached him, becoming his first friend in Texas.

With blue eyes and blond hair, Christina was friendly, though often serious, very smart and a fantastic artist. For Christmas, she'd given him an old movie poster of HG Wells' *The Time Machine*. Christina loved to read and had helped edit *The Alien Bicycle,* which had led to her drawing incredible pictures for his story.

Danny wished he could tell her *The Alien Bicycle* wasn't just a story.

"Hi," Danny greeted her. They hugged.

"Your artwork is a major hit. Mrs. Patterson loved it. There's only one problem with it."

"What?" Christina sounded concerned.

"Now my writing has to live up to the artwork. That's going to be tough!"

They laughed together. Cynthia looked at them, chewing gum and obviously thinking they were warped.

"Hi Cynthia," Danny said. "Where's Jason?"

"Outside. Something about getting his bicycle back."

"Come on, Christina!" Danny gently guided her outside. "I was afraid of this," Danny said as he stepped into the red-brick courtyard.

Near the bicycle rack, a crowd gathered. Jason and Spike stood at least a head above all the onlookers. A pale face hid in the masses behind Spike. Was that Reggie Tuckett? Danny saw a flash of orange. Was the entire gang of Headbangers here?

As Danny took a step forward, he spotted a second crowd a little beyond the first. A group of a half-dozen guys swarmed around a beautiful girl dressed in green; she reminded him of Christina. The girl across the way had long red tresses, and her eyes . . . were . . . .

Oh no! They were lavender! Krindee was here! Hoping she hadn't blown her cover already, Danny rushed forward.

"Danny, what's wrong? What's going on?" Christina asked.

"Didn't Jason tell you that Spike stole his bicycle?" Danny asked.

Spike saw Danny coming. "Hey! Puke boy! King of the

Wimpoids!" Spike yelled and shook a fist. Even Spike's knuckles were bruised. The damage along his face and eye had changed color, green and yellow spreading out from the sickly purple hue.

Jason glanced over his shoulder. He tried to glare Danny away. "My fight," he mouthed.

Spike shoved past Jason and bulled his way toward Danny and Christina. Kids staggered out of his way. With a flushed face and eyes glinting murderously, Spike suddenly loomed over Danny. "My stepdad gave me something last night! Something I'd like to give you!" Spike reared back, his huge fist poised to strike.

"NO!" Jason yelled, charging Spike from behind.

As if a magician performing a stage trick, Krindee appeared next to Spike. She grabbed his wrist and twisted. Spike yelped and crumpled to his knees. Krindee held his wrist above his head, still clutched in her slender hand. Her red nails gleamed as though the bloodied talons of an eagle.

"YOU WITCH! LET ME GO!" Spike cried.

"Wow! Did you see that?" someone asked. "She knows Kung Fu!"

"Who is that girl?"

"A babe and a half. Tough, too."

"I've always wanted to do that to Spike." Cynthia loudly popped her gum.

"Who is that?" Christina asked Danny.

"My cousin, Krindee, from Paris." Danny's heart sank.

"You have a cousin from France?" Christina asked.

"My dad's side," Danny fibbed smoother than he expected. "My uncle's also in the military." That at least was the truth. "You could say she's an alien."

"Out of this world, all right," some boy behind Danny said.

"*Bonjour,* Daniel." Krindee smiled at him. She looked very satisfied with herself, some of the Siamese showing through. Krindee completely ignored Spike, a bored feline with its paw atop a frightened bug.

Even though he felt ill, Danny forced a smile.

"Hello, Krindee."

Jason stared back and forth between Spike to Danny. "You know this girl?"

All gazes shifted from Krindee to Danny. He could see it on their faces—guys amazed that he knew her. For some reason, it granted him more respect and a fair amount of envy. He felt he was going to have some unwanted friends.

Reggie Tuckett and Page abruptly burst from the crowd, rushing toward Krindee. Reggie smiled wickedly, his gaze sizing Krindee. Page appeared flushed, the red wash creeping down his neck along his snake tattoo.

"If I were you, despite being big, strong boys, I would not dare anything rash," Krindee said without looking back. She didn't appear to do anything, but Spike screamed as if stabbed. "If you pull me the wrong way, something might snap. We understand each other, yes?"

"Spike?" Reggie asked. "What do you want us to do?"

"WHATEVER THE WITCH SAYS!" Spike bawled.

"You can have him back once I teach him some manners," Krindee told them.

"This isn't over, sister! Not by a long shot! Right, Chase? You know, don't you?" Reggie snapped. Reggie and Page glared at everyone, casting daggers, then turned and left. Several of the onlooking girls cheered and clapped.

Krindee looked at Danny as if to ask him what she should do. The kids picked up on it. Cynthia turned down her thumb. A second girl followed, casting her vote. Soon, as if condemning a gladiator in a ring, everyone held their thumbs down.

"Danny, what does thumbs down mean?" Krindee asked, cocking her head. "A new American gesture like 'the finger'?"

"Roman times," Danny replied. "Spike's popular, as you can see."

"CHASE!"

"Oh. Oh! I understand now. How barbaric," Krindee replied. "Children can be so cruel."

Spike glanced up and let out a wail. "What are you doing to me, witch?!"

"It's called Aikido," she replied. "A non-violent way to restrain someone. If you quit fighting, the pain subsides. Be glad I'm not using Savate, a martial art of the feet that was perfected in my beloved France."

"Chase . . . ." Spike tried to surge to his feet. With an agonizing cry, he dropped back to his knees.

"*Bonjour mademoiselle,* you must be Christina," Krindee said, putting out her hand toward Christina. "I'm Krindee LaFleur, pleased to make your acquaintance."

Christina stared at Krindee's outstretched hand.

Krindee looked to Danny. "Danny, isn't this the way you greet someone in America? Should we kiss on the cheek instead?"

"Oh!" Christina replied, snapping out of it. "I've just never shaken hands with someone restraining a psychopath before." The girls shook hands.

"This is Jason and Cynthia." Danny gestured toward his friends.

"You really know this bad martial arts babe, Danny?" Disbelief still highlighted Jason's features. Krindee introduced herself and shook hands. "A firm handshake, no surprise there. Reggie and Page made the right decision."

Cynthia looked back and forth between Christina and Krindee. "You know, you two could be sisters!"

"Hey, she's right," Jason agreed.

"*Merci bien.* You are kind," Krindee replied. "You are beautiful," Krindee told Christina. "Danny has written so much about you. That you were the first person nice to him at school and helped him write his paper for English. I feel that I know you."

Christina blushed.

"HEY!" Spike groaned. "What about me!?"

"I came here specifically to meet you and Jason," Krindee continued.

Christina turned to Danny. "Why didn't you tell me?" "It was a surprise," Krindee responded for him. "I saw your drawings," Krindee told Christina. "You draw beautifully." "Danny, your cousin knows how to make a good first impression." Her eyes laughing, she said, "You could take some lessons."

"Hey! HEY!" Spike wailed. "Let me go! Please?"

"Speaking of manners," Krindee told them, then turned to address Spike. "*Monsieur*, do you know what manners are?"

"Being polite? Playing nice?" Spike replied. "Not hurting anyone, like me, maybe?"

"Well, Mary Little Wilson said politeness is one half good nature and the other half good lying," Krindee informed him. "I have a feeling you are a liar *magnifique*."

Someone nearby laughed.

"Mary who?" Spike squawked.

"Why are you doing this?" Christina asked Krindee.

"The most difficult thing in the world is to know how to do a thing and to watch someone else doing it wrong, without commenting."

"Hey, that's from T.H. White!" Christina cried in surprise. "I love T.H. White!"

Krindee nodded. "Spike, do you promise to leave Danny alone?"

"Yes, I promise never to touch him!"

Krindee looked to Danny and grimaced. She knew about promise-twisting. "You'll never harm him again?"

"I'll never harm him again, promise."

"You'll stay away from him?"

"YES! I'll stay away from him!" Spike promised.

Krindee let go of his wrist. With a sigh, Spike collapsed onto his side. He crawled to his knees, then struggled to his feet. When he rounded a corner, Spike peeked to see if Krindee watched, then glared at Danny. Like a consuming fire, hate radiated from his eyes.

"How come I have a feeling this isn't over?" Danny wondered aloud.

EIGHT

The Haunted House

As Spike walked home, he couldn't believe what just happened. Whupped by Mademoiselle Van Damme! Held helpless by a girl in front of the whole school! And the Headbangers! They just stood and watched!

Spike shook his throbbing head. His ears still rang from his most recent beating. How far had he fallen? From king of the hill, leader of the football team, to whipping boy for the likes of Jason, Chase and any old girl that came along. Spike spat. He'd have to lie to his stepfather, and lie very well at that. If Ike found out . . . .

Besides Ike marrying Mom, when had things started to go wrong? The Oktoberfest 20K bicycle race? When Chase had outraced his friend Hank and his brother Rocky? The Wimp would have beaten him too, but Chase had crashed. What a spaz. Since Chase lost, he should have to honor his bet. For some reason, Hank, Rocky and Jason didn't think so. Despite having a broken arm, Jason had been ready to fight, warning him to stay away from Chase.

How could he pound someone already injured? Beating a crip would only hurt his image.

Spike sighed. Not long after the race, he'd injured his ankle and missed playing a couple of football games. Somehow—miraculously—they had won both games. Adding insult to injury, Christina had turned the girls at school against him.

Except for Reggie, Vargas and Page—all newcomers to school—Spike didn't have any friends; but the four of them were tight. They thought alike, which is why they formed the Headbangers. None of them liked Chase or Jason.

How had those two outrun motorbikes? That should be impossible. They would have to be riding alien bicycles, Spike thought, recalling The Wimp's story for English class. Could it be? Nah, that was absolutely ridiculous. Chase and Jason riding alien bicycles to escape the Headbangers.

Spike shook off that thought. But unless he did something fast, Reggie would become the leader of the pack. Besides the Headbangers, he had nothing. He'd tried to redeem himself, but he hadn't been able to handle Chase, Jason or even Mademoiselle Van Damme. Next, Rocky would start beating on him. Or his younger brother, Raymond. Even his sister, Tabitha. He could just open up a stand. Throw a pie at Spike. Dump Spike in the water tank. Smack a Spike, the new hit game show!

Spike couldn't take it any longer, wound so tightly he was ready to snap. If he had any money, he'd leave home right now! Anything was better than getting beaten every single day. When he'd been playing football, it hadn't been like this, but now . . . .

Chase. What was up with Chase? He used to run away at the sight of big, bad Spike. What changed? Today Chase walked up to him like they were having a Showdown at the O.K. Corral. He'd never done that before. What made him so bold? So brave?

Spike thought long and hard for a while. He didn't want

to go home, so he wandered around, thinking about Chase. Something about The Wimp made his blood boil.

Eventually, Spike found himself in a familiar place. When Hank, Rocky, and he had pursued Chase, The Wimp had raced off the road at this very spot. They'd followed his trail to an old mansion—to the haunted House of Blue Lights. Had something special happened there? Something that not only inspired Chase to write *The Alien Bicycle*, but encouraged him to be braver and bolder? That sounded ridiculous but . . . .

Spike thought back to standing on the back porch. A strange light flashed, unnerving him. He still would've gone inside, but neither his friend nor Rocky would join him. If Chase had been able to do it, why hadn't he?

"I'm tougher than The Wimp!" Spike snarled. "I'm not frightened. I'll go there right now!"

As Spike raced deeper into the woods, it grew as quiet as the lull before a Texas thunderstorm. Spike saw the fence just in time to slow down. Finding a hole in the chainlink, he sprinted inside the estate. The weeds stretched tall and the brush wildly overgrown. The ghost gardener had been slacking.

After passing what appeared to be a ramshackle stable, Spike paused to catch his breath. So this was the place where Chase had 'met the alien.' What a chump!

At the bottom of the hill, the gray stone mansion hulked in the shadows. The westward light peeked weakly through the trees, barely illuminating the three story edifice. The House of Blue Lights emanated the air of an above-ground tomb—an ancient mausoleum to house all those legendary ghosts. Its stone walls and roof crumbled, edging closer to collapse and ruin.

The back entrance hid in heavy shadows. At the end of the pool loomed a tower which jutted skyward as though a huge nose. The top still bathed in light, the diving board stuck out like a sickly white tongue.

A gust of wind brought the shutters to life, banging open and closed like old bones being shaken. Spike felt watched. Did he see something dart across one of the windows? Spike pulled his eyes away; his imagination played tricks on him. Same as before. Same as Chase. Whoa, that was a scary thought.

Spike remembered the stories. One said the family had been poisoned with the extract of an exotic blue flower. When the victims died, their body radiated an eerie blue light. The other story involved secret government tests and a leaky nuclear reactor. In both cases, the ghosts stalked the mansion and its grounds. It was said that if they stole enough life force, they regained their lives lost.

Spike spat. He didn't believe a word of it or anything from The Wimp's *The Alien Bicycle*.

Spike marched down the hill and through the dead garden. As if skeletal hands, weeds snagged his feet, pulling him down. Spike caught himself with his hands; but still scraped his nose. With a mighty struggle and lots of cursing, Spike yanked himself free. Glancing back with a baleful glare, Spike continued toward the back door. He walked left around the scum-covered pool, staying away from the diving tower.

Spike stopped in front of the back door. On bent hinges, it hung off-kilter. The steps were cracked and crumbling, leaving a metal railing on the ground.

The wind gusted again, slamming the shutters. Spike jumped, then took a step back. Another stiff breeze shook the door, then with a *creak,* it opened invitingly.

Spike swallowed, then he snarled at his cowardice. Chase had done it! If The Wimp could do it, so could he!

Anger bolstering his courage, Spike entered the haunted house, walking into a ragged laundry room where the wallpaper peeled as if shedding. The mansion groaned, sounding like a beast awakening. Spike stepped back but refused to retreat. He marched boldly forward, his hand trailing along the wall. His footsteps echoed emptily through the house. Even slight *creaks* and *squeaks* made him start and jump.

Recalling *The Alien Bicycle,* Spike kept waiting for the blue flash of light. Obviously they hadn't imagined it, because

Chase mentioned it in his story. What had it been? Would it happen again? If so, what would happen then? Might the light make him braver? Able to stand up to his stepfather? To leave and live without Ike? That would be worth any risk! But *The Alien Bicycle* was just a story. A product of Chase's overactive imagination. Wasn't it?

Spike edgily eased past the opening to the kitchen, then the basement. He kept an eye on the basement stairs just in case. By now, the alien should be long gone. Spike tried to keep a firm grip on his imagination; but it continued to squirm.

At the end of the hallway, past several doors and doorways, the front door waited. It wasn't far. Maybe fifty feet. He'd staggered that far with two tacklers trying to drag him down!

Spike's breathing came in rasps. His leaden legs shook. What's wrong with you?! Chase had done it! Forty feet, passing a bathroom. Forced himself. Thirty feet. Drove himself. He could almost hear Chase, the skinny wimp, taunting him.

Spike ignored the holes in the walls. Nothing creepy lived in them. They didn't have tentacles for arms and eyes set upon stalks. Twenty feet. This place wasn't haunted. Ghosts didn't exist. It was just stories to stir up his fear. Ten feet, passing a door.

He felt something poised behind him, claws sprung and ready to jump him. Stop him before he reached the door. Someone or something was always trying to stop him.

Spike yanked open the rickety front door and stepped outside. "Whew!" He wiped away the sweat pouring down his face. "I did it! I did it!" Spike roared to the sky. "Chase, this isn't over yet!"

NINE

First Flight

"Danny, we should be going." Murg reclined on the steps, her eyes gleaming as emeralds in the bright moonlight. The night air wafted chilly, becoming biting when a breeze brushed through the backyard.

"Where are we going at this hour?" Krindee sat on a lower step.

"To Germany to see our friend, Gretchen." Voices carried too loudly at night, calling attention, so Danny replied telepathically. He looked for Comet, unable to find the black dog in the deep shadows. "She knows about Kalyde II."

"Benjamin Disraeli said, 'Travel teaches toleration'."

"I have been a stranger in a strange land." Murg lifted up a paw to glance underneath it. A cricket scooted forward a few inches, then the calico dropped her paw upon the bug.

"Exodus. I didn't know you studied their religion," Krindee projected.

"George Bernard Shaw—a great lover of cats, as are all wise men—said, there is only one religion, though there are a hundred versions of it." Murg lifted her paw, batting the cricket back and forth.

"Can you gals be a little more quiet? My head's ringing. Doesn't the wise cat speaketh little, silence is golden or something?" Danny 'heard' a sullen silence in response.

"Comet?" Nothing stirred in the shadows. "Comet? Comet! Come!"

A black blur, Comet streaked across the back yard. Danny scooped up his puppy, laughing as he tried to avoid the retriever's lightning-fast tongue. "I hate to put him inside and leave. He gets lonely."

"Bring him along," Krindee thought.

"NO!" Murg replied.

"He's too young." Danny gave Comet a big hug, then put him in the laundry room.

Back outside again, Danny glanced up at his dad's window. Was he watching, per covert orders from Colonel Hawker? Just waiting for him to go in search of aliens? "Murg, what if the Shadow Daggers are watching me by satellite?"

"They aren't. They have a homing signal on your bike sitting in the garage. What more do they need to keep track of a fourteen-year-old kid?"

"Are you sure?"

"I have a sixth sense about these things. Now, let's go."

Danny snuck through the shadows to the far, dark corner of the yard, then climbed the fence. When he landed, Danny listened for calls of alarm or pursuit. The calico took the lead, disappearing into the moonlit and shadow-striped woods.

"Why not change Kalyde II into a bicycle in your room?" Krindee asked.

"It makes too much noise, but I'm working on it." Danny moved farther into the woods, staying in the shadows. The trio crossed a creek, then climbed an embankment leading to a road.

Danny waited in the woods, pretending he was a cat, listening and watching. No secret agents and no black sedans. The farm road was deserted and quiet, except for the muted symphony of buzzing bugs and chirping crickets. "Let's go before I'm eaten alive. We need a good winter freeze to get rid of the bugs." Danny took off his watch. Closing his eyes, he pictured Kalyde II in bicycle form, shaped as the red Bowden Spacelander but with mountain bike handlebars. A flash of light enveloped the threesome, then the sound of a balloon expanding hissed throughout the night.

When Danny felt the Spacelander's frame in hand, he opened his eyes and smiled. Thought working magic! "Let's ride." Danny climbed onto the Spacelander. Krindee hopped gracefully to the carrier, then into Danny's backpack. "Coming?" Danny asked Murg.

The calico sauntered to the bicycle. With a lithe hop, Murg landed on the book rack— or the feline palanquin as she'd come to call it. " The Egyptians, who worshipped cats as deities, carried pharaohs and queens on a throne atop a platform lined with poles. It was called a palanquin."

Danny remembered to turn on the headlight. The beam was brighter than a lighthouse beacon, splashing the road with near daylight intensity.

"Can't you see in the dark?" Krindee asked.

"Humans can't see in the dark," Danny replied.

"But you're on a magic bicycle."

Danny turned off the headlight, then imagined being able to see in the dark. "I . . . I can!" The world's colors were subdued, mostly dark and gray. Trees, bushes, fences and telephone poles lined the roadway heading into the rural lands of north Texas.

"Let's go!" Quickly settling into a rhythm, Danny pedaled down the road.

"What's Germany like?" Krindee asked.

"Lots of mountains, alpine valleys and rolling hills cut by streams and canyons made by melting snow. I'm concentrating on the stream where Gretchen will be waiting." The area was a branch of the Isar River, one of several shallow rock-filled creeks not far from her school.

The bicycle raced faster, the surroundings blending into one long, gray-black blur. The road ahead seemed endless, the black asphalt melding with the dark somewhere far ahead.

Danny thought of Gretchen: her huge, dimpled smile and apple cheeks. Her eyes radiated the warmth of the sky on a sunny day. She made him laugh and think positively about things, lifting his spirits when he was downhearted, just as Sarah had done during troubled times.

With a resounding roar of thunder, darkness gave way to a flash of lightning. The threesome burst from the cloudy mists onto the rainbow highway. After the darkness, the colors shone blindingly.

Kalyde II rocketed ahead, following the skyway's arc high into the clouds, where it shot through a wispy mass, reminding Danny of a deserted toll booth. The bicycle crested the peak of the rainbow, threatening to touch the stars, then plummeted downhill, joining the falling stars' plunge.

Murg unleashed a wailing caterwaul of pure pleasure.

They disappeared in a wash of light, then with a *whoosh* that wafted through the alpine canyons, Danny, Murg, and Krindee appeared in Germany. The road stretched before them, running along the Isar River and down a mountain canyon. As usual, Danny's smile threatened to burst free from his face.

"There she is." Murg's tail flicked to and fro.

"Hi Danny! So nice you could join me again for our secret rendezvous." Gretchen laughed. "And Murg!" Gretchen picked up the calico and hugged her. "Danny, you're riding with two cats?! When did you get a second cat? She's gorgeous!"

"What am I?" Murg wondered aloud.

"What you wish to appear to be." At first, Gretchen had been surprised when Murg spoke; but now Gretchen liked matching wits with the calico.

"I now have two new friends, Krindee here, and a puppy named Comet," Danny said.

"Great! I'll bet you're thrilled about the dog," Gretchen told Murg.

The calico's tail snapped.

"Is anybody else around?" Danny watched for the sudden arrival of Blackhawk helicopters.

"Just ghosts," Gretchen replied. "Why so secretive?" Danny gave her a skeptical look. "More secretive than usual?"

"Well, first, Krindee isn't a Siamese cat. Her full name is Kri-neee-dee."

"Kri-neee-dee? That makes me think of Kah-laye-dee."

"She is smart." The Siamese jumped to the ground.

"Gretchen Heinrich, I would like you to meet Kalyde's sister."

Gretchen watched in open-mouthed and wide-eyed amazement as the Siamese's body glowed, then grew, an expanding balloon gone wild. A ripple of light washed across Krindee, then she suddenly appeared human.

"You look like Sarah! It's uncanny." Gretchen studied the Cor-ror-o'lan turned human, then pulled Krindee into a hug. "From his description of Kah-laye-dee, this isn't what I expected."

"Were you expecting someone less human appearing?" Krindee asked.

Gretchen nodded.

"Murg, do you sense anyone?" Krindee asked.

The calico yawned, apparently bored to near slumber.

"Good." Krindee changed to Kri-neee-dee. Her long blond hair and girlish features melted away, reshaping into a silver woman with lavender eyes and a crossways magenta Mohawk.

"W... wow!" Gretchen stammered, then she smiled. "Very punk."

"Don't show yourself off too long," Murg said. "Somebody might come along."

Kri-neee-dee waved her hands along her body. A glow washed from her palms, bringing claymation-like change. In moments, the Cor-ror-o'lan was once again the Siamese cat, Krindee.

"Girls, can we ride and talk?" Danny asked.

They nodded. "Where to?" Gretchen asked.

"We're going to fly!"

Gretchen paled. "I thought you said—Kalyde said—that the magic bicycle couldn't fly."

With a thought and a touch, Danny transformed Kalyde II into a tandem. "He did. But then he didn't think it could travel time, either. Here." He handed her a brain bucket.

Gretchen donned the helmet. "You're not planning on dropping off the rainbow, are you? Or launching?"

"You've been hearing bad things from Murg." Danny glanced at the calico. Her eyes were closed. "I've been studying." Danny told Gretchen about what he'd learned about avians and aviation.

"You really think that will help?" With one eyebrow raised and her head cocked, Gretchen's opinion appeared obvious.

"I'm ready this time. I've prepared myself, just as I did with traveling back in time."

"Have you ever been hurt on this bicycle?" Gretchen asked.

"Just his pride," Murg replied.

"Never. And neither will you," Danny replied. "Let's go fly!"

"If we lacked imagination enough to foresee something better, life would indeed be a tragedy," Krindee said. "Laurence J. Peter."

"She studied earth history and now she's showing off," Danny said. Gretchen rolled her eyes. Krindee just blinked slowly and unevenly. "Everybody ready?" Danny received a 'yes,' a meow and a caterwaul as replies. "Today, we are going to fly!"

Together, the foursome concentrated on Nevada and the Loneliest Highway. They pedaled at a normal pace; but Kalyde II devoured ground as though starved for asphalt. A roaring flash enveloped them, then they soared across the dazzling rainbow.

With an explosion of light and a bellowing *whoosh*, they appeared on a highway atop a snow-covered mountain. The full moon presided over the desolate land. The dark stripe of the road sloped away, disappearing around a black curve in the whiteness. Danny looked both ways. "I don't hear or see anything. Let's go!"

"Aren't you going to turn on your headlight?" Gretchen asked.

"We can see by the light of the moon, or just see in the dark," Danny replied. "Imagine you can. Go ahead, just try."

"Danny. . . . Ok. I'll try," Gretchen whispered. *"Wow!* What do I do now?"

"Think lightweight thoughts and pretend the bicycle has wings."

Danny pushed off, letting gravity seize the bicycle. "Gretchen Heinrich, Kri-neee-dee, Danny Chase and Murg, the wonder cat, are about to make history."

The chilling wind flowed around them. Those currents gathered force, swirling behind and propelling the magic bicycle faster and faster down the mountain. "Elemental winds are pushing us!" Danny imagined the creatures of air behind them, cheeks billowing as they blew.

Danny pictured the bicycle; it was lithe, sleek, and made from the material of ultra-lights. Two sets of wings slowly unfurled from the bicycle, one in the rear and the other between Danny and Gretchen. The pinions stretched wide, fluttering in the winds. Danny added flaps, then adjusted them to catch the wind. Gravity eased its grip.

"Danny! You're doing it!" Gretchen cried.

Danny smiled. He felt overwhelming lightness, then he grew light-headed.

"Hey! Do you see that?" Danny asked. For just a moment, until his eyes focused on it, he'd seen a brilliant emerald orb floating nearby like an observing eye. "It's . . . it's gone." Could it have something to do with the Shadow Daggers?

"What . . . ." Gretchen began.

Kalyde II abruptly whipped sideways, spinning as a top across a stretch of gleaming black ice.

"Danny!" Gretchen screamed, her words flailing around him. The world whirled faster and faster.

Danny held tight, just trying to ride it out and keep the bicycle upright. At the speed they were going . . . . He changed his thoughts. They were safe. Kalyde II was safe. Tucking in the wings, Danny imagined they spun with the grace of Olympic skaters.

"Hang on!"

The front wheel jerked, then the rear caught. Danny hung on as the spinning abruptly stopped. Gretchen slammed into his back. Squashed in between, Krindee wailed. Murg's claws spread wide, digging into the palanquin.

As though nothing had happened, the tandem raced downhill, tearing air and squealing tires through a curve. Danny pulled onto the side of the road. Gretchen slumped against him. Krindee jumped to the ground, landed awkwardly and then threw up.

Murg sprawled across the carrier, eyes still spinning and her tongue hanging out to one side. "That," she thought to Krindee, "is undignified."

"Everybody okay?" Danny asked.

"I *never* want to do that again." Gretchen replied.

"An understatement if I ever heard one," Krindee projected.

"We were almost flying!" Danny told them, his eyes alight and face flushed. "And . . . and now that we've hit ice, we know how to handle it. It was . . . sorta fun. Wasn't it?"

The threesome looked at him as if he were stark raving mad.

"I wish I was wearing body armor to go along with my helmet!" Gretchen straightened. "Krindee, surely you didn't visit us just to go flying."

"I'm here to learn about the Human Race."

"See if we're fit to socialize with?" Gretchen asked.

"In a manner of speaking, yes," Krindee replied.

Danny explained about Krindee's mission, the Shadow Daggers and their tracking devices. "And that's why I'm here," Krindee finished, "To find out if there are more Gretchens and Danny Chases than Spikes and Mr. Picketts populating this planet."

"Danny, I'm concerned," Gretchen said.

"I'm very, very careful."

"Thanks for trusting me."

Although it hadn't happened in this time, Danny remembered the trouble caused by confiding in Gretchen before. While sick, she'd told her father, who'd told his dad. They'd tried to confiscate his bicycle. Danny thought with the back-tracking and replaying of time and history, Gretchen would've forgotten about the bicycle; but she still remembered, thinking they were dreams. He needed to confide in someone, so he told her, again; but he'd never told Jason and Christina.

"Danny, is Spike still bothering you?" Gretchen asked.

"Yeah, and since that new guy, Reggie, moved from LA, it's gotten worse." Danny explained about his recent encounters with Spike and the Headbangers.

"Krindee did more than observe, violating her charter," Murg said, commeting on the alien's encounter with Spike at school.

"You are right to chastise me, Murg. There is plenty of fighting in Terran history." Eyes downcast, the Siamese's expression appeared grave. "So much it might be contagious. That concern distresses my people. Evolved races have better ways to resolve disputes."

"When I think back across our history, I'm not surprised you question our cosmic sociability," Gretchen said thoughtfully. "Danny, you *have* to do something about Spike. Krindee won't always be around to use Kung Fu."

"I *don't* want to help Spike."

"Danny, if you can go out of your way to help an alien stranger, you can certainly take the time to help—choose to help—one of your own kind," Gretchen said.

Danny sighed. "Suggestions?"

"I don't know, but avoiding him hasn't really helped, has it?"

"I'm healthier for it," Danny replied.

"But it's escalating!" Gretchen waved her arms.

"Danny, this could be an important question about your race," Krindee said. "What makes your people hostile?"

"A lot of things," Danny replied.

"That is an understatement." Murg yawned.

"Is Spike a good example of the hostile people of your world?" Krindee asked.

"Americanized but prime." Murg yawned again.

"Well, unless it's genetic or drug-induced, hostility is learned," Gretchen announced. "Danny, I think you should really think about Spike. Solve the problem instead of avoiding it."

"How?"

"How should I know?" she replied. "You're the one with the limitless imagination. How would you imagine the problem resolved? I mean, in a sense, you were able to 'imagine' your mom and Sarah alive when you traveled back in time."

Danny was silent for a long time. "We could make sure Spike's mom never meets his dad. Reverse the storyline from the movie *Back to the Future*."

"Humor to handle distress. Our races have that similarity," Krindee said. "I believe it to be a good one."

"I don't like you traveling time," Gretchen began, "But if you do, I suggest taking Spike back in time."

"Not a good idea," Murg stressed.

"My mom says abuse is a vicious circle," Gretchen said. "You pass it on . . . like a disease."

"That's right, your mom's a psychiatrist." Danny recalled.

"Marie, a friend of mine, shares a common past with Spike," Gretchen said sadly. "She just handles it differently. So if you go back, show Spike that he's violent because his stepfather beats him. Who knows, perhaps his stepfather's father beat him and so on and so on. You see? Maybe seeing that would help break the cycle. Someone must. With Kalyde II, you could even take him to the future and show him beating his own kid. Odds are he will."

"No time travel," Murg maintained.

"By then Spike won't care," Danny said. "He hits his brother now."

"Brothers hit brothers a lot and it's not always abuse," Gretchen told him. "Think on it."

"I have. Murg won't let me leave Spike in the middle of the Atlantic Ocean or in Antarctica, either." Danny smiled. "I think the penguins would love Spike. Sharks, of course, would like him even better. Spike versus the Great White Sharks!"

All but Murg laughed, trading dire suggestions for Spike's justice: cement shoes, introductions to a basalisk, captivity in a Tibetan monk's temple, and working the Salt Mines of Grundge on the black moon of Tavias in the Alpha Centari system.

"Danny, I really do think you should do something about Spike—help your fellow man. Put your imagination to work."

Danny was thoughtful. "I will, IF, you'll try flying one more time today. Tonight! This morning! Whatever time it is! The time is now!"

Gretchen looked at him for a long while, then she smiled slowly. "Deal! But if we fly, you have to try something different with Spike, okay? You can't just avoid him anymore."

"I promise."

"Then let's fly." Gretchen flipped her ponytail over her shoulder.

When everyone was settled, Danny pushed off, letting gravity seize them, hauling them gradually faster downhill. Danny imagined the wind aiding him, cloud giants putting their massive shoulders behind them and shoving. Danny began pedaling, this time driving on the upstroke.

Pulled, pushed, and driven, Kalyde II raced down the mountain, a rocket on wheels. The cold air howled defiance, the wind screaming. The landscape blurred, light and dark flickering as areas of moonlit snow and hollow-blue shadows flashed by.

In his mind, Danny imagined riding a mechanical pegasus. Its wings majestically unfurled, spreading wide. Kalyde II shifted, its star metal flesh altering. Wings protruded from behind Danny's seat and from next to Murg. The feathers ruffled, whistling and sometimes humming in the winds. He added flaps to the feathers. An eerie sense of weightlessness, as if he were falling, welled up from Danny's stomach.

"Danny, you're doing it!" Gretchen cried.

"Of course. He's my protege," Murg replied. "Impossible is not in his vocabulary."

Danny looked down. The falling sensation was actually rising! "We're pulling away from the road! Gretchen, keep pedaling for balance!" They floated a few feet farther above the ground, gaining altitude and drifting skyward. "We're flying! We're really flying!" Danny let out a big *whoop* and a holler. Gretchen joined his cheering.

They glided away from the road, the metal pegasus carrying them aloft. The snowy hills and white-blanketed trees seemed to rise and fall as they sailed over its peaks and gullies.

Danny tilted the bicycle. A night breeze wafted up a canyon, further lifting them. They circled ever higher as if an eagle riding the currents, around and around, reaching for the stars. The bright pinpoints grew larger and brighter, urging them on. Mars hung in the sky as a glowing red dot. Venus shone as magnificently as a giant diamond.

Danny guided the magical bicycle toward the valley, soaring as straight as a lazy arrow. "I knew we could do it! Yee-haw!"

"Danny! This is incredible! The air tastes so much better! Sweeter!" Gretchen breathed deeply and sighed.

"Great works are performed not through strength but perseverance," Krindee told him. "Your Samuel Johnson."

"Not without imagination," Danny replied. "Imagination lets us see where we're going."

"A dream come true," Murg said. "I believe Kalyde telling you that the magic bicycle couldn't fly created some sort of mental block. You didn't believe it could be done, so doing it became difficult."

"Yes, anything is possible," Krindee said. "But first you must put your mind to it."

"Maybe Cor-ror-o'lans and Terrans will become friends," Danny suggested hopefully.

"Four already have," Krindee replied.

"Danny! Thank you! This is the most incredible thing I've ever done! Thank you!" Gretchen hugged him. "There's something about seeing far that's inspiring."

"It certainly gives one a different perspective on the world," Murg told them.

"If I can fly," Danny said thoughtfully, "I can figure out a way to deal with Spike. Imagine a better way."

TEN

Hunted

The next day, Danny still felt exhilarated from his flying adventure. Drifting. Gliding. Sailing. Soaring on air, light as a bird. "I think having Gretchen with us helped us fly." Danny put the last of the evening papers into his carrier bag. "That was quite a morning, night, whatever it was, wasn't it?"

Krindee meowed. Nearby, Murg quietly slept on the grass.

Danny checked his watch, then sighed. The paper truck had arrived late. A winter nip chilled the air. Soon, after sunset, temperatures would plummet. "If we don't want to deliver the papers in the dark, we'd better hustle."

Krindee jumped up and climbed into his backpack. With a bored look, Murg leisurely climbed onto the back and waited like a queen being carriaged to a formal banquet.

Danny lost himself in the routine of delivering papers; he could almost do this blindfolded. Riding Kalyde II no-handed was easy and allowed his mind to drift.

It had been a good couple of days, Danny thought. Yesterday, he'd aced a pop quiz in algebra. Comet was a new joy in his life; flashing tongue and wagging tail, he was always glad to see Danny.

To top it all off, Danny hadn't seen Spike in days, not since the incident with Krindee. Danny had heard more than one version of the event. In a few, he felt embarrassed by the way he was portrayed. In all of them, Spike was thoroughly shamed and totally slammed. "Ernest" was skipping school and hiding his face.

This frightened Danny. Alert and wary, he didn't expect Spike to keep his promise not to harm him. Danny wished he could talk with his friends about Spike; but Jason was at basketball practice, and Christina attended cheerleading practice.

Danny tossed a pair of papers. "Are you two going to help me figure out what to do about Spike?"

"It was your promise," Murg replied.

"If you can turn Spike around," Krindee began, "there is hope for just about anyone of your race. Especially the young that are not yet completely jaded."

"Yeah, but it's not like I can come up to Spike and say, 'Hey big fella, I think I know what you're going through. Why don't you get some help? Talk to the counselor? Or a teacher? Call one of the hotlines.' How's that?"

"That would certainly be a different approach," Murg agreed.

"The bashing would be the same." Danny sent another paper spinning, then glanced at the sky.

The sun sat upon the horizon where dark clouds boiled. The growing storm rapidly swallowed the sinking red orb. The light peeking through the clouds was an eerie purple-crimson, washing over houses and reflecting off windows.

"I'd better pick up the pace." As Danny zipped along the streets and darted through neighborhoods, he kept thinking about dealing with Spike. Wishful thinking didn't help any.

"A waste of time," Murg agreed. "Imagining, yes. Wishful, no."

"Besides talking to him, what would work?" Danny wondered. "I can't use the bicycle to help him. That would probably lead to disaster. Spike already had his hands on Kalyde II once. He used it to hurt somebody."

"He was injured, too." Murg thought. "And remember, that didn't happen in this Time."

"I guess I could go to the school counselor. But if Spike doesn't accuse Mr. Pickett of abuse, what good would that do? Maybe I could talk with his brother first. If they both saw the counselor . . . ."

"That's a start," Murg thought.

Danny reached the end of the street. Here, new houses were under construction. The gravel road led to dirt lots crammed with stacks of brick and piles of lumber. Some plots were little more than holes in the ground.

"I have one of those feelings of deja vu. Hey!" Danny cried. He felt pinched! "Which one of you did that? OUCH!" Danny slapped at his neck. He'd been stung!

"I'm hit too!" Murg growled. "Someone's firing on us! Get out of here!"

Something *whizzed* by Danny's ear. He jumped on the pedals and thought speed. As if catapulted, Kalyde II shot away, racing farther into the construction. The magic bicycle struck gravel and slowed. Danny imagined a smooth ride. Running easily, as though across a newly paved road, the magic bicycle rocketed away.

"GET HIM!" Somebody cried. From between houses and out of a garage, three motorbikes barreled toward Danny. Two boys carried rifles; the third one smoked a cigarette and wielded a bat. As if a sound track, hard-driving and headbanging music kicked in.

"Spike and the Headbangers! I knew it!" Danny cried.

"They're carrying BB guns. Hmm. I don't see Spike." Murg calmly appraised the terrorists.

"Nor I." Krindee cocked her head. "That boy with the bright orange hair. If his skin was shiny, one might mistake him for

Don-lowe-mor, a friend of Kah-laye-dee's."

"Did this Don-lowe-mor snarl in that pleasant way?" Murg ducked. A BB ricocheted off the seat spring.

"Thankfully, no."

"Does he pierce himself for adornment, like flame-top?"

"No, but some do," Krindee replied.

"Another wonderful commonality between Cor-ror-o'lans and Earthlings."

"The guy with the face metal is Vargas," Danny breathed. "I don't know his first name. He's from Houston."

"Do Cor-ror-o'lans tattoo themselves?" Murg asked. "Turn themselves into walking billboards?"

"No." Krindee ducked inside the backpack.

Danny glanced over his shoulder. "Reggie's leading them."

The gaunt boy with the dark hair and eyes wore a red-leather jacket. With the practiced ease of an Old West gunslinger, Reggie stuffed his rifle in a saddlebag and pulled out a bat. "Coming for ya, Chase!"

"I'll bet this is Spike's fault!" Danny twisted the handlebars. Kalyde II swerved, throwing out rocks behind it.

The nearest rider, Vargas, screamed as he covered his face, then veered away. Reggie and the tattooed boy gave their motorbikes more gas. With a whining roar, Reggie closed on Danny. "Coming for ya, chicken boy!" Reggie snarled. "First you, then Jason!"

"Danny he's getting close," Murg projected.

"I'm trying not to blow my cover!"

As Reggie closed, he swung his bat. "Get him, Page! He's sucking up good air!"

"HEY!" Murg complained as she dodged Reggie's swing. "Now would be a wise time to initiate some evasive tactics."

The tattooed rider roared along Danny's other flank. Writhing snakes breathing fire covered his arms. "We got ya, Chase!" Page yelled, the cigarette sticking to his lower lip.

The Headbangers grew closer. Moved tighter. Page hefted his bat. "Batter up!"

Danny quit pedaling and stopped on a dime. In a cloud of dust and bouncing rock, the riders blew by him. Danny pivoted and turned behind them, heading for an unfinished house.

Reggie cursed and steered back around. Muscling his motorized horse, Page followed.

"I don't believe it!" Page cried. "Get him, Vargas!"

The orange-haired boy was closest now.

Danny noticed his rifle was larger than a normal BB gun. "That's a 410 shotgun! I knew this was going to happen! I knew it!" Danny steered for the boards ramping to the front door.

The shotgun roared.

Danny gunned his imagination. As though fired from a cannon, Kalyde II exploded forward. The magic bicycle hit the boards leading to the front door and shot airborne, flying into the house. Buckshot whizzed by Danny, taking bites out of the doorframe.

The magic bicycle bounced twice in the unfinished entryway, then raced through the house. As though bars on a cell, two-by-fours rushed together.

"Danny!" Murg squeezed her eyes shut. Claws seized the padded carrier.

Vargas ramped into the house, bounced once, then slammed into a doorframe.

"One down!" Danny guided the rocketing bicycle left into the living room and past the fireplace. Kalyde II burst out the back door, soaring long to a smooth landing.

"Launch practice came in handy!" Danny laughed.

"Danny! This is nothing to laugh at! That was a shotgun!" Murg thought. "The Headbangers are not trying to scare you anymore!"

Danny turned right, heading to the next unfinished house. Insulation panels and sheet rock gave him more cover.

The harsh roar of an engine announced the boy with the

tattoos closing the gap. Danny glanced back. Page carried a bat. Danny glanced right. Reggie gunned the motorbike, racing between buildings. He no longer carried a Louisville slugger but a .357 Magnum. "This is special, just for you, from LA!" The handgun roared, spitting fire. A bullet ripped into the rear tire. Kalyde II shuddered, then hit the ramp to the back door at an awkward angle. The boards went flying, slipping into the dry rut below. The magic bicycle twisted in the air as though a wounded bird.

"I don't like jumping!" Murg closed her eyes and hunkered down.

Danny fought for a moment, then relaxed. He imagined Kalyde II's frame flattening to better catch the air. The magic bicycle soared a little slower, giving Danny time to straighten their line. He twisted the handlebars just in time, allowing them to slip through the doorframe. They landed softly, then raced inside.

A bullet shattered a nearby board. Wood chips swirled in Kalyde's wake.

Danny turned into the bathroom. Drywall had been erected, giving him some cover. Through the unfinished window, he saw Reggie race around front, trying to cut him off.

"Spike kept his promise. He's not harming me," Danny snapped. "Spike's having the Headbangers do it for him! We're out of here."

A bike roared up the front ramp, then *thumped* into the house.

"Where are we going?" Krindee asked.

"To Jason's. Spike didn't promise not to hurt him," Danny replied. "I hope and pray the Shadow Daggers think this little jump is just a blip on their screen."

Danny closed his eyes and imagined himself elsewhere.

ELEVEN

A Matter of Trust

With a *whoosh,* Danny, the two felines and Kalyde II appeared in a stand of trees near Jason's house. Danny searched the neighborhood for trouble, then rode to his friend's house. The long, one-story home was brick with white trimming around arched windows and doorways. Danny walked Kalyde II to the door and knocked.

After a minute, Jason opened the door. "Hey, Speed-demon!"

"Hi Jason."

"Is everything okay? As my mom would say, you look stressed."

"Jason, who is it?" came his mother's call.

"See? Moms. It's Danny Chase!"

"Remember, you have homework to finish."

"I'll only be a minute, Ma. I promise. Man! Moms!" Jason

stepped outside and pulled the door closed. "Between school, basketball, Cynthia and riding with you, I'm swamped."

"Have you seen Spike recently?" Danny asked.

"No! Why would I? He's in hiding! When I see him, I'm going to kick his butt! I told him that last time. Why? Has he been bothering you?"

Danny nodded, then explained what had just happened.

"Guns?! Guns!" Jason's eyes widened. "Man-o-man-o-man! You're serious, aren't you?"

"I was afraid they might've split up, with Spike coming here."

"Naw, he wouldn't do that. If it's just one on one, he's scared of me. Danny, what are you going to do? Call the police?"

"Tell my dad, first."

"Sounds like a good idea. Hey, thanks for warning me." Jason clasped him on the shoulder. "If you want, I could ask my mom to give you a ride home."

"I think I'm all right tonight." Danny climbed on his bicycle. "See you tomorrow!"

"Murg, what if Spike went after Christina?"

Once out of sight, Danny pictured her neighborhood. A little down the street from her house grew a thin gathering of trees. Fortunately, it was dark, so no one could see them arrive. With a rumbling *whoosh* and a dim flash, they appeared among the dark copse of trees. "It looks peaceful."

"Feels good," Murg agreed. "But let's check anyway."

They conducted a sweep of the area, even turning Kalyde II into a road-bike. The streets seemed clear, the woods free of thugs. "Let's head home." When he saw Andie Mayfair's car in his driveway, Danny became even more distressed.

"Give her a chance," Murg said.

"I think I've taken enough chances tonight," Danny replied. After circling the neighborhood, he parked in the trees near his normal bicycle. He made the quick change, including switching homing devices, then rode home. A minute later Danny stopped at his garage doors.

"You better slip away," Danny told Krindee. "I left my window open. If Dad closed it, I'll let you in when I visit Comet."

"Lucky you," Murg thought.

"You are just prejudiced." Her Siamese smile radiated satisfaction.

"I am not. 'A dog teaches a boy fidelity, perseverance and to turn around three times before lying down.' Robert Benchly. I have higher hopes for Danny."

Once inside, Danny heard his dad pacing. Danny shut the door to the garage and walked into the kitchen.

"Danny?" A bit flushed with ruffled hair, his father appeared upset. "Where have you been?!" His father rushed forward, putting his hands on Danny's shoulders. "Are you all right? You look tired."

"I am."

Petite and dark-haired, Ms. Mayfair sat at the kitchen table. Her warm smile reached her dark brown eyes. "Hi Danny."

"Hi." Danny looked back to his father. "Dad, I have a . . . . problem? Can we talk?"

"It's all right. You can speak in front of Ms. Mayfair. You should thank her for Comet."

"It would be proper," Murg agreed. "You should thank someone even for a gift you don't like. In this case, a worthless gift. But it's the thought that counts."

"It's serious, Dad," Danny whispered. "It's sort of like the alien thing but not quite. Please?"

His father's stare scrutinized Danny. "All right. Andie, we'll be back in a minute." His father motioned to the family room.

"Ms. Mayfair. Thanks for Comet! He's a great dog! I think he's going to be very smart."

"You're very welcome. He needed a good home. I think he's found one."

Danny walked into his father's office and waited. Murg sat next to his feet.

His father closed the door. "As bad as the alien?" Captain Chase asked, his expression serious. His eyes flattened, sharpening into interrogation mode.

"Not exactly. Do you remember Spike?" Danny asked.

"Of course. He's the bully at school. You think he stole your English paper, right?"

"Yeah," Danny replied. "There's a new kid at school. Reggie. He's friends with Spike. Tonight, Reggie and his buddies shot at me!"

"Shot at you . . . Danny . . . ."

"Yes, Dad. They shot at Murg and me! Shot at us with BB guns, a 410 shotgun and a .357 Magnum!"

As if examining a new recruit, his father looked him over from head to toe. "Are you all right?"

Danny was shaking. "Yeah. So's Murg. We weren't hit, except by BBs."

Murg meowed pitifully.

"BBs. Hmmm. Danny, are you sure you're not just imagining things?"

"Yes."

His father sighed. "Why would somebody shoot at you?"

Danny explained about Spike stealing Jason's bike, the visit with Mr. Pickett, and then gave an altered recount of the confrontation with Spike. Danny finished with the ambush and guns blazing.

"Spike sent hit men on motorbikes after you?" His father's eyebrows arched skeptically above a long, dead-pan expression. "Did they hit anything, son?"

"Careful," Murg warned.

"My bicycle once and some of the houses a bunch of times."

"Your bicycle. What did the bullet damage?"

"Uh . . . ." Danny suddenly remembered Kalyde II had been hit, not his bike in the garage. Could he make the change in time, swapping one for the other? No, his father wanted to see it right now. "A bullet just . . . just grazed the paint."

"Let's take a look." His father turned to the door.

"Wait! Let's go to the houses at Red Stone instead! There's bullets stuck in the 2x4's."

"Danny, it's dark and a ten-minute drive. Let's just look at your bicycle." His father turned toward the door.

"But . . . ."

"There's nothing wrong is there?" his father asked over his shoulder.

"Dad, they really shot at me. Really, really shot at me! I'm telling the truth!" He sounded as if he were pleading. He hated that.

"This is about Andie, isn't it? You don't like me spending time with her, do you?"

Danny stiffened. That was true but . . . . "Dad, they could've killed me! Come look!"

His father pulled Danny into a hug. "Danny, I think I understand. I miss Mom, too. But she'd want us to make new friends. Nobody will replace your . . . ."

Danny wanted to scream. "Mom would believe me."

His father's face tightened. "Yes, she probably would. Tell you what, son, I'll check out the houses. You're safe here, Danny."

"Dad . . . ."

"Danny, I am not going. Come join us for dinner. Andie cooked a fabulous lasagna."

"I'm not hungry!" Danny raced upstairs, yanked open the door and hurled himself onto his bed. Unable to lay or sit, he paced the room. Danny grabbed the pillows and threw them. He wanted to scream and break things.

After a while, Murg slipped into the room. "Finished ranting and raving yet?"

Danny sniffed. "Dad doesn't believe me. Why is this any wilder than meeting aliens?"

"Danny it's not what you're saying, it's when you're bringing it up. You would have had a better chance if your Dad had been alone, giving him less reason to think you're trying to keep him from Ms. Mayfair." Murg sighed. "Even though you've traveled time, your timing could definitely improve."

"Murg, what am I going to do?" Danny asked.

"It seems you're now forced to do something about Spike," Murg replied.

TWELVE

Games

"It was nice of Christina to invite me to Jason's ball game," Krindee said from the back of the tandem. In Gretchen's style, her hair was tied into a long, red-gold ponytail.

"Uh-huh." Danny scrutinized every single shadow. Even with his dark-vision, Danny didn't see any threats; but he couldn't shake the feeling someone followed them. He preferred staying home; but he just couldn't miss Jason's first basketball game. After last night, Danny felt lucky he was allowed to go to the game at all.

At least the Shadow Daggers hadn't confronted him, asking for an explanation about the sudden distance change; although someone had checked on the homing devices. The clumps of cat hair Murg had intentionally left had been moved, meaning someone had snuck into the garage. Were they doing this with his father's permission?

"Something wrong?" Krindee asked.

"Lots of things. Yesterday we were shot at! Tonight, if Reggie and the Headbangers show up, we could be dodging hot lead again. I wish Murg was with us; she'd know if we were being followed."

"Why can't she come along?"

"Because she can't change into a human like you can," Danny replied.

Krindee chuckled. "Not even cats are perfect."

"Well, here we are. Back at school." As Danny ramped onto the sidewalk, he wished he didn't have to leave Kalyde II at the bicycle racks. He felt something bad might happen.

"Take it with you."

"Somebody might see me change it."

"Well, if it's damaged, can't you just reshape it?" Krindee asked.

"Yes. I'm more worried about it getting stolen. In another time, Spike stole it. Boy, was that a mess. I make sure Spike can't do that now."

Danny disconnected two locks from under the seats, then wound an unbreakable chain through Kalyde II's frame and wheels. "Safe and sound. Come on. We want to say hi to Christina before the game. Remember, you don't know much about basketball."

"I can manage that."

"And your English is only okay. Misunderstand something every now and then."

"Danny," Krindee reassured him. "I've done this before."

"Sorry." Danny opened the door to the gymnasium foyer. From inside, the sounds of milling, bouncing basketballs and the squeaking of shoes mixed to create an air of excitement.

"Let's go enjoy ourselves! I've never attended a basketball game!" Krindee cried. Danny showed his school ID, then paid for Krindee. "I could have snuck in as a cat. No one would be the wiser," she whispered. "This place has a nice feel to it. Upbeat with lots of energy. Except," Krindee rubbed her ears, "the chirping of the sneakers hurts my ears."

The gymnasium was noisy but not very crowded. Straight ahead stretched a set of folding bleachers pulled out from the wall. A few students, but mostly parents, stood waiting for the game to begin. Several devout fans waved flags. Two teams, one in green and white and one in red and yellow, performed lay-up drills.

The cheerleaders danced and performed in front of the near sideline bleachers. Christina was the closest. She nodded at him as if telling them to wait.

"Is this jv or varsity?" Krindee asked.

"Don't talk like that!"

"I am sorry, monsieur. I know nothing of the game of baseball."

"That's better."

"The need to belong to something—a club, a gang, a church or a family—is a very powerful force in your species," Krindee observed.

"Most people don't enjoy being alone as much as I do," Danny replied.

"Blaise Pascal said, 'Most of the evils of life arise from man's inability to sit still in a room'."

"Here comes Christina." Danny walked forward to greet her. They hugged, then Christina moved to Krindee, who kissed her on each cheek.

"Bonjour," Krindee said.

"Bonjour! I'm glad you could make it! The game's about to start."

"Have you seen Spike? Has he given you any trouble?" Danny asked. "He or Reggie?"

"No, why?" she asked. The overhead buzzer sounded. Krindee grabbed her ears. The teams walked to their respective benches. "Go sit. You were almost late." Christina gently shoved Danny toward the bleachers. "Have a good time!"

"Merci'."

Danny led Krindee up the bleacher steps. When an official's whistle sounded, five boys from each team walked out to center court. Jason wore a green and white jersey, like the Celtics of old, he would say.

"Cool! Jason's starting," Danny told Krindee.

"Is he good?" she wondered.

"You know . . . I don't know. I guess. Jason says so. I've never seen him play. I've only seen him ride."

The Eagles won the tip. Jason snatched the ball and raced to the goal, beating everyone and scoring uncontested. The rhythm of the game didn't change much after that; Jason dominated, scoring, blocking shots, making steals and passing to the right teammate at the right time. The home crowd loved it, yelling and whistling wildly. Danny was thrilled for his friend; Jason had worked hard to be able to play again.

"Why do they have to dribble?" Krindee asked.

"Otherwise they'd be traveling. A violation. If you have the ball, you have to dribble to move your feet."

"Dribble to move your feet. Reminds me of a baby at play," she laughed. "If I remember right, they don't dribble in football or baseball. They can run with the ball." Danny frowned. "I do agree that it's a foul if you hit someone. Hitting does not lead to camaraderie." Danny just shook his head. Krindee laughed. "Why are free throws only worth one point? And are they really free if you have to get hit to shoot them? What's goal-tending?"

Danny answered each question patiently. It allowed Krindee to look around and study the crowd. It kept Danny's mind off Spike and other unpleasant thoughts.

At a timeout, the applause was thunderous. "Nice energy. Excitement. Pride. Definitely good vibes."

"We're winning," Danny told her. "And Jason is dominating!"

"On the other hand, there's a few papas who appear fairly . . . dogged. Even war-like. Kill 'em and destroy them aren't great cheers. Wasn't it Vince Lombardi, the Packer coach, who said, 'Winning isn't everything. It's the only thing'?"

"My dad agrees with him."

"You don't?" Krindee asked.

"I think having fun is important. When I'm having fun, I seem to do well at things. When I'm not having fun . . . well, I seem to suck." Danny noticed she appeared baffled. "As in suck eggs. You really should have brushed up on our slang."

"So suck is bad, right?"

"Definitely. Stink is another term."

"That one I've heard."

After a timeout late in the half, Danny wondered if Spike waited outside. If so, was Spike doing something to his bicycle? Maybe Spike carried chain cutters. Or a welding torch. What if he'd brought a truck, and at this very moment, was loading the entire bicycle rack into the back?

"Your imagination is running away with you," Krindee whispered.

"Yeah, I know," Danny checked the clock. Less than thirty seconds remained until half-time. "I'm going to check on my bicycle."

"I'll come with you. This game is a—how do you say—a blowout?"

"That's right. A massacre. A slaughter."

"Another fighting term. You have lots of them."

"I guess we fight a lot," Danny replied.

"That is what worries us."

Danny and Krindee descended the steps. When they reached the floor, the half-time buzzer sounded. "We have fifteen minutes before the second half starts."

Once outside, Danny jogged to the bicycle rack. Kalyde II stood untouched by time, weather, or hands of ill intent. Danny smiled and ran his hands over the magic bicycle's frame.

"Chase," came a gruff voice from behind him. "I've had enough of you!"

Danny turned, expecting the worst. "Chris! You almost scared me to death!"

Something about his tone struck her. Christina stifled her laughter and grew serious. "Danny, what's wrong?"

Danny told her about the motorbike marauders and their blazing guns.

"They shot at you!" Christina exclaimed, her blue eyes wide. "What did the police do?"

"I didn't report it. First, I checked on your place and Jason's, then told my dad. He didn't believe me. If he doesn't believe me, why would the police? Dad thought I was just trying to keep him away from Ms. Mayfair."

"I believe you, Danny."

Again, Danny wished he could confide in her. "Thanks." Danny hugged her. "I want you to be careful, too. They might come after you."

"I'll mention it to my mom and dad."

"HEY! CHRISTINA! Get back in here!" Cynthia yelled. "They're getting ready to start."

As they rushed inside the gymnasium, a big shadow stepped out from behind the bushes. "One of these days, Chase." Spike hefted his bat and slapped it into the palm of his hand. "First your bicycle, then you."

THIRTEEN

Unseated

"A tandem. How many bikes does The Wimp own?" Spike glanced toward the gymnasium entrance. Chase and that French witch were inside. Spike studied the parking lot and shadowed areas around the building. He was alone.

Spike smiled as he walked toward the bicycle rack. "Since hitting seems to be the name of the game, let's hit The Wimp where it hurts most."

Spike positioned the tandem, eyed it for a moment, then, taking the aluminum bat in both hands as if it were an axe, struck the magic bicycle. Kalyde II squealed, its front cross bar crumpling. Spike smiled broadly. "That felt good!" He struck again and again, pounding the crossbar into a V.

"Whew! Take that, Mr. Speed-demon!" Spike hefted the bat. "And I'm just gettin' warmed up."

Spike took a bat-swing, striking the wheel. The spokes bent, some springing out the other side. Grunting, Spike disentangled the bat. "One more time." Spike swung again. Spokes exploded free as the back wheel caved in. For this wheel's finale, Spike axe-stroked the rear wheel. It crumpled into a U.

"Oww!" Danny jumped up and clutched his back. Krindee glanced his way. "Are you all right?"

"My back!" Danny arched backwards, trying to stretch out the ache.

Krindee touched his back. "Some sort of spasm."

"It's getting worse." Danny grimaced. "I may have to lie down."

Krindee looked around, then slid her hand under Danny's sweatshirt. "Relax."

Danny felt a warm glow swell from her hand, washing over his back. The muscles unclenched. He abruptly felt fine, reminding him of when Kah-laye-dee had healed him. "That's better! Thanks, Krindee! Thanks a bunch! You know, I wish I could do that. OW!" Danny suddenly grabbed his left leg.

"A cramp?" Krindee laid her hand on his knee.

Danny writhed. The pain grew worse, rocketing up into his hip and down his leg into his foot. "People are staring at me."

"Because you're groaning and writhing. Is the cramp feeling any better?" Krindee asked. The warmth radiated from her hand again, sweeping away his pain.

Danny nodded. "It feels like something is happening to Kalyde II."

"Feels?"

"Yeah." Danny stretched and tested his leg. "I'm going to check on it." He started to rise and quickly slumped back to his seat.

"Stay here until your leg feels better. Is Kalyde II being stolen?" Krindee asked.

Danny concentrated. "No."

"Even if someone does damage the Xenozilit, you can repair it?"

"I'm still worried about it." Danny rubbed his leg.

"Well, then imagine it's fine," Krindee suggested.

"Okay." Danny closed his eyes. On his mental drawing board, Kalyde II the tandem appeared perfect, its long wiry frame straight and its red skin gleaming as if newly painted.

Outside, Spike repositioned the magic tandem. He wedged it firmly so it wouldn't twist when he bashed on the front tire. Just as he finished his backswing, the tandem shifted, listing to the side. "Hey!" Spike halted his swing.

The frame straightened to perfection. The back wheel and tire swelled to roundness as it reinflated. Just as before, the spokes were all in place perfectly.

Spike dropped the bat.

Everything about the crimson tandem appeared brand new. Untouched. What happened? Spike rubbed his eyes, then reached out and touched the bicycle. Running his hands along it, he confirmed he hadn't imagined the restoration.

Spike knelt and picked up the bat. He looked around, then with a mighty swing, he axe-chopped the front tire. The wheel crumpled into an M, the tire exploding with a hiss. Rearing back, Spike swung again and again in a frenzy of frustration and rage.

"Ow!" Danny hissed. He grabbed his right knee and sat quickly.

"What's wrong? Your other knee?" Krindee's lavender eyes searched his as if she could read what was wrong.

Danny nodded.

"Breathe through it." Krindee placed a hand on his shoulder. "Think through it. You're fine. It's just a cramp."

"That should do it!" Spike smiled. The front tire was beaten into scrap iron, a mass of twisted metal and claw-like spokes.

The wheel suddenly expanded, swelling into roundness. As though soldiers lining up for formal dress, the spokes snapped into place. The tire seemed to patch itself together, rubbery flesh regenerating to wholeness.

"HEY!" Spike threw down the bat. He didn't understand this at all.

Spike knelt, eyeing the combination locks. He wasn't going to get those off without a chain cutter. Even then, he mused, they might just knit themselves back together.

Spike kicked the bicycle, then picked up the bat. He couldn't do anything to hurt this damn thing! He'd tried to beat the life out of it, and it still looked brand-spanking new!

Where did Chase get such a bicycle?

With a flash of insight, Spike suddenly thought back to Chase's story—the one about the alien bicycle. Spike laughed at himself. An alien bicycle! "Heh!" One that changed shape and time-traveled. "He-he! Right." Ike's blows had damaged his brain.

But what . . . what if Chase had been serious? The alien bicycle had repaired itself, just like the tandem. "I'd love to have a piece of E.T. technology. That'd be worth big bucks. I could sell it and move out."

Spike ran his hands along the tandem's frame. It seemed to undulate under his hand. Spike laughed. Was Chase's imagination infectious?

Spike touched the seat. Nice padding. Must be comfortable.

The seat. Spike smiled evilly. "This will do just the trick!"

"How's your knee?" Krindee asked.

"Better."

"Only three minutes left to go. Patience."

"I hate being patient."

"Patience is best courted by observing the now and not hurrying the future," Krindee told him.

"Who said that?"

"That's loosely quoted from the great Cor-ror-o'lan philosopher, Zen-rahe-gan."

"Oh." Danny stood and stretched. He suddenly stopped.

"What's wrong."

"My bicycle . . . . Someone's stealing it!" Danny raced to the aisle and ran down the steps. As he reached the floor, Krindee caught up with him.

Danny abruptly stopped. "Weird. It's still there, and yet. . . ." Danny rushed outside and sprinted to the bicycle rack.

Kalyde II still stood there, gleaming in the lamps' light.

"It's all right." Krindee smiled

"Hey! The seats are gone!" Danny ran his hand along the frame and over the socket where the seat posts should be set. "Somebody stole our seats! Why would they do that?"

"Because they couldn't damage it?"

Danny's eyes widened. "Then I didn't imagine it."

"Maybe you're somehow linked to Kalyde II. Imagine the seats coming back to you" Krindee suggested.

"I'll try."

As Spike approached his Honda 150, he tucked the seats under his arm. They were his! His to do with as he pleased! Spike wished he could turn them into a big bat that released electric shocks when it hit so he could pay back Ike.

The seats seemed to squirm out of his grasp. Spike juggled them, catching them before they hit the ground. "Slippery devils! You're not going anywhere. You're mine!" For a moment, Spike had the feeling he'd done something like this before. He smiled evilly.

Danny closed his eyes. Holding his hands out in front of him, he imagined the bicycle seats appearing in his hands. He felt a tug, some distant connection, then nothing. Trying again, he pictured the seats swirling into existence, sitting in this hand. He didn't care if they teleported or appeared from thin air. The how didn't matter. Just come. Just appear. He didn't feel anything. Danny opened his eyes. "Nothing."

"Can you tell where they are?"

Danny nodded. "I think so."

"Then let's find them. You can track them, right?"

"I think so. But first." Danny looked around. He didn't see anyone.

He touched the bicycle. In his mind, Danny pictured the tandem with its seats intact. Two blobs oozed out from the shafts as though metallic fountains, then coalesced, gathering and assuming the shape of two seats.

After removing the locks, Danny lifted Kalyde II from the rack. "Get on, Krindee." As he pushed away, he said, "I hope Christina isn't mad that we didn't stick around."

"Why would she be mad?" Krindee asked.

"I imagine I'll find out," Danny groaned. "I can't even think of a good excuse. But we have to find those seats! Nothing is more important than that! If Spike or someone else discovers they can change shape . . . ." Danny shuddered, then kicked Kalyde II into high gear.

FOURTEEN

Unexpected Changes

Spike hid his motor bike in the woods, then peered over the backyard fence, looking for his stepfather. The porch and yard appeared deserted. Lights illuminated his mother's and stepfather's upstairs window. Spike watched for movement but saw neither shadows nor silhouettes. He didn't want to be surprised by Ike again. Feeling all was clear, Spike darted to the back door.

He tried the door, finding it locked. Spike moved to the garage door, then the front after that. All the doors stood locked. He searched for the spare key; but it wasn't hidden under the large rock by the door to the garage.

Spike crept to his bedroom window. He should've done this last time. When he tried to open the window, it didn't budge. The lock's lip was bent, so when he lifted the window just right, it slipped off. Groaning and grunting, Spike tried to shift it, then heave the window open. Again, it didn't budge at all, rock solid.

The window next to his became illuminated. What luck, Rocky was home!

Spike moved to his brother's window and knocked. Rocky looked around. He almost could have been Spike's double, a big boy with broad shoulders, a stout build, and a flat face with close set eyes below protruding brows.

Spike rapped again. His brother slowly turned toward the window. Rocky put his fingers to his lips, then immediately rushed to the door and closed it.

"Where have you been?" Rocky whispered when he opened the window. "Ike is really, really mad. School called today. You've skipped two days in a row, haven't you?"

"Yeah. Can I come in? My window's locked."

"It's nailed shut. Ike discovered you're sneaking out. He's furious about that, too."

"Are you going to let me in?" Spike asked. Rocky reluctantly moved out of the way. "Take these."

"These look like bicycle seats."

"You are so smart," Spike replied as he climbed inside.

"You're going to get in even more trouble."

"I'm not going to get caught this time."

"Spike, you always get caught," Rocky groaned. "Sometimes I swear you want to get caught."

"That has to be one of the stupidest things I've ever heard you say," Spike snarled. "Sometimes it's hard to believe you're my brother." He snatched the seats from Rocky's hands. The two brothers stared at each other for long moments. "I'm thinking about leaving."

"You're always thinking about leaving," Rocky replied.

"Ike hits me more than you. I'm his whipping boy."

"You fight with him all the time. I try not to."

"I fight with him because he's wrong all of the time! You don't fight because you don't have a spine! Chase, The Wimp, has more backbone than you!"

"Shh! You can't leave! If you do, Ike will start hitting Raymond."

"He's already started," Spike replied brusquely.

"What?"

"You heard me." Spike listened at the door, then turned to Rocky. "Stay quiet." Spike listened again, then opened the door. "We'll talk later." Slipping into the hallway, Spike snuck to his room.

The place was a mess. Spike rarely spent any time here. The Headbangers' quarters felt more homey than this place.

It had been so long since he'd done anything in the room besides change clothes that the posters hung half-fallen, limply draped toward the floor. His bed lay unmade, the cases missing from both pillows. His clothing lay scattered like carpeting.

Spike dropped the stolen seats on his bed. Tossing his clothes into a pile atop the bed, Spike cleared a path to his closet. He opened the door and grabbed his backpack, then hunted for his duffel bag.

"Ernest!" The door whipped open, *whacking* against the wall.

Spike froze.

"I know you're here!" His stepfather grabbed him by the shirt collar and hauled him out of the closet. "What are you doing hiding in there, boy?"

Spike's foot caught on something. He stumbled backwards, trying not to fall on the floor. He landed sprawled half onto the bed.

With hands clenched, Ike Pickett loomed over him. His face twisted and his lips compressed into a thin white line. From deep sockets, his eyes blazed as though stolen from the devil.

Spike threw the clothes aside and jumped to his feet. He wasn't going to take this anymore!

The tall bony man stuck a finger into Spike's chest. "You and me, Ernie ole' boy, we're going to have a talk."

"That means you're going to hit me again!" Spike stood poised and ready.

Ike Pickett struck quickly. The blow snapped back Spike's head. With a single blow, his head was already ringing. "You asked for that, boy."

"Yeah. Right."

Ike Pickett hit him again and again, to the head and stomach. After the third blow, the big man asked, "You ready to listen?"

Spike wiped the blood from his nose and nodded. "Yes, sir."

"Good. You been skipping school, so the principal's calling again. It makes your mom look bad. That makes her cry. I don't like to see your momma cry, and I don't like to be embarrassed. You listening?"

Spike numbly nodded.

"Now, you're going to do as I say. You're going to school tomorrow. You'll attend your detention. You won't get in any more trouble. You won't skip any more school. You will clean up your room. You know why?"

"Because you'll hit me some more if I don't," Spike coldly replied.

"And trash that nice dirt bike you been riding," Ike Pickett told him. Spike's head snapped up, his eyes and expression a mixture of anger and worry. "That's right! I found it! I've been waiting on you. You mess with me, I mess up your bike. You do what I say, you can have your bike back in the spring. Think on it." His stepfather turned and left the room.

Spike crawled up onto the bed, then sprawled out. His head rang loudly, and his vision jumbled. Without his Honda, he couldn't run away! Couldn't escape! Spike squirmed. Something dug into his back. He pulled it out from the blankets and held it up.

A seat! One of those damned tandem seats. He was lucky Ike hadn't seen them. That would have led to more blows. Venting his rage, Spike twisted the seat. It resisted him, so he tried harder, pretending it was his stepdad's neck.

"Who do you think stole it?" Krindee asked from the back of the tandem. No one thought an answer was needed.

Astride a restored Kalyde II, they raced along the road, following the bright light of the headlamp. The wind was cold; but Danny didn't notice. He concentrated on the link between his bicycle and the missing pieces of Xenozilit. "We're headed toward Spike's house," Danny replied. "I hope we don't have to meet Mr. Pickett again. That man scares me."

"Be glad he isn't living at your house."

Danny shuddered. "I guess I'm a lot luckier than I thought."

Spike squeezed harder, seeing his hands wrapped around Ike Pickett's neck. No . . . no, choking him to death would be too quick. While he'd like to see Ike's eyes bulge and his face redden, it would be over in a matter of minutes. Spike didn't want that. He wanted Ike Pickett to suffer.

What he needed was a bat. A very special bat. Light but one that hit hard. A big nightstick. The special Spike electrified nightstick!

Moving as if a squirmy cat, the seat shifted in Spike's hands. His eyes popped open as wide as golfballs. The seat flattened some and elongated. "Just like the bicycle in Chase's *The Alien Bicycle*. Like the bicycle tonight. Hmm. Nah!

"Ah hell, why not!" Spike closed his eyes. He mentally pictured a bat, seeing the shape, feeling the grains and the engraved monogram.

With a smile, Spike opened his eyes. His smile dropped away. He held what appeared to be a long beige sausage. "That's not what I pictured. Hell, maybe I'm just hallucinating. I've been hit in the head enough."

Spike thought he should probably see a doctor about his headaches and the ringing in his ears. Suddenly, as though it were a memory released from captivity, Spike remembered riding Chase's bicycle—The Alien Bicycle.

He raced along a stretch of farm road. First, Spike imagined running over Ike. The squirrel died quickly. All the bicycle needed was a cow-catcher, so he could drive people off the road. The bike changed shape, an inverted shovel protruding from the front of the bicycle. Now he would win every race! Nothing would stand in his way!

The world seemed to tilt. Spike felt ready to slide off. He didn't know where those weird thoughts had come from.

Spike grabbed the second seat. Closing his eyes, Spike imagined them as one big bat. He could feel them melt together. When he opened his eyes, Spike held a long bough with all the branches trimmed. The seats now appeared to be a rough-hewn walking stick.

"That's closer, but I want a bat," Spike muttered. "One with spikes like a medieval mace."

He closed his eyes and tried again. When Spike opened them, little had changed. "This is gonna take some work, but if Chase can do it, so can I! What did Chase say in his story? To not only see it, but to feel it? Believe it to be true? He claimed Einstein said imagination and thought were more powerful than knowledge. If one can imagine it, it can come true.

"If I can get them to work for me like they did for Chase, then I'm outta here. Long gone, bye-bye. Money won't be a problem for someone who can travel time. Heck, I've always wanted to meet the Big Bambino. Hello Babe, here I come."

Danny steered Kalyde II onto Whippoorwill Road. "We're almost there. Spike's house is only a couple down on the left."

Danny cocked his head, then slowed to a stop. Straddling the tandem, he stood and looked around. "It's gone! The star metal pieces are gone!"

FIFTEEN

Night Stealth

Danny opened the garage door, then guided Kalyde II inside. He leaned the magic bicycle against the wall and locked Kalyde II to some pipes. "Krindee, Murg's going to freak when she hears about this! I can't . . . ."

"Hear what?" The calico crawled out from under the car. Murg stretched, then studied Danny. "Didn't you have a good time at the ball game?" Murg looked to Krindee. "I understand completely. I never cared for sports either, bicycle racing aside of course."

"The ball game wasn't bad. Jason was great."

"But?"

"You're not going to believe this." Danny took off his helmet and hung it on the handlebars. "Spike stole part of Kalyde II." Danny wrung his hands.

"Spike stole part of Kalyde?" The calico slowly blinked. "What part? It looks fine to me."

"The seats," Krindee replied. "Spike stole the seats."

Murg's tail flicked in irritation. "Danny, it appears we overlooked a detail that could get us in a great deal of trouble." Murg sighed. "Live and learn. Experience is a great teacher, though rarely a gentle one. Do you know where Spike took the seats?"

Danny explained about following his feelings to Spike's house. "About the time we arrived, they felt . . . I don't know . . . different."

"I'm afraid Spike has control of them," Krindee added.

"Did you try summoning them?" Murg projected.

"Yeah. Nothing happened," Danny replied. At first—back when Kalyde II was brand new—Danny couldn't believe he could summon it. Now, Danny couldn't believe he was unable to summon the magic bicycle's seats.

"That is odd and worrisome. You could feel them but could not get them to return to you. Did they feel a different shape?" Murg asked.

"I think so. But I don't see how Spike could figure out anything. Spike is such a blockhead."

"As you discovered earlier, accidents often lead to discoveries."

"I thought I heard someone," his father said as he opened the door. "Danny are you talking to Murg again?"

Krindee hid, slinking to the shadows.

"Yes."

"I thought you said you could speak to her telepathically?" he asked sarcastically.

Danny shrugged. "My brain's tired."

"I see. Bring some Puppy Chow with you. How was the game?"

"Jason was the best," Danny replied proudly. His friend had schooled them, all right. Danny wished it hadn't been necessary to race off. Jason deserved congratulations.

"You should try basketball," his father suggested.

"Dad." Danny's expression was deadpan. "I'm short."

"You'll grow. Your grandfathers and uncles are tall. Do you still have homework to do?"

Danny nodded.

"Okay, feed Comet, then do your homework. You can play with him when you're through." Captain Chase headed back into the kitchen.

Once upstairs, Danny opened the window, letting in Krindee. "What are we going to do?" Danny wondered as he slumped onto his bed. "I wish I could just storm Spike's place and take back my bicycle seats."

"Sounds war-like." Krindee rubbed against Danny's leg. "You can do better than that. Murg, go ahead, I'll relay your thoughts for you," the alien telepathically projected.

"Put on your thinking helmet," Murg suggested.

Danny went through the motions as he imagined putting on a spectacular thinking cap. The golden contraption held numerous dials, flashing lights and wires stretching from one spot to another.

"Do you know what the pieces of Xenozilit look like?" Murg wondered. "That could be why you're unable to summon them."

Danny closed his eyes and concentrated. Reaching out with his mind, he searched for the seats. "Nothing. I'm going to supercharge the thinking cap." Danny imagined flicking a green switch. "I can feel them. They're not seats, but I don't know what they are. I . . . I'm not getting an image."

"Spike has definitely discovered something. Done something to them," Krindee thought.

Murg nodded. "If we can find out what shape they've become, Danny might be able to call them back."

"How do I find out what shape they're in? Sneak back tonight and look in through the window?" Danny asked.

"That sounds fine to me," Murg replied.

"I have homework."

"Do it now. Then when your dad's asleep, we'll go cat-sneaking around Spike's lair, leaving the homing devices in the garage, of course. We wouldn't want the Shadow Daggers to inform your father that you're sneaking out at night, would we, Danny?"

Time crawling toward midnight, Danny walked Kalyde II into the woods behind Spike's house. The moon shone brightly, its silvery light creating sharp contrasts of light and dark.

Although Danny could see in the darkness, he still made noise. Whenever a stick cracked, it sounded as loud as a gunshot. Each misstep made him even more nervous.

After a particularly loud snap, Murg thought, "You still need to work on stealth for your feline merit badge." At her noisiest, Murg was the breeze rustling through fallen leaves. Behind the calico, Krindee tagged along as a beige and black shadow.

"What do you think Spike will do with the seats?" Danny wondered.

"Most of my guesses scare me," Murg replied. "And my imagination is tame compared to yours."

"Do you think Spike was being vindictive? Or does he know about the bicycle's properties?" Danny asked.

"Accidents happen," Murg replied. "I think Spike knew nothing about Kalyde II's shapechanging ability. Unfortunately, I believe he now knows at least a little about the Xenozilit. Krindee, please enlighten us, what is Xenozilit?"

"It is metal from the very heart of a star—one of the many Hearts of Creation."

"When the star metal is mined, is the star still living?" Murg asked.

"Yes. Solar flares—what we call Rhaewinds— are caught in large . . . let's just say energy nets, for the sake of keeping things simple. When it cools, you have Xenozilit—star metal which can be reforged and recreated with thought. Imagination is its fuel."

"Its?" Danny asked.

"Yes, some posit . . . ."

"Sounds like a Vulcan word from Star Trek," Danny thought.

The Siamese smiled, her eyes twin orbs of lavender luminosity. "Some hypothesize that coming from a Heart, Xenozilits are simply dormant. In a sense, potential energy or life, if you believe life is energy. Thought feeds them. Some of our sages and scientists believe that with enough feeding, a Xenozilit can become sentient."

"Alive?" Danny whispered.

"Possibly. At this time, it is just a hypothesis. Kalyde II seems different from any other Xenozilit. Maybe because it's fed by your imagination. Have you seen any sign of intelligence?"

"No, but I guess that could be due to my lack of intelligence," Danny replied thoughtfully.

"Sometimes your astuteness surprises me," Murg thought wryly. "The important thing though, is to get the seats, or whatever they are now, back from Spike without drawing the Shadow Daggers' attention."

Next to a fallen tree and a big rock shaped like a stone hammer, Danny parked Kalyde II against a dying oak, wrapped a cable around the trunk, then locked it. He'd modified the seats so nobody could take apart the bicycle. Although the pieces moved independently, they were all one piece. He wasn't sure that was scientifically possible; but he had imagined it so.

"I could wear Kalyde II as a watch so I could see in the dark," Danny whispered. "I could probably even see telephoto. You know, imagine having binocular eyes."

"It didn't make you stealthy."

"I wasn't wearing it."

"Danny, please let us scout ahead first." Murg nodded to Krindee. "We can search quietly and inconspicuously."

"We'll act normal," Krindee told him. She gave him a broad, ear-stretching smile, then stuck out her tongue, not acting at all like a Siamese cat.

Danny chuckled quietly.

Murg frowned at her. "Danny, wait here. We'll be back in a few minutes. If you have to leave, we'll meet you at home."

Danny sighed. He hated waiting. He could change time and travel quickly; but he still had to wait. Murg often told him he should try to do something—anything—besides simply enduring the passage of time.

The shadows seemed to abruptly darken. What if more than just Mr. Pickett lived here? What if this was a community of android Mr. Picketts? What if the Mr. Picketts were programmed to end humanity by killing all kids? It could happen. Right now, one of the Mr. Picketts could be letting his robotic dog out for the night. What if they could see in the dark, the better to capture kids? Might he wander into the woods? Might . . . .

To his right, Danny thought he saw a face peeking from the shadows. The stranger's brow was so thick Danny couldn't see his eyes. His face was gauntly bony and scarred as though ritualistically cut with curved knives. The android smiled, crooked silver teeth flashing . . . .

Jarred to reality by a dog's angry barking, Danny bolted to his feet. Cats hissing battled with the hoarse barking. That sounded like Murg!

Danny was very tempted to check on the cats. Of course, Murg would tell him that she could take care of herself. The calico wanted him to stay put here. Danny sat, again.

What was he going to tell Christina? He hated leaving the game, not saying good-bye to her or Jason; but getting Kalyde II back together was more important than anything else. If the secret of Xenozilit became known, he was sunk—losing the bicycle meant losing his freedom—and others might sink with him. Krindee would have to leave in a hurry, aborting her scouting mission. How would that affect Cor-ror-o'lan judgment?

Danny sighed. How had things grown so complicated? So out of control? It almost made him sick to his stomach. Danny imagined it feeling better. That helped some, until he thought everything would probably get worse before it grew better.

His stomach! He could tell Christina his stomach bothered him! That would be the truth. Sort of. Danny sighed. He was afraid he was getting too good at skirting the truth. What did lying to his friends say about his character?

"Ah, excellent. You stayed where we left you," Murg thought as she returned.

"All I heard was your breathing," Krindee thought.

"What next?" Danny whispered.

"As you suggested earlier, put on the magic watch and we'll show you."

"Was that you I heard?" Danny stood and unlocked the cable.

Murg nodded. "We led Bubba the Pit Bull on a merry chase, and now he is stuck under the fence." On cue, the dog whined pitifully.

Krindee's eyes were still wide. With a ghostly air about her, she nearly glowed in the dark, her fur somehow lighter than before.

"Were you hurt?" Danny wrapped the cable under Kalyde II's seat.

"By a dog? Perish the thought. Bubba is a buffoon," Murg replied. "Now come on. Even if he's a typically stupid dog, he won't stay stuck all night. He'll dig his way out."

Danny rested the bicycle in his hands, then pictured a watch. With a shrill squeal of metal being twisted, the shape shifted and writhed in his mind, trying to become a walking stick. Danny wrestled with it, then focused, very clearly visualizing the watch. The weight lessened in his hands. When Danny opened his eyes, the glow was just fading.

"That took a while and was louder and brighter than usual," Murg thought. "Is something wrong?"

"The bike seemed to . . . resist the change. It wanted to be a walking stick."

"Interesting. Come on. We are sneaking to the fence. From the proper position, you can see through Spike's window. He's there now."

"What was he doing?"

"Lying on the bed cradling a stick," Krindee told him. "Interesting, wouldn't you say?"

With Murg in the lead and Krindee close behind, Danny wound between trees and bushes. Any contact, any noise, might give him away. The cats moved irregularly, darting from shadow to shadow and hiding spot to hiding spot.

Danny stepped on a stick; it snapped loudly. Both felines

turned, their expressions not hiding their annoyance. "Sorry."

"Stay right behind me," Murg told him.

As the forest grew less dense, the shadows fell away, leaving less places to hide. Fortunately, Danny wore dark clothing—usually a big no-no when riding at night—but they helped him blend with the shadows.

Murg and Krindee stopped near two short trees and a bush atop a small knoll. "Here," Murg thought.

When Danny stopped and knelt, he looked under the trees' leaves and over the fence. Spike sat on his bed. Beyond that, Danny would only be guessing about what he saw. "I'm going to try seeing telephoto." Danny closed his eyes, then drawing on the magic of the watch, he imagined being able to see far as if he were looking through binoculars.

"Wow!" Danny whispered. "Very cool! I can see Spike clearly, like I'm standing at the window peering in."

Eyes closed and forehead furrowed, Spike looked depressed. His bruises were still prominent, some now black instead of purple. The yellow and green had spread out from the dark, ugly splotches. Why was he cradling a walking stick?

Danny blinked, then examined the stick more closely. All the branches had been removed, and the surface area appeared smoothly sanded. One half was fatter, growing thicker toward the end. The other end finished in a knob. Danny watched in fascination as the branch seemed to change. What was that writing slowly appearing on it? LOUISVILLE SLUGGER?

"He's creating a bat!" Danny whispered. "Why?"

The snap of a stick shot through the night. Danny's head whipped to his left. A mammoth figure walked through the woods. He carried a flashlight and something shiny. It gleamed in the moonlight. Was that a rifle?

"IT'S MR. PICKETT!" Krindee almost thought aloud.

SIXTEEN

Cats and Mice

"Danny, keep quiet and stay very, very still." Murg's thoughts seemed to hiss through Danny's brain.

Although the mammoth man appeared to be part shadow, Danny could see Mr. Pickett all too clearly. The darkness wrapped around Spike's stepfather like a massive black overcoat. The shadow of his baseball cap hid all but his eyes, which gleamed beadily in the cold moonlight. In one huge hand, Mr. Pickett held a dark flashlight; in the other, he carried a rifle, its metal glinting silvery.

As if Spike's stepfather knew they were near, the big man slowly approached the threesome. Mr. Pickett suddenly paused, looked around, then knelt to check the ground.

"He's looking for tracks," Murg thought. "Hunting something."

When Mr. Pickett looked up, Danny could see his face. Spike's stepfather appeared angry, his mouth tight. Gaunt lines cut darkly across his ghost-white flesh. His eyes seemed to have taken on a reddish hue, pinpoints of laser sight seeking a target.

"He's hunting us!" Danny mindspoke as he started to shake.

"Maybe not. We saw digging near the fence, signs of armadillos at work," Murg thought. "He might be hunting them."

"Let's get out of here," Danny projected. His stomach lurched queasily. He remembered imagining Mr. Pickett stalking him.

"To conquer fear is the beginning of wisdom. Bertrand Russell," Krindee quoted.

"I'm trying." Moving quietly in a crouch, Danny snuck away from Mr. Pickett. The deep woods provided better cover. He could lose him there, hiding behind trees and in the shadows. When Mr. Pickett looked his way, Danny stopped next to an oak, pretending to blend with its trunk.

"Krindee, you lead. Danny, stay close behind her. I'll follow last," Murg ordered. The Siamese darted ahead. The calico dropped behind Danny. "When we get to the road, change Kalyde II back into a bicycle and we'll race out of here."

Staying near trees, Danny followed closely, keeping out of the moonlit swaths. He imagined the shadows as a cloak of darkness and wrapped himself in them.

Danny stepped on a stick. It snapped loudly, echoing in the woods. Danny didn't dare move. Mr. Pickett looked at him, laser optics sighting, taking deadly aim.

Danny inhaled deeply to relax and waited. Long moments later, when Ike Pickett looked away, the threesome darted off, sprinting in spurts from one tree to the next. Each time they paused, Murg checked behind them. "Mr. Pickett is still following."

"He's closer! Maybe he can see in the dark." Danny's mind raced. He was reminded of the relentless android gunslinger in the movie *Westworld*, long before *The Terminator* stalked the silver screen. Danny's heart jumped into his throat. Despite the cool air, sweat streamed in rivulets down his face.

"Calm down," Murg replied. "He stopped to check your tracks again. Move quickly, but quietly. As outlandish as it may seem, imagine you are a cat." Murg looked to Krindee. "It's the current rage."

Krindee darted ahead. Danny followed, imagining he was a cat with softly padded feet.

Danny felt Mr. Pickett's eyes on him. Following him. Locking on target. Mr. Pickett's footsteps grew louder. Readying his rifle, the android drew closer.

"Stop!" Murg thought. "Danny, rein in your thoughts. See your way clear."

Danny stopped abruptly and tried to slow his breathing, which raced like a stallion's after a sprint. "Is he still coming?"

"We're gaining ground. He'll be out of sight soon," Murg replied.

Danny looked back through the shadowy trees. Kneeling in a patch of moonlight, Mr. Pickett bent close to the ground. Danny swore Spike's stepfather sniffed the earth. After a moment, Mr. Pickett stood and tucked his flashlight into his coat pocket. Both hands now grasped the rifle.

"He knows where we are!"

Krindee darted off into thicker trees. Danny followed closely behind the Siamese. Tail dancing, Murg joined the sneaking parade.

The Siamese stopped so suddenly Danny almost ran her over. "Someone else is coming," Murg projected.

Danny slid behind a pair of oak trees, hiding partly behind a barren bush. Now he heard the crunch of footsteps. He—they— weren't trying to be quiet.

"Why aren't we going to the front door, Reggie?" a boy asked.

"Because, Page, Mr. Pickett hates kids. Haven't you seen what he's been doing to Spike? He does it to Rocky, too. I ain't gonna let him do that to us. He hits me, I kill him." *Snikt.* "He bleeds, too. My switchblade will see to that."

It was Reggie Tuckett with Page and Vargas! Their footsteps grew much louder, crunching dead leaves and cracking dry sticks. Danny could see them now. "They're headed directly for Mr. Pickett!"

"We can take off when he notices them." Murg thought.

"But Pickett has a gun!" Krindee replied. "He might shoot them!"

"Hmm. A man of Mr. Pickett's character just might at that," Murg replied.

"Man, this place has bad vibes," one boy groaned. "I hope Spike's all right. He hasn't been to school or our place for a couple of days now."

"We'll just tap on his window and ask him where the hell he's been."

Danny looked over to Mr. Pickett. The mammoth man looked up and left, noticing the three boys. His meaty hands seemed to caress his gun.

"He'll shoot them, Murg! I've got to do something!" Danny snatched up a rock.

"But they tried to hurt you," Murg reminded him. "They tried to shoot you." Danny missed Murg's wink to Krindee.

"I know, but I can't let them get shot!" Danny whispered, his voice hoarse.

"What do you have in mind?" Krindee asked.

"A diversion." Just before the threesome stepped into the moonlight, Danny hurled the rock high into the sky. After a few moments, it crashed through the branches of a tree. The stone landed with a dull earthen *thud* behind Mr. Pickett. Gun trained, Spike's stepfather whirled.

"HEY!!" Page yelled. "Did you hear that? Something's out here!"

"Over there!" Vargas cried.

Krindee sprinted away. Danny raced after her. Murg loped almost underfoot.

Danny felt eyes follow him. Was that a rifle sight poking him between his shoulder blades? No, think invisible. I am invisible. Light reflects off me. People see through me. I appear as air.

"Danny, where are you?" Krindee asked.

Danny looked down at himself. He could perceive a vague outline of his body. "I'm . . . I'm invisible! Wow!"

"Keep moving, Mr. Invisible Man," Murg projected.

"I swear I saw something," Vargas continued. "I did, I'm tellin' ya."

"Probably just an armadillo or a coon," Reggie replied.

Danny heard a metallic double *click*. He hoped everything would work out all right and kept running.

"Who's there?!" Reggie cried.

A gunshot flashed throughout the trees and rang through the woods.

SEVENTEEN

Blackmail

Danny ramped onto the sidewalk and rode toward school. The morning hung cold and gloomy, the day starting with many of the hallmarks of winter. A chilly wind swirled, kicking up leaves and dirt. Above, black clouds threatened freezing rain.

Danny still couldn't believe it. Spike with his minuscule brain had somehow imagined forming the seats into a bat, thinking the Xenozilit to change. What was next, another magic bicycle? One with a cowcatcher? Had Spike actually read *The Alien Bicycle?* If so, Spike was familiar with how the star metal worked.

The story had been a good idea, helping him deal with the deaths of Happy, Sarah and his mother. On the other hand, the story gave away too many secrets. Danny never suspected that anybody would take him seriously, especially Spike.

"In another Time, Spike stole your bicycle. Remember what I said about Time wanting to reassert itself?" Danny recalled

Murg's comments. "Repeat what had happened before being changed? This may be Time's way of doing that. History repeats itself unless monumental efforts are made not only to change it, but to keep it altered. That's why worrying about what is past is wasted time. Working in the present, based on past experiences, is the best way to remedy any problem."

Danny had to get back those pieces of star metal! But what could he do? Keep trying to sense and guess the current shape of the pieces, then summon them? He could try talking to Spike but doubted that would do any good. Demanding was certainly pointless. Offer something in trade? But what? Kalyde II was priceless.

Danny steered between students walking from the buses to the front door. The brick courtyard was crowded, so Danny climbed off and guided Kalyde II toward the bicycle racks.

"Morning, Speed-demon," Jason said as he walked past. He appeared amused by something. "You'd better wake up!"

"What?" Danny turned around to watch Jason depart. When Danny turned back around, he smiled weakly. "Hi Christina!"

His girlfriend stood in front of the bicycle racks. Looking cold and displeased, Christina waited with her hands on her hips. Her eyes gleamed as blue as ice, giving a biting edge to the wintry air. Christina pulled up her collar, then tugged her jacket closer. "Hi Danny."

Cynthia stood next to her. Her stare was unfriendly, lashing out.

Danny parked. "I'd say good morning but it's so very cold . . . ."

"It's about to get colder," Cynthia muttered around her chewing gum.

"Christina," Danny began, "I'm sorry I had to leave early last night. I really am. And I apologize for not saying good-bye. I really do. I . . . ."

Christina's brow furrowed. "You look cold."

"Everyone is cold." Cynthia frowned.

"Danny never looks cold. Are you sick?" Christina reached up and touched his forehead.

"I'm feeling better. I felt worse last night." Danny felt heartsick, disaster impending. Things spinning out of control. Something fragile teetering. "A little after half time I began to feel lousy." He wished he could tell her why.

Cynthia snorted.

"That's why you left in such a hurry." Christina's expression softened. "See," Christina looked at Cynthia, "I told you he had a good reason."

Cynthia rolled her eyes.

"Are you sure you feel well enough to be here?" Christina asked.

Danny nodded. "I wanted to see you. To apologize."

"You could've called."

"Last night I was so wiped I didn't feel like talking." Danny wished he could tell her the truth. Why couldn't he trust her? Because of what had happened with Gretchen in another Time?

"How's Krindy?" Cynthia's tone accused. "Did she catch a chill on the tandem?"

"She's feeling all right," Danny replied. As a Siamese, the Cor-ror-o'lan was tailing Spike. Murg tagged along in case her expertise was needed.

"I'm sure she is," Cynthia replied.

"What did she think of the game?" Christina asked.

"She asked me stupid questions the entire time," Danny replied. "About traveling, charging, free throws . . . ."

Christina burst out laughing.

"I don't think she's much of a sports fan," Danny finished.

"Meow."

Danny turned around. A tabby with lavender eyes stared at him. She sat on the bench being petted by a trio of girls. If Krindee was here in a new cat form, then Spike was here!

Cynthia glanced over to the tabby. "Speaking of your French cousin, that cat reminds me of Krindy."

Christina glanced at her watch. "The bell is going to

ring. We'd better hurry to class." She gave Danny a hug. He returned it. "Will I see you at lunch?"

"If you come to the library."

"Stick in the mud. After school?"

"I have to take Comet to the vet for shots."

"On your bicycle?"

"How else? I'll try to stop by tonight. If not, I'll call you." Danny waved farewell, then locked the magic bicycle to the rack. A hand fell on his shoulder. Danny whirled around, surprising Jason.

"Whoa, Speed-demon. I saw Christina smiling, so whatever you said went over well. As my granny used to say, she was madder than a hornet. What's your secret?"

"I can't tell you. Then you'd be good at everything! You were fantastic, incredible, and spectacular on the court last night."

"Thanks, man!"

"I'm sorry I had to leave. I . . . I didn't feel well."

"That's all right," Jason replied. "You were there! Hey, we'd better run. Otherwise we're late." They sprinted to the front door. "Later, you fill me in on what has you down," Jason said as he grabbed the door. "Is it Spike? Or that Mayfair lady? You know you'd feel better if you'd come watch some NBA hoop with me."

Wishing he could say more, Danny waved and kept running, heading toward the gym. That seemed to be the way things were going, running from one thing to the other. Rush. Rush. Rush.

With his mind on Spike and the stolen star metal, Danny went through the motions of gymnastics like a zombie. Fortunately, he only fell off the parallel bars once and didn't hurt himself.

During class changeovers, Spike was always just ahead. Just around the corner. Just out of sight. Danny could feel the pieces of Xenozilit; but he never saw them.

At lunch, Danny headed for the library. He didn't feel like seeing anyone. He had to figure out what to do! Render himself invisible and sneak inside Spike's house to steal back the star metal? What if Mr. Pickett was waiting?

"Still doing research?" Jimmy Chang asked. "How's your paper coming along?"

Danny snapped out of his woolgathering. "Huh? Hi Jimmy! Fine. How about yours?"

"Going just great!"

"What are you studying?"

"The formation of professional baseball."

"Mr. Gordon's letting you do that?"

"I told him that the changes in the American pastime reflected the issues of that time."

Danny laughed. "That sounds convincing."

"What are you looking for?"

"I want to mention how fiction and imagination helped develop flight, you know from Icarus to *War of the Worlds* to *Star Trek*." Danny glanced at the clock. "I'd better get at it. See you." Danny walked along the aisles, letting his mind and hands drift, fingers dancing along book spines. He wasn't watching and bumped into someone, head to chest. "Spike."

Spike stepped back to study Danny. Spike carried a walking stick—the stolen pieces of Kalyde II!

"You don't look like you feel so good," Spike told him. "You know, I'd think that with a bicycle like yours you'd always be feeling good!"

"What do you mean by that?"

"The inspiration for *The Alien Bicycle*. I got pieces of it, you know." Spike looked around conspiratorially.

"I know," Danny replied.

Spike appeared surprised. "You aren't as dumb as you look, but then, no one could be."

"You *stole* my bicycle seats!" Danny hissed.

"Don't get prissy with me." Spike jabbed a finger at Danny. "I know your secret. I put it all together." He tapped his bruised forehead. "Or at least enough to get you in big trouble. If you tell anyone I took the seats, I'll tell everyone about the star metal. I'll bet the government," Spike leaned close, "would be *real* interested. Hey, I could probably sell this," he shook the stick and smiled, "for big bucks!"

"Spike! Don't!" Danny cried, thinking of the Shadow Daggers.

"*Shush!*" A nearby girl hissed.

"Hey, don't worry, Mr. Speed-chump," Spike chuckled. "I ain't going to say nothin' if you don't say nothin' to nobody . . . *and* you tell me how the star metal travels time."

"Only if you're going back to prevent your own birth."

"Very funny! Four months ago you were never this uppitty. Walking through a haunted house sure is liberating, isn't it? I guess I'll just have to turn this in." Spike hefted the walking stick.

Danny's gaze narrowed. "Go ahead. Tell the authorities. They'll take it from you. I know you don't want that to happen. You want the star metal. You want to use it to run away from home."

"What do you know?" Spike's glare radiated loathing.

"I know what bruises look like. I know you're not a wimp."

"That French . . . ."

"I know Rocky gets bruised, too. I saw your stepdad hit Raymond. I know, Spike."

Spike bristled.

"I know about the bat," Danny continued. Spike appeared surprised, his block jaw slack. "I'd want to leave, too. Anybody would."

For a moment, Danny thought Spike was going to ask for help, but he abruptly straightened. "I'm not just anybody. I'm Spike. Don't worry, I'll work it all out. Then, I'll score some collectibles, turn them into cash, and *whoosh*, I'm gone—long gone. Don't worry about Spike."

"You should talk to the school counselor."

"What do I have to talk to a counselor about? Star metal that reacts to thought? That flies and time travels. Sounds like science fiction to me. Hell, soon, it won't matter. I'll be a rich man! Then nobody will mess with Spike!"

"Spike . . . ."

Spike leaned close and snarled. "Don't you even think of trying anything. It's mine! Mine do you hear!" Spike looked around. No one paid any attention. "If you try to steal it back, you're dead meat. I'm not fooling around. Dead, got it?" Spike's fists clenched, jabbing the walking stick under Danny's nose.

"Yes." Danny replied. Spike needed help all right.

Before Spike walked off, he turned and said, "Hey, Mr. Speed-demon. Don't look so worried. I ain't gonna do nothin' that affects nobody but me. Hardly anyone will care. And nobody will notice. So chill, okay?"

"Spike . . . . " The boy kept walking. Danny wanted to tell Spike about the dangers of traveling time; but he wasn't about to listen to Chase the Wimp.

"Hey, Danny! What was that all about?" Christina smiled, interest twinkling in her blue eyes.

"You came to see me at the library?" Danny exclaimed.

"*Ssshush!*" A blond, pig-tailed girl hissed.

"Where else can I see you? Things are so busy. Are you worried about this paper for Mr. Gordon's class?"

Danny closed his eyes. "This semester started off with a bang."

"Are you feeling okay?" Christina touched his forehead. "You're warm."

"Going home isn't going to make me feel any better," Danny sighed.

"What's the problem with Spike this time?" Christina asked.

Danny wished he could start from the beginning and explain it all. "He stole something again; and I can't prove it, yet."

"What did he steal this time? Your research?"

"No, the seats to the tandem."

"Last night?"

"During Jason's ball game."

"I see. So you and Krindy stood and pedaled all the way home?" Christina looked skeptical.

Danny nodded, then felt trapped. Sinking. Fast.

"Do you want to stick to that story? You know what, maybe Cynthia is right!" Christina snapped. "IF so, I'm an idiot!

Danny, when you want to tell the truth, come see me." Fists balled and head held high, she stormed away.

"Christina . . . ." Danny tried to find words, but could not give up his secret.

EIGHTEEN

Two Magic Bicycles

In the woods behind the Pickett house, Danny slumped against a tree. His Saturday slipped away, the way days quickly fade in midwinter. To his left, the Siamese and calico slept in a patch of sunshine. Without wind, the day felt pleasant, *IF* you wore fur. Danny sighed loudly.

"Spike probably heard that." The calico yawned, her mouth growing cavernous.

"Who cares?" Danny gestured toward the brick house. "Spike already knows I'm watching, so he won't go anywhere *until* I leave. Once I'm gone, though, he'll be out riding."

"Are you saying he's scared of you because you know more about the star metal than he does?" Murg asked.

Danny hadn't thought of that. "I'm tired of spying. I want to do something! Don't you ever get tired of lying around? No? Of course not, you're cats! Or acting like them, anyway."

"You suggest charging in?"

"Where is your white horse?" Krindee wondered. "Or should I be more modern? We are talking aliens. Where is your black car, silk suit and dark glasses? Just remember, fools rush in where angels fear to tread."

"Who said that?" Danny asked.

Krindee looked at him, yawned, then the Siamese rolled onto her back, belly fur now catching the sun.

"I know you're upset about Christina, Danny. Now what do you suggest?" Murg asked.

"I don't know." Danny threw up his hands in frustration. "I've been watching Spike for almost three days now, but I haven't learned anything! Everybody's mad at me because I'm busy and can't tell them what I'm doing. My dad would probably be mad, too, *if* he noticed anything besides Ms. Mayfair."

Murg climbed into Danny's lap, then glared up at him. "Danny, in the last few days, you learned to sense what Spike is doing to the star metal. You know where its parts are and what shapes they hold, correct?"

"Yeah, right now he's trying to make a mountain bike." Danny nodded toward the house.

"And you feel Kalyde II echo these shapes, right?"

Danny nodded and glanced at his watch. Since Kalyde II sometimes mimicked its missing pieces, Danny kept the Xenozilit in bicycle form as little as possible. He didn't want to help Spike create a mirror image of the magic bicycle.

"From a distance, you've exerted your thoughts on the missing star metal and learned that it doesn't work. You can't change their shape, draw them to you nor summon them."

"Maybe I'm not close enough," Danny said.

"That could be. Or, possibly, the longer Spike thinks on the star metal, the more the Xenozilit becomes linked to him."

Danny paled. "What do you suggest I do?"

Murg closed her green eyes. "I am still pondering the possibilities."

"How's his bicycle-creating coming along?" Krindee asked.

Danny closed his eyes. "Unfortunately for us, better.

Spike's been studying a Specialized Bicycle brochure. Who'd believe Spike could study anything? I mean he's actually trying to use his brain. He . . . he must be desperate." As Danny pondered that, he chewed on a blade of grass.

Murg open her eyes. Wonder in her green orbs, the calico cocked her head. "Eating grass is good for the digestion. Are you nervous?"

Danny nodded.

"Just wondering if you're being sympathetic."

"After all Spike has done to me? Sympathetic?! Ha! Sarah might have been sympathetic, but not me! Not . . . me."

"Sarah was very kind and understanding," Murg replied. They shared a moment of mutual pain and longing.

"This is all Spike's fault," Danny moaned. "He's always screwing up my life! I'm either hiding from him, running from him, or trying to find him because he's stolen something."

"If it wasn't for Spike, you wouldn't have met Kah-laye-dee," Murg projected.

"I'm sure that's what he intended when he was running me down," Danny replied bitterly.

"That's not what I meant. Sometimes bad things result in something good."

"A silver lining, you mean?"

"Something like that. Unintended consequences," Murg replied.

"Would pity be a better word when describing your feelings toward Spike?" The Siamese's eyes were closed again.

"Sort of in between," Danny replied. "I feel he kinda deserves it. That's not particularly right, I know; but I feel that way anyway. Still, I don't like being hit. Who does? Why would anyone?"

"Don't some people, called boxers, make millions of dollars by hitting people?" Krindee asked. "Modern day gladiators?" She shifted a little to get all of her tail in the sun.

"Professional sports don't reflect real life," Murg thought.

"Don't tell my teacher, Mr. Gordon, that," Danny chuckled. "He might make Jimmy Chang do a different report."

"How's your report coming?" Krindee asked.

"All right, I guess. Can you believe Spike spends lunch in the library now? He's doing research! Research!" Danny threw up his hands, then sighed heavily. "I miss Christina a lot. I really, really wish I could tell her and Jason what's going on. Cynthia keeps saying I'm more interested in Krindy LaFleur than Christina."

"Of course you are," Krindee purred. "I am a cat."

Murg appeared quietly pleased. "Danny, relationships take time. Look at all the time we spend together. We learned to trust each other. Trust is earned."

"Jason's peeved, too. He thinks I'm hiding from Spike. Thinks I shouldn't be afraid of Spike."

"Are you?" Murg asked.

Danny was thoughtful before admitting, "Not like I was, no."

"And if you told him that Spike had stolen something, he'd go charging in?"

"Yeah he would, but that really doesn't matter. I can't tell him about Kalyde II. We agreed that nobody else should know about the magic bicycle. If Spike gets busted, he'll tell the authorities. I can't let that happen."

"Then Spike has to willingly give up the bicycle."

"I could be sneaky and steal it back. Even if he reported me, little would happen. The Shadow Daggers would question me and search around; but they wouldn't find anything. Spike can't point to *The Alien Bicycle* as proof. They'd think he's more whacked than I do."

"This might require a bit more brain power than you're currently using. Simply stealing the star metal might not work. You might get beaten or worse, killed, depending on the extent of Spike's desperation. Unless you plan to move, I would not recommend, as a course of action, stealing back the Xenozilit."

"You won't let me go back in time and prevent the seats from being stolen!" Danny snapped.

"No time traveling. It can severely disrupt the way of things. Living in the present is better than trying to manipulate the past."

"I haven't thought of anything better. I'd be embarrassed

by my stupidity, except a cat and a highly evolved alien I know can't help me." Danny glanced at his magic watch. "I have to get home. The papers will be arriving soon."

"I will continue to watch and follow Spike, if necessary." Krindee cracked open an eye. "This way we can keep track of his progress. And truth to tell, I've enjoyed being a bird during these periods of observation."

Murg eyed her with cocked uncertainty.

"I wish I didn't have to leave." Danny took off his watch.

"You'll know if Spike goes somewhere,then you can follow us," Krindee told him. "Now go, since you've assumed a responsibility to keep people in touch with what is happening in their world."

"Danny, come on." The calico darted into the woods. Danny glumly followed.

Once far enough away, Danny transformed the Xenozilit watch into Kalyde II. As the duo rode away, Danny felt the star metal shifting underneath him. "Did you feel that?"

"No."

"I'm afraid we just gave Spike a clue."

"A bicycle template to match the magazine picture? Metal, especially forged or shaped, can have memory. The Xenozilit might already know the shape, especially if it is sentient."

They arrived home, coasting into the driveway seconds before the delivery truck pulled up. Danny signed for the papers, then started folding. He was about halfway through when he shivered.

"Are you all right?" Murg quit playing with a rubber band to look at Danny.

"That was odd." Danny looked at the bicycle. "I think . . . I think Spike is out riding a Chase-Stomper One or something."

"Is Spike having a good time?"

"Who doesn't on a magic bicycle?" Danny finished folding the papers, then stuffed them into his delivery bag. As he started to climb onto the bicycle, Danny suddenly stepped back.

"Something wrong?" Murg asked.

"I thought I saw Kalyde II ripple." Danny watched

carefully, but nothing happened, except the sun sank closer to the horizon. The air grew colder. "Come on."

After Murg settled in, Danny pushed off, racing down the street. The quicker he finished work, the sooner he could find Spike. Danny was almost done delivering papers when the magic bicycle shimmied. Danny looked down; Kalyde II appeared normal.

"That was odd," Murg thought.

"Yes it was. Hey!" Danny cried..

From top to bottom, the magic bicycle rippled, then wavered as if wanting to change shape. Danny thought Kalyde II briefly grew a huge blue nose, then returned to normal, an old red ten speed bicycle with a bookrack over the back tire.

"Spike is getting better. That's too bad."

"Let's finish, then go find Spike!" Dodging cars, dogs, and people, Danny sprinted through the rest of his deliveries, finishing with the sun still above the horizon. "Spike, here we come!"

"What are you thinking about?"

"Clay, memory metal and magnetism."

A friend of Cynthia's, Manny, was doing his science project on the force of magnetism. The link between the bicycles, Danny imagined, was a magnetizing force.

Danny concentrated, mentally reaching out for the stolen pieces. A connection existed between them and Kalyde II, so Danny let his bicycle be drawn to Spike's bike. Whenever Kalyde II drifted one way or another at an intersection, Danny turned, racing through the coming twilight and away from the neighborhoods. Spike rode the open farm roads, testing, sprinting as fast as he could imagine. Danny thought he could feel Spike's exhilaration.

Kalyde II picked up speed, nearly flying along the northerly farm road. The asphalt lay rutted here and there; but the magic bicycle rode as smoothly as ever. The light from the setting sun cut low and long through the trees, washing Danny in a kaleidoscope of dark and bright. The flickering grew hypnotizing as Kalyde II raced faster and faster, homing in.

In his mind's eye, Danny could clearly see Spike's bicycle as if he stood next to it. The distorted mountain bike was deep blue with flat black trim, seat and handgrips. Instead of standing straight, the mountain bike seemed twisted and brooding. The brakes along the handlebars appeared spiked, dark hair plucked from a porcupine or the many horns of a nightmare—a hellbeast stallion that breathed fire. Two lights adorned the front, a set of blazing eyes with a searing stare. Big knobby tires stuck out from the front and rear, claws ready to run over and rend anything in their path.

"Does it really look that way, or is that your imagination?" Murg wondered. Leaning into the wind, her fur lay flat.

"I don't know." Danny opened his eyes. Somewhere to the right . . . "There!" Danny nodded across a field. Ahead along a crossroad, Spike rode toward the sinking sun. The monster bike's headlights shone brightly enough to draw attention in the waning daylight.

"Sorta looks like a motorbike. If I time this right, we'll coast in, meeting him at the intersection. HEY! " Danny jumped as something landed on his helmet, setting his head rocking. Wings gently batted away his grasping hands.

"HI! It's me!"

"Krindee as an owl," Murg told him.

"What's going on?" Krindee changed into a Siamese. The cat slithered down his back and into the delivery bag.

"Clay, memory metal and magnets. Kalyde II and the Xenozilit remember being one, which draws them together. Once they're near each other, I should be able to imagine them—bring them together—as one again."

Danny bent low across the handlebars and relaxed, letting Kalyde II draw them together. He wanted to swing alongside as smoothly as a hawk swooping down upon on its prey. Even from this distance, he could tell Spike smiled. His grin was huge, pushing his ears back into his batting helmet.

They could hear Spike yelling now. Arms above his head, he pumped his fists. Besides his Yankee blue batting helmet, Spike wore a Texas Longhorn jersey and red-orange football pants.

Kalyde II glided into the intersection, swinging alongside Spike's bike. Less than a foot separated the two-wheelers.

"CHASE! What are you doing here?!" Spike appeared startled, as if he'd been daydreaming.

"He looks scared," Krindee thought.

"I'm taking back what's mine!"

Murg groaned.

Danny thought metal, clay and magnetism. He imagined two bikes combining into one.

The bicycles raced forward, wheels spinning in time with each other. Flashing spokes circled in rhythm. The air between them shimmered, then the bicycles slowed as if slogging through molasses. Their colors bled together, red and blue creating a purple haze between the two-wheelers.

"NO! You can't!" Spike whirled around, reaching for his bat.

"No hitting." Murg flexed a claw, then pricked Spike's thigh.

"OWW! DAMN!" Spike whirled about. "I dropped my bat! I hate that cat! Devil cat! HEY!" Spike suddenly noticed his bike. As if soft clay, the two bicycles oozed toward one another. The tires seemed to melt together, the purple glow between the bikes growing misty, then muddied.

"STOP! You can't do this to Slugger!" Spike swung a fist.

Danny ducked. "It was a gift!"

"You don't need it all!" Spike roared. "Let it go! Let me go! If the Headbangers were here, things would be different!" Spike suddenly closed his eyes, his face becoming a mask of concentration "Or- or if we were there. Let's go alien bicycle! *Yee-haw!* Bye sucker! I've been practicing with Slugger . . . ."

"Danny stop him. He's going . . . ." Murg began.

With the loud and long sound of fabric tearing, then a cable snapping, Spike and his monster bike disappeared in a blindingly bright flash.

"HE'S GONE!" The magic bicycle careened wildly across the road. Danny regained control as Kalyde II dove off the asphalt toward a fence. "I wish I'd never written *The Alien Bicycle*. Now, let's see if we can follow," Danny growled.

"Danny, that may not be . . . ."

Danny closed his eyes and concentrated on following Spike. Looking for a trail, Danny kept thinking about magnetism. The distance didn't matter. Kalyde II would be drawn there; the bicycle would take him wherever it needed to be reunited. Brightness surrounded them, then seemed to swallow them.

" . . . a very good idea."

"Where is this?" Krindee whispered.

"The Headbangers' hideout!" Danny hissed.

Overgrown with weeds and wild bushes, the old shack sat among a copse of trees. The roof appeared ready to collapse from the weight of years of neglect. Light speared from between boarded windows, illuminating the nearby barn, a shadowy companion to the once abandoned house.

"I have a bad feeling about this," Danny groaned.

"He teleported much too easily. He's obviously been studying *The Alien Bicycle*."

"I never should've written it," Danny moaned.

"If the Xenozilit is growing intelligent, it would remember how to teleport," Krindee told them.

Danny paled. "If Spike tells Reggie and the Headbangers about Kalyde II and—Slugger, I think he said—we're in big trouble. They'll be coming for the rest of the magic bicycle."

The front door and barn doors opened simultaneously. Shadows lunged for Danny as someone large jumped out from the barn. Danny braked, stopping abruptly.

"Hey Reggie, Chase is here!" Spike yelled from the barn.

"I see him." Reggie stepped from the door. He cradled a shotgun. Bursts of fire exploded from its twin barrels.

Suddenly the world seemed to slow down; but Danny was still able to move. "A trap!" Danny thought, then backpedaled furiously. Seeing the shotgun's fragmented buckshot gaining and racing against their sudden impact,he imagined himself elsewhere. With a roar, white light engulfed him, buckshot hot on his trail.

NINETEEN

Going Bad

Pedaling with all his might, Danny and the felines raced backwards across the fading rainbow bridge, the buckshot racing closer. Danny could clearly see their deadly, jagged fragments bulleting nearer and nearer. The tips glowed white hot.

"Think faster!"

Danny thought faster, then started weaving. The magic bicycle picked up speed. Kalyde II hit a rut and bounced airborne. Like guided missiles, the bullets followed their erratic trail.

Out of the corner of his eye, Danny clearly saw a green ball of light. It grew larger quickly, as though catapulted.

The slugs crossed the handlebars, heading for Danny's face. "I can't lose them!" Danny leaned back, away from the buckshot.

"Yes you can!"

"Should I try a quick stop?!" Danny yelled. The buckshot ripped closer, now less than a foot away.

"Think of being somewhere else," Murg projected.

The shot suddenly surged.

"The woods near my bicycle! A couple minutes ago!"

A fragment finally reached him, cutting into his cheek and forehead.

"MY RED BICYCLE!" In a roaring flash, Danny appeared in the dark woods, nearly slamming into a tree.

"Whew! That was close," Murg mindspoke.

"Let's head home. I'm too tired to think straight. That was way too close. Th-that's the second time I've been shot at." Danny shook. "I could've been k-killed. You guys could've been killed." Like a punctured balloon, Danny suddenly sat, placing his head in his hands. He wished he had nine lives. Then he'd be nonchalant like the cats.

Changing from an 'I told you so' expression, Murg's reaction softened. "But none of us died. Your quick thinking saved us. Just think ahead a bit more, then thinking quickly will be less vital. Now, take a few deep, cleansing breaths—you're all right—and let's go home. But stay cautious. The Shadow Daggers might be watching your place."

"Danny, let me heal your face." Krindee transformed into her normal self, touched his face, healing his cuts, then changed back into a Siamese cat. "Now you don't look so suspicious."

"I feel better too." Danny touched his cheek, thinking of what might've been. This was all Spike's fault!

Danny switched bicycles and homing devices, then rode home. What was he going to do about Spike?

Hours later, Danny rolled over in bed and sighed. Spike must be smarter than he looked, learning to teleport so quickly. Or, maybe Danny had written *The Alien Bicycle* too well.

Danny massaged his temples, working to keep away a headache.

Had Spike told the Headbangers about the star metal? If so, what would happen then? Would Spike, Reggie and the Headbangers come for the rest of the magic bicycle? Danny rearranged, then beat on his pillow. He would be ready for them.

What if Spike hadn't told them? That was better, but what was Danny supposed to do? Thievery didn't appear to be a great idea. Danny tried to put on his super-charged thinking helmet; but he was tired and too worried.

When the time drew close for the paper delivery truck's arrival, Danny crawled out of bed and dressed. If he couldn't sleep, he would visit Comet. He needed to talk with somebody. The pup was a good listener.

As soon as Danny stepped out of his room, Murg and Krindee appeared at his feet. "Isn't this early?" the transformed Cor-ror-o'lan asked.

Murg rubbed against Danny's leg. "Good morning."

"What's so good about it?" Danny glanced at his dad's door. "I can't figure out what to do about Spike. I should have never written *The Alien Bicycle.* Then he'd still be in the dark about using star metal."

"Worrying less would probably help."

"Do you think Spike told Reggie?" Danny descended the stairs.

"What do you think?" Murg replied. "Think it out. Pretend Socrates is around to answer your questions."

"With more questions, you mean. I don't want to give myself a headache." Danny opened the laundry room door. Comet bounced to his large feet. Sending newspapers sliding, the retriever wiggled and wobbled toward Danny.

"Hi, Comet!" Danny scooped the black bundle of energy into a hug. Comet's tongue darted fast and furious, lapping across Danny's face. "Good morning!" Danny laughed uncontrollably.

"The boys are good for each other," Krindee told Murg. With a bored expression, the calico simply stared at the Siamese.

Danny stood up and carried the squirming retriever outside. The backyard was dimly lit by the amber light of the setting moon. "Okay Comet, take care of business! If he could, I'll bet Comet would tell me what I should do about Spike stealing my bicycle." Danny plopped onto the back steps. "I promised to help Spike, but I didn't promise to do it all by myself."

Murg began cleaning her tail.

"If Spike tells Reggie and the Headbangers about Kalyde II, I'm in trouble," Danny moaned. "I'll have to move away or something. Funny, I like it here now. If Spike hadn't stolen the star metal, his absence would be a heaven-sent blessing."

"Just three months ago, you hated it here," Murg thought.

"But I don't now. I guess it's a time thing."

"Now, since Socrates isn't here, I shall endeavor to help you come to terms with whether Spike has told Reggie and the boys about the pieces of Xenozilit."

Danny put his head in his hands and groaned. "Is this the past coming back to haunt me?"

"Han Suyin said you only understand the present when it is past," the Siamese quoted.

"Now what does that mean? Hindsight is twenty-twenty? Well, if I had to do it all over again, I wouldn't have gone back to the past."

"Really?" Murg asked.

"I think I just had high hopes. You know, boy hero goes back in time to save mother and sister." Even though Danny thought he had accepted things, their deaths lingered as a heavy shadow.

"You respected their wishes. That is very important," Murg thought.

"You met Socrates. Many would be envious," Krindee told him.

Danny rolled his eyes. "That old man was so confusing. That's probably where the saying 'it's Greek to me' came from. Socrates would never, ever, answer anything straight out."

"And he smelled funny. He needed to take more olive oil baths. When you don't stink, people take what you say more seriously, which is why we cats are so fastidious."

"Many revere him as a great man and thinker," Krindee projected.

"Krindee, please. Socrates would cross-examine you if you told him to have a nice day. What is nice, he'd ask. We must look at the context of what is nice, so we can not only know that this day is nice, but what niceness is, so we can apply it to any day and judge whether or not it is nice."

Murg appeared bemused. "Danny, why do you believe Spike has turned the star metal into a bicycle?"

Comet returned, vigorously attacking Danny's pants. Danny fought back. Comet growled as he was slung about.

"Just what he needs, a soul brother and great minds thinking alike." Murg stepped away from the rough-housing. "Danny, why would Spike make another bicycle?"

"Riding a magic bicycle sounded like fun? It would take away his cares? Let him escape them? Oh! Let him escape!" Danny stopped wrestling. Comet kept at it, dogged and growling. "He's thinking of running away to escape being beaten," Danny continued, holding Comet at bay. "That sounds all too familiar."

"Then you and Spike share some experiences," Krindee pointed out.

Danny's jaw dropped. "That was not funny, Krindee."

"Exactly. Danny, do you think Comet would run away if you beat him?" Murg asked.

"I'd never beat my dog!" Danny scooped the puppy into his arms once more. Comet squirmed every which way.

"But if Comet were abused, do you think he'd run away? Go find a better home?"

"Sure. But that's not going to happen. And Spike is not like Comet, either. Spike is mean and spiteful."

"You think he was born mean and spiteful? Never young and innocent?"

Danny's look was deadpan. "Murg, kids can be very mean."

"In a straightforward and teasing way. You were very annoying as a youth. That's why I spent so much time with Sarah. Do you think you were young and innocent?" Murg asked.

"Yeah. I guess. Young and ignorant might be closer to the truth."

"You consider yourself experienced and knowledgeable for a Terran?" Krindee asked.

"Yeah, I guess, for a kid." Danny shrugged. "I dunno. I

know more than I did a year ago—a lot I didn't want to know."

"If you were beaten, would you have run away?" Krindee asked.

Danny was silent.

"Maybe if Spike had been born into a loving family, he wouldn't be such a bully. Unless you're saying he was born a mean-spirited bully. Can Terrans be born bad?"

Danny thought back to his biology class. "Bad genes? I don't know if science has discovered anything in DNA that contributes to someone being born bad. And about that original sin stuff, I still don't know what to believe. If it's true, then it's very unfair."

"If Spike couldn't be born a bully, then he would have to learn to be a bully. His stepfather probably instructed him more than Spike would like to believe," Krindee mindspoke..

"What if at one time, even if just for a while, Spike was like you, Danny? Young and ignorant. If Danny Chase was in Spike's situation, living with Mr. Pickett, what would he do with the bicycle?" Murg asked.

"Escape. Go live somewhere else. That would take money. I guess I could run an overnight delivery service. Working for a living is better than being beaten."

"That sounds quotable." Krindee's expression was thoughtful.

"Would you tell Reggie?" Murg asked.

"Heck no! If Reggie knows, he might tell someone else. As we talked about, Murg, the more people that know about the magic bicycle, the more likely it is to be stolen. Look what happened." Danny threw his hands into the air. Comet leapt from his lap. "I certainly don't think Spike would trust Reggie. I wouldn't. I might lose my chance to escape."

"That being the case, then our secret is probably safe. But what could he do to raise money?"

Danny heard the delivery truck arrive out front. "I'll think on it." He hugged Comet, who licked him, then scratched both cats behind the ears. "Time to go to work."

"So what are you going to do?" Murg asked. "Spike knows how to teleport. He could be learning about time traveling. That would be disastrous."

"If Spike won't talk, now that I know I can influence his monster bike, I have some tricks in mind. Today, he won't escape us. We'll follow him wherever he goes, even to the ends of the earth!"

TWENTY

Cross-Country Chase

Danny glanced at the school clock. Another minute was all he must endure, then he'd privately confront Spike about the star metal, among other things. Danny wanted to find out what Spike had planned, then make a decision about what to do.

The bell finally rang. "Remember your assignments!" Mr. Gordon tapped on the board.

Danny bolted for the door, escaping into the hallway. Weaving in and out of students, Danny sprinted out the front doors. This time he was going to catch Spike and free the star metal from its torturous existence.

Danny quickly unlocked Kalyde II, then whipped around the corner before most of the students left the building, especially Jason and Christina. He didn't want to run into his friends and twist the truth again. For the hundredth time, he wished he could totally confide in them.

Danny rode across the school's rear lawn, heading for the trees. If Spike wanted to avoid him, Spike wouldn't be leaving by the front doors. Spike might try to flee by the gym exit or use the doors to the football field. Danny knew the various escape routes from school all too well; he'd used them on numerous occasions.

"Greetings, earthling." Krindee sat on a branch several feet above his head. Next to the Siamese, Murg rested with eyes closed, apparently asleep.

"Hi, Krindee. Are you cats ready to roll?" Danny pulled into the woods and hopped off his bicycle.

"Is that a term from the sixties?" Krindee asked.

"I was being literal," Danny replied. "When Spike leaves, I want to be ready to fly."

"Literal again?" Krindee asked.

"Hey! The star metal is moving! He *is* leaving by the front doors. Let's go!" Danny cried.

"I'm on my way." A winged Siamese, Krindee glided out of the tree to land on Danny's shoulder. She flapped her receding wings, then reverted to a normal cat. "Birds are so graceful," Krindee said as she climbed into his backpack.

Murg watched in disgust. "I fear you still have much to learn about being a cat." Using her claws, Murg descended and leapt onto her leather palanquin.

Danny allowed the bicycle's magnetism to work its magic, letting Kalyde II be drawn toward Spike's monster bike. Kalyde II shimmered, then writhed. "He's playing with the star metal's shape again." Danny kept the picture of his old red ten speed on the drawing board of his mind, reinforcing Kalyde II's bicycle shape.

Danny suddenly wondered if he could reverse this process. Molding the two bikes into one took too long, giving Spike time to escape. Could he change it while Spike was riding? Give the monster bike flat tires? Or make it smaller?

When they exited the woods, a chainlink fence confronted them. "Nothing's going to stop us." Danny imagined being on the other side. With a bright flash, they blinked beyond the fence to the road. Danny let Kalyde II follow the link connecting the "twin" pieces of star metal, drawing the two bicycles ever closer.

Soon, after many turns, Danny ramped onto a back road.
"He's close by!"
"Look out!" Krindee yelled. A red truck rumbled toward them.

Danny thought fast, as if the pickup were parked, to swerve around the truck. He could clearly see his reflection in its shiny front bumper. As the pickup and bicycle traveled in opposite directions, time no longer seemed to stand still, the wind suddenly tearing at the threesome.

"That was close!" Danny laughed.

"Youth always believes it is invulnerable," Murg thought.

Seeing Spike astride Slugger in the distance ahead, Danny thought speed—focused on being there. Kalyde II rocketed forward.

Spike heard them coming and looked over his shoulder. With a loud curse, the large boy pedaled harder and faster. As if spurred, the monster bike bolted forward.

"Standing still." Danny focused on Spike's knobby back tire. Kalyde II sped along the asphalt like a bike-seeking missile. Distance melting away, Slugger's rear tire grew larger as Kalyde II raced closer.

Spike glanced over his shoulder again. Grunting and straining, he pedaled even faster.

"Spike! I just want to talk! Running away won't solve your problems!"

"Yes it will!" Spike snapped.

"And stealing to create a better life will just lead to a life of crime!"

"A life of crime is better than my life now! Go away! Leave me alone!"

"Spike, please stop and talk!" Seeing that talking wasn't working, Danny concentrated on strengthening the link between the magic bicycles. In a moment, he would flatten Slugger's tires.

"No!" Spike cried. In a flash, he and the monster bike disappeared.

Kalyde II ripped through the spot where Spike had just been riding the monster bike. "Hang on! We're going after him!"

Danny could sense the distant star metal. "He's not far!" He concentrated on the link, seeing Kalyde II drawn to the monster bike.

With a burst of brilliance, the threesome appeared elsewhere, racing along a rural road toward a small town. Most of the houses were single-storied with winter-brown lawns. Several homes stood still adorned with Christmas decorations. One flew a Texas state flag, the star snapping proudly in the wind. All the mail boxes sported sidecars, extra orange boxes for the local paper, the Palestine Gazette.

"Since we didn't transverse the rainbow highway, we didn't travel very far," Murg thought.

"There he is!" Danny pointed. "I wonder what he's doing here?"

"Pointing at you, now speeding away. *Oops!*" The Siamese put a paw over her mouth.

Hearing the cat talk, an elderly man walking his dog stopped abruptly, his eyes wide as he watched them pass. Pulling at his chain, the dachshund barked excitedly.

"That was out of character," Murg thought. "I warned you about not thinking as a cat when you're acting like one. I fear you are slipping. Maybe you should shapechange into a Pekingese."

"Sorry."

Pedaling with all his might, Spike raced into Palestine. He immediately swung left at a corner with an auto body shop, then down a street of quaint one-story homes. Danny followed, shortening the gap.

As they raced by the houses, dogs barked, the canine crescendo building. Murg covered her ears.

At Erma's Antique Shoppe, Slugger darted down an alley of driveways. The monster bike slid through the turn, knobby tires spitting gravel that bounced as tossed marbles into the street.

Danny followed, whipping around the turn and into the alleyway. *"WHOA! "* Danny dodged a scruffy, white-haired mutt. He quickly corrected their path, barely missing a stack of concrete bricks but sending a cluster of trash cans *clattering.*

A roar buffeted them, then a bright light washed over the

bicycle, bleaching everything white for a moment. The world seemed to slowly reappear.

"He left again." Danny thought of the star metal and Spike. He could see himself there, right now, close behind Spike. Danny reached for the monster bike. Slugger and Kalyde II—two would become one.

With a flash and a ripping roar, Kalyde II and its passengers soared across the rainbow bridge, then appeared less than ten feet behind Spike. Danny barely noticed passing an abandoned gas station and a dilapidated general store.

"We're not in Texas anymore." Krindee pointed to an old faded sign that read, LAGNIAPPE. Corner of Third and Orleans in Lafayette. Below it, someone had paint-scrawled, Geaux Cajuns!

"We are in Louisiana. I smell bayou." Murg delicately rubbed her nose.

Spike looked over his shoulder. "HOW'D YOU DO THAT?!" Spike stood on Slugger's pedals as if running. The black and blue monster bike jumped ahead.

Danny thought faster. The bicycles were linked, one to the other like twins, Spike's monster bike hauling along Kalyde II and its riders.

Spike glanced over his shoulder and screamed in frustration.

Danny smiled grimly, then suddenly wondered if Spike felt what he, The Wimp, used to feel. Chased. Hunted. Hounded.

"Spike! Let's stop and talk about this! Please. You're making a terrible mistake!" Danny yelled. With his thoughts, Danny reached for the monster bike.

"You can't have it back! No way! No how! It's mine! You have no claim to it anymore!" With a wild cry, Spike veered off the road, dropping down a hill. Over sticks and tree roots, Spike bounded through the woods toward the brown water. Moss and shiny webs hung from the branches of the green-sheathed trees standing in the bayou.

"He's stretched the link!" Danny exclaimed. "It's barely there!"

Krindee peered ahead. "That doesn't matter. He's cut off. There's only water ahead!"

Slugger slammed into the bayou, drenching Spike. For a moment, Danny thought Spike was going to sink, but the monster bike slogged on, caught about a foot below the surface. Spike desperately pedaled, Slugger plowing through the water and leaving a rolling wake behind.

With light thoughts, Danny guided Kalyde II atop the bayou. The magic bicycle slowed for a moment, then gathered itself, rising smoothly onto the surface. Bounding gently over the swells, Danny guided Kalyde II toward his nemesis.

"Spike, if you'd just listen to me for a minute, listen to what happened to me when I tried running away . . . ."

Like a leviathan, the monster bike surged from the depths, exploding onto the surface. In a wave of water, Spike sped away.

The liquid wall slammed into Kalyde II. The magic bicycle sank a foot before Danny recovered from the swamping. "Yecch!" Danny spat. He was soaked to his skin.

"No more sympathy from me!" Murg's fur lay plastered thick against her.

Krindee wailed loudly. "This feels horrible!"

"Where's that famed feline indifference?" Danny asked.

"It's acceptable conduct to be enraged when your fur is soaked to your skin!" Murg snapped.

"Hey!" Danny stuck a hand under his shirt. A small squirming fish tried to escape his grasp.

"I'll deal with that!" Murg snatched the sunfish from his hand. "Get Spike!"

Danny couldn't see Spike, but he saw the rippling trail atop the water. Focusing on it, Danny let the magic bicycle follow the monster bike's wake. Kalyde II squirted through a narrow space between three moss-smothered trees, then slipped under a dripping branch.

The ripples grew larger and larger, becoming waves. When Danny spotted the water groove left by the monster bike's tires, he knew Spike was nearby.

Just ahead, Spike raced drunkenly between the trees, careening off spongy trunks. Pondweed clung to him, hanging like a witch's green hair. Danny spotted a clearing Spike would momentarily reach. He breathed in the smell of the swamp, then pictured himself racing through the clearing. A flash of light carried them to the watery alleyway and next to Spike. Danny mentally strengthened the link between bikes.

"There must be someplace!" Spike screamed. In a flash of white, he disappeared.

Danny steered into the flash and let Kalyde II be carried along in the monster bike's blinding wake. The two-wheelers briefly flew across the rainbow sky bridge, then reappeared, Kalyde II and Slugger racing side by side on a road surrounded by tall berms of snow and trees plastered white. They rocketed past a gas station advertising tire chain sales and houses nearly buried in snow, their facades peeking out from under thick white hats.

Murg sneezed, then snapped. "I'm wet and cold now!" The calico unleashed an agonizing wail that doubled as a siren.

"This could be Colorado. Maybe New Mexico." Krindee sneezed.

Spike and Danny passed a car with a ski rack atop it.

"Spike . . . ." The cold wind ripped at Danny's words, tearing them away.

They blew past several outlying buildings concealed as snowdrifts and burst into town. The wind gusted, driving snow through the intersection. Spike swerved around a UPS truck. Danny slipped around the other side of the boxy brown vehicle. Almost too late, Danny saw the stop sign.

"Spike!" Nearly laying the bicycle aground, Danny whipped around the corner, just ahead of a bus.

"No!" Spike suddenly recalled *The Alien Bicycle* and backpedaled, wishing he were elsewhere. With a roar as though a thousand lions charged, Spike disappeared in an explosion of white light. The bus barreled through the spot where Spike had been moments ago.

"I don't believe it!" Danny cried, looking over his shoulder.

"Watch where you're going!" Krindee cried.

Kalyde II slammed into the back of a VW bug, racing up its trunk, then ramping up and over the automobile. They skidded across the flat bed of a truck, then landed firmly atop a black Jeep. Danny guided them down the windshield and onto the snowy pavement.

"HEY!" A woman jumped out of the Jeep.

Kalyde II spun around, then shot back toward the intersection.

"Do you feel anything?" Murg asked.

"Nothing," Danny groaned.

"The worst has happened. Spike has just learned to time-travel."

TWENTY-ONE

Boys of Summers Past

By late the next day, Danny still hadn't seen Spike or felt the star metal. Danny hoped to find Spike in the library, but doubted he'd be there. He was lost somewhere in the past. But where? Unfortunately, even with Spike absent, Danny felt he absolutely had to resolve things. That included more than just getting back the star metal. He wanted his friends back.

For a moment, Danny felt a kinship with one of Marvel's first popular comic book characters, the Amazing Spiderman. Danny was amused to think he was living a secret life, just like Peter Parker.

Danny walked into the library where the bookshelves created a maze. The usual suspects sat here, studying or simply reading for pleasure. Many of the kids were called nerds, among others things, some even more objectionable. Whatever Jimmy Chang was reading had him thoroughly engrossed. Next to him, his laptop computer sat open, text printed across the screen.

Danny quietly walked over and tapped him on the

shoulder. "Hey!" Jimmy jumped.

"*Shush!*" a nearby girl hissed.

"Sorry! Hi, Danny," Jimmy whispered. His hand rested over his heart. "You really scared me!"

"Must be some interesting reading." Danny pointed to the open book on the table.

"I'm reading Babe Ruth's biography."

"Oh. Baseball." Danny's interest waned. "For your paper."

"Yes. It's coming along great! The boy you mentioned—Spike was it?—has been a big help."

"Really?" Danny was nearly floored. "You've seen him today?!"

"No. We spoke yesterday and the day before, talking baseball. He discovered what I was researching and asked lots of questions. Several of them made me think. Led me to new avenues to explore."

"Baseball." Danny scratched his head. "I thought Spike was only interested in football. You don't hit anybody in baseball."

"Spike must be a big fan. I've seen him with a bat and a Yankee ball cap."

"What were some of his questions?"

"They were usually about important moments in the game. You know, historic moments."

"You mean no-hitters and World Series games?"

"Those too, but Spike must be a big home run fan," Jimmy replied. "Most of his questions were about big flies."

"Home runs? Game winning ones?" Danny felt he was close to a revelation.

"Some," Jimmy nodded. "Many were milestones of great players like Lou Gehrig, Mickey Mantle, Willie Mays, Hank Aaron and Reggie Jackson. Spike was especially interested in the Big Bambino."

"Who?"

"Babe Ruth. Despite what you say, anyone who loves baseball as much as Spike can't be all bad."

"But is half a percent enough?" Danny asked. Jimmy laughed. "Seriously, you must have seen him at his best. Spike isn't pleasant to anyone. He . . . he must have wanted something from you," Danny finished thoughtfully.

"My baseball knowledge?" Jimmy's expression was doubtful.

"That does sound absurd," Danny replied. History. Time traveling. Why had Spike gone backward in time to see old baseball games? For the thrill of it? That didn't sound right, not in light of his current situation. How would traveling back to past baseball games help him escape? To forget his current woes? Nah. Gambling in Vegas? Knowing the outcomes would ensure he'd win, giving him enough money to run away from home, except that Spike was underage to gamble legally. Illegally then? That still didn't sound right. And why was Spike interested in homers?

"Danny, are you okay?" Jimmy asked.

"Just thinking."

"I thought I smelled oil burning," Jimmy laughed.

Danny chuckled.

"How is your paper coming?"

"Better than I expected," Danny replied. "My only problem is there's too much material. I think I need to focus better on my topic. Mr. Gordon agrees."

"Focus is one of his favorite words. Do you fly?" Jimmy asked.

Danny started to nod, then caught himself. This double life stuff was getting difficult. "Sorta. My dad works in the Air Force, and he used to take us flying a lot; so I've had my hands on the joystick."

"Wow! I'd love to fly a jet."

Danny smiled. What he flew was even better than a jet.

"You read the sports pages?" Danny asked.

"Every day, during the season or when the hot stove league is cooking." Danny appeared confused, so Jimmy said, "Winter when there are trades, drafts and signings."

"Oh. Well, anything interesting happen recently related to baseball history?"

"Now that you mention it, yes! Just yesterday, there was a closed bid auction for the largest collection of autographed and dated baseballs ever! It was an amazing collection!"

"Shush!"

Jimmy looked guilty and quieted. "It had Hank Aaron's first, 500th, 700th, 714th and last homer. All three of Reggie Jackson's '79 World Series blasts. Roger Maris 61st season record-breaker dinger. Gosh, and so many others."

"Any of Babe Ruth's?" Danny wondered. This couldn't be a coincidence. No way.

"Yeah!" Jimmy suddenly looked thoughtful. "Ruth's first homer. First when he was pitching. His last with Boston. First with the Yankees and on and on. It's incredible! —How could one person get all these? The Babe basically invented the modern day autograph. Some say he signed over 600,000 baseballs; but not only is each ball signed, but dated and marked significant by the players. All have been authenticated. The collection is worth millions!"

"What's the seller's name?"

"It hasn't been released yet. It's hush hush, a big secret, ya know. It's made for a big media story. The Mystery Home Run Collector."

"I see." Danny thought he knew where Spike had gone and the identity of the Mystery Home Run Collector. "What about Mark McGwire's or Sammy Sosa's milestone home runs, 70 and 66?"

"Nope. The balls are all older."

Danny hid a smile; that meant Spike hadn't radically altered time. On the other hand . . . Would Danny have known the difference? "Can you tell me about Babe Ruth? Any pictures of him in that book? Or the stadium he played in?"

"Yeah! There's some great black and whites! Have a seat!"

Danny sat and studied. He learned more about Babe Ruth and the Yankees than he'd ever wanted to know—Ruth changed the game from a pitcher's game and base to base baseball to a game of home runs; they created the foul pole because of the Babe; he hit 54 homers in 1920 which was more than seven other teams all put together; and on and on. When Danny was done, he was ready to chase Spike into the past.

TWENTY-TWO

The Bambino's First

As the blinding flash faded, a cold wind lashed at Spike's back like a hundred whips. He cursed his inability to see and hung on tightly. Slugger bounded and hopped, the rainbow bridge as rough as an old-fashioned washboard.

"HEY!" A large chuckhole sent the monster bike flying, surprising the still blinded Spike. When it landed bone-jarringly, his chin grazed the handlebars.

What happened? Where was he? As long as Chase wasn't around, it had to be better.

When Spike's vision finally cleared, he couldn't believe his eyes. He rode backwards at an incredible speed, rocketing through a washed out rainbow tunnel, its colors as faded as an over-bleached shirt. The walls appeared ready to collapse, the relentless waters of days upon days creating long tears and ragged gaps.

"I k-know this p-place," Spike stammered, the jarring making him stutter.

In *The Alien Bicycle,* Chase had ridden the worn and rutted rainbow highway back in time to save his sister and mother. If most of that story was true, which it appeared to be, maybe The Wimp wasn't as big a wimp as Spike thought. Just maybe . . . naw.

Chase had tried to describe how frightening the rainbow tunnel felt, but he'd failed miserably. The time passage reminded Spike of the haunted mansion. The bridge felt ancient and abandoned, ready to crumble. And yet, it wasn't abandoned. He felt watched. The wind keened hauntingly, echoing the despairing cry of unfulfilled dreams. Were those eyes watching him from the gaps? They blinked, the darkness returning.

Spike shook himself. Get a grip. This is my chance to escape Ike!

Where was he going? Grand Slam Slugger raced somewhere. "What was I thinking when Chase interrupted me?"

The monster bike continued to thrash, but now it also seemed to drift. Slugger swayed about, then bounced awkwardly from a chuckhole, bounding toward the dark purple wall. Spike yanked on the handlebars, barely steering the monster bike away from a gap where darkness plunged forever deep.

Spike shook himself again. He was letting this get to him! He had to be brave. IF Chase could really do this . . . .

What should he be thinking? Shouldn't he be focusing on something—a person or place? If Spike remembered correctly, when Chase had lost concentration, he'd ended up in the age of dinosaurs. Did he really believe this? The monster bike shuddered as if warning him.

Since lunch, he'd been thinking about Babe Ruth. Spike would love to travel back in time to Fenway Park, Yankee Stadium, Forbes Field and other ballparks to catch a few of his home runs.

"That's it!" Spike cried. Ruth's first home run ball, signed, might be enough to bankroll his freedom. More signed balls would give him and his brothers, Rocky and Raymond, even his sister, if Tabitha wanted, enough cash to start a new life! One without Ike!

Spike laughed. If Chase could do this, he could certainly do it, too!

Spike concentrated on the entrance to Fenway Park. In the book that Chang kid had been reading was a black and white photo of the entrance to the Boston Red Sox's stadium. The street was unpaved, packed dirt where horse and carriage traffic jockeyed with early automobiles. The cars sported open- spoked wheels with thin tires and only a front windshield, so the drivers wore funky goggles. Besides headlights, lanterns sat along the edges of the windshield.

Over the years, the stadium hadn't changed much, so Spike added coloring from what he'd seen on TV. Fenway's entrance plaza was laid brick, just like the sprawling walls of the park. They stretched far to the left and right, slanting toward the outfield. Windows topped with awnings lined the walls. Above them, green painted beams of iron held up the roof of the grandstands. The gates and turnstiles were also bright green, nearly matching the ballfield's grass.

Slugger settled some, no longer weaving drunkenly along the highway tunnel. The ride still wasn't smooth but seemed direct, line-driving toward a historic moment in baseball's past.

Spike remembered being amused by the clothing people wore in 1914. Most of the men dressed in suits to attend the gentleman's game. Many wore bowlers, berets, funky hats made of pleated straw, and sometimes even top hats looking as if inspired by stovepipes. Women dressed in long, baggy dresses that left no skin exposed from neck to shoe tops. Many even wore gloves. Their hair was pinned up or tied into a bun, making them all look as severe as school marms.

What a bunch of stiffs, Spike thought. Eighty-some years ago holding hands was considered bold, especially in public. Even scandalous! Cursing at an umpire would get you thrown out of the game and probably suspended. Nowadays, they didn't kick you out of junior high games for cussing.

In a ripping explosion of light, Spike and Slugger appeared in Boston, 1914. He sped backwards across the crowded brick courtyard, the monster bike gobbling up the cobblestones. The marquee above the brick entrance read: Welcome to Fenway Park. The NEW YORK YANKEES versus The RED SOX.

"Way cool!" Spike slammed on Slugger's brakes.

"Uph!"

Spike whirled around to look behind him. An elderly man dressed in black with a white collar staggered forward, falling onto his hands. Oh no! A priest!

Without a second thought, Spike raced away, dodging between people, startling men, women and children. Horses reared as he cut between wagons. Drivers angrily shook their fists. "Danged metal beast! Get that thing out of here!"

Maybe he hadn't been seen! Spike didn't spy any policemen. Had that old geezer really been a priest? Spike hoped not. Here some eighty years back in time, he could use God on his side.

People stared curiously as Spike raced by. Their dress appeared as he remembered: heavy and conservative. Whatta bunch of stiffs! People sucking up good air, Reggie would say.

Spike whipped around the corner of Mrs. Smith's Bakery and hopped off the monster bike. People stared at the bicycle, so he rolled Slugger into the alley behind a stack of crates.

After checking to make sure he was alone, Spike placed his hands on the bicycle, then closed his eyes. He imagined a baseball bat. The star metal squealed as if caught in a vice. A flash of light filled the alley but was mostly lost in the daylight. When Spike opened his eyes, he held a wooden-looking Louisville Slugger. "Cool!"

Spike looked down at himself. Except for his Yankees ball cap, he wouldn't blend in very well. Nobody in the city wore jeans or anything with writing on it. Where was Dallas? Who were the Cowboys? What would these people think of his sneakers and B.U.M. equipment?

Spike knew he'd have to find out. No matter what, Spike vowed, he'd watch Babe Ruth hit a home run. His first round-tripper had been—would be—a mammoth shot. Spike knew what inning the blast occurred and that it landed in the right field bleachers. He could change the star metal bat into a mitt and catch the ball. Anyone getting in his way would be hurt.

Spike peered around the corner. Nobody seemed to be

looking for him, except for the priest. The old geezer walked to the other side of the entrance, farther away from horse, buggy and wagon traffic. Clouds of dust filled the air, creating a dirty fog.

As Spike stepped around the corner, a policeman crossed the dirt-shrouded street. Calling out, the priest waved to him. The man in blue walked toward the stooped man in black.

Spike jumped back, hugging the wall. They were looking for him! He snatched his cap from his head. What was he going to do? They knew how he was dressed.

Spike suddenly whipped off his jacket and reversed it. The inside of the jacket was all blue without any writing. Spike also turned his shirt inside out. Redressed, he peered around the corner. Quite a crowd stood around the priest and the policeman.

While they were distracted, Spike ran around the corner. He slowed and mingled with a family of five hustling toward the main entrance.

The man wore a pinstriped and double-breasted suit and sported one of those hats worn by members of a barbershop quartet. The woman was adorned in a long white dress that fell to her ankles. In one hand, she carried a frilly umbrella; the other rested around the shoulders of a young boy. The three kids were all boys clad in brown pants, flannel shirts and plain baseball caps without much of a bill.

"Hey! That's a great jacket!" the eldest lad pointed out. "Where'd you get it?"

Spike looked down. The reversed Cowboy jacket was shiny and brilliant blue. "Uh, it's from . . . France," Spike replied.

"And your shoes. Haven't seen anything like them! Hey Mom, look . . . ."

"Jeremiah, I told you . . . ."

"Later, Jeremiah! Gotta go!" Spike jogged ahead.

As he reached the box office, Spike suddenly realized he had a problem. Just like he didn't own any old clothes to blend in with the times, he didn't have any old money to buy a ticket. All his money was from the end of the century, not the beginning of the 1900's! What did old money look like? Had coins and dollars changed? Surely they were different. He recalled somebody else was on the half dollar before Kennedy. What else had changed? What was he going to do? He had to get into the ball game!

Spike glanced over to the entrance. As several people walked through the turnstile, a young boy ducked underneath. The ticket-checker never saw him. A moment later, another lad slipped in for free. Spike wondered if he could do that. But if he was caught, the policeman might recognize him. Then the priest would file a charge . . . .

He could try to steal the money, but again, if he were caught . . . .

Could he find a quarter? Did he have time? It sounded like the game was going to start.

Spike stepped up to the box window. He hoped the man wouldn't notice the difference in the coins. They were probably the same size and color.

"Good afternoon, young man. Would you like a ticket?" the pockmark-faced man asked as he looked over the top of his spectacles.

"Uh, yes. One for the outfield bleachers."

"That will be twenty-five cents."

"Only a quarter?" Spike couldn't believe the price.

"Quite a bargain to see the professionals play, isn't it?"

Spike nodded. He hoped 1914 quarters didn't look much different than the modern ones. As he dug in his pocket for change, his heart thundered, ready to stampede from his chest.

The quarter slipped from sweaty fingers and bounced across the bricks. Spike dropped it twice more before getting a good grip on the coin. Wishing there was another way, he gave the ticket seller his quarter. While Spike waited, sweat dribbled down his face.

"Are you all right, son?" the old man asked.

"Just excited!"

"I understand. Yankees versus the Sox. It doesn't get any better." The man held out a ticket, then suddenly pulled it back. "Hey! What's this?" He looked at the quarter again. "What are you trying to pull, kid?! We don't take foreign money! Hmm. On second thought, this looks American, but the date's 1991. Heh.

Looks real though. Listen kid . . . Hey, kid!"

Spike was sprinting. He darted around a corner and rested against the wall, trying to catch his breath. What was he going to do?! He had to get into the game! He took a deep breath, then sighed. Maybe he'd be lucky and find a quarter. Yeah, right, Mr. Lucky was his nickname. He'd have to either sneak in or find a quarter. He'd try scavenging first. It'd be easier to sneak into the game once it started.

Avoiding the courtyard where the priest and policeman were still surrounded by a crowd, Spike searched the sidewalks along a side street. He found two pennies near a tree and compared them to a 1988 penny. Lincoln adorned both on the head's side, but on the back, wheat ears surrounded "one cent" instead of the Lincoln Memorial. Spike checked his pocket. In all, he had eight modern pennies. If he could find fifteen more, he could mix them and maybe nobody would notice. He sighed and kept looking.

In front of an ice cream parlor, Spike spotted a coppery glint. Another penny! Hands snatching, Spike darted for it.

With an "Ooph!" someone slammed into him. Spike rolled over, ready to let loose a string of profanity, then swallowed his tongue and held back his anger. He even managed to smile. Fate was on his side. "Jeremiah! I thought you'd already be at the game."

"Mom left her pillow in the car, so I ran back to get it. I'm the fastest." Jeremiah held up a seat cushion. The boy's face was flushed. His eyes kept drifting to Spike's jacket.

"You like this jacket, don't you?" Spike asked.

"I've never seen anything like it! I'd love to have one!"

"It's your lucky day. I need some money. I'll sell it to you for two dollars."

"I only have seventy-five cents," Jeremiah replied.

Spike couldn't believe he was selling his favorite jacket for seventy-five cents. But he had to get into the ball game! With a couple of signed Babe Ruth baseballs, he'd be rich and free of Ike. "It's a deal!"

"All right!" Jeremiah cried.

After the exchange, the boys raced for the gate. Spike went to a different window and paid a quarter. With a ticket in hand, Spike felt lighter, as if wings had sprouted from his ankles. He didn't even think about his jacket anymore. He was going to catch Babe Ruth's first home run!

Once inside the gate, the smell of hot dogs, popcorn and cotton candy overwhelmed him. Spike was tempted to buy something, then decided not to risk it. He followed a crowd through the tunnel to the grandstands.

At a railing, Spike stood amazed. Fenway Park was smaller than he remembered, seating no more than a few thousand. The grandstand roof appeared stark and rickety compared to modern architecture. Instead of plastic seats, green wooden chairs lined the concrete tiers.

With a huge smile on his face, Spike walked down the aisle toward the field. The teams were warming up, tossing the ball back and forth and fielding bunts. The Boston Red Sox' uniforms drooped baggily and were plain white without letters or numbers. Even their hats were white, although red stripes adorned their socks. The drab gray Yankee uniforms read NEW YORK in dark blue across the front. Their hats were also navy, matching their socks.

Spike stared slack-jawed at the players' gloves. How could they field with those tiny things? The mitts barely covered their hands.

Spike searched for Babe Ruth. The Sultan of Swat sat in the dugout swinging a bat. Even at the age of nineteen, young Ruth was big and more than stout with massive arms, tree-trunk legs and a sizable belly. His pudgy face was flushed and his dark eyes bright from the excitement of his first major league baseball game.

Spike couldn't believe this! If he had a baseball, he would have it autographed and dated right now instead of waiting for a homer. Spike thought about joining the throng of boys along the railing between home and first, pleading for balls. How much would a baseball cost? Did they sell them here?

Spike glanced around, then looked to the outfield. In the sixth inning, he planned to catch a very special baseball. It would land in the bleachers, right below the Fashionknit Neckwear sign, between the Coca-Cola and Ever Ready Safety Razor placards.

The players quit what they were doing and headed for the dugout. Both managers walked toward home plate where the umpires waited.

"Good afternoon ladies and gentlemen!" the announcer's voice boomed, "and welcome to Fenway today for a game between the New York Yankees . . ."

"*BOO!*"

"Losers!"

"Go home Yankees!"

". . . and your beloved Red Sox," the announcer continued.

"Yeah!"

"Go Jumpin' Joe!"

Feeling as if he were floating in a dream, Spike sauntered toward the outfield bleachers.

"I wish I were strapped in," Murg thought over the wailing winds. The calico hunkered low across her palanquin, claws dug in at the four corners to hang onto the bucking bicycle. Whenever traveling backwards in time, despite being in what had been the rear, she became a living hood ornament of fine distinction.

The tattered rainbow seemed to undulate, arranging holes and bumps for Kalyde II to hit. The magic bicycle slammed into a large pothole and careened airborne. Murg hissed. They landed violently and immediately swerved into another chuckhole. "I don't like this."

"I—I don't either, b-but you agreed t-to it, too!" Danny's words stuttered with every rut Kalyde II hit along the bleached rainbow bridge. Clad in a helmet, a plain white sweatshirt, blue jeans and a backpack, Danny was dressed for 1914. His watch appeared a bit futuristic, but he'd keep it hidden under his sleeves. Right now, the hour and minute hands raced backwards crazily, emitting a low *whirring* noise.

"Yes, I agreed to this," Murg replied. "It was my choice, just as helping Spike was your choice."

"I don't want to let down Krindee and the Cor-ror-o'lans *and* embarrass the Human Race!" Danny yelled over his shoulder.

"You aren't. Of course, getting back the pieces of the star metal is also good incentive."

"Yes it is!"

"Just remember, your mom said, people are more important than things."

"I remember, and minister-to-be Big Jim said caring is the greatest gift. Of course, they never met Spike. I wonder what the homing signals are sending back to the Shadow Daggers?!"

"There won't be any change," Murg projected. "In the present, you are still there. When you return to the same spot in time, the Shadow Daggers won't notice anything."

"I w-wish I could've j-just left it on my other bike!"

"The Shadow Daggers are already suspicious. They might have found your other bicycle. We must stay smart."

They hit a big hole. Kalyde II jumped airborne, then landed hard.

"This is not fun!" Krindee wailed. Nearly ripping away her words, the wind tore at Danny's backpack.

"Going b-backward in time this t-time is worse than last t-time! We're n-not even going back as far this t-time!" Danny stammered.

"Think of it as a rough sea, worsened by Spike's wake. Remember, time traveling is always dangerous serious business. Your thoughts are wandering, Danny. Remember the Jurassic period we visited?"

"Krindee! Keep your mind on Fenway Park in Boston, spring 1914! Can you see it?! It's brick with green trimming, beams and roofing!" Danny continued describing it, clarifying it in his own mind as well as the Cor-ror-o'lan's thoughts.

"Hey! What's that?" Krindee pointed back along the battered tunnel. Sickly green flickered along the ceiling and walls, washing forward and brightening. An emerald dot appeared in the distance, rapidly growing larger and larger. Dark smoky tendrils writhed around the orb like fouled halos. It almost seemed as if they approached the thing, instead of racing away from the storm-shrouded orb.

"I don't like the looks of it!" Danny moaned. He'd seen it before, and just as before, dread seized him. Somehow, he just knew the storm orb was after the star metal.

"Stay calm, Danny. All goes well. Glance behind you."

Danny looked over his shoulder. "Hey! That's somebody . . . on a bike! That's Spike on Slugger!"

"You are arriving close to the same point in time."

"Before the game!"

A witchy green light washed over Danny, causing him to turn around. "That thing's gaining!"

"Stay focused!" Murg told him. "We are nearly there."

Danny stared into the writhing green light but he no longer saw the orb. In Danny's mind, the green darkened, becoming a sprawling construction of green metal beams and orange brick walls. The avenue in front of the ballpark clarified, Danny visualized green fading to black and white, just like the picture in the book. The front gate loomed before him. The marquee above welcomed them to Fenway and announced the The New York Yankees versus the Red Sox.

The green radiance brightened to nearly blinding intensity.

Danny looked across the park toward the setting sun. "C-can you see it, K-Krindee?"

"Clearly."

The storm orb raced closer, now just above the front wheel. The wind grew biting and nasty as though angry Arctic snakes. The green sphere and swirling clouds reached the handlebars, now inches away from Danny's face. Within the globe, large eyes blinked at him.

A white light roared bright, then with an implosion, swallowed Kalyde II. The radiance faded quickly, leaving the quartet on a stadium street corner in Boston.

"*Ooph!*" a man cried as he was knocked over by Kalyde II's abrupt arrival.

Danny squeezed the brakes and stopped. "I'm sorry."

A tall policeman helped the man dressed in black rise to his feet. "Twice in one day, may the Lord have mercy upon me," the priest prayed.

With a snarl, the angry officer grabbed Danny's arm, pulling him away from the magic bicycle. "Son, you're coming with me to the station."

TWENTY-THREE

Play Ball

Krindee leapt onto the officer's feet, then hissed angrily.

"Hey ya!" The whip-thin lawman jumped back, then drew his club. With eyes as hard as agates, the man in blue glowered back and forth between Danny and the Siamese cat.

"Relax," Murg thought to the Siamese. "Cats are observers. When annoyed, we simply ignore the offender or casually depart."

"Behave, Krindee! I'm sorry, officer." Danny gestured and shrugged as if to say, 'you know cats'. "She's upset because you're blaming me for something I didn't do, well, at least not twice." Danny turned to the priest. "Father, I'm sorry. Please forgive me. I should've paid more attention to where I was going. Are you all right?" He tucked his helmet under his arm.

"Forgive you?" Again, the policeman seized Danny's arm. "You're dangerous on that contraption of yours, running around with these nasty cats!"

Murg lifted her nose high. The calico's tail snapped back and forth.

"Please, Father, I am sorry," Danny asked.

"Give obeisance," Murg suggested.

"What's that?"

"Kneel but don't beg, plead or grovel."

Danny kneeled.

"H-hey!" The policeman let go of Danny's arm. "Something wrong with ya, kid?"

The elderly clergyman appeared surprised, his gray caterpillar eyebrows nearly touching his thin, steely hair. The stooped priest cupped his chin, his expression thoughtful. *"Hmm. Officer, we may be making a mistake. We were told that the assailant was much, much larger and wearing a white, blue and silver jacket. There was no mention of cats, nasty or otherwise."*

"You're right, Father. Come to think of it, we were told that bicycle was blue. Sorry, son." The policeman put away his club, then stepped forward. Admiring Kalyde II, the officer ran a hand along the bicycle's frame. "This is quite a piece of work. Nicely done. Haven't seen anything quite like it."

Danny didn't like where this was headed. He needed to get into the ball game and find Spike before he knew Danny was here. If he could sense the monster bike, then Spike could probably feel the magic bicycle.

While most of the crowd looked at the bicycle, an elegantly clad woman with her hair pinned high scrutinized his clothes. He wore blue jeans and plain white sweatshirt. Although his backpack might be mistaken for a sailor's bag, his sneakers were a dead giveaway.

"This looks brand new. And so red! All the bicycles I've seen are black," the officer said.

"Newly built," Danny replied, inwardly berating himself for not changing the color. "We just moved here from . . . Philadelphia. My dad's going to manufacture these. He's searching for a place to set up shop."

"Interesting," the policeman murmured. "Riding looks like fun. It would make patrolling easier."

"More fun than riding a horse, sir." Danny glanced around. In the distance, he thought he heard the baseball teams being announced. "I guess it's so much fun I got carried away. Again, I'm sorry, Father. Can I buy you a ticket as an apology? "

"No, young man. I have a ticket, but thank you. Now get going, they'll be . . . glory be, they're starting! Go on! You don't want to miss the first pitch. Go Sox!"

"Thank you, sirs!" Danny carefully rolled the magic bicycle through the crowd toward the box office.

"That was smooth," Murg told him.

"I thought my heart was going to explode." Danny's tension disappeared as if a freshly untied balloon.

Murg and Krindee sat on the back carrier, studying people. "1914. In some ways, a kinder, more refined time in your history. More people had manners."

"Or at least had the courtesy to put on airs." Murg added. "But then World War I is just about to start."

"Danny, instead of buying a ticket, why don't you just use the star metal's magic to carry you inside?" Krindee asked.

"I don't know where to appear. Someone might see me. Besides, it's not right, and it's against the law to sneak in. I should pay for a ticket." Danny stepped up to the box office. The pockmark-faced man put on his glasses, then looked expectantly at Danny. "One please."

The man adjusted his spectacles, then asked. "What type of ticket, son?"

"Outfield bleachers. I want to catch a homer!" Danny mustered false enthusiasm.

"Be a quarter."

"Danny, wait a minute. Your money is futuristic—far ahead of this time," Murg told him. "He might notice."

Danny dug around in his pocket. "I . . . I must have left my money in my other pants," he said lamely.

"Go on! Get out of here! People are waiting!"

His mind whirling, Danny rolled the magic bicycle away from the box office. People stared at him, not surprisingly, because the bicycle was bright red and two cats rode atop it.

"What are you going to do?" Krindee asked.

"Use my imagination. I can't believe I forgot about money.

I remembered about clothing. Do you know what old coins look like?"

"Certainly," Krindee replied. "You need quarters. From 1892 to 1916 quarters were known as Barber quarters. They had a Caesar-looking head on the front, you know a man with a wreath circlet. Tails had an eagle spread wide with stars encircling it. Here." She projected the image into Danny's mind.

"I see." Danny leaned his bicycle against the wall, then looked around. If he stood right, he should block people's view so they couldn't see what he was doing. Digging into his pocket, Danny removed two quarters. He stuffed them in the little black case suspended underneath the magic bicycle's seat. As he stood facing away from the wall, Danny reached back and laid his hands on the black case. He imagined a transformation, the current design restamped into an old minting.

The case contracted as if a fist squeezing. A squeal of metal preceded a burp, then the case returned to its normal size. "Excuse me," Danny said to a couple staring at him. When they were gone, Danny removed the coins and examined them. "Perfect. I think."

"Let me see," Krindee thought. Danny held the quarters before the Siamese's eyes. "Looks good. How did you do that?"

"Magic and imagination."

"How did you know how to do that?"

"The first time we traveled to the desert, I forgot to take a water bottle. With magic and imagination, we—Kalyde II and I—created a full water bottle," Danny replied.

"You could drink the water?" Krindee asked, her expression incredulous.

"You're not acting as a cat," Murg thought. The Siamese sobered.

"It was delicious. Now, let's go buy a ticket!" Danny walked to a different ticket window. "One outfield bleachers ticket please."

"That's a quarter," the young man told him.

Danny gave him the coin and waited, his legs trembling. The ticket seller looked at it, rubbed his eyes, then looked again.

Danny nervously licked his lips.

After a jaw-cracking yawn, the cashier put the quarter in the drawer and handed Danny a ticket. His legs still shook as he walked along the brick wall toward the outfield entrance. "I was worried there for a minute," Danny murmured.

"He was just bored," Murg replied.

They walked past the gate leading to the outfield bleachers. "Where are we going?" Krindee asked.

"I need to find a place to transform Kalyde II. I can't just roll a bicycle inside the gate."

"All right. While you do that, I'll go find Spike," Krindee replied. "Once I do, I'll be waiting inside the gate."

Danny nodded. "Be careful."

Krindee darted between a man's legs and through the gate. "Hey!" The ticket taker whirled around. For an instant, Danny thought the man was going to chase the Siamese; but he turned around and took the next person's ticket.

"Now let's find a place to change." Danny rolled Kalyde II down a street stretching along the back of the stadium. A roar sounded from behind them, signaling the beginning of the game.

With hands full of popcorn and Coca-Cola, Spike sat down. Resistance had been futile. The low prices were unbelievable! Now he was prepared to wait another six innings.

Spike thought about what he'd felt while waiting in line. He swore he'd felt The Wimp nearby. Spike reached down to ensure the bat was still against his leg. Thinking of Chase had to be pure paranoia. There was no way Chase would think to look for him here, in the early nineteen hundreds. Spike sighed. Relax and have fun, he told himself.

"GO YANKEES!" Spike yelled.

Annoyed people glared at him. A woman huffed, pulling her child closer as if he were infectious.

A big man, reminding Spike of Ike, leaned toward him. "That'll be enough of that cheering, kid. We're all Red Sox fans here."

The man's hands were huge scarred bricks. Was this Ike's grandfather? Spike laid his hand on the bat, then decided being seen and not heard would probably make it easiest to catch Ruth's homer. Swallowing his tongue, Spike smiled. "Sorry. I'll cheer quietly." No more Ike. No more Ike, Spike kept repeating under his breath.

"Murg, do you see any place to change?" Danny looked around downtown Boston. He was surprised at the number of people out strolling, walking and busily working.

"I think you made a wrong turn. I doubt Spike had this trouble. Find an alley."

"But I might be seen."

"Yes, you do seem to be drawing a lot of attention."

"Hey, that garage looks like a good place." Danny pointed to the shop: The Beantown Mechanic. The sign in the window read: CLOSED.

Danny rolled the bicycle to the front window and looked inside. The door from the office to the garage stood wide open. The work area appeared deserted. Danny knocked, hearing it echo. After a minute of silence, a second knock, followed by more silence, Danny asked, "You ready?"

"How are you going to get inside?"

"Magic."

"Isn't that breaking and entering?" Murg asked.

"I won't break anything. And I'll only touch the door on my way out."

"Interesting interpretation."

"I know. It's a good thing Krindee isn't here to see this. She'd be disappointed."

Resting his hands on the handlebars, Danny looked through the window, concentrating on the garage. Being inside the garage. Seeing himself there. Be there—be there now. With a flash, they disappeared, blinking to reappear standing on the greasy dirt floor of the garage.

"Oil. Grease and horse dung. A marvelous combination that clogs the olfactories."

Danny placed his hands on Kalyde II and concentrated on quietly making it a watch. With an eruption of brilliance and a metallic squeal amplified by the confined spaces, the star metal transformed from a two-wheeler to a timepiece.

The front door opened. "WHO'S IN THERE?!"

TWENTY-FOUR

Storming

At the top of the fourth, Spike turned around and stretched. He saw a woman returning to her seat and performed a doubletake. As his mind contemplated the impossible, his face slowly drained of all color. That woman looked just like that French witch, Krindy what's her name! Could she be following him? That was ridiculous, but so was traveling back in time!

"Are you all right, young sir?" a nearby woman asked. "You look pale."

Spike nodded. "I think so." Spike looked up again at the woman with the purple eyes.

"You are a brave young man, wearing a Yankees cap to a Red Sox home game," the elderly woman continued.

"Hey, I'm a Yankee fan, but I'm here to see one of the Bosoxs, George Herman Ruth."

"You're here to see the newcomer from Baltimore? He already struck out twice. My husband believes he should be sent packing back to the minors."

"Just you wait and see, the third time's a charm for the Babe," Spike glanced at the scoreboard.

When he looked back behind him, the woman with Krindy's eyes was gone. There was no way it could be that French witch. No way. Spike rubbed the back of his neck. Maybe it was his imagination. In *The Alien Bicycle*, Chase said that he thought using the star metal expanded his imagination. Spike thought The Wimp must be right. His imagination raced a mile a minute.

"What am I gonna do!" Danny panicked, looking wildly around the garage.

"Breathe and think! How did you get in here?"

"I used the bicycle's magic and my imagination," Danny replied. "Oh! That's right. I don't have to be on the bicycle to use its magic!" Danny snatched up Murg.

"HEY JACK, I THINK I SEE SOMEBODY!"

Danny clutched the watch and closed his eyes. He wanted to be out front. With a flash, he appeared outside the garage. "That was cool!"

Danny glanced to his right. "What was that?" A large, gangly man followed a stout fellow into the front door of the repair shop.

Danny scooted around the corner, then took off at a dead run. He kept thinking he'd hear calls to stop, but no one shouted at him. His outstretched ticket seemed to explain everything. "I wonder how far along the game is?"

"Keep running."

As a Siamese, Krindee paced back and forth near the outfield gate. The Cor-ror-o'lan felt Danny before she saw him enter the park. "There you are!" She bounded to his side. Murg joined them, fresh from slipping in unseen. "Are you all right, Danny? You appear flushed."

"I ran all the way. We had trouble finding a place to make the change. What inning is it?"

"The fifth."

"Man, time flew, but we're still here in time." Danny sighed in relief. A passing man looked oddly at Danny, a reminder not to talk aloud to the cats. "Where's Spike?"

"He's in the outfield bleachers. He has turned the star metal into a bat."

"Getting around as a cat has worked well?" Murg asked.

"Actually, I became human for a while."

"Did he see you?"

She nodded. "Unfortunately."

"Did he recognize you?"

"I don't think so. I am sorry. The feeling, the uplift of emotions here is more powerful in my human form than when I'm a cat."

"A small price to pay for the privilege of being a cat. Danny, how are you going to approach Spike?" Murg asked.

"I can't just grab the bat and run, but I like that idea."

Murg just stared at him. She finally blinked slowly, then thought, "Just when I think you're beginning to think . . . ."

"You want me to just sit down next to Spike and start chatting? Howdy, Spike. How's it going? Good weather for a ball game some eighty years in the past, isn't it?"

Krindee looked to Murg. "Sarcasm?" The calico nodded. "Danny, Spike doesn't appear to have changed anything around him yet, but I think he's changed. He's laughing and having fun," Krindee told Danny. "Please try talking first. It is the high evolutionary way. Oh no, I think it's too . . . ."

"CHASE!" Open-mouthed and staring wide-eyed at Danny, Spike stood in the ramp to the stadium. He had dropped his drink but kept a tight grip on the Louisville Slugger.

". . . late."

"Damnation!" The mammoth boy exploded forward, shoving Danny aside as he ran at full speed. Spike vaulted the turnstile and raced out the gate. A brown and beige streak, the Siamese hotly pursued the bully.

Murg waited for Danny, who jumped to his feet and sprinted after them. "This is fruitless. Why keep doing what you've been doing when it doesn't work?"

"He can't get away from me!"

"Testosterone," Murg groaned.

Danny raced out of the gate, then slid to a stop. "Where'd he go?" Danny looked about wildly. "There he is!" Danny pointed. A team of horses pulling a milk wagon passed by. Beyond it, Danny spotted Spike ducking into an alley.

"Fruitless is right. Let's take a short cut." Danny scooped the calico into his arms. Looking left then right, he clutched the watch and briefly wondered what these people were going to think. Danny focused on the alley. See there. Be there. The walls of the alley stretched to his left and right. Spike was . . . .

With a flash of light and a low whoosh, Danny and Murg reappeared across the street and in the alley some distance ahead of Spike, giant-stepping without ever taking the first step.

As he ran clutching Slugger in both hands, Spike looked over his shoulder, watching for them at the mouth of the alley. The star metal bat slowly transformed into the monster bicycle. As if sensing Danny, Spike looked ahead. "CHASE!"

The bat spread from Spike's hands, pouring to the ground and geysering upward and out, changing into the monster bike. As it finished altering, Spike climbed aboard and raced into the street.

Danny screamed in frustration, then removed his magic watch. His imagination shaped the star metal into the magic bicycle. Before it had completely settled into the Spacelander, Danny hopped astride Kalyde II. The felines were barely aboard when Danny rocketed out of the alley.

"To your left!" Krindee projected.

Whirling dust devils spun in Spike's wake. He darted between a horseless carriage and a horse and wagon. The driver screamed at him.

Danny followed. He dodged one person, then two women crossing the street. The ladies screamed and threw their parasols.

"I've had enough of this!" Danny visualized himself riding next to Spike. In a wash of bright light, Kalyde II and its passengers blinked ahead, appearing immediately next to Spike.

"CHASE! Damn your hide!" Spike slammed on the brakes and backpedaled.

Danny reacted quickly, also reversing direction.

The white sun erupted, swallowing Spike and his bike in the brilliance.

Danny followed. When he could see again, they rode through the rainbow time tunnel, neck in neck with Spike, speeding forward toward the present. "You can't lose me, Spike."

"CHASE! I don't believe this!"

Danny reached out with his thoughts, contacting star metal. The monster bike quivered. Did he feel resistance? Danny sighed; he'd promised he'd try talking first. And his mother had told him that people were more important than things. "Spike. Let's stop and talk. I might understand what you're going through! Be able to help!"

"You don't understand anything!" Spike roared.

"He won't listen to me." Danny seized control of the monster bike and thought small.

Slugger abruptly squealed and shrank. "HEY!" Spike appeared to be riding a two-wheeled tricycle. Spike was hunched over, his knees springing up around his ears.

Danny changed his mind, thinking giant-sized.

The miniature monster bike hissed like a balloon and suddenly expanded, growing to triple its original size.

"No!" Spike appeared to be an ugly toddler on a normal bicycle. He slipped off the seat, barely hanging onto Slugger with one hand and a knee crooked over the center bar.

Danny pulled the monster bike toward him, then shrank Slugger to normal. The center bar smacked Spike in the chin, stunning him.

The monster bike swerved closer. Its frame wavered, the metal appearing to warp. Colors swirled between the magic bicycles, blending with each other. A humming vibrated throughout the air, growing into a song as the bicycles melded together. Once the two bicycles were one, a tandem under Danny's control, he could guide it as he wished.

"Danny, look!" Krindee pointed ahead. In a wash of sickly flickering green, the emerald storm orb flew along the tattered rainbow tunnel toward them.

"Not again! I . . . I think it wants my bicycle! Uph!" A blow from Spike stunned Danny, causing him to lose focus.

"YEAH!" Spike yanked on the handlebars. With a *pop*, Spike's bicycle abruptly regained its monstrous form and pulled away.

The Spacelander bounced, careening toward a wall.

"Danny! Get with it!" Murg yelled telepathically.

Danny yanked the handlebars right. The Spacelander grazed the crumbling purple wall. It collapsed, spewing dust. Kalyde II bounced over and through several chunks, then skidded sideways. Danny fought mentally and physically to right the magic bicycle.

"It's still coming."

"I can't avoid it! Hang on!" Danny slammed on the brakes, then raced backwards.

"Sucker!" Laughing, Spike raced away.

"WHERE ARE YOU GOING?!" Krindee asked.

"AWAY FROM THAT THING!"

"IT'S FASTER THAN YOU!" Krindee cried.

"Your excitement is ill-representative of the feline species."

"NOTHING'S FASTER THAN ME!" Danny thought light speed. He thought warp speed. The fastest speed was being there.

"It's still closing!"

Danny thought faster, bending time. Jumping from place to place, riding the tunnel connecting the overlap of time as the years folded atop each other. The crumbling walls became mottled purple streaks, black gaps and violet stretches blending together. The rainbow's colors became even more drab, nearing bone-dry whiteness. The ride grew rougher, the bicycle bounding about as though a crazy Superball. Danny could barely hold on.

"WHERE ARE YOU GOING?!" Krindee cried over the howl of the wind.

"I DON'T KNOW!"

"Danny, this is a mistake. Think. How did you escape this thing before?"

As though an undertow, something suddenly seized the magic bicycle. Danny was nearly thrown off. Murg and Krindee lay sprawled across the book carrier.

"WHAT WAS THAT?!" the Siamese asked.

"A time tide. Danny and I have been this way before. We're heading for the Jurassic period again, my friend."

"NO!"

The storm orb closed, now less than five feet away. Malevolent green eyes appeared within the orb. The sense of evil was so strong, Danny felt ill.

The rainbow tunnel pulsed with the eldritch light of a dark emerald. Smoky tendrils spun outward, reaching for Danny. One seemed to form into a hand.

"HANG TIGHT!" Danny slammed on the brakes, thinking himself into the now. With a thunderous implosion of glittering light, Kalyde II abruptly disappeared.

TWENTY-FIVE

Greek Philosophy

"Spike! Stop! Listen to me!" Danny's words were lost in the winds' piercing wail as they screamed along the faded rainbow tunnel. Kalyde II shook and shuddered with every rut and bump. The magic bicycle struck a fallen chunk of crumbling wall, then rattled as if ready to fly apart. Danny held on tightly, the quakes leeching strength from his hands and arms. One foot slipped off a pedal, almost causing him to fall off. "This gets worse every time!"

"I have a bad feeling about this." Murg's claws were buried in the bike's book carrier.

"I wish there was another way," Krindee said from inside Danny's backpack.

"Spike . . . ." Danny began again.

"Leave me alone! You'll never get this back!" Spike yelled over his shoulder. He jumped up on his bicycle, running on the pedals.

Danny stayed calm, focusing on catching Spike. "You can't have the star metal. It was a gift! This is wrong! This won't solve your problems!"

"You're wrong! Soon I'll be rich and famous!" Spike shouted back.

Danny steered closer, Kalyde II drafting the monster bike. The two bicycles drew together as if magnetized, rear wheel meeting front wheel. Rubber melting to rubber and spokes merging, the two tires became one, linking the bikes into an odd tandem.

"Got 'em!" Danny cried triumphantly.

"Danny, we've tried this before," Murg mindspoke.

"If at first you don't succeed, try, try again," Danny replied.

"That can also mean trying something different. Think!"

Danny was ready to duck when Spike whirled around. The blow was aimed low, the bat slamming into the Kalyde II. The impact drove the twin bicycles apart. The magic bicycle swerved sideways, hit a rut, then skidded across the tattered time bridge. Out of control, Kalyde II slid toward the crumbling wall, heading for a cavernous gap.

"Look out!" Krindee cried.

A dark breach swallowed the magic bicycle. Spinning head over heels, Danny and the felines plunged into the darkness.

"Murg!? Krindee!?" Danny gasped. With a drumming headache, he awakened from his nightmare to someplace strange that smelled of olive oil.

The ceiling appeared to be made from the same white marble as the walls. They glistened in the sunlight slanting through the open window. The sounds of carts, mules and people walking and talking drifted into the room. From the direction of the door, Danny heard a distant conversation that he didn't understand; although the language sounded vaguely familiar.

"Murg?! Krindee?! Where are you guys?"

Danny looked around. A small, nearby table held a pewter goblet, a pitcher, a bowl of dates and a vase cradling flowers; his gaze didn't settle there but beyond, his attention immediately seized by what stood in the distance outside the window. He knew that building! It was the Parthenon atop the Acropolis! The temple to Athena! "I'm in ancient Athens!"

The sacred shrine appeared new, its white steps and tall columns freshly cut. Against the blue backdrop of the Aegean Sea, the Parthenon appeared to be a white helm sitting atop the blunt coastal summit.

He had to be in ancient Greece—the time of the Hellenes, somewhere 300 or so BC, a time of legends. Athens was the center of philosophy, architecture, mathematics and much, much more. Danny had visited ancient Greece before to ask Socrates about the rightness of changing time and preventing his mom and Sarah from dying in a car accident.

Danny closed his eyes. This was just a bad flashback—a hangover from Time. Or maybe this was another nightmare. Danny hoped and prayed but the conversations *did* sound Greek.

Where were Murg and Krindee? Where was Kalyde II? A bolt of panic surged through Danny. Without the magic bicycle, he was stranded in Time! Alone! He'd never see his friends or his father again. He already missed Christina and Jason. He wished he'd told them about the magic bicycle.

He had to find Kalyde II! Danny jumped to his feet. He reached out, feeling for the magic bicycle, but dizziness overwhelmed him.

What had happened? Really happened? He was having trouble struggling through the fog. The last Danny recalled, that storm orb thing was chasing them. They had tried to elude it by racing back in time. When that hadn't worked, he'd focused on the present—now—wherever that was at that moment.

Danny vaguely remembered the landing. It had been hard and jarring. Had he run into something? Lost a grip and been thrown off the magic bicycle? That would explain his headache. He had the strange feeling he'd done this before. That sensation was called deja vu, except, Danny felt this had happened many times before.

"Murg! Krindee!" Danny peeked under the bed. "Please be all right, wherever you are! We're in trouble!"

A tall stately gentleman in a long white robe pushed aside the curtains and entered the room. The elderly Greek said something that sounded friendly.

"I'm sorry, I don't speak Hellene," Danny replied. "I'm sure you don't speak English or German."

The Hellene's features were strong but wrinkled with deep set eyes, a pronounced nose and a square jaw covered by a thin beard. It matched the vague wisps on his nearly bald head.

"Do you know Socrates?" Danny asked.

"Socrates . . . ." The old man nodded and smiled.

Danny threw up his hands and paced. Socrates wouldn't understand him either. Last time, Kalyde II translated the language. Danny's thoughts still whirled when he thought about his conversation with the Father of Western Thought.

"Danny Chase, meet Plato." Murg's voice sounded inside Danny's head. The calico led the Siamese through the curtain. The cats appeared alert and prissy.

Danny scooped up Murg and hugged her. "Murg! You're all right!"

"Of course," Murg replied, appearing indignant, then she stuck her head under Danny's hand. He ruffled the calico's ears.

"Hi Krindee! Where were you guys?" Danny thought.

"Enjoying Hellene hospitality. They treat felines grandly."

"You mean you were relaxing and eating while I was worrying?" Danny projected.

"Worrying about something you can do nothing about is a major contributor to shortening Cor-ror-o'lans' lifespans," Krindee mindspoke.

"I'll remember that." Danny touched his head, fingering a sore spot. "Murg, did we crash land?"

"Yes. You slammed into the Parthenon. Only the bicycle's magic protected you. Even then, you were knocked unconscious."

"Why did we end up in Ancient Greece?" Danny asked.

"Time currents. As we discussed before, they flow along old channels, sometimes righting themselves, or taking the path of least resistance. Now Danny, be polite. This is Plato, as in *the* Plato of Ancient Greece circa 360." The calico looked around the room and suddenly wrinkled her nose. "Sometimes I forget the future is much more sanitary and smells better than the past."

"Oh! I'm sorry, sir. I didn't mean to be rude. Hello, I am Danny Chase." He offered his hand to the Greek scholar. "I'm just excited to see my friends." Danny looked to Murg. "Does he understand me?"

"I am telepathically interpreting for both of you," Krindee replied. "In your mind, you hear him speak English. In his mind, he hears you speak Greek."

"How do you do that?" Danny asked.

"I turn words into thoughts and project them into your minds."

"I understand your concern," Plato replied. "Animals can be dear friends and bring one much joy. Greetings and salutations, Dannychase, I am Plato. How are you feeling? You have quite a lump on your head."

"I'll be all right." Danny gingerly touched his head again. "Thank you for letting me . . . rest here." Danny had almost said 'crash' here. "How did I get here? Where am I?"

"You are at my academy." Plato spread his arm in an all encompassing gesture.

"The one you built in honor of Socrates?" Danny asked. "A school dedicated to thought? The first European College?"

"I know not what Europe may be, but it is obvious that you are a young scholar." Plato fondly patted Danny on his shoulder. "That must be how you come to speak Greek. For you are certainly not of Athens, or any other part of these lands." Plato's gaze studied Danny's clothing, especially his sneakers. The scholar touched Danny's backpack and appeared thoughtful.

"I am a wanderer in search of knowledge." Danny certainly wasn't going to explain that an alien appearing as a Siamese cat was telepathically relaying their conversation. That almost made him laugh.

"Don't start," Murg warned him. "Remember where you are."

The crush of being twenty-three centuries in the past abruptly sobered Danny. "The crash confused me," Danny apologized. "For a time I didn't understand you."

"You spoke in tongues," Plato replied. "I feared you were addled."

Danny still felt a bit confused. "How did I get here?"

"A student named Aristotle found you unconscious at the Parthenon. He said he saw you appear out of nowhere and crash into a wall. I assumed the gift of the grape had affected his judgment, but saw no other sign of intoxication."

"Is my bicycle okay?! Where is my bicycle?!"

"You speak of that . . . person cart with two wheels?" Plato asked.

"It's called a bicycle."

"Kalyde II is waiting in the courtyard," Murg replied. "It's perfectly fine. No worries. Remember, worry ages you. Transforms you into your dad."

Danny blanched, unsettled more by that thought than being twenty-three centuries in the past.

"I have only seen one . . . bicycle—you say?—before." Plato appeared contemplative. "It was many years ago. Upon it rode a boy much as yourself and a cat similar to this one." He gestured to Murg. "Even then, according to Socrates, the young man sought knowledge, questioning what was right."

Danny was speechless. When visiting Socrates, Danny had seen Plato—a much younger man then—from a distance as he left the philosophers' daily discourse atop the steps of the Acropolis. That had been about 387 BC, about a year before the Trial of Socrates.

"Could you take me to my bicycle?" Danny asked.

"Certainly. Come this way." Plato parted the curtain and gestured outside.

Danny stepped into the hallway. The floor changed from hard clay to flagstone. Bright silk tapestries lined the walls depicting scenes of the sea. Others honored Zeus, Hera, Ares, Aphrodite and of course Athena, among the twelve gods and ten heroes of Greece.

"Why are you here?" Plato asked.

Danny was thoughtful, then said, "I have a moral question—a question of what is right."

"Ahh. A question of Justice, one of the true cosmic Forms, which can only be found through reflection." Plato appeared thoughtful, then said, "The quest for what is Just requires a search of the soul, which is as boundless as the seas. The journey is worth exploring, for the unexamined life is not worth living. What has happened to send you questing?"

"I've been robbed by a . . . vicious man."

"And you are wondering what act in response would be just?" Plato asked.

Danny's mind whirled. As a student of the Socratic Method, Plato answered questions with more questions. He believed that the immortal soul already knew the Truth, even if you didn't realize it yet. These Truths could be understood through discussion, rejecting irrational contradictions and embracing reason. Whew! Just thinking about it made Danny's head hurt more.

"Bravo!" Murg projected.

"Danny, I didn't know you were a student of history and philosophy," Krindee mindspoke.

"I wasn't until recently," Danny replied. "I read some Socrates, Plato and Aristotle while writing *The Alien Bicycle* to help me understand my visit with Socrates. It didn't really, since he talked in circles."

"But Plato differs from Socrates," Krindee thought.

"Plato thought the senses could be poor judges to rely upon when answering philosophical questions. He rejected the idea that knowledge is derived from sense experience."

"As have other great minds," Murg mindspoke, "including Einstein and Mark Twain. Remember, Einstein encouraged you to keep questioning."

"Well, it seems to me that all Socrates and Plato do is ask questions, hoping you'll come up with the answer yourself. I've seen kids in class do that all the time. They don't get away with it."

"Should I rephrase my question?" Plato asked patiently.

"Do you only answer questions with questions?" Danny asked.

"Questioning, seeking, is good for the soul. If people were to ask you the same question time and time again on many occasions and in many ways, in the end you would have knowledge as accurate as any other on that particular question."

"I think I could be asked algebra questions a million times," Danny thought, "and I'd never come up with the answers by myself."

"We must take care with the answers we find," Plato continued. "True beliefs run away from a person's soul until one ties them down with reasoning and explanations. That is why knowledge has more value than simply true belief."

"The stolen object is special . . . ."

"But it is just a possession."

"It's more than *just* a possession. It is tied to my imagination, which I believe is a part of my soul."

"Where did you get such a gift?" Plato asked with a raised eyebrow.

"Uh, it is a gift from a . . . god."

"I can never tell Kah-laye-dee of this. His head would swell!"

"Well, some relate alien visitations to ancient gods," Danny lamely explained.

"Then you are a lucky man." Plato was quiet for a long moment, then offered, "Or are the gods being contradictory, as they often are? The gods often serve their own interest."

Danny certainly didn't believe in the whimsical Athenian gods. Often times, Danny wasn't sure what to think about spiritual matters. According to Socratic argument, if he kept questioning—kept seeking—he would learn the answers one day.

"Few truly know if the gods are on their side. But let us discuss Justice, for in discussing the different aspects of it and Good, we might find a definition that will clearly direct us to act rightly in any situation."

Danny inwardly groaned; he'd run these mental circles before.

"Tell him you want to discuss the soul. Does doing an evil act make someone evil?" Krindee asked. "Remember, I am curious regarding what makes Spike how he is and you who you are."

"Plato, does evil spring from the soul, or is it learned in some way?"

"You inquire as to whether this man has an evil soul?" Plato asked.

Danny nodded. He actually just wanted to get his bicycle, find Spike, and get back the star metal.

"Souls are not evil. They are as the Forms, immutable and just. The soul knows the Truth. Those that seek possession and the facade of virtue make irrational decisions based upon physical desires."

"Then you say Spike isn't thinking? He's just acting on physical desires?" Danny asked.

"You have a quick mind for one so young."

"It's spinning quickly in circles," Danny thought.

"If you spoke with this 'Spike'—a very odd and troubling name I must admit—he might, with great reflection and discourse, eventually understand the benefits to the soul of leading a virtuous life. For there is no compensation for a vicious soul."

"That belief hasn't been well embraced over the centuries," Murg thought.

"A well-ordered soul is based upon the right beliefs, right choices, aims and good character. Any conflict between self-interest and morality is based upon a false image of self."

"Upon sensations and physical desires?" Danny asked. "Short term wants?"

"Truly."

"But Spike won't listen to me. He's blinded by what has happened to him," Danny replied. He thought of the beatings and how they might change a person. How would he change if he'd been beaten every day?

"I believe there is an effective technique for turning the soul around," Plato began, "for changing its direction as easily and effectively as possible. When you deal with ignorance, you are not trying to make a blind man see; but to simply guide the uneducated eyes in the correct direction, so that he will see the Truth and make reasonable choices. Virtues such as Justice and Good are not only good for everyone but good for the soul."

"But what if he's so overwhelmed by sensations that he's now blind?" Danny asked.

"You need to turn Spike's attention away from his body and possessions and more to his soul. Is he better off being wealthy and unjust, or unwealthy and just?"

"That's a tough question."

"Not for most. Most people prefer wealth over anything, except possibly health," Murg mindspoke. "And they don't consider being unjust unhealthy."

"Dannychase, I have faith you can show that a well-ordered soul functions best when tempered with wisdom and courage. These are very important to our souls. Suppose someone explained that the causes of each thing I do, walking for example, is because my body is composed of bones and sinews. It is utterly absurd to call such things causes.

"But if someone said that without bones and sinews I would not be able to walk or do what I have decided upon, he would be right. But to say that these physical things, and not my choices, are the cause of my doing what I choose, that would be incorrect. Our thoughts control our bodies as well as our actions. We make choices and our flesh obeys. Thought is the master to the body."

Danny nodded. "Meaning don't blame it on hormones."

"Eh? I'm not sure I understand."

"Physical wanting." Danny could barely stand—he couldn't wait to see Kalyde II.

As they entered the sunny courtyard, someone played a flute, the sound drifting elegantly on a soft breeze. A fountain gurgled from the shadows of the pillars surrounding the grassy area. Below the bright blue sky, nearly a dozen men, young and old alike, rested on the benches and the lawn to discuss ideas and philosophies.

On a day as this, Danny could imagine unfurling the magic bicycle's wings, as Icarus had done with pinions dipped in wax, and flying high, soaring toward the glorious sun. Danny sobered when he thought of the fate of Icarus. His wings had melted, and he'd fallen to earth.

"The lack of women studying here is a grievous oversight and a common fallacy among your species," Krindee thought. "Higher species believe in the Form of Equity."

"Yes, cats don't care about gender or the color of another feline's fur," Murg agreed.

"Look! Only a couple of men have books!" Danny thought. One man was taking notes, using some kind of quill and ink on parchment. Danny wondered what it was like for paper to be rare. He took it for granted, as he probably did too many things.

"Your bicycle is this way." Plato turned right, walking along the pillared hallway surrounding the courtyard.

Danny suddenly realized the source of his discomfort and restlessness. "I don't feel Kalyde II! If it was near, I should be able to feel it!"

"Easy, Danny."

"Hmmm. I don't see your bicycle," Plato told him. "I wonder what happened to it?"

TWENTY-SIX

The Seer And The Thief

"Kalyde II's been stolen!" Danny railed. "We're stranded in time! We'll never get home!Never see Dad, Christina, Jason or Gretchen again!"

Plato looked at Danny as though he were a raving madman. "Stranded in time, you say?"

"Danny, be quiet! We don't want to change things. Now get a grip. Focus on finding the magic bicycle," the calico projected. The force of that thought worked as a slap in the face, checking Danny's growing hysteria.

"I meant to say strapped for time. I'm in a hurry, you know, to find my bicycle and get going."

"I see," Plato said, appearing perplexed as he rubbed his bearded chin, "Last I saw, young Aristotle was examining your bicycle. My student appeared to be fascinated by this . . . Kalyde Tu, you called it? I suspect Aristotle has taken the bicycle to learn how it works."

"Aristotle believes in the power of observation as a learning tool," Krindee mindspoke.

"This could be disastrous. What Aristotle might learn from the bicycle could change history." Murg mentally groaned. For once, the calico looked a little worried.

"Worry less and focus on finding the magic bicycle," Danny thought.

Paws over her mouth, Krindee stifled a chuckle. Murg appeared indignant.

A round-faced youth with wheat blond hair approached them. "Damocles," Plato began, "have you seen Aristotle?"

"When I last saw him, he was rolling something strange," Damocles replied. "It had two wheels and was the color of blood. I thought it might be a wagon or a chariot, but there wasn't any place to stand or carry anything."

"My bicycle!"

"Where is he?" Plato asked.

"I asked him what he was doing. He said he was going for a ride," Damocles replied.

"Then that is where we shall look for him. Thank you, Damocles."

"Let's go," Danny said. "You guys want to ride?" Both did, so Danny put the cats in his backpack.

"Come this way." The elderly philosopher led Danny through a long stone hallway lined with colorful silk tapestries. Students looked curiously at Danny and his feline cargo. The scholars clearly wanted to ask questions, but none of them spoke, instead nodding in deference and respect.

"You are so fortunate," Krindee told Danny. "You've met Socrates and now Plato!"

Danny rolled his eyes.

"Oftentimes wisdom is wasted on the young," Murg projected.

"At least I don't put on airs," Danny thought back.

"The fool doth think he is wise, but the wise man knows himself a fool," Krindee continued.

"That sounds like Shakespeare," Danny replied.

"Someone we should visit. He knew much about the human condition," Krindee told them. "I have questions I'd like to ask him. It's on our way back to the future."

"First, we have to find Kalyde II," Danny said. "Or we're not going anywhere!"

Once outside, Danny immediately concentrated on finding the magic bicycle. As though questing fingers along an invisible chain, his thoughts followed the link tying him to Kalyde II. Danny fought through a bit of a headache to sense something off to the left. "Krindee, can you do something about my headache?"

"Once I return to my true form, I can heal you."

"Are you all right?" Plato asked. Danny nodded. "Shall we go for a walk through Athens? It is a beautiful city."

"Even if it does reek," Murg thought. "This is before the Romans had invented sewers, aqueducts, roads, and plumbing. Hellenes are so used to the stench, they hardly notice it. Perfumed scarves should be popular."

Danny breathed deeply. Murg was right; the place smelled like a barnyard. The air was warm, humid, and laden with many unpleasant smells—animal droppings, rotting food and too many bodies in too close a space.

When they reached the bottom of the stone steps, Plato turned right. Danny still felt a faint tug in the other direction. "Let's go this way," Danny said.

"In this direction lies the Acropolis. That way passes Demosion Sima, the graveyard where Pericles is buried. He was as close to a philosopher king as they come. Pericles gave us democracy, encouraged thought and built the Parthenon. I think Aristotle would ride to the most magnificent structure in our city to gaze out over the sea."

"The Parthenon's uphill," Danny replied. "He probably started downhill. It's easier and more fun."

"As you wish, Dannychase." Plato headed inland toward the Demosion Sima.

Danny breathed shallowly through his mouth as they

shouldered their way along the narrow dirt street. Grand buildings of limestone with terra cotta roof tiles and magnificently pillared entrances towered over nearby slums. Barefoot and rag-clad beggars slumped against walls, looking filthy and pitiful.

"Despite claiming that Pericles brought democracy to Athens, only a small portion of the Hellenes were citizens with rights and a voice in government," Murg thought.

"Look out!" Plato cried, pulling Danny to the side. A wagon hauled by a strange looking donkey raced past, leaving them choking on a cloud of dust.

"Thanks. That was close," Danny told Plato.

"A wise man knows when to have his head in the clouds and when to have his feet on the ground," Plato replied.

"What was that thing?" Danny thought.

"They're called onagers," Krindee told Danny. "They're early evolution donkeys."

Concentrating again, Danny focused on locating Kalyde II. He was having more trouble than usual, as if the magic bicycle were playing hide and seek.

"What are you going to do about this man who has wronged you?" Plato asked.

"I don't know," Danny replied. "I don't know if I can turn his eyes in the right direction. He'll hardly talk to me. In some ways, Spike has been treated as a . . . slave, but he is not one."

"Are you saying his beliefs have been whipped into his flesh?" Plato asked. "If so, you must simply guide him to a place of safety where he may cast his eyes more freely."

From somewhere ahead, the sounds of a flute drifted along the street. Hawking and bartering carried from the street market. Tents and rickety stalls lined the boulevard, reminding Danny of a festival. Impassioned vendors sold pottery of all shapes and sizes, woolen carpets, silk tapestries, and freshly tanned leather goods, along with vases of oils and clay jugs of wines. Aloft on a soft coastal breeze, Danny smelled fresh bread over the distasteful odors.

A pig squealed as it escaped captivity, running across the road to hide among a cluster of cages holding doves. The gangly, white-haired owner sprinted into the streetside menagerie, knocking Danny into a table. That sent his head spinning. He caught himself with his hands. "Hey! I don't feel Kalyde II."

"Not at all?" Murg asked.

"I think your headache is dampening your abilities," Krindee projected. "I will try and soothe your head with my mind. If that doesn't work, I will have to find someplace to make a transformation."

"Would you like your fortune told, young one?" came a gravelly voice.

"I . . . ." He turned to find a wizened woman whose eyes were covered by cloth. Her hair was snowy, much whiter than her shift. A gaunt young girl with a pinched face sat behind the fortune teller, watching with bright blue eyes. "How?"

"I am blind but can still clearly see the future, boy of tomorrow."

Danny blanched. "What? If you're really a seer, then you know I don't have any money worth anything to you."

"Do not worry. My words are for your ears only, and only you will hear them."

"Seer Ophalia speaks truly, Dannychase. I shall await you down here." Plato handed the fortune teller a coin, then walked away.

She called after him, "Thank you, kind Plato." The woman peered at Danny for so long he grew alarmed. He was just about to bolt when she spoke in a high, fluted tone, "Though you think otherwise, boy of tomorrow, the gods smile upon you. They lay travails upon your path so you may learn from them. For we do not receive wisdom, but must stumble upon it. Wisdom is discovered on a journey no one else may take for us—a journey which no one can spare us. For wisdom is the point of view from which we finally come to regard the world in light of what we have experienced. And we should experience it with our mind, body and spirit, three acting as one."

"What does that mean?" Danny asked. Her words made him shiver.

"Few learn from others' mistakes, but those who fail to learn from their own are true fools and thoughtless, for thought is true power."

Danny's mind spun.

"Remember, boy of tomorrow, that thoughtlessness is cloaked in laziness and weakness. Thoughtlessness is the bane of caring, calculation and creativity."

"There! How's that?"

Danny's head abruptly felt fine. Now he could clearly feel Kalyde II, coming closer. Danny searched through the bustling market.

"Ah, your chariot arrives." The elderly woman laughed, then coughed, "Go."

Elated at feeling Kalyde II, Danny rushed to find Plato. Standing further up the street, the elderly Hellene waved to Danny.

"Ah! I see Aristotle coming!" Plato exclaimed. "He's riding your bicycle." The philosopher waved toward the slender man atop the red bicycle. His once white clothes were dusty brown.

The tall scholar stopped before them. He was flushed with excitement and his chin was scraped. "A fine morning to you, Plato!"

"You appear invigorated, friend Aristotle."

"To feel the wind push at you and your heart pound . . . ." For a moment Aristotle stood speechless ". . . is truly magnificent. I can only compare it with riding a horse and yet also running, the two as one; and yet, I feel as if I fly faster than either man or horse." Aristotle looked down at himself, his clothes dirty and his knees bleeding. "That is, once I learned how to stay astride it."

Danny smiled. "It is fun, after you quit falling. Hi. I'm Danny Chase." He offered his hand. Aristotle's hand looked scratched and dirty.

"What is this invention?" Aristotle asked, patting the magic bicycle. "It is the most incredible thing I have ever seen. Its body is as sturdy as wood but lighter. Unlike our wheels, yours turn separately from the axle and are made out of some strange leather filled with air. And I could stop the wheels from turning by squeezing these handles." The young Hellene pointed to the hand brakes.

"I was afraid this would happen one day if we kept traveling into the past," Murg thought. He glanced at Aristotle who still raved about the bicycle.

"Danny didn't plan this," Krindee reminded the calico. "You agreed that Spike must be stopped before he changed time and damaged the future."

"I'm beginning to think we're doing more damage trying to stop him. One of us should have stayed behind to watch over the magic bicycle. What might Aristotle do with this information? Danny, we have to leave. Leave right now."

"But what are we going to do about that storm orb thing?" Danny asked.

"We'll worry about that later."

"Who would think to use a chain to aid travel?" Aristotle continued, his eyes bright.

"I would let you examine it more," Danny told him, "but I must be going. I have to stop a boy before he steals again. I was chasing him when I crashed."

"Falling is too easy," Aristotle agreed solemnly. "Perhaps, I can craft a better cart."

Danny smiled uneasily and took the bicycle from Aristotle, who gave it up with obvious regret."Good luck, Dannychase." said Plato. Just remember, anybody can become angry—that is easy; but to be angry with the right person, and to the right degree, and for the right purpose, and in the right way—that is not within everybody's power and is not easy."

"Nothing is ever easy for me," Danny replied.

Aristotle smiled. "What we learn to do, we learn by doing. I learned to ride by falling and getting back on, never giving in."

"I know, and if I don't learn something from falling, then I am a fool," Danny replied.

"In the beginning, we are all babes and fools." Aristotle laughed.

"Thanks for taking me to the academy," Danny told him. "And thanks for taking care of my bicycle." Danny climbed onto Kalyde II. "Plato, uh, thanks for advising me."

"I hope it stirred thought," Plato said. "Good fortune settling your dispute."

Danny smiled and waved. "Good-bye!" As they rode down the street, they left a trail of curious onlookers. "Now what?" Danny whispered.

"How's your head?" Krindee asked.

"Great! I feel whole again!"

"Then let's find Spike and convince him to return the star metal," Murg told them.

"What about that storm orb?" Danny asked. "It's probably still waiting for us in the rainbow tunnel."

"Maybe not. It might just have been a hiccup in the stream of time."

"But what if it wasn't?" Danny asked. "It's been there twice already. I think it's intelligent."

"Why?" Murg asked.

"The last time I saw eyes. Green eyes."

"Really? What do you think it is?" Murg asked.

"Even though it has eyes and is green and stormy, it feels a lot like . . . like Merlin's spell that carried us to his tower in October."

"Yes, now that you mention it, there are similarities." Murg appeared thoughtful.

"You met Merlin?" The Siamese appeared astounded. "The greatest wizard your planet has ever birthed?"

"Briefly. Merlin didn't want to meet us," Murg replied. "Like a bad-tasting fish caught in his net, the Grand Vizier of Camelot threw us back into the ocean of time."

"Somebody wants to catch us," Danny said. "But who? And why? And what are we going to do to avoid him and catch Spike? Hey! Maybe Merlin would help us! Let's go see him!"

TWENTY-SEVEN

Time Hopping

Danny rode out of Athens, then stopped on a rocky outcropping. Looking over the Aegean Sea, Danny paced along the ridge and restlessly tossed rocks, watching them disappear into the green-blue water.

To bolster his thinking, Danny donned his thinking cap. He fashioned it after the helm of Athena—the goddess renowned for her wisdom. As Danny pondered what to do next, the helmet gleamed brighter and brighter, radiating a golden light.

"I've been thinking," Danny finally said.

"That is almost always a good sign," Murg replied without opening her eyes. The calico and Siamese lay atop a rock, basking in the Mediterranean sunshine.

"I shouldn't have to run from the storm orb thing. Nothing can harm me as long as I'm on the bicycle. I think I just panicked; it really spooks me."

"I was scared, too," Krindee said. "I sensed malevolence, an evil that stems from the soul."

"Then you agree it's intelligent?" Murg asked.

"Possibly."

"If it's magic like Merlin's, who could have sent it? How do they, whoever they are, know about me?" Danny words tried to keep up with his racing thoughts. "What if it's a being or a spirit, like a djinn, what some call genies?" Danny suddenly snapped his fingers. "Merlin snagged us with that spell, brought us to him. A rival magician might know about us because we've been to the dark ages. The storm orb's master might be a powerful druid or even a witch."

"Indeed. You have been thinking," Murg said. "Did the eyes you saw look male or female?"

In his mind, Danny pictured the storm orb. Clouds parted and emerald eyes opened. Long lashes framed the eyes. "Definitely female."

"It could have been Nimue or Morgan Le Fay; both are accomplished and power-hungry sorceresses, as well as bitter enemies of Merlin. Nimue covets Merlin's magical powers. Morgan Le Fay wishes to rule Camelot, thereby all of England. I fear the bicycle's magic might not protect you from their magic, just as it failed to protect you from Merlin's spell."

"But it's only been protecting me unconsciously," Danny replied. "If I consciously protect myself, that might be different. I could create an impenetrable force field."

Murg opened her eyes, appearing skeptical as her whiskers twitched.

Danny climbed back on Kalyde II. "Get on. I'll show you."

Krindee sauntered toward the bicycle. Murg strolled behind her, joining the Siamese on the palanquin.

"Watch." As though made of molten silver, Danny scooped a clump of star metal from the center bar, then imagined himself afire. Purple flames engulfed him. In the fiery forge of his mind, Danny crafted a silver orb. "Stronger than adamantite." The star metal grew hotter, glowing brighter than the sun. With imaginary hands, Danny seized the golden globe and pulled. It expanded like a shiny balloon, surrounding the bicycle.

Danny thought it transparent, much like the Invisible Woman's force field. Then he pulled it tight as a second skin, outlining the threesome and the magic bicycle. "Stronger than Brainiac 5's or Doctor Doom's personal protective fields," Danny mumbled. "Tougher than the shields of the Starship Enterprise." The air around them shimmered, rainbow highlights dancing brightly.

"I can still breathe," Murg said. "That's a good sign."

"Let's go after Spike!" Danny began pedaling, heading back to the dirt road.

"Danny. Stop. We *must* be cautious," Murg said. "As I said before, if Merlin's spell captured us, then so might the storm orb. It might not need to harm you to transport you."

"Then let's get Merlin to help us!" Danny kept pedaling, now heading downhill toward the Mediterranean coast.

"I like that idea," Krindee said.

Murg frowned.

"Yeah, if that thing's following us, we'll just lead it to Merlin's tower. I remember what it looks like inside. It was cool! All those books, maps and the talking owl, Archimedes."

"Okay, if we see the storm orb again, we'll lead it to Merlin. I'm sure he'll be thrilled." Murg rolled her eyes. "Better yet, let's avoid the sorceress' spell all together."

"How?" Danny asked.

"Short hops forward through time. That allows us to hide among the ripples."

"But I have to study places to jump there," Danny groaned. "I'm not prepared."

"A good reason to keep learning," Murg replied. "You never know when you might need knowledge."

"A lot of good that advice does me now."

"I can provide images and information about certain points in time," Krindee said. "I have what Terrans call a photographic memory. Together, if we focus on the same place, we should be able to travel even faster than before."

"Through an exchange of memories! A mind meld, just like I did with Kah-laye-dee!"

"Are you willing?" Krindee asked Danny. "Remember, there are risks involved. It might burn out your mind."

"I've done this once already," Danny pulled onto the side of the deserted road. Krindee transformed back into her natural state. The Cor-ror-o'lan placed her hands on Danny's head. Fire seemed to erupt from her fingertips. Burning daggers sliced into his mind, then exploded, scattering fragments of images throughout Danny's brain, and he saw Earth's history through Krindee's thoughts.

Eight men in armored breastplates and wearing golden torques shouldered the ornate palanquin, carrying a handsome man of noble air for all to see. In the distance were the Great Pyramids and the stone lion called the Sphinx. "Alexander the Great—King of Macedonia—isn't Egyptian," Danny thought. "He's Roman."

"He just finished organizing Egypt. Now he guides his armies across the Eastern Desert to the Euphrates and Tigris rivers, then beyond to Persia to fight another war. This is just barely tomorrow, 331 BC."

Danny raced through a desert city, fighting through a crowd to follow a staggering man carrying a giant cross. Some people threw stones. Others wept and wailed, praying for Jesus.

"History shows Terrans often slay those who speak of peace and benevolence."

As if a mirage, the throng quickly wavered into colors, clarifying into a magnificent city. Wagon after wagon hauled statues and monuments used to adorn the city.

"In 324, the city of Constantinople was decorated with pirated statues and monuments of pagan gods and goddesses. It is now called Istanbul."

The carts disappeared but the horses remained, now burdened with sallow-skinned riders. Wielding curved swords, wild-eyed Huns whipped their stallions into combat, slaughtering men, women and children. A dark-haired man, his eyes glittering as obsidian, led the riders. "Flee for your souls! The Scourge of God comes."

"Attila the Hun, 436 A.D."

The scene shifted. A man adorned in a white robe with a circlet around his head stepped up to a magnificently carved lectern. The crowd below was restless, waiting for him to speak. Justinian the Great announced the codification of Roman law. No longer would rulings be arbitrary, but based on the written word, called laws.

"That was after the Romans were invaded and conquered in 532."

In 782, Danny reluctantly watched Charlemagne direct the mass execution of 4,500 people. Danny felt devastated and ashamed, wanting to weep. He'd never imagined such death and carnage. "The Saxons. Not long before Arthur."

"Stop," Danny whispered. "No more, please."

A cluster of knights, swords held high and red sashes flying behind them, charged into an army of dervishes astride awkwardly loping camels. Blades *clanged* against each other and *banged* off armor. Riders fell and blood stained the sands.

"The Crusades. Europeans were inflamed when Muslims refused to let Christians make holy pilgrimages."

"Stop," Danny whispered.

A towering man rose as though carried aloft by a giant fire centered among the tribal chieftains. "We fight as one people. All others are our enemies."

"Gengis Khan unites the nomadic Mongols," Krindee said.

"Stop! Please!" Danny tried to close his mind's eye. He didn't want to see any more! Know any more! So much fighting and killing. Is this what Kri-neee-dee saw when she looked through their history? Danny thought back to his history class. Earth's heritage was full of war and death, fighting over rule, property and religion. Events were calendared by whether they happened before or after a certain war. With such a legacy, it was amazing everyone wasn't like Spike, thinking first with their fists.

Danny recalled men of wisdom fostering peace, tolerance, and brotherhood. Confucius. Socrates. Plato. Jesus. Did Krindee see them? How could people change? A Renaissance? Another search for beauty, wisdom and knowledge?

"There have been many bright spots," Krindee said.

More images flashed by. Danny knew he saw Milan, Italy, where a bearded man with knowing eyes stepped away from a painting depicting a group of shocked men sitting at a dinner table. Leonardo da Vinci stared out the window, studying the flight of a flock of birds. Jotting notes, he wrote from right to left.

Images of a spectacular church suddenly filled Danny's mind. A man rested on his back atop scaffolds, painting the ceiling. Danny knew it was Michelangelo decorating the Sistine Chapel.

With a change of mind and memories, Danny stood among the crowd, staring up at a stage. The roof was open above, the building and its balconies surrounding the yard. A mustached man, his hair thick on each side, spoke eloquently, "To be, or not to be . . . ."

"Enough," Danny whispered. "Please, no more." When Krindee pulled away her hands, Danny collapsed. The Cor-roro'lan grabbed him before he could fall to the ground.

"So much. Too much." Danny clutched his head, trying to stop the spinning.

"There is good and bad in your world, although it seems war outweighs knowledge."

"It certainly gets more press," Murg said. "Terrans are fascinated by it. Knowledge is dry and intellectual. Killing is juicy and stirs emotions."

"Be that as it may," Krindee began, "I have passed landmarks every several centuries or so. Now we may make more precise hops forward in time."

Danny groaned. "I think my brain's swollen."

"Even before we began this melding of consciousnesses, your merging with Kah-laye-dee linked both hemispheres of your brain—the logical and the intuitive. You are now using more gray matter than most Terrans."

"When he isn't driven by hormones," Murg said.

"That is why your imagination is powerful enough to create things with the star metal."

"Spike can do it."

"True, but you were the first of your species. Once one

has started, little can stop the wave of thought as it washes over the world. One day you might not need the star metal."

"Then anybody can do it?" Danny asked.

"Of course. You must simply change what you believe and what you do. Oftentimes, simple things are difficult because they seem so simple and are given less effort and thought. Simple is not necessarily easy."

Danny was silent, trying to absorb everything. While he pondered things, Krindee transformed into a Siamese. "I don't want to go to those places," Danny finally said.

"What do you propose?" Murg asked.

"Let's go someplace that has endured the ravages of time and remained unaffected."

"Such as?"

"The Great Pyramids or Stonehenge. Both exist now and in the 20th century. We could stay at one of those places, and yet still ride to the future, sort of riding in place but moving forward."

"We're listening," Murg said.

"You told me that time is just a concept invented by man, especially the linear aspect, because our minds work that way," Danny continued. "We go forward and back better than sideways. Well, I could set my mind to linear and just imagine the years rolling by. By riding from time to time instead of place to place, we'd limit our exposure. Sort of like running through the woods, darting from tree to tree. Does that make any sense?"

"Or going from ripple to ripple, hiding instead of bouncing atop the waves. Sometimes you are frightening," Murg said, sounding pleased. "I suggest the Pyramids. Stonehenge is in Nimue's and Morgan Le Fay's backyard."

"Then she might not look for us there," Danny said.

"The mystic energies Stonehenge emits might conceal us," Krindee said.

"And I studied Stonehenge after meeting Merlin."

"More research for your story?" Krindee asked.

Danny nodded. "It was originally designed around 4500 BC. It was a small, circular stone ditch with thirty-six wooden posts on the inside. Later, wooden structures were built inside the circle. Then in about 2600, stones were removed from Amesbury. They erected thirty-six sarcens, stones some fifteen feet tall, and set lintels atop them to complete the circle. Years later, they erected five sets of taller sarcens creating a U in the center."

"And why did they do this?" Krindee asked.

"It's a sacred place of power. Stonehenge lies on the ley lines. You see them on a globe. Some say these lines contain mystical properties. Others say the electromagnetic strength is greater along the lines. Nobody seems to really know exactly why Stonehenge was built or how or by whom. Maybe they moved the stones by thought." Danny shrugged.

Krindee smiled.

"Let's go there," Murg said. "Stonehenge 200 BC."

"Easy," Danny said with a smile. He pushed off, riding downhill. When they reached a flat section of road, he pictured the great monument of stones some hundred and fifty years in the future. The towering rocks still wore wounds from carving, although some were patched with dark lichen. The grass was lush and green, the fog slowly rising from it. A breeze blew through Stonehenge, the standing stones singing an eerie tune like a giant flute.

With a roaring flash, Kalyde II and its riders appeared on the tattered rainbow bridge, racing forward in time. The wind still whistled but no longer ruffled or chilled them.

"I don't feel the wind," Krindee said.

"The force field makes the ride a bit more bearable," Danny said.

"Even better, I don't see the storm orb," Murg said.

Kalyde II bumped along for a few more moments, then disappeared in a ripping flash of light. A spinning sensation assailed them, then they reappeared, stopping in the center of Stonehenge. As though grim giants, rocks glowered down upon them.

"That was a different sensation," Murg said.

"I was trying to appear outside the circle," Danny said.

"Not your fault, Danny. You were drawn in," Murg said.

"I wish I knew exactly when we were."

"We're close to 200 BC," Murg said.

"Shall we try again?" Krindee asked. "Beginning of the first millennium?"

Danny rode outside the stones, then around and around the circle. With his eyes closed, Danny sought the future at this very spot, some several hundred years ahead.

A flash of thunderous brilliance engulfed them, then they raced along the time passage. The surroundings blinked in and out, then another eruption of light swallowed them. Kalyde II spun around and around, appearing once more in the middle of the standing stones. Long shadows crisscrossed the center of the circle, falling across the trio.

"Here we are, back in the middle again," Murg said.

The English night was warm, calm and quiet, except for the symphony of crickets. The full moon hung high overhead, the lunar face appearing radiant and joyful as if thrilled at their arrival.

"Wow," Danny whispered in reverence. "There's a feeling of power here."

"And a sense of expectation," Murg said. "Let's go."

Without moving outside the circle this time, Danny repeated the thought process, firing his imagination and leaping forward in time. Light danced with the faded rainbow, then they reappeared once more without incident. They hopped again and again, stopping to rest after three consecutive jumps.

"So far so good. No sign of the storm orb," Krindee said.

"We're around the turn of the first A.D. millennium," Murg said.

"Eerie," Danny murmured. Thick fog covered the night, blanketing the stones and all beyond. As though ghosts, the sarcens seemed etheral, standing on the edge of the spirit world.

"How do you feel?" Krindee asked.

"I have a bit of a headache."

"Let me help you." Krindee transformed into her true form, then placed her hands on Danny's shoulders. Warmth washed along his neck.

He relaxed until he saw the fog swirl. Something moved within the mists churning around the stones.

A pair of emerald orbs appeared, growing larger as they neared.

"It found us!" Danny pointed.

TWENTY-EIGHT

The Sorceress

A second pair of green eyes accompanied the first. Yellow orbs joined them, then twin eyes the color of blood appeared along the circle. More and more faceless eyes silently gathered. Soon, a hundred glowering eyes surrounded Stonehenge, Danny and the felines.

"What are they?" Danny asked.

As if one, the floating eyes moved forward. Dark shapes appeared, the eyes now no longer disembodied. The wolves sat, staring at Danny. A chill skittered along his spine.

"What do they want?" Danny asked.

"I think they're telling us to move along," Krindee replied.

"Or warning us," Murg said. "Let's try the Great Pyramids this time."

"No problem." Closing his eyes, Danny pedaled. He imagined traveling into the future, to the Sahara desert where camels roamed and sirroccos whirled. Standing against parching dryness, the blazing sun and scalding winds, the timeless Great

Pyramids of Egypt loomed before a backdrop of endless blue sky.

Sound and light assaulted the riders, then they appeared in the faded rainbow tunnel. Kalyde II rocketed forward.

"Still clear!" Krindee called out. Ears perked and eyes searching every direction, the Siamese and calico were vigilant watchcats.

Something seized the bicycle, yanking them off course and sending them spinning. Danny tried to right their course, seeing the Egyptian Pyramids; but the shadow of standing stones kept intruding.

With an angry roar of fire, they reappeared atop a blazing pyre in the center of Stonehenge. Red, orange and yellow tendrils licked across the force field as if taste-testing dinner.

"This isn't what I pictured! What happened?!" Danny could barely see beyond the flames; but above the fire's roar, he heard chanting.

"At least the force field is working," Murg said.

"Who are those people?" Krindee wondered. The shadowy figures wavered and writhed as they intoned an ancient ritual.

Danny pointed to the charred carcass next to him. "They're burning somebody!"

"Not somebody. It looks to be a stag," Murg replied. "It's a religious sacrifice. Common in Britain during this time. But why now?"

Despite standing in the flames, Danny shivered. "Something is wrong. Very wrong. I'm outta here."

As Danny began pedaling, he caught a woman's gaze. Long lashes seemed to caress her emerald eyes but failed to dim a malevolent gleam. She smiled a wicked leer, as though some foul wish had just come true.

Danny closed his eyes, imagining Shakespeare's London, circa 1590. The magic bicycle erupted through the roaring blast of brilliance to appear in the rainbow tunnel.

"She's coming again," Danny said. "I can feel her. Almost . . . almost as if this has happened before. I mean, this particular time, not the last time."

Murg's expression was unfathomable. "Just concentrate on London, late 1500's."

Even before Krindee pointed, Danny could feel the storm orb. Its witchy radiance preceded its arrival, washing the tunnel in a sickly emerald glow.

"Just keep in mind what we discussed," Murg said.

Calling upon the magic of thought and the bicycle, Danny fortified his imagination, strengthening it until it glowed radioactively. The force field was more powerful than the shield around the Empire's Deathstar and as impenetrable as the Power Cosmic globe protecting Galactus' planet-dwarfing spaceship.

Struck by foresight, Danny could see the glowing green sphere latch onto the protective shield. Dragging him . . . . Danny fought off those thoughts.

The emerald storm orb raced closer, the strange missile growing larger and larger. As it homed in on Kalyde II, the clouds swirling about the orb became clearer.

"Stay calm," Murg suggested.

"Should we take evasive action?" Krindee asked.

"We've been running away," Danny said. "That hasn't worked."

The storm orb suddenly slammed into the shield, stopping less than a hand's width away from Danny. He swerved wildly, trying to dislodge the sphere. It slowly expanded as though green wax spreading across a windshield. A devouring blob, the green radiance slithered along the force field.

Danny swerved again and again. He even slammed on the brakes, jarring everyone to a stop; but the storm orb clung to the shield.

"I smell something burning." Krindee said. The air around them glowed ruddily.

"I can't shake this thing!" Danny cried.

Shoved mightily, Kalyde II abruptly hurtled backwards.

"It's forcing you back in time," Murg said. "Probably back to Arthurian times."

"Morgan Le Fay!" Danny yelled, taking a guess. "What do you want from me?"

"You have divined my true identity." Boiling black clouds parted to reveal narrowed eyes blazing with emerald radiance. "No matter. Soon we will be home, then nothing, Daniel Chase, not this protective aura nor your meddlesome familiars will stop me from seizing your wondrous artifact of power. The passage of time will soon be at my command, then, Merlin will grovel at my feet! Camelot will be mine! All of England shall bow before me!"

"As evil and vindictive as they come," Murg thought.

Danny changed tactics. Instead of resisting, he added his will to the sorceress' magic, hurling Kalyde II back in time. He focused on Merlin's tower. He imagined being there, standing next to the wizard.

Along the canvas of his thoughts, Danny pictured Merlin's chamber. It was crammed with alchemical apparatus, books laying atop maps, tables and teetering stacks of books. The shelves appeared swollen, ready to collapse from the weight of ancient tomes. Maps spread across the walls and each other, leaving little visible of the stone walls. The aroma of an apothecary full of herbs, oils and incense mingled with the air of a neglected attic.

Archimedes flew in through the window to alight on Merlin's shoulder. The wizard's eyes gleamed bright blue and as fathomless as the sky. His white beard and mustache stretched down to his chest. The stars on his robe sparkled and soared as if comets . . . .

"No!" Morgan Le Fay screamed. "Not there! Not him!"

For a moment, Danny thought they'd made it into the wizard's chamber. Then Kalyde II slammed into something unseen. Merlin's ward repelled the magic bicycle, catapulting Kalyde II forward faster than ever before along the rainbow bridge.

"Yeow! What was that?" Krindee's lavender eyes spun.

"The power of Merlin. He didn't want to be interrupted. And may I say," Murg continued over the howling wind made by the bicycling cutting through time, "that your exclamation was a very improper reaction for a feline."

Danny shook his head and rubbed his eyes. He tried to focus, but constellations were still spinning through his mind, dislodging his thoughts.

"Danny. Concentrate."

"I can hardly see." Danny sounded woozy, his words a bit slurred.

"You don't need to see. Just think."

"I feel Morgan Le Fay coming after us again. She's furious."

Searing the walls and bursting from the gaps as though blow holes, a wave of emerald fire raced in front of the storm orb. Lightning flashed from the clouds, jagged bolts propelling Morgan's sphere closer and closer.

"Quickly now. She's gaining."

"We're almost up to to 1450. Danny, you've been studying Shakespeare and Elizabethan London. Concentrate. See us there at . . . at The Globe Theatre at the turn of the 16th century. I think we can make it that far."

The storm orb flew closer. Over the screaming of the wind, Morgan's anger raged thunderously.

"What theater?" Danny asked.

"The Globe. The one you've been studying for Shakespeare. Where *Julius Caesar* and *Hamlet* were performed. Aren't you reading *Hamlet?*"

"Shakespeare?" William Shakespeare, Danny mused, the most renowned bard of the ages had been born the son of the high bailiff of Stratford, England. By 1592, Shakespeare had become a successful actor, performing in *Henry VI* and receiving rave reviews. "And The Globe Theatre, you said?"

"Yes. See us there," Murg said.

Danny pictured Kalyde II appearing under the open sky, in the yard where peasants stood watching the show for a penny. Practicing tonight's play, the actors rehearsed on the lowest level of the stage.

"Danny hurry!"

Danny could see William Shakespeare rehearsing his part. Gentle William stood tall and lithe, a man skilled in acrobatics and fencing—two essentials to acting in London during the Elizabethan times. Shakespeare wore a kindly face, an outward expression of his patience and easy-going temperament. A rapier-thin mustache accented his rounded features. Below a prominent forehead, dark eyes peered into one's soul, seeking character motivation for his next story.

A wave of green washed over the riders. Kalyde II bucked.

"Danny! Hurry! She's right behind us!" Krindee cried.

Murg gave the Siamese a withering stare.

Danny stayed focused. He pictured Shakespeare rehearsing the final act in *Hamlet*. The bike shuddered, then slowed. A sickly green aura flared to surround them.

TWENTY-NINE

Merely Players

With a fiery roar and a blinding burst of light, the riders and bicycle disappeared from the faded rainbow tunnel. Danny, Murg, and Krindee atop Kalyde II, appeared just as suddenly in a roofless theater to the blare of trumpets, followed by a cannon's thunderous *booming*. The building shook, the blast echoing through the empty seats and the balconies.

"We're here," Murg thought.

"Magnificent! Nothing in your current time compares to this theatre," Krindee thought.

Glistening with newness, The Globe Theatre radiated an air of elegance. Plush seats created a 'U' under a balcony protected by a beamed roof. The sun glared down on the trio, illuminating the peasant yard but not touching the quartet of staggered stages.

"My ears are ringing. I still can't hear anything," Danny mindspoke.

Actors, burning sconces, several tables of food and a set of thrones transformed the stage into a king's audience chamber.

Most of the royal entourage stood back, watching a pair of men battling with rapiers. The combatants darted, danced and slashed, trying to find a way around the other's steel.

Danny did a doubletake; the queen was obviously a man wearing a wig. All the women were men wearing wigs and gowns!

"Remember," Murg began, "women aren't allowed to act—in fact, they aren't allowed to do anything that might compromise their purity—so men play women's roles. Romancing was couched in words and never enhanced by touching. These are puritan times, even in London, although the actors consider themselves above such staid constrictions."

With their attention wholly on the swordsmen, no one noticed Danny and his entourage. "The trumpets and cannons must have drowned out our arrival," Danny thought. "I wonder which one is Shakespeare." Danny pointed to the actor playing Hamlet. "Him, I think."

With his rapier-thin mustache and a goatee, the actor-playwright appeared perfectly cast as the confused and melancholy Prince of Denmark. His height, lean build and gypsy grace matched with his baldness gave the impression of a young man turning old before his time.

Murg cleaned a paw. "Shakespeare has a great mind, one which fathoms the depths of Terran souls. Whether he plagiarized or not, he knew that action was character and character sprang from the soul and the events they'd endured."

"First reason, now the human heart and soul," Krindee mused.

"Hey! This is the final scene!" Danny mindspoke. "Hamlet is dueling with Laertes. Hamlet accidentally killed Laertes' father, then his odd behavior drove Ophelia, Laertes' sister, to suicide. Laertes seeks Hamlet's death in payment. Actually, the King is the real villain here. He murdered Hamlet's father, then married his mother. The King has poisoned the wine and Laertes' sword."

Their expressions grim, the actors cut and stabbed at each other. The swords' blades flashed in the torchlight, leaving slashing trails of fire. When the roaring finally died in Danny's ears, the first sounds he heard were grunting and the clashing of metal against metal. "Hey, the acoustics are great!"

"In these times, people heard plays more often than seeing them."

"Another hit! What say you?" Hamlet asked.

Laertes looked down at himself. "A touch, a touch, I do confess."

"Our son shall win," the King whispered to his Queen, a far from comely man with blond hair tied in a bun beneath a golden crown.

"He's fat and scant of breath," the wigged man replied in a sottovoce. "Here, Hamlet, take my napkin, rub thy brows. The queen carouses to thy fortune, Hamlet." The Queen picked up a bejeweled goblet.

"Good madam!" Hamlet appeared shocked.

"Gertrude, do not drink!" the King cried.

"I will, my lord. I pray you. Pardon me." The Queen hoisted the cup to her lips.

His eyes wide, the King turned aside. "It is the poison'd cup! It is too late!"

The queen offered the goblet to Hamlet.

"I dare not drink yet, madam; by and by," Hamlet said.

"Come, let me wipe thy face," the Queen cooed.

Danny squirmed. He felt uncomfortable watching this and yet, also fascinated. This was happening, live!, nearly four hundred years ago!

"I am honored," Krindee thought.

"My lord, I'll hit him now," Laertes whispered to the King.

"I do not think it."

Laertes looked over the empty seats, not seeing the threesome and the bicycle in the low peasant's yard. "And yet 'tis almost 'gainst my conscience."

"Come, for the third, Laertes!" Hamlet cried. "You but dally. I pray you, pass with your best violence. I am afeard you make a wanton of me."

"They really did talk funny," Danny thought.

Once again, Hamlet and Laertes wielded cold-steel death. Feet shuffled to and fro, and blades slashed, the air whistling angrily as if crazed snakes attacked in a frenzy. The rapiers *clanged* together, then squealed as the swords slid to lock at the crossguards. Now nose to nose, the duelists sneered.

"Say you so? Come on," Laertes whispered hotly. He shoved Hamlet away, then leapt forward. "Have at you now!" Laertes knocked away Hamlet's foil, then drove his rapier into Hamlet's stomach. The sword buried nearly halfway along its shaft, blood gushing freely.

Danny gasped. All but Laertes and Hamlet stopped. The combatants wrestled, rolling across the stage. With a triumphant cry, Hamlet jumped to his feet, Laertes' bloodied foil in hand. As Laertes arose, Hamlet struck, driving the rapier into his opponent's chest. The blade bit deeply and blood spurted.

"William! Richard! Stop! A patron come early eagerly watches!"

Still bleeding but walking just fine, the man playing Laertes came to the edge of the stage. "Pardon me, but pray tell, for what reason doth thou stand there? We are not yet open."

Still confused and shocked by the sight of blood, Danny stammered incoherently.

"I'd measure the urchin's tongue hath been seized by our resounding performance," someone said. The company laughed heartily, the sound echoing through the rafters.

"Or the artful use of a bladder and sheep's blood. Kemp, the effect is truly excellent, as you plainly witness."

"Thank you, Cuthbert."

William Shakespeare stepped forward. "Gentle youth, why art thou here?"

Danny finally managed to find his voice. "My name is Danny and I work for . . . the *London Crier.* I'd like to interview you about the play, *Hamlet.* You are William Shakespeare, the author and actor, yes?"

"Times must be hard." More laughter pranced about The Globe Theater.

Danny frowned. With a flash of insight—seeing Morgan Le Fay arriving here—Danny suddenly felt time slipping away. "What is that you art astride?" Laertes asked. "A carriage for cats?"

Danny flushed. He'd been so frightened, enthralled, then shocked, that he'd forgotten to change the bicycle into something conforming to 1601. A walking cane would have been more appropriate. That made him think of Spike and his bat. He had to find Spike!

"Richard, please still thy tongue. You art frightened," Shakespeare said to Danny. "And while thou art a fair liar at best, time the truth to tell."

"Okay, I don't work for *The London Crier.* I come seeking your advice."

"And . . . ."

"Well, I'm being chased by a wicked woman . . . ."

"I wish I was," the Queen jested. The actors roared, some slapping him on the back.

"Fah!" Shakespeare frowned and waved in disgust. "Young man, with a new play opening tonight, I am too busy to advise a lonely soul on matters of the heart. Off with thee!" His cape swirling, Shakespeare turned to walk away.

Danny's shoulder slumped, his expression crestfallen. He didn't know what else to say. That he was pursuing a villain who could travel time and change the past which might wreck the future? He had to say something! He needed help, desperately! This was more important than a play. This was real life!

Danny's mind raced, then threatened to lock. What could he say to change the master bard's mind? A quote? A future quote?

"Yes! Tonight is opening night, and nothing has been published. Quote something you can't possibly know. That will get his attention." Krindee projected.

Danny took a deep breath, then spoke loudly, as if addressing the entire company of players, "As thou art a man . . . ." Danny paused, forgetting the words. Shakespeare turned, a singled eyebrow raised and questioning.

"Give me the cup: let go; by heaven . . . ."

"Thanks Krindee. Give me the cup! Let go; by heaven, I'll have it! O God! Horatio, what a wounded name! Things standing thus unknown, shall live behind me." Danny paused to send thanks across time to Christina. Over the holidays, he'd helped her practice for Hamlet, the school's spring play. "If thou didst ever hold me in thy heart, absent thee from felicity awhile, and in this hard world, draw thy breath in pain to tell my story! "

Pale with eyes wide, then narrowed, Shakespeare appeared shaken. "How doth thou knowest these words which art mine and still newly penned?"

"Mr. Shakespeare, I know the future."

"A seer?" the playwright asked. "What art thou called?"

"Danny Chase."

"Well, young Danny Chase, we shall speak." Shakespeare turned to his companions. "Friends, I bid thee rest well awhile. I will return anon. Come, lad. I could sorely use a moment's respite from being someone else and turn my face to the sun. 'Tis a rare day indeed when light most fair shines long upon the City of Churches."

Rolling Kalyde II across the yard, Danny met Shakespeare at the base of the stage steps. The playwright now wore a hat, a clean white blouse and a crimson cloak. "This way," Shakespeare pointed toward an archway, then led Danny out of the peasant area and into the mezzanine where refreshment booths lined the wooden walls. A pair of stout double doors waited ahead, sunlight slanting between doors and frame.

"This is a fantastic place! Future theaters will copy The Globe's design," Danny said.

"The Admiral's company hath already done thusly, yet a grievous error hath been made designing The Fortune as a square." Shakespeare opened the door to the outside world, then made a grand, sweeping gesture. His red cloak billowed, leading the way outside.

Danny blinked, blinded for a moment, then guided Kalyde II outdoors. Cobbled streets wound through the maze and mixture of new and old inns, shops, and tenements. Above the rooftops in every direction, churches towered over London. In the distance, a bell tolled. Others chimed in, mixing joy and solemnness.

"Time to stretch." Murg jumped to the ground. Krindee followed.

"Ah...London on a sunny day!" Smiling broadly, Shakespeare removed his plumed hat.

"We're in Southwark?"

"Yes, the district of the Liberty Clink. Populated by sailors, actors, guards, gamblers, and ladies of the evening, it is a bit livelier than the St. Helen's district: but that kind of excitement is not for one so young. Now why art thou here?"

Danny watched a horse-drawn carriage pass. Not far behind bounced a milk wagon and a cart carrying chickens. The driver yelled out a greeting to William Shakespeare. He nodded in reply but kept his gaze on Danny. "Well?"

"I . . . I'm a rider . . . ."

"A writer and a seer," Shakespeare mused. "Talents of an interesting blend. Does such maketh you a prophetic scribe? Such would certainly create powerful enemies. This wicked woman, did you abase her with your well-crafted but too sharpened words? The slash of a quill cuts deeper than a sword."

"My riding got me in trouble all right." Danny looked over his shoulder. He could feel Morgan, lurking somewhere inside The Globe Theater. "I'm trying to escape the witch, which is why I hid here, and so I can catch the thieving villain who has stolen part of my . . . soul."

"A wicked woman and a rogue, excellent material for a play it sounds," Shakespeare mused. "But if thou art a seer, as thou say, how canst these two bring injury against thee?"

When Danny thought of Morgan Le Fay, her presence grew stronger. She was here, somewhere!

A roar bellowed from down the street. Danny whirled, afraid of what he might find. The workers guided a wobbly brown bear toward the open warehouse door.

"Just another warrior for The Bear Garden." Shakespeare sounded disgusted.

"Bear fights?" Danny asked.

"Aye. They be baited, too." Shakespeare replied sadly.

He closed the doors to The Globe. "Come this way. We shall move away from the Bear Garden and the Bishop of Winchester's handsome palace. Both are fraught with peril."

The Siamese jumped onto the bike. Murg stretched once more, then joined her.

"Now, Danny, tell me of thine enemies."

Sounds of boatmen seeking work carried from the Thames River. "Only a penny to ride to London! Faster than the bridge. Only a penny!" "The nicest boat on the Thames. Fit for the Queen. Only a penny." A boat bounced against the dock. Several people waiting atop the steps clambered down to the quay.

Danny wondered how he could explain his situation. Did he dare tell the truth? He'd already concluded that the saying the truth never hurt anyone had been uttered by a fool. "Mr. Shakespeare may I tell you of a tale I've written?"

"The one that hath thou in dire trouble?"

Danny nodded. Passerbys looked at him strangely, but seemed to accept him as just another one of the many foreigners roaming the streets.

"Certainly, tell thy tale. As history hath shown, a tale that incurs trouble is often one of interest."

They passed a building with the sign "The Green Lady". Danny could almost feel Morgan's anger, making it difficult to think. Was she coming? Had she already arrived? And why did he feel as if he'd met William Shakespeare before now?

"It began with a death . . . ." Danny started.

"As many a goodly and tragic tale shouldst," Shakespeare said.

Danny explained about the death of the hero's mother and sister, their royal stage overturned by some dark sinister force. The hero, Chastan, was falsely accused of causing their deaths. Danny paused to blink back the tears that always came with thinking of his mom and Sarah.

"While fleeing his evil stepbrother, Pickett, and the King's men, Chastan hid in an old haunted castle, where a mage—a foreigner in exile—hid from the royal law," Danny continued. "In gratitude for helping him escape, the wizard gifted Chastan with a magical staff made of two interlocking parts. This artifact of power allowed him to do anything his mind could imagine. Chastan practiced with the staff, discovering that its magic could even take him back in time. He returned to the scene of death, where he couldn't prevent . . ." Danny stammered, " . . . prevent the tragedy, but discovered that an evil sorceress, Morgan Le Fay had brought about the deaths . . . ."

"The sorceress from Arthurian times?" Shakespeare asked. Danny nodded. "And the wizard was Merlin?" Danny nodded again. "It is wise to use characters commoner and royalty alike recognize. A sense of knowing the heroes, heroines and villains be very important, as long as they be not tritely contrived."

Danny explained about three hags who'd foretold Chastan getting the staff.

"Ah, likened to the witches in Holinshed's *Chronicles*. One of my favorite tales. *Chronicles* hath inspired a play I have yet to name."

Danny wanted to say like *MacBeth*, but didn't, continuing to explain that Morgan tried but always failed to steal the staff from Merlin. "Stealing it from Chastan is a different matter. The sorceress enthralled Pickett, using her wiles to convince him to steal the staff."

"That will be a most popular part of the tale," Shakespeare said with a wink.

"Pickett stole half the staff before Chastan escaped him, fleeing back through time," Danny continued. "Morgan Le Fay pursued him. With only half the staff, Chastan couldn't defeat the sorceress. He fled, barely able to stay one step ahead of her magicks."

"Am I correct in guessing that this Chastan needs the staff whole to slay Morgan Le Fay, but can't regain the stolen part until she's defeated? Quite a conundrum. Is this Pickett truly evil? Or simply enthralled, a noble but tortured soul slaving under the yoke of the witch? If the latter be true, then brave Chastan must save the very one trying to slay him. Quite a tale, my young friend. How does it end?"

Danny swallowed. He barely looked up in time to dodge a staggering man carrying the stench of whiskey. "I fear with the death or imprisonment of Chastan."

"I foresee an angry audience," Shakespeare replied. "Unless proper that the characters' actions hath appropriately led to such a tragic ending. Never forget the power of rewriting. Now, who is this wicked woman pursuing you?"

"The real Morgan Le Fay."

Shakespeare laughed. "Your mind is certainly aflame with fancy."

"I don't know how to escape her."

"How would Chastan escape her?" Shakespeare asked, obviously amused.

"He tried to contact Merlin but failed."

"Where else might yon hero find magic? In these times, another word for magic, though some shudder at the very thought, wouldst be religion. Said power performs miracles. Pray thee, let me ponder anon."

They walked in silence for a time. Danny's dread heightened. He kept feeling Morgan Le Fay's presence. They passed a stone building with fortress walls and guards armed with swords.

"If thee can choose from all times, who wouldst be a proper foil for the evil English witch?" Shakespeare murmured.

They crossed an intersection where Danny pulled Shakespeare along so he wouldn't get struck by a horse and rider. At the far corner, Danny steered right at MacP's Pub, keeping the Thames River on their starboard.

"The latest from France!" A chronicler held up an illustrated wood cut.

"France?" Shakespeare mused.

"Drawings and news in English about the Queen's ruling on gambling. Good news! Bear and cockfights stay open on Sundays!"

"The first tabloids," Murg thought. "A curse that still plagues man."

Danny guided the musing playwright around a pair of men talking over a paper. The one smoking a pipe said, "Yes, as fine a fellow as I've known. Pity he be not an Englishman."

"Hmm. France. Yes. Yes! I would suggest Joan of Arc," Shakespeare finally said. "but that wouldn't go over very well with English audiences. She is generally regarded as a tramp who used her enchanting wiles to build an army that was lucky enough to repulse the Britons."

"That's it!" Krindee thought. "Joan possessed spiritual powers rivaling any magic. And she's not far away in time. She would probably be glad to help, since an English witch led to the downfall of the French government."

"That might work," Danny mused.

"The Londoners would care little for it, but we speak not of a play, do we?" Shakespeare arched an eyebrow.

"What do you mean?" Danny asked.

"I know not why, but I feel as if I hath dreamt this very moment time upon time again. Odd though, 'tis not a dream I wouldst expect. When thou spoke of Chastan's mother and sister, thou nearly came to tears. When thou speaketh of Pickett, I felt thine anger. The magical staff brings a whimsical smile and light to thine eyes. And when thou speaketh of Morgan Le Fay, thou cast a spell of fear. A writer thou may be, but an actor thou be not."

"Uh . . . don't you write plays by adding parts of yourself to them? Add your experience and emotions?" Danny asked. Shakespeare nodded, lips pursed and thoughtful. "Don't you live it? Breathe it? Sometimes even believe it, so that when you speak of it, it seems true?"

"The knack of storytelling falls upon thy shoulders. Despair not, Danny Chase. Unlike Hamlet, thou art not blackened by whatever has happened and not yet slipped into melancholy. Hiding from thy dreams and shadows be not true to thine heart. Be not afraid of greatness: some are born great, some achieve greatness, and some have greatness thrust upon them. Sadly as I am to bear the news, I believe thou art a victim of all three."

"Mr. Shakespeare, I need help. Fast!" Danny suddenly thought he sensed Morgan Le Fay's arrival. In a flash of green light, she appeared in The Globe Theater. Her evil beauty enthralled the actors. They eagerly pointed the way to Shakespeare and his strange company.

"What am I going to do about Pickett?" Danny walked faster. Shakespeare moved at an easy pace, longer legs keeping stride.

"Is he ensorcered?" the master bard asked.

"In a sense. A wise man told me to turn his eyes in the right direction."

"Methinks he's read Socrates or Plato. Be that as it may, that be sound advice. The miserable have no other medicine but hope. The magic staff be his hope. A beacon of light guiding him through the murky fog to a place of comfort."

"I tried talking to him, but he won't listen to me," Danny moaned.

"Give him thine ear, but hold thy voice."

"You mean listen?" Danny felt time slipping away. Cold gusts of wind cut the warmth of the day. Were they tendrils of magic searching for him? "You mean walk in his shoes. Empathize?"

"Surely. Thine young mind be sharper than a barrister's."

"How will that help?" Danny looked around nervously. Lots of strange faces, but none of them housed green eyes.

"Thou must understand the motivations of thine characters, this Pickett and Morgan Le Fay, before thou can appropriately resolve the play. All the world's a stage, and we are merely costume-clad players speaking the lines of the roles we have chosen."

"I heard something like that in a Rush song," Danny murmured.

"Rush? Be they a boys choir?" Shakespeare asked. "Danny, I speak with sincerity. Thou art playing thy role. Pickett, whoever he be, acts his, as this . . . Morgan Le Fay plays hers. Our lives art roles we've chosen," Shakespeare continued. "What we do, we hath chosen. What we do not do, we hath chosen. There be no destiny but what we believe and what we hath chosen. We live by thought and act with thought. To not do so, is to be less than human and fail in the doing."

"Wow." Danny wasn't sure he understood all this.

"If we do not like our lot—our life, then we must look at ourselves—our character—find what be our motivations, and discover what needs changing. Nothing be cast in stone, certainly not destiny. We decide whether to continue acting in the roles we hath chosen, or to change our lines and speak and act anew, adding freshness to what otherwise might be a trite though true play."

"All the world's a stage?"

"Exactly. This above all: to thine own self be true. And it must follow, as the night day, thou canst not be false to any man. You must be true to yourself, and do what you feel is right for thy soul."

"William! William!" a man running toward them yelled. "She is here!"

"Who?" Shakespeare asked when Richard "Laertes" reached them.

Richard paused, hands on knees, to catch his breath. His outfit still showed sheep's blood. "The most beautiful woman I hath ever laid mine eyes upon. She appeared at the theater looking for this boy. When Kemp flirted with her, she froze him with a stare. He hasn't moved. That's when Winston and I ran out looking for you. William, she may be beautiful, but she feels so . . . evil. Trust her not. I fear she be close behind me."

"She's here!" Danny whispered. "Just like I keep seeing. Not a ball of light, but in the flesh."

"I believe your act reaches its zenith, hopefully, not as you have foreseen, seer of the future." Shakespeare smiled wanly.

"So Morgan wishes you to think." Murg looked down the street. "Richard probably guided her to us."

As though a green sun rose, an emerald light washed along the boulevard. Wherever the radiance passed, it left its mark, deepening the shadows and stopping horses and Londoners in mid-stride, their feet frozen in step. Carriages and wagons bumped into draft horses that stood as still as stone. Unfinished conversations and the calls of paralyzed news venders hung in the air.

"'Bye, Mr. Shakespeare. I'm outta time!" Danny jumped onto his bicycle, then waved as he pedaled. "Joan of Arc, here we come!"

"I can guide us there." Krindee jumped onto the bicycle. Even Murg appeared to hurry.

"Thank you!" Danny called back.

"Remember, seek the truth of Pickett's heart! A flock of blessing light upon thy . . . ." Shakespeare called out, then stopped. The green wave of light splashed along the street, washing over Richard Burbage and William Shakespeare, leaving them as still as statues.

The storm orb flashed forward, closing the gap between it and Danny. "You are mine, Danny Chase!"

THIRTY

The Maid of Prophecy

Leaving Shakespeare's London behind, the magic bicycle erupted backward through the roaring blast of brilliance to materialize in the rainbow tunnel. A flash of smoky green shot from the brightness as though a vileness spat out.

"She's right behind us!" Danny cried.

"It's not far. Just keep focusing on Joan of Arc," Murg said. "Take yourself there. Be there." The calico stood as though a captain atop the prow of a boat.

"This is a nightmare!" Danny stammered. "Haven't we done this before? I mean, this particular time, leaving Shakespeare in 1601. I should be able to outrace her. Right?"

"Danny, my friend. Calm down. Use your imagination. Focus," Murg projected.

"Jeannette d'Arc," Krindee reminded Danny, lightly touching his arm.

"Even Shakespeare thought he knew me from a dream. Why would we be in Shakespeare's dreams? Murg, what's going on?" Danny continued.

Murg's expression was unreadable. "Contemplate later. Now calm down and concentrate on 1420 and Joan of Arc." Murg's words carried a calming effect.

Just behind Danny, the witchy radiance raced closer, washing the crumbling walls. They turned inky as though shadow-swathed. Darkness and the cavernous gaps blended into one long black strip.

"Joan of Arc! Uh! I'm drawing a blank!" Danny panicked.

"Let me help," Krindee said. "Jeannette d'Arc was often called the Maid of Prophecy. In the 1300's, Marie of Avignon predicted that a young woman from Lorraine would save France from an Englishwoman's betrayal—Isabeau of Bavaria, the King's mother."

"That's why Jeannette will help us!" Danny tried not to watch the dark swath devour the tunnel to the future. In moments, the storm orb's green radiance would reach his front wheel. "Hurry!"

"Forcing yourself doesn't help. Shake once like a dog," Murg projected. "Like Comet after a bath."

Danny shook, releasing some tension.

"On January 6th, 1412 in Domré my, France, Jeannette was born to a pair of peasant farmers. Kind, caring and pious, Jeannette prayed often and gave alms to the poor. At thirteen, she heard the voice of God and received guidance from angels to drive the English from France."

"Hurry! What's she look like?!" Danny asked. A fleeting image came to mind.

"At seventeen, some saw the tall young woman as beautiful, perhaps due to the aura of light she radiated. Her dark hair is cut short, in a page fashion. Her eyes are dark and, while fueled by holy fire, they are not without humor nor compassion. She'll be dressed as a page or a messenger in a black hat, brown tunic, surcoat, leggings and high boots called gaiters."

In Danny's mind, Jeannette appeared with surprising detail. He'd met her before! He just knew it! Her radiant smile caused her eyes to glow. Brightness surrounded her and seemed to benevolently reach out to him.

"We must find her after she's heard the voice of angels, but before she meets Charles the VII! After that, she's always in the company of squires, pages and followers!"

"Hmm . . . about February of 1429?" Danny asked. He'd never learned this in school. Was it from the mindmeld? It had to be? Didn't it?

"Good! Jeannette is traveling from Vaucouleurs to Chinon to see King Charles VII. She just received a sword and blessing from the governor of Vaucouleurs. Accompanying and protecting Jeannette will be two knights, cavaliers they call them, a messenger, and another, all returning to Chinon to meet with the King. These brave souls travel through a frozen countryside at night. Brits control the roads, and bandits roam the forests. For France and much of Europe, it is a time of death and famine."

Almost as if it appeared from nowhere, the witchy sphere expanded in a wash of green light. Then the storm orb slammed into the magical thought shield, stopping a breath away from Danny's nose.

He swerved wildly, trying to dislodge the sphere. The magic of Morgan Le Fay softened and oozed. It flowed around the front of the bike and Danny, attempting to totally engulf Kalyde II and its riders. Danny swerved again and again. The time winds tore at the edges of the green ooze, causing it to flutter and flap. Danny slammed on the brakes, jarring everyone to a stop, and dislodging some of the gooey light; but the storm orb was tenacious, continuing to stick and spread.

"Is that sizzling?" Krindee asked. The air around them suddenly glowed ruddily.

"I can't shake this thing!" Danny suddenly swerved, heading for a wall. Kalyde II swiped close, knocking free more of the orb ooze. It trailed away, slapping the handlebars and dangling ahead in time.

"We almost lost her!" Krindee cried.

"Stay calm. We're almost there. I can see the woods," Murg peered into the bright flash.

"You cannot escape me!" Morgan Le Fay's voice swirled about them. As the breach in time opened, the storm orb darted into the blast of sunlight, following her prey.

With a dazzling blast, night briefly exploded into day. Danny and the felines appeared in a snow-blanketed forest. Kalyde II whipsawed sideways, spinning through the mud and slush.

"HANG ON!" Danny cried. The tires became tiger paws. Kalyde II snapped to a stop. Anchored by claws, Murg didn't budge. Krindee lost her grip, slipping partly free, her tail lashing Danny.

Sizzling as it raced by, the storm orb missed. It circled around, growing larger as it returned for another attack. The dark forest was cast in a witchy emerald light. Contorted shadows writhed through the woods as if dark soldiers.

"Jeannette d'Arc!" Danny called out as he looked around wildly, searching for the French Saint.

Three people from a dark camp of seven cloaked figures jumped to their feet. Swords drawn, two armored men flanked a tall young page clad in white and black. The others rose and stepped back deeper into the woods.

Kalyde II slid to a stop before the threesome. "Jeannette! Help!" Danny cried, looking for her among them.

"Sacre bleu!" the taller of the cavaliers exclaimed. His blue eyes reflected the witchy light and shone with fear. Trembling hands held a broadsword and shield.

"Stand fast!" the page commanded in French. He sounded young. "Have faith! The Lord is with us!"

"It is she! The Maid of Prophecy!" Krindee exulted.

"She?! Where?!" Danny asked. He didn't see any girls.

The storm orb darted for Danny and the group. As it neared the page, the brave cavalier intercepted it. "Jeannette, beware!"

Danny looked around. Jeannette? Where?

The cavalier's sword flashed harmlessly through the emerald sphere, whistling as the stroke cut only air. The orb shot forward, passing through the knight's shield. He screamed, then danced about as though shocked. When the sphere backed away, the cavalier collapsed.

"Bertrand!" the other knight cried as he leapt forward.

"Be wary, Sir de Metz," the page warned him.

"I believe we are blessed in your presence, Jeannette." The cavalier advanced, sword held steady, ready to attack or defend.

"Jeannette?" Danny asked, looking at the page. He was a she, tall and handsome with short, dark hair, bold features and a faint golden aura that danced in her eyes.

"Young sir," Jeannette began, "what is this thing of evil?" The storm orb bobbed backward and cavorted angrily. A harsh cackling filled the air as though a pack of hyenas taunting their prey. "She will not help you, Chase!"

"It speaks!" Jeannette cried.

"It? IT? I AM MORGAN LE FAY! I have come for Daniel Chase and his magical artifact!" The orb expanded and elongated, stretching to the ground like a waterfall of smoky light. As though a fountain, detail and definition geysered upward, leaving a beautiful woman clad in emerald mists. Morgan Le Fay stood scornfully, her dark hair framing green eyes and a cruel visage. Dark skull-carved gemstones hung from her ears, around her neck and nestled among her bodice. "You are the key to destroying Merlin! He is vulnerable to the Tides of Time!"

The sorceress leveled her staff at Danny. A bolt of black light flashed toward him. Murg jumped in front of Danny intercepting the bolt. With a wail, the calico crumpled, lying unmoving in the snow.

"MURG!" Danny leapt off the bicycle.

Sir de Metz took a step forward, then hesitated.

"It is a demon, not a woman!" Jeannette told the cavalier. "Le Fay means dark faerie. Hear me, dark queen of Briton! You are banished from this land! Leave willingly or suffer the consequences. Sir de Metz, it is our duty to defend France against such evil! Stand fast!"

Morgan Le Fay pointed her staff at the onrushing knight. A jagged bolt of lightning surged forth, striking Sir de Metz. He screamed and staggered backward, then collapsed onto the snow where he lay twitching and smoking.

"Danny, you must do something!" Krindee whispered.

Danny held Murg in his arms. He couldn't believe that

she was dead! His best friend, gone! Sarah would be furious! He'd let down both Sarah and Murg.

"Thank you for your faith, Father. I shall not fail you." Drawing her sword before her, Jeannette d'Arc rose from genuflection and strode toward the sorceress. "Be gone, foul demon."

"Aside child, or you shall share the fate of these armored churls."

"I do the will of the Lord. Angels bring me charges. You are not the first vile English woman to set foot upon my land. As the hand of God, I will first cleanse my homeland of you, then the rest of the English barbarians!" Light as bright as the sun sprang from her hands, running along her sword. When the holy fire reached the tip, the blade exploded with white flames.

Morgan Le Fay grimaced, then directed her staff at Jeannette d'Arc. The dark lightning struck Jeannette's white shielding, shattering as obsidian upon marble.

Jeannette charged, swinging her blazing sword. Morgan countered, blocking with her staff. The forest shook as blade and staff clashed again and again, black and white lightning flickering across the trees. Branches shook and snow tumbled to the ground, sounding as giants stalking the woods.

"A child may not vanquish me, I am Morgan of the Woodland Folk!"

"I fear neither faeries nor shades, for the Lord fortifies me." Jeannette attacked again.

The sword bit into the staff and held fast. Screaming in anger, the sorceress of Camelot jerked on her staff. Jeannette yanked back on her sword, then surged forward, fighting a tug of war.

Morgan let go with one hand, then pointed to the ground. Snow and earth changed to mud, swallowing Jeannette d'Arc. She staggered, nearly dropping her sword. With a maniacal laugh, Morgan Le Fay struck, knocking the blade aside, then bludgeoning Jeannette. She reeled, but stayed upright, trapped by the mud pit.

"Danny, do something!" Krindee cried.

Danny looked at Murg, lying so still. Must he do something violent? Must he?! What would Murg say? Don't change the past. Don't wreck the future!

"Murg wouldn't want you to give up!" Krindee cried.

As his mind raced frantically, Danny wrung his hands. What choice did he have? If Morgan slew Joan of Arc, that would change the past; France might become part of Britain. What other disasters might occur? And if the evil sorceress seized the star metal, then destroyed Merlin, taking over Camelot, what havoc might she wreak?

He would not let Murg down. As Danny charged, he changed the star metal into a bat.

Morgan reared back, ready to crush Joan of Arc's skull.

He wasn't going to get there in time!

Danny scooped up a handful of snow. Saying a prayer, he let the slushball fly, prevailing on the magic of snowballs. The icy sphere sailed true, striking the sorceress' face. Hands going to her eyes, Morgan screamed. "A snowball! A snowball! Who dares!"

Jeannette d'Arc surged from the mud pit. With all her God-inspired might, the Maid of Prophecy struck the surprised sorceress. Morgan Le Fay crumpled silently, then shimmered, transforming back into the storm orb.

"Be gone foul demon!" Jeannette drove her sword into the glowing ball. It erupted with a flash and *whoosh* that ripped through the woods as a vicious blast of winter. Snow flailed at them. Branches broke free to *clatter* through the woods. As suddenly as the violence arrived, silence and peace returned.

Danny ran to where Murg lay. Looking forlorn, Krindee sat next to the calico. Danny tenderly gathered his friend and lifted her into his arms. He hugged Murg, then began to weep. "Krindee can you help. . . ."

"I will try, but my healing gifts have limits. Hold her out to me."

"Fear not, my young friend." Jeannette d'Arc reached out and touched Murg. Danny thought he saw her aura surround the calico in a warm glow.

Murg spasmed, then briefly open her eyes. With a yawn, Murg snuggled closer to Danny.

Danny hugged her tightly. "Murg! You're alive! Thank you, Mademoiselle!"

"Of course I'm alive. And too much affection, while certainly appreciated, must be spurned if it endangers the perception of all felines."

Jeannette smiled, then moved to aid the fallen cavaliers. "Arise, Sir Jean de Metz," she commanded the tallest of the knights. "The Lord still has need of your strong right arm." She touched the other armored man. "Arise, Sir Bertrand de Poulengy, the angels tell me your time has not yet come."

Sirs de Metz and de Poulengy slowly stood, Jeannette assisting the latter who still appeared dazed. The cavaliers dropped to their knees and renewed their pledges and vows.

Leading two horses, a small, hunched man wearing a heavy cloak approached. "Mademoiselle, we must move quickly! A filthy Burgundian patrol might have seen the lights or heard the battle."

"Peace, Monsieur de Vienne," Jeannette told the King's messenger.

"Murg, how are you?" Danny mentally asked.

"A bit tired. I could use a nap."

"Are you well?" Jeannette asked Danny.

"Yes. Again, thank you, Mademoiselle," Danny replied. "I am Daniel Chase and am forever in your debt."

"Nay, not mine, but that of the Lord. I am simply his humble servant."

"Where are we?" Danny asked, looking around the woods. A blanket of white seemed to have been laid, readying the area for the morning's sacred service.

Jeannette looked at him strangely, then said, "We are in the forest south of Auxerre along the river Yonne. Rouvray has fallen and the cities and roads swarm with Englishmen."

"And the date? "

She eyed him with uncertainty. "February 27, 1429."

"Then you are on your way to Chinon to see King Charles the VII?" Danny asked.

"I do what I do by commandment. How do you know of me?"

"Uh, voices tell me things," Danny replied weakly.

"I, too, hear the voices of angels and do their blessed bidding. Daniel Chase, who are you? You dress and speak strangely. Do you come to France from afar?"

"I am from far across the waters to the west," Danny replied.

"Did you come to join the crusade of angels?"

"Uh, no. Sorry. I came here because I needed your help."

"With the English witch?" Jeannette asked. Danny nodded. "Why was she following you?"

"Morgan Le Fay was trying to prevent me from a very important mission. I seek to regain possession of . . . a very special relic before it's misused, causing a disaster."

"Is this thief a companion of Le Fay's?" Jeannette asked. "If so, he is evil and should be vanquished."

"I don't think he's evil, just confused," Danny couldn't believe those words had just come from his mouth.

"Evil are those who turn a deaf ear to the words of the Lord. If you are to do battle, you shall need a weapon. Aldrette!" She called for a sword from a squire, then handed it to Danny. "Take this to aid you in the Lord's work. I sense that what you do is important." She appeared to listen for a moment. "Souls hang in the balance."

Danny blanched and hefted the sword. "Ugh!" The second time he wrapped both hands around the leather hilt, using the sweeping silver crossguard to help hold the long sword upright. What was he supposed to do, go in swinging? Spike, give me the star metal or lose your head?

"Do not look so grim, Daniel. If this man is not wholly evil, he may yet be saved. Redemption is the greatest blessing of our Lord! If God be for us, who can be against us? For with God, nothing is impossible. Go, friend Daniel, be a messenger,"

Jeannette said. "Remember, show the one you seek the truth, and that will set him free."

Plato had said something similar—guide the eyes of the ignorant in the proper direction. Danny didn't know what to say, so he knelt, then departed. Once far enough from Jeannette's camp, Danny climbed aboard the magic bicycle.

"Inspiring isn't she?" Krindee sighed. "We had our own Jeannette d' Arc, Met-reee-han, who was moved by The Creator to change a land. Too bad those in power conspired against them and executed Jeannette and Met-reee-han."

"What am I supposed to do with this sword?" Danny asked. "Slay the wicked? Somebody, I don't remember who, said violence begets violence."

"A cat, I'm sure," Krindee replied.

"Then you need to handle things differently. The word seize includes violence," Murg told him. "Convince Spike to return the star metal."

"You are lots of help!"

"You've received plenty of advice. Plato suggested turning Spike's gaze in the proper direction. Shakespeare spoke of roles and choices and knowing one's own heart, as well as the other characters' motivations. Jeannette d'Arc preaches redemption."

"So speaks reason, heart and spirit," Krindee said.

"Let's go find a baseball game. I'll think of something." Danny glanced down at the sword, then turned his thoughts to time travel.

CHAPTER THIRTY-ONE

SULTAN OF SWAT

Standing on a Boston street corner in 1919, Spike waited for Babe Ruth to leave Fenway Park. A team of horses hauling a wagon of ice passed by, kicking up a cloud of dirt. Spike waved away the dust, looking for Babe's funky, bright red sports car.

In the past, Spike waited for Babe at the park;but now that Ruth's popularity had swelled, the gate area was crawling with kids. The brats made it difficult for him to spend any time with the baseball legend, so Spike had moved to this corner.

He smiled broadly and looked at the baseball in his hands. Everything was going great! Even better than he'd dreamed. Today, he'd caught the Babe's 100th home run.

The Babe always graciously signed his home run catches, so Spike thought history treated the Big Bambino unfairly. Instead of a party animal, Babe Ruth was a kind and gentle man, often giving Spike a smile and talking to him as if he were family.

A loud honking followed by uproarious laughter rebounded throughout the street. Horses and pedestrians jumped, the traffic parting as if the President approached. The horn honked again, then driving out of the dusty haze chugged a scarlet Cord, a flashy topless car with golden lamps, bumpers and wheels. Smoking a cigar and drinking a beer, George Herman Ruth steered the fancy car through the milling throng. Even the animals appeared to stop to watch the greatest home run hitter who'd ever lived.

"Babe! Babe!" Spike yelled as he ran into the street.

The car squeaked to a stop. "Hey there, partner!" Babe wore a flat hat and driving goggles. "Are you following me, son?!"

"Of course! You're the home run king!"

"Aw, you'll make me blush!" With a flourish, Babe stuck a huge cigar in his mouth and puffed. A gigantic cloud of smoke surrounded him.

Spike held the baseball forth. "I caught your home run today! It's your hundredth! Will you sign it? Please? Date it, too?"

"Again? Do you catch all my home runs?"

"Not hardly!"

"Then I guess it just seems like it."

"You're going to be famous one day, and I want to be part of it. I'm keeping track of your dingers."

"Dingers?"

"Big flies. Roundtrippers. You know, home runs!"

"Dingers, eh? I like that. The Big Bambino hits dingers." With a belch and then a smile, Babe signed the baseball, finishing with a flourish. "There! You are now the proud owner of the Babe's John Hancock."

"Who is he?"

"He signed the Declaration of Independence in big, bold letters. Hey, I'm going out for dinner. Are you hungry? Want to join me?"

"Sure," Spike replied.

"Hop in."

Spike tossed his bat, Slugger, into the car, then jumped inside. Once seated, he suddenly realized what he'd done. Babe Ruth's hands appeared huge, oversized even, compared to his girth. Was he like Ike? Did he hit kids? Lured them in, then . . . . wham?! Babe guzzled the last of his beer and chucked the bottle into the back seat, then belched mightily. Spike almost bolted out of the car.

"You okay? Got ants in your pants?" Babe asked.

"I'm fine." Spike mustered a smile. He felt uneasy, and yet, comfortable at the same time. How could that be? He experienced the oddest feeling of deja vu.

"What are you hungry for?" the Babe asked. He waved to someone calling his name. This inspired more calls and waving.

"Uh . . . ." Spike stammered.

"How about a steak and some fried potatoes at McGinty's? They dump cheese on them." Babe smacked his lips.

"Yeah, cool!"

"Cool? No, they serve them hot. Piping hot."

"No, cool is good. Like . . . great!"

Babe laughed. "You talk strange . . . . What's your name? We've met, but never been formally introduced. And since we know each other like old buddies, we'll skip the formal introductions. Never liked standing on formality, anyway. Wait, don't tell me, it's Ernie, isn't it?"

"No, it's Sp . . . . Ernest is fine." Why had he said that? Did Spike sound too weird? How had Babe come so close to guessing his name, calling him Ernie?

"Spernest Isfine? That's a strange name. No wonder you talk funny," Babe chuckled.

"Not Spernest! Ernest!"

"Got it. Sorry. Where you from, Ernie? Mind if I call you Ernie? Seems like we're old friends."

Spike smiled. He felt a familiar feeling, too, as if they'd been more than acquaintances, but friends many times. "I'm from, uh, Baltimore." Spike cringed. That was the first place that came to mind.

"Uh, Baltimore. That a suburb of Baltimore proper?"

"No!"

"Heh-heh! Baltimore. What a small world! That's where I was born!" Babe belched, then laughed.

"Must have been scary."

"What's that? Living in Baltimore? It's not a bad place at all. Played my first ball there."

"No, I meant your parents abandoning you at St. Mary's Industrial Academy."

"My parents did not abandon me," Babe replied mirthlessly. "My mom wasn't well and Dad worked the docks, so they couldn't care for me. So they packed me off to school. I learned to use my hands, and I learned to play baseball." He let go of the wheel to swing an imaginary bat. The car weaved, heading toward a milk cart.

"Watch out!"

"You worry too much!" Babe grabbed the wheel and righted them. "The Babe's driving."

"So your father didn't abandon you? That's what a newspaper article said."

"No, they didn't abandon me. It just makes for a good story, I guess."

That sounded defensive to Spike, just as he sounded when people asked him about his true father. He hadn't told the truth then either—that his father had left without a word late one night.

"The docks. Did he load ships?"

"No, he ran a bar," Babe replied. "Not a good place for a kid to grow up."

"Oh." Spike swore he'd read Mr. Ruth worked the Baltimore docks handling materials.

"Oh? Something bothering you, Ernie?"

"Just thinking about my father."

"Where is your old man? Why wasn't he there with you to enjoy the game?"

"He split when I was very young," Spike replied.

"I'm sorry." Babe didn't say anything for a while. The sounds of the Beantown streets filled the silence.

"Mom remarried." Spike said. Why was he telling this to the greatest baseball player who'd ever lived? Because he felt a kinship?

"That's good."

"No, it's not! Ike's a mean, nasty s.o.b. He hits me, my brothers and my sister, even when we don't do anything wrong. He just likes to hit people. He hates kids."

The Babe appeared thoughtful when he said, "You might be better off at a school."

"I've been thinking about running away, but I'd have to leave my family."

"Thinking about it? Have you run away?" Even through goggles, Babe's stare pierced Spike.

"Not yet, I'm trying to save up money."

"You know, family is important. I think it's probably the most important thing. Having someone you can depend on, care for you and care back, is important. I'd like to have sons one day, so they could watch me play baseball. I could teach them to play. We'd have a family game going, and when I grow old, I could go watch them play. Dinger, Jr.," he chuckled.

"But what if they don't care about you? If they hate you?"

"Your mom, brothers and sister hate you?"

"No, they just won't do anything about my stepdad, Ike."

"But you would?"

"If I was bigger, I'd smack him back."

"That would stop it?" Babe asked. People waved at him, but he no longer saw them.

"If not, I'd kill him."

"I see. That would solve everything?"

"A lot."

"Have you talked with your mom?"

"She wouldn't believe me. She never believes me."

"I see. How about if all of you kids talked to your mom? I mean, talking can be hard to do sometimes. Heck, I know that, my dad and I hardly ever talked; but now, I wish we had." Babe appeared sad.

"But you're always yelling at umpires," Spike said.

"We're just talking about a game. When you get all emotional and want to win so badly, you do a lot of shouting. You don't listen because you want to win. Winning seems so important. The only thing. Heck, if you have good friends and a good family, you're already winning in the game."

"Life isn't a game," Spike snapped.

"Oh, I don't know about that. I've heard some people say it is. I don't know if I really believe them, but there seems to be something to the thought that it isn't whether you win, but if you're enjoying the game. Hell, it's no fun to play a game alone, is it?"

Spike's head whirled. What was Babe trying to say? Stay home and endure the beatings? That it was better to stay with a bad family than have no family at all? If so, man, was he screwed up.

Just as Spike started to ask a question, a roar preceded a dazzling flash of light. Spike covered his eyes with one hand and clutched his bat with the other. The star metal quivered as if sensing a sibling's presence nearby.

"Please let it be an alien invasion and not Chase," Spike pleaded. When he uncovered his eyes, his worst fears appeared— alongside Babe Ruth's car, a boy and two cats rode a red bicycle. Stuck behind the seat sat a gleaming sword of silver. Chase planned to take back the bicycle by force!

"Hi, Spike," Danny said, his smile a wicked leer. He reached for the silver sword.

THIRTY-TWO

TRY, TRY, AGAIN

With a scream, Spike leapt out the other side of the moving car. He landed hard, rolling across the dirt road.

"Hey!" Babe cried. He slammed on the brakes, kicking up a heavy dirt storm.

"I think you scared him," Murg projected.

"I find that hard to believe. I'm a wimp, remember?" Danny rearranged the sword before it fell out of its sheath.

"A wimp wielding a sword," Murg continued.

"Spike! Listen to me!"

"Leave me alone!" Spike jumped to his feet. As the big boy rose, the bat changed shape, enlarging and changing color as it transformed into the blue-nosed monster bike. Even before the two-wheeler was finished, Spike rushed aboard Slugger and pedaled frantically. The monster bike bolted, a blue streak ripping through downtown Boston, leaving behind a dumb-struck Babe Ruth rubbing his eyes in disbelief.

"You can't lose me, Spike!" Danny cried. With a thought, the magic bicycle exploded ahead, continuing the chase.

"Threatening him is a great way to open a dialogue," Murg thought dryly. "Nor should we be chasing him. It calls attention."

"I'm tired of chasing him. I want my bicycle back!" Danny snapped.

"Remember what Plato and Aristotle said. Are you being mad at the right person?"

"Yes! Spike is a bully and a thief! Besides, he isn't listening to me!"

"You can lead a horse to water." Murg sighed. "Shakespeare suggested listening. Why don't we just return to the present? To before Spike stole your story, *The Alien Bicycle*? You could rewrite it, leaving out anything that would help Spike."

"That might prevent this; but it wouldn't solve the Spike problem. You, Krindee, Gretchen, everybody, wants me to deal with Spike. Well, he's going to learn he can't just steal from everybody. Run over anybody!" Danny snapped. "Besides, you said time flows like a river, looking for the path of least resistance—where it had flowed before. Wouldn't this just happen again?"

Murg sighed. "I did say that. Well, at least turn yourself invisible so nobody sees you."

"Okay." Danny imagined light wrapping around them, cloaking them, making them blend into their surroundings. "Happy now?"

"No. I'm going to be disbarred."

"From who?"

"The time cats, of course. Now watch where you're going."

Rapidly closing on Spike and his monster bike, Danny thought-weaved his way through traffic. The magic bicycle darted between horses, carts, wagons and automobiles as if they stood still. As Danny raced around a team, the horses whinnied and reared, shying away from the 'breeze'.

Spike turned suddenly, laying down Slugger like a

motorcycle to take an abrupt corner into an alleyway. Open-mouthed, Bostonians stared.

"We're fouling the past," Danny moaned. He steered Kalyde II in hot pursuit, cornering on a dime. His knee brushed the ground, tearing his pants. "Now I have him! That alley's a dead end!"

Spike glanced over his shoulder. "Hey! Where'd he go?! I know you're there, Chase. Damn! I wish I could see . . . There you are!" Spike hunched over the handlebars, urging Slugger faster.

"The wall! He's heading for the wall and not slowing down. Well . . . then I'm not either!" Danny cried.

A split-second before he would have crashed into the wall, Spike yanked back on his bike's handlebars. The monster bike reared, then scuttled up the side of the brick wall. It disappeared over the edge onto the roof.

"If he can do it, I can do it! Here we go!" Danny leaned back and imagined spider-wheels of speed. Kalyde II leapt forward, bending and twisting to latch onto the brick wall. As though racing along a flat road, the magic bicycle rocketed to the top, then snapped over the edge to speed across the rooftops.

Just ahead, Spike hit a loose board, ramping over an alley onto the next roof. Danny steered for the same board. Kalyde II struck the ramp; the boards twisted, flipping around to smack them like a fly swatter and driving them toward the ground.

"Hey!" The magic bicycle tumbled fender over handlebars. Rutted dirt rushed to meet them.

"Wonderful," Murg mindspoke.

Wind whistling past him, Danny imagined appearing on the rooftop. Without losing a beat, the magic bicycle space-jumped, landing on the roof and speeding after Spike. "Now, let's see if I can make Spike invisible, too. He'll never know." Danny concentrated on the link between the magic bicycle and the monster bike. Suddenly, Spike disappeared. Danny focused, imagining he could see invisible and feeling for the star metal. Spike and Grand Slam Slugger reappeared, their coloring muted. Now, no one could see them!

The monster bike raced up a steepled roof, then down the far side. Pulling a wheelie, Spike dropped onto a lower roof. The monster bike skidded, throwing Spike off balance. Danny took advantage, closing the gap. Spike recovered, leaping onto another rooftop. Below, people looked up for the cause of the noises but saw nothing. Danny followed, moments behind. He grew impatient, tired of leapfrogging from building to building. Closing his eyes, Danny imagined appearing next to Spike, wheel to wheel and nose to nose. With a whirlwind of color and sound, Kalyde II appeared next to the monster bike. "Spike, talk to. . . ."

Spike swerved suddenly, steering Slugger off the roof and plummeting toward the docks. The monster bike bounced once, then splash-landed in Boston Harbor. With a gasp, Spike resurfaced, urging Slugger faster across the water's chopping surface.

"I should've grabbed him," Danny moaned. "Here we go!"

"I hate plummeting," Murg groaned.

As though a Superball, Kalyde II rebounded off the pier to fly over Boston Harbor. Workers nearby jumped, startled by the thudding.

"Stay dry. Picture staying dry."

Kalyde II landed with a small splash, then bounded across the waves. Water splashed around them, Danny keeping them dry. He thought about flying fish and magnetism.

As though yanked by its tail, the monster bike floundered, slowing as it hit a wave sideways. Spike cursed as he was swamped. Kalyde II catapulted ahead, closer and closer.

As the bicycles touched, Spike disappeared into an explosion of light, separating the two. Danny darted through a brilliant burst to appear on a cloudy rainbow skyway.

"Where's he going?" Krindee asked.

Danny thought faster. As both bikes blew through the cloud, Spike appeared and disappeared. When Danny burst through a gray mass, he saw Spike fade, swallowed by another dazzling flash. Danny doggedly continued the chase.

Kalyde II reappeared, spitting white sand and bogging down. For miles in every direction, the rolling dunes met the washed-out blue sky. The sun hammered down mercilessly, causing the harsh whiteness to shimmer. Spike and the monster bike crested a hill into a cluster of shifting cacti.

"Where'd he go?" Krindee asked.

"He's still here. He's hidden by a mirage and heading over that dune," Danny coughed on Spike's dust. He pictured Kalyde II's tires widening, then the magic bicycle shot forward, following the monster bike's dusty trail. Slugger kicked up enough sand to create a storm. Danny erected a windshield. When that didn't work, he swerved out of it, still following the dusty tail.

"We're in White Sands, New Mexico, aren't we?" the Siamese asked.

"I think so," Danny replied. Hot on the trail, they ripped over the dune, heading for a lake of quicksilver. Spike disappeared without a ripple into the phantom water. Dust rose as if steam. As Kalyde II dove in, the water disappeared, leaving only the starkness of sand. Across the way, Spike raced up another dune.

"I've had enough chasing." In his mind, Danny pictured the black fender of the monster bike. Kalyde II disappeared in white to the roaring of a jet. The magic bicycle reappeared, bouncing about as though caught in a storm. A second white eruption engulfed them; the bellowing roar sounded enraged. The magic bicycle shuddered and quaked. Danny felt stung by angry hornets. His skin burned and his muscles ached.

"YEOW! That hurts! What's going on?!"

Krindee also let out a very undignified scream.

"You teleported as he bridged. A bad combination, creating a riptide of space." The calico sounded worried. "I really wish you'd just go back and rewrite *The Alien Bicycle*. We are damaging a fragile fabric."

The roaring slowly died, but the whiteness lingered long. "Are we stuck?" Danny asked.

With an ear-shattering whistle, Kalyde II shot forward,

sliding sideways across rock toward a cliff. The edge plummeted to a lake. Danny thought STOP. The magic bicycle screeched to a halt inches away from tumbling off the edge. A handful of rocks tumbled into the chasm. Burnt rubber wafted past Danny, who held his nose, then whispered, "Wow!"

Below him, a mammoth red stone arch like the legs of a colossus arched across a river canyon. As if a gateway to the realm of sky, the air within the Rainbow Bridge shimmered.

"Danny, you're covered in welts." Murg touched one.

"Ouch!"

"I barely touched you."

"Are you letting Spike go?" Krindee asked. Ahead, Spike raced across the flat plane of water toward the natural bridge. The monster bike charged ashore, rumbling over rocks and bushes.

"No. We are going to resolve this, this time." Danny visualized Kalyde II appearing across the water next to Spike. Whiteness raged over them. This time, Danny felt pelted by hail, stung again and again. "Oww! He must've gated! Bridged! Teleported! Whatever!"

Somewhere ahead, Spike screamed.

The roaring faded, leaving wind and high desert. Rocks, cacti, manzanita bushes and rugged mountains whirled around as though caught in a blender. Despite Danny's efforts to right it, Kalyde II continued to spin and whirl.

"What's going on?!" Danny grew dizzy. Nausea billowed in his throat, overwhelming the pain from his welts and bites.

"We're caught in a time vortex," Murg replied. "Rare and nasty. Want to stop now?"

"NO! How do you know this?" Danny asked.

"I am a cat."

As if the tires dug in with claws, Kalyde II stopped, then abruptly sprang, racing like a jaguar toward a giant canyon with buttes and free-standing table-top mesas. Striations of many colors lined the rocks. "What's a time vortex?!"

"It occurs when an area experiences multiple gates opening within a short period," Murg replied.

"There he goes!" the Siamese pointed. Spike and the monster bike disappeared over the lip, dropping into the Grand Canyon where the Colorado River waited far below.

"Hold on!" As though riding atop rollercoaster rails, Kalyde II steamrolled to the edge, then snapped over the lip, barreling down the walls of the canyon. Danny used the magic of the bicycle to heal himself. The improvement came slowly, the pain grudgingly subsiding to dull throbbing.

Kalyde II struck an outcropping, bouncing airborne. Danny imagined wings appearing. The magic bicycle soared, sweeping around, trying to cut off Spike.

Slugger struck a boulder, flying across a gap and raced by Danny before landing atop a free-standing mesa. The monster bike skittered across the table top, then disappeared down the other side.

Kalyde II landed gently, skipping across the mesa, then dropped over the edge and plummeted like a stone.

"Danny, this must stop. You don't look well. Try something different," Murg said. Danny ignored her. The calico rolled her eyes. "Creator, please save us from youthful enthusiasm."

When Danny saw Spike, he thought magnetism, picturing and feeling the bicycles slamming together. Kalyde II rocketed forward, slamming into the rear bumper of the monster bike.

Spike was thrown forward onto the handlebars. "Get away from me!"

The magic bicycle flew backwards as if repelled. Kalyde II raced backwards up the side of the table top mesa. Before Danny regained control, they slammed into an outcropping. His head snapped back. For a moment, his dizziness, throbbing aches and the whiplash ganged up. As Danny tried to shake it off, Spike raced away.

Through the haze, Danny imagined the monster bike having a flat tire. Surprised for a moment, Spike hung onto the bucking bronco, then righted the ugly two-wheeler.

"That got him!" Danny cried. Kalyde II closed the gap, racing alongside Spike.

A black-streaked white light engulfed them.

After a brief burst of mist, sky, and rainbow, Danny reappeared right behind Spike, plunging down a long waterfall. Water sprayed far and wide, drenching them. Murg shook violently, caterwauling in utter misery. "You shall rue this day! You are right, Danny, we must deal with Spike."

The magic bicycle plowed ahead, spitting falling water. The front and rear fenders suddenly met, Kalyde II hitting Slugger. Kalyde II shuddered, but held its ground, a dolphin after a shark. The monster bike skidded sideways, threatening to spin. With a string of profanity, Spike fought to right his ride.

"Look out!" Krindee yelled.

Below, a great plume of water erupted from the rocks, geysering into a valley surrounded by granite walls and domes that loomed as giant sentinels. A river cut through the enchanting valley, heading into the sun over the rolling lowlands.

"Brace for impact!" In his mind, Danny pictured the invisible force field wrapping round them—a body glove protecting them.

The monster bike smacked the ledge sideways. The magic bicycle crashed right behind it; only the force field kept the trio aboard Kalyde II. Danny imagined flaps sprouting out to catch their fall.

As he fell, Spike appeared dazed, barely hanging on with one hand. His legs dangled behind him. Spike splash-landed in the river. The magic bicycle landed much more gently.

Spike snapped alert and swam aboard the monster bike. As if a small whale, the bike surged to the surface.

"Spike we can work . . . ." Danny began.

With a deafening explosion, black-ripped whiteness engulfed them. Mists whipped by, swirling in Kalyde II's wake.

Just ahead, Spike whipped the monster bike across the rainbow bridge. Clouds churned in its wake as if chilling exhaust, creating misty tornadoes that erupted as Kalyde II burst through.

Danny thought about a flat tire again. Spike immediately fixed it. Both of the magic bicycles' tires flattened. Danny made his solid. "He learns faster than I ever imagined. You know, I swear this has happened before!"

As the words left his mouth, deja vu like a tsunami swept over Danny. This *had* happened before, even if not exactly like this; but it had happened. Danny remembered driving down the side of the Grand Canyon and plunging madly 2200 plus feet down Yosemite Falls. He recalled being fired upon more than once. He'd already met Plato, Aristotle, Shakespeare and Joan of Arc many times. "T . . .this—this all is a . . . a repeat!"

Danny felt slugged in the stomach, breathless with a feeling that he'd never, ever breathe again. Why bother? How many times had he failed over and over and over again. He might as well die. Sickness soul-deep washed over him. A failure. A loser so many times over and over. "W . . .we're caught in a cycle, I guess. Kind of a do-loop; I keep failing."

"A do-loop? Isn't that a computer programming term?" Krindee asked.

"Yeah, the program repeats itself until something changes, but I've tried a bunch of times to change things and always failed." Tears of frustration welled in Danny's eyes. "We've done this a bunch of times . . . so why keep trying? I can't win." He was tempted to stop and sit, let things move on. He was insignificant, unable to make a difference.

"Danny, don't believe that."

"Murg, have I tried different things?"

"Not a change of thought, which can lead to true changes. And you have always wanted to chase Spike, as you namesake implies. That is understandable, for so long you have been pursued."

"Oh." Danny sank even lower. "Yeah. I guess I'd love to run Spike into the ground. So this set of events repeats itself, going faster and faster. I am an idiot. A lame-brain."

"You have to think of something different . . . do something different to break the cycle."

"Murg I'm so very, very tired and I hurt. I give up. Spike having baseballs isn't so bad. What's the harm of letting Spike be rich?"

"Danny, don't give up," Krindee projected. "I have faith in you. When it's all over, you will come through."

"Why bother?"

"Are . . . are you telling me you have no imagination left? Nothing to mine for inspiration? A hero is judged by the obstacles overcome and villains defeated."

"You sound like Shakespeare."

"I just never expected to see you getting stuck. Plato, Aristotle, Shakespeare and Jeannette d'Arc gave you pearls of wisdom. You must mount them in their proper setting."

"And show the Cor-ror-o'lan that we're not idiots. Okay! Okay. I'll try one more time. I really want to end this; but if this doesn't do it . . . it's not worth the aggravation and pain. I'll go back and rewrite my story."

"Danny, the same problem confronts us until we solve it," Krindee mindspoke.

"I said OKAY! Spike, here I come!"

Danny thought of springing. Kalyde II leapt forward, landing next to the monster bike.

Spike swung the newly created baseball bat. Danny lay back, ducking below the blow. His hand fumbled atop the sword, knocking it loose. It almost fell free before Danny could grab it, then was surprised by his idea. Try something different!

Spike coiled, readying to strike again. This blow would be aimed at Kalyde II.

"Not this time. This should slow you down!" Danny adjusted his grip, blocked the bat, then jammed the silver sword between the monster bike's rear spokes and tearing into the rainbow. Spectral fire erupted from the rip, cavorting along Danny's arm. He jerked away, letting go of the sword. Danny lost all sensation in that arm.

Slugger's rear wheel crumpled, its rubber slapping against the magic bicycle's front tire. Suddenly, two wheels became one—bicycles becoming an odd tandem again.

"HEY! LOOK OUT!" Krindee cried.

The monster bike floundered, then suddenly veered toward the edge of the rainbow, taking the magic bicycle with it.

Danny pictured separation. Imagined pulling away. The bicycles remained one. He tried again, reinforcing the thought as they slid closer to the void. Danny thought-created spiked tires digging into the rainbow.

The monster bike slowed, but continued dragging Kalyde II. As though skidding across ice, Slugger slowly, relentlessly, slid toward the edge.

"Danny, stop us, now!" Murg sounded near panic.

Almost stopping, Slugger reached the edge of darkness, hesitated, then plunged into the void, taking Kalyde II and its riders. With a spectral burst of fire, both bicycles disappeared in the nothingness of time.

THIRTY-THREE

Time Breach

Spinning and whirling, Danny rose and fell as though riding a white tornado. He couldn't see anything, the brilliance all-engulfing. "What's happening?! Murg! Murg?! Where are you?!" Danny felt hemmed in, the white nothingness growing tighter. A chill seeped into his bones, making him cold and stiff. Was he dead or dying? "MURG! KRINDEE!"

Out of the blinding blaze, Kalyde II suddenly stormed into a hot, humid place, the rain driving as hard as bullets. Wet vines slapped at them, green whips lashing. One smacked Danny across the face, stinging him. With a thought, Danny hastily erected the force field. "Whew! We're alive!"

"And in a jungle," Krindee replied. The Siamese backed away, staring at the bushes slapping and slithering by the protective field. Unable to see anything, Danny slowed the magic bicycle.

"That was the dumbest thing you've ever done!" Murg's damp fur stood like porcupine quills.

"Why?" Danny felt all stiff and achy, his joints and muscles protesting.

"Why? Why?! What if the Xenozilit *is* alive? You may have injured it."

"I just tried something different—tried to trip it. You know, you girls haven't been much help!"

"You just tried something different, not better. Danny . . ." Murg took a deep breath. "Danny, you damaged the rainbow. Why did you use the sword of all things?"

"Because the sword didn't feel like part of the cycle. It felt fresh and new."

"War is a poor chisel to carve out tomorrows. Martin Luther King Jr.," Krindee quoted.

"Well, you broke the cycle all right." Murg sighed, sounding very disappointed. "For the worse. Now you're adrift in time."

"Adrift in time? We're lost? How can that be?"

"You damaged the rainbow. Now you're no longer on a linear path. You can travel in any direction."

"That's bad?"

"It is for you. Humans think better forward and back, not sideways."

"I'm sorry. I'm so dumb sometimes. What about Spike? Did the same thing happen to him? Before I was blinded, I thought I saw him tumbling over and over again."

"Over there! See the brush moving?" Krindee pointed through the sea of green growth to where black and blue flashed.

Danny steered toward that spot. They blew past a surprised panther who skidded to a stop, eyes wide and limbs akimbo. A large snake slapped the shield, its eyes wide and long tongue flicking. It slithered a bit, then stuck, one wide eye peering at them. "I can't see! Get off!" A second wet vine joined the snake.

Kalyde II dropped suddenly, landing with a splash. The wave washed away the vines and the snake.

"There he is!" Danny pointed.

Ahead across the water, appearing haggard, Spike rode across the white-capped waves, leaning atop the handlebars, urging Slugger faster.

Danny pictured teleporting ahead of Spike. Kalyde II space-jumped forward, appearing ahead of Slugger.

"What's that roaring I hear?!" Krindee projected.

"Hey!" Danny cried. The water dropped out from under them. Thousands of feet below, white water thrashed and roiled, plummeting to the river below.

"I believe we're riding Angel Falls in Venezuela and plunging over 3,000 feet toward a series of falls," Krindee said.

"Spike! Stop! Rocks ahead." Danny roared as Spike raced by him down the falls. How could anyone be so much trouble? Anger fueling him, Danny urged Kalyde II faster down the falls. "Spike!"

Spike glanced over his shoulder, his expression tired and his face aged, then the brightness roared, swallowing them. Kalyde II ripped through the mists, finding firmer riding atop a ragged rainbow. From dark holes in the crumbling purple walls, worried eyes watched and the wind howled.

"We're in the time tunnel. How did we get here?" Danny asked. "And if we're going forward in time, why does the bridge look so bad?"

"As I said, all our racing around is causing damage," Murg replied. "The barriers between times are fragile things."

"Danny, did you notice how old Spike looked?" Krindee asked. "Something's wrong."

Spike raced ahead, cresting nearly out of sight. Danny thought of appearing farther ahead.

"Danny wait until . . . ." Murg began.

Even through the force field, a twisting and tearing sensation assailed Danny. Black-streaked white light engulfed the world.

Danny screamed as thousands of cold needles pierced him. The tiny ice pains seemed to last forever, then he reappeared next to Spike.

They raced across a cobblestone road high above the land. Crenelated walls blurred into a long gray streak. Westward from the Great Wall, clusters of bamboo and hills covered with Japanese cherry blossom trees rolled into the misty mountains beyond.

Even through the force field, Danny felt scraped raw. His legs and knees ached, so cold and stiff they felt as if they needed lubricating. Danny could barely see through his tears; but he heard the monster bike ripping through the nearby air.

Spike appeared worn and battered. His clothing rustled behind him in tatters. His bruises appeared larger and blood ran from his nose along deep set lines into his gray temples. Heavy bags surrounded his glazed eyes. "He won't beat me! He won't beat me! Can't stop! Can't stop! Won't beat me. Won't . . . ."

"Danny . . . ." Murg began, then groaned. "I feel awful."

After a groan, Krindee projected, "Danny, this wall, The Great Wall of China, looks newly built. If I remember correctly, work began 221 BC and was completed 204 BC. This wall of earth, stone and bricks runs for fifteen hundred miles and was created to hold off the hordes."

Danny unclenched his teeth. Blood ran down his chin. "How'd we get here?"

"With the rainbow damaged, you fall through holes, going in any direction," Murg replied. "I think that's why we feel so bad, we're being torn in different directions."

"Hey Wimp, you're not tough enough to catch me!" Spike smiled grimly. With graying hair, deep age lines and sagging skin, he looked over fifty. The monster bike disappeared in a flash of brilliant colors. Kalyde II dove into the burst.

"Did you see Spike? He looked . . . he looked really old! What's going on? Do I look old?" Danny asked. His stiffness, aches and pains intensified, enfeebling him. Was . . . was he growing old, racing toward death?

They appeared on a curvy, snow-covered road. In the distance, the Matterhorn jutted skyward, protruding through the clouds.

"Danny, you don't look as old as Spike, probably because of the force field, but you're aging, looking about fifty."

"FIFTY! I'M FIFTY?" Danny, stunned beyond belief, could not imagine it. Could not imagine being fifty. Devastated, his mind locked. He never thought of being fifty! Had . . . had he been chasing Spike thirty-five years?!

"It's not just the years, it's the mileage."

"Fifty. Fifty! I'm . . . I'M DYING!" Danny felt sick and leaden, his joints and muscles stiffening. No! It couldn't be! HE COULDN'T HAVE WASTED THIRTY-FIVE YEARS!

"The tides of time are ravaging. Keep this up, we'll be . . . ."

Another flash of light and the cyclists reappeared, Kalyde II racing behind Slugger through the snow. Night had fallen long ago across the wooded hills, but they were neither dark nor still. The light of ethereal spirits danced among the groves and copses, colors cavorting among the shadows.

Shifting in the sky above the hills, a shimmering carpet of colors cast its magic. Pinks, blues and greens lapped among each other like ocean waves. Long, lean columns of gold swayed as if oriental maidens, drifting through fiery arches and sparking curtains. Dragons sprang from the arches, streaming skyward, their tails lashing behind them.

The beauty of the Aurora Borealis was lost on Danny. He could feel himself aging, dying, by the moment. "SPIKE! LISTEN TO ME! SOMETHING'S WRONG! TERRIBLY WRONG!"

Spike appeared frail and bewildered but still grimly determined. "No way!" his voice shook. "Go Slugger, go!" The monster bike put on a burst of speed, spitting snow as Slugger climbed the hill. As if hooked to Slugger's rear bumper, Kalyde II followed. Snow slopped against the force field, blinding Danny for a moment. Spike became a silhouette, racing toward the shifting waves, filaments, columns and archways of spectral color.

With a splash of pink, Spike disappeared. The backlash drafted Kalyde II. Danny and his feline companions disappeared.

In a wash of fading color that sputtered into shapes, the cyclists appeared in a magnificent garden. Through a receding haze, three colorful brick terraces stepped up from the ground. Each layer of flowers grew brighter and more beautiful as they neared the sun. From hand-carved columns and towers housing waterfalls, pots overflowing with flowers swayed far above the earth.

"Where now?" Danny wondered, rubbing the brightness from his eyes.

"One of the Seven Wonders of the World, the Hanging Gardens of Babylon," Krindee said.

Danny's eyes seemed highly sensitive. On second glance, things at a distance seemed blurred. "I'm going blind! Spike! Stop! We're tearing up things! We're getting old! You look sixty, going on seventy! WE'RE GOING TO DIE!"

Spike wasn't listening, chanting over and over, "I can't stop!" Spike's tongue lolled and his eyes bugged, ready to pop.

White light flickered, carrying them away to someplace and somewhere else. Side by side, they raced across the sandy shore along a river. Against the setting sun, a pair of pyramids stood silhouetted. A third one stood unfinished, but appeared to move, teeming with workers.

"Oh no, we're on the River Nile, more than 2000 years BC."

"SPIKE! WE'RE DYING! IF WE KEEP THIS UP, WE'RE DEAD. LOOK AT YOUR HANDS!" Danny yelled.

"I can't stop!" Spike looked exhausted.

"Has he gone deaf? I'm going to ram him!"

The brightness swallowed them, then the cyclists exploded from the mists, bouncing wildly across the rutted and pot-holed rainbow tunnel. The walls appeared ready to collapse, the stars falling as fiery streaks to crash upon the bridge. Geysers of fire sprayed far and wide as though miniature volcanoes erupting.

"SPIKE!"

"You're never getting this back! NEVER! If I can't have it, no one can!" Spike's hair receded, a bald spot growing larger and larger.

The magic bicycle hit a chunk of wall, sending it airborne.

Kalyde II landed bone-shakingly hard and swerved wildly, rattling as if ready to fly apart.

Laughing, old man Spike pulled away.

"After a half-dozen times, even your mutt, Comet, would have learned by now," Murg said.

"Six times?! We've done this six times!" Danny squawked. He stopped pedaling, his legs leaden. Arrows of pain raced into his hips and up his back. He could no longer sit up straight, stooped and bent.

"I could be underestimating. After about the third time, the trails overlap and merge, causing plenty of chaos. But then the sword was a new twist; you were right about that. It made things worse! Danny, use your imagination. I wish I could help, but I can't. In a little while, we're going to all be dead."

"Danny, I have faith in you," Krindee said. "You can make things right. Repair the damage we've done."

"I . . . I guess you're right. I'm tired and not thinking straight. What else can I try? What else? I tried grabbing. I tried talking." Danny stammered. "Doing as Plato suggested, turning Spike's eyes in a different direction."

"Did you? Did you change roles as Shakespeare suggested? Or were you the same old Danny?"

A thought struck Danny. Spike needed a friend. "I'd rather impale myself on the sword."

"Have you ever thought of it before?"

"Being Spike's friend? Never!"

"You once needed a friend," Murg said, staring at him with large green eyes.

"I'll help, but he's not my friend." With a thought burst, Danny caught up with Spike, who appeared thin and skeletal, his skin ready to fall from his bones.

"Spike, if you'll listen, I'll help you catch all of Babe Ruth's baseballs. Hank Aaron's too!"

"WHAT?!" Spike slurred, then Danny's words appeared to hit home. "Catch baseballs! You will?! No more chasing?!" Spike spat out several teeth. "Wha . . . what's happening?"

"Spike, the sword damaged the rainbow. We have to fix it."

"You said we'd catch baseballs."

"We will, after we fix things, we'll talk, then we can go catch baseballs. Spike, look at your hands. You're old and tired."

"I'm not tired. Never tired. Never stop. I'm Spike. Spike's never tired."

"SPIKE! WE'RE AGING! YOU LOOK EIGHTY! YOU DON'T HAVE ANY HAIR!"

Whiteness flashed. They reappeared next to a mountain. The peak suddenly disappeared, vaporized as earth became an explosive storm of mud, dust and fire. "GRAB ON!" Danny cried. With shaky hands, Spike grabbed the magic bicycle. Danny imagined a force field around all of them.

The volcanic blast slammed into them. As if riding inside a ball, they tumbled together into the aborning grayness. They reappeared in the faded time tunnel. Dust fell, clouding the shaft as the ceiling and walls crumbled, moments away from a massive collapse.

Danny grabbed the crossbar of the monster bike. "Spike, we have to combine our imaginations. Restore the star metal to full strength. Concentrate, using both your hands and your mind, pull us together into a tandem. Otherwise, we're going to shrivel up and die." Danny coughed, then spat out a tooth and something black. "CONCENTRATE! ONE BICYCLE!"

The metal slithered together, shimmering and shifting to become a red and black tandem. Spike rode up front with Danny and the felines behind.

"Now what?" Spike asked. He didn't have any teeth left. His lips were brown and curled under.

"We travel back to the rip. The one we fell in. Do you remember the sword?"

"How could I forget? You stabbed at me!" Spike snapped.

"I was just trying to flatten your tire."

"You were trying to take my head off!" Spike swung

around. "You just want to get back to the sword so you can stick me!" Hands shaking, Spike grabbed at Danny's throat.

With a thought, Danny caused Spike's seat to fall away. He let go, hands questing for a grip.

"Boys!" Krindee snapped. "We don't have time for this!"

Hanging on precariously, Spike stared, his jaw hanging open. "A talking cat! Just like in the story. You must be Murg."

The graying calico glared.

The magic tandem bucked, almost throwing them all off. A scalding whiteness engulfed them.

They exploded into a prehistoric jungle. The sky appeared murky. The air blew hot and sulfurous. In a nearby swamp, a herd of Apatasaurus dined on trees, bending them forward, then snapping off the tops.

"DINOSAURS!" Spike cried.

From behind them roared an angry bellow.

"Not again." Danny wearily searched for the protective field. It wasn't there; it'd been blown away. Danny focused on erecting it, sweeping it out around them. It felt weak and unstable. His mind was going, too. Soon, he might not be able to imagine anything!

Spike glanced over his shoulder. His jaw dropped, his face paled, and his eyes widened. "A T-REX! That's a T-Rex. I'm outta here!" He jumped on the pedals to ride, then slipped. Spike's jaw met the handlebars with a *crack*, leaving him stunned.

"Danny, concentrate on the sword. See yourself there, holding it! We have to repair the rip!"

"I'd rather poke out my eyes than help you . . . but I don't want to die here!" Spike climbed on the pedals and joined Danny.

The ground shook. Trees thrashed as though a tornado approached. Rocks bounded down the hill. The second quake shook stronger, a miniature earthquake.

"IT'S GETTING CLOSE! OH MY GOD, IT'S HUGE!"

"SPIKE! Stop panicking! You're slowing us down!" Danny cried.

A roar buffeted them, then the air jumped. Inches away, the T-Rex's blood-stained jaws slammed together, all too close. Had the field held? Danny couldn't tell through his blossoming headache.

The great beast gathered itself, then lunged forward, spear-like teeth slashing just behind them, the impact throwing them forward. The T-Rex gathered again, then lunged. Danny drug a foot. Kalyde II suddenly swerved. Right next to their ears, teeth crashed together with the sound of cars colliding.

Danny felt a stabbing headache. The shield was surely gone now! Spots danced before his eyes. He could barely see, his vision becoming a tunnel.

A low branch crashed into Spike's forehead. He fell, knocking Danny back. The branch rushed overhead.

"I should let him fall off. That would eliminate my problem." Danny pushed Spike forward, letting him drape over the handlebars.

Trees burst and splintered, the T-Rex tearing after them. Another roar assaulted them.

With a final burst of imagination, Danny pictured the sword. The long sweep of the blade ending in a simple, argent crossguard that led to a dark, leather-wrapped hilt ending in a silver ball. Danny reached for the sword.

Blackness washed over them, churning and hammering, trapping them in an undertow. The tide sucked them away. The pressure grew, squeezing. Danny could barely think straight, but he remained focused on the sword—grabbing the sword, feeling it in his hands and wrenching it free.

With a piercing scream and a blast of spectral light, they appeared next to Joan's sword stuck in the rainbow. Black mists streamed from the rip, coiling about the blade and spinning around the hilt. Darkness hung along the walls and clung to the ceiling, slowly eating away at them.

His vision collapsing to darkness, Danny grabbed the hilt, then yanked with all his might. The sword didn't budge.

"I'M BLIND!" Danny cried. He desperately tugged at the sword. It wouldn't budge. He no longer had any strength. He wouldn't be holding onto the sword if his hands hadn't frozen around the hilt.

"Pull it with your mind." Murg sounded ancient, her voice harsh and raspy. "On three. One. Two. Three!"

Danny imagined he was Hercules, Atlas, Thor and Superman all rolled into one. With a metallic ring, the sword slipped free.

A sun aborning, a bleaching brilliance turned everything white. Warmth washed over Danny, then as the time storm suddenly broke, the winds died to nothing.

THIRTY-FOUR

The Deal

Cows turned to stare at the bright flash, then returned to chewing cud as the magic tandem coasted to a stop in the field. Across the gravel road waited a brand new, bright red tractor with a bushhog attached. The stately white home appeared to be much more than a farmhouse; although well kept, it seemed empty. Beyond the gray barn bustling with prized chickens, dew-glistening hills gently rolled into the woodlands that disappeared in the morning mists.

Murg jumped to the ground. "The farm appears deserted, but I hear raking behind the house." A cow cocked her head as she looked at the calico, who ignored it. "The great news is the rip in time is repaired and you look young again."

"Thank heavens. I feel normal. Getting old is the pits." Danny stuck the sword in the ground, then stretched. He felt much better, no longer arthritic and feeble, but still stiff and tired.

Danny climbed off the bicycle, then eased Spike to the ground. "You're lucky I don't push you off into a cow patty," Danny said to the unconscious bully. No longer bald and wrinkled, Spike still looked a little worse for the wear. A large welt, like a headband, spread across his forehead, the redness growing darker and uglier. Blood still stained his lips and chin. Danny couldn't muster feeling sorry for him. "You brought this on yourself."

"Crime doesn't pay," Krindee quoted.

"Another dubious quote that sounds like propaganda, wishful thinking, or philosophy instead of truth," Murg replied. "If humans believed such, their world would be vastly different."

Danny took the magic tandem in his hands, then concentrated, visualizing a sword sheath. The bicycle shrank and squealed, scaring off the herd of cows. Still weary from aging and racing, he tried five times before getting it right.

Spike groaned and rolled over onto his side. "What happened?!" He touched his face, then his head. "I have hair! I'M YOUNG AGAIN!" Spike jumped to his feet; teetering unsteadily dampened his enthusiasm. "Getting old bites. I don't ever want to be old, bald and fat." He shuddered, then rubbed his eyes. "Where are we?! Where'd you bring me, Chase?! And where's the bicycle! Hey, wait a sec, I know this place!" He smiled. "It's Babe Ruth's farm outside Boston. Why'd you bring me here?"

"I told you that I'd help you catch homers."

"Yeah, right! Those who can't fight always want to talk. Where's the bicycle?"

"Safe. I'll go get it once we're through talking." Danny slid Joan of Arc's sword into the magic scabbard.

" 'Fraid I'll take off again? That you can't catch me?"

"You can't lose me. The bikes are connected."

"So that's why I couldn't lose you! Lucky you! Otherwise you were toast, just like in the Oktoberfest race. Chump."

"Why should I trust you?" Danny replied angrily. "You hounded me for months! Stole things! Beat on me! Frankly, I think turnabout is fair play."

"This isn't helping," Murg thought.

Spike flipped him a coin. "Here's a quarter. Call somebody who cares." The coin bounced off Danny and landed in the dirt. "You don't know what trouble is." Spike touched his forehead. "What happened to my head? Did we drop by and see Ike?"

"You hit your head on a tree branch when we swerved to escape that T-Rex. If I wasn't afraid that it might . . . ." Danny glanced at Murg, " . . . adversely affect the future, I would've let the T-Rex eat you. Heck, the future might have been better for it! I know mine would've!"

"Crybaby! I see you found that blasted sword. Did that make a happy ending? Is the cosmos safe?" Spike laughed harshly. "I guess so. We're young again and not being thrown from place to place."

"Time seems to work like before," Danny replied, looking toward Murg. The calico nodded. "Spike, aren't you tired of running away?"

Spike slowly stood. "Yeah. I am tired of running. Time to fight. Give me the bicycle or I'll beat it out of you. If they're really connected, I can't let you have any of it." He teetered a bit as he stepped toward Danny.

Danny's hand itched to grab the sword. "I never figured you as a chicken, but running away is being chicken, Ernest."

"Danny . . . ."

"I ain't running!" Spike snapped. "And don't call me Ernest. I've got a plan."

"To get a bunch of money together so you can run away from home?"

"I ain't running, I'm starting over. Now give me the bicycle!" Spike dove for him.

Danny easily dodged. Spike lurched after him. Danny jumped aside, giving Spike a small shove. He landed hard, his nose inches away from cow droppings. After a moment, he rose to his knees, shaking his head to clear it.

"Spike . . . ." Danny began.

Spike suddenly lunged, grabbing Danny's shirt. Danny spun away, slipping free. Spike lunged again and again, clutching only air each time. Finally, Spike collapsed, where he lay retching. After a while, Spike wiped his mouth, then climbed to his feet. "Keep the bicycle! See if I care! I'm going to stay here. The Babe'll probably take care of me. We're kindred spirits. Maybe I'll learn to play baseball. Yeah, I like the sound of that. I can be a star! I'm bigger and stronger than most guys my age, especially now, eighty years ago, and I know about weightlifting."

As Spike turned to walk away, Danny asked, "What about your brothers and sister?"

"They'll be okay."

"You think so? Ike's already hitting Raymond," Danny called out.

Spike turned around, walking back to confront him. "Say what?"

Danny told him about the night he and Jason had visited Mr. Pickett. "If you leave, Raymond will probably take your place. Who's next, your sister?" Danny thought of Sarah and flushed angrily. "How can you leave her with Ike?! Why don't you tell somebody?! I wish I had my sister back! You . . . you don't even care about your sister!"

"She's a ditz, but she's still my sister! I won't have to leave her with Ike if you'll give me the bike!"

"I said I'd help you catch baseballs. Why do you want the bicycle if I help you get what you want—take you back and let you carry out your plan?" Danny asked.

"I . . . uh, this sounds crazy," Spike laughed, then said, "but it's my friend. I even named it Grand Slam Slugger. Sometimes I swear the thing was trying to talk to me."

"Not so crazy. I've thought that, too. Kalyde II is like a friend. How would you like it if somebody stole your friend?"

"You already stole my friends! Hank and Rocky were my friends until that Oktoberfest race. After that, they wouldn't listen to me. So I know how it feels!"

"They weren't your friends. They were like robots, doing whatever you told them to do!" Danny snapped. Eye to eye, the two angrily stared.

Danny thought about his friends. He wished they were here. Jason and Christina were still mad at him, maybe even madder than before since he didn't know how much real time had passed. With the jumbling of things, could he go back to moments after he left? He thought of Gretchen. She could help him figure this out. End the feud. Break the cycle—the cycle of violence.

What had she suggested? Show Spike his past and his future!

"Spike, I guess everybody needs a friend."

"I don't need nobody. I just need some cash."

"Well, I'm not your friend, and I don't plan on being one. But, well, if you'll keep your end of the deal, come travel with me . . . ."

"You didn't say nothing about traveling . . . ."

". . . listen to what I have to say, I'll do what I said I'd do. Take you to where you can catch home runs, then take you home. You can sell them, move out, break up the family, and start all over."

"What's the catch?" Spike asked suspiciously.

"None. Just time-traveling, sight-seeing and talking."

"I do that, you'll help me gather baseballs and return me to the future?"

"I said I would, yes," Danny replied.

"I don't trust you."

"Then an act of good faith." Danny unsheathed the sword, then held the scabbard in one hand. With a thought and an image, he recreated the magic tandem. "Get on. I'll show you how to heal yourself."

Spike climbed on the front seat, all the while glancing warily over his shoulder. "This ought to be interesting. Don't try anything tricky. I'm getting my strength back."

Danny and the cats settled on the magic tandem. "Ready?" With two meows, Danny shoved off.

"Where we going?" Spike asked.

"Just around. Moving seems to make the magic more powerful." As they rode through the countryside, Danny explained using the power of the magic to heal.

Spike closed his eyes and concentrated. Moments later, he touched his face, a look of amazement spreading across his features. "Wow! Way cool! This is the best I've felt in . . . in, I . . I don't know how long. Nothing hurts. Nothing at all! So how come I'm still tired?"

"I think it's mental fatigue."

"Well, let's get this show on the road so I can catch some baseballs, sell them, and tell Ike *hasta la vista!*" Spike smiled. "I got places to go! People to see!"

"I want you to picture Ike as a kid."

"He was never a kid."

Danny admitted it was difficult to see the looming, lurching Frankenstein of a man as a youth. "How old's Raymond?"

"Eight."

"Picture Ike at eight years old," Danny began. Spike scowled. "Did you ever visit Ike's home, where he grew up?"

"Yeah. About two years ago, we visited Ike's father on the Pickett Ranch outside Amarillo. That's near the panhandle for you foreigners."

Danny refused to take the bait. "Picture the Pickett ranch in your mind. See Ike as eight and his father, your step-grandfather, at Ike's age. Those two probably look a lot alike."

"They do. I've seen pictures."

"Use those pictures to create an image, then add feelings, smells and sounds."

"I know how ta do this!" Spike snapped. "I've traveled time, too, ya know."

"Fine. Tell me what you're seeing in your mind, so I can help."

"You mean link imaginations? Like you did with that alien, Kalyde? I want no part of that."

"Then I won't help you . . . ."

"Danny . . . ." Murg began. "Must we do this?"

"Yes. We'll only watch. I promise. Spike, just take us there."

"Why?" Spike's lower lip stuck out.

"Because it's important to know why! When I visited Socrates, he told me asking questions is important. Plato agreed. He also said something about turning one's eyes to the truth. Your truth and . . . motivation stem from the past."

"Aw, the truth is based on who won and wrote history."

"Don't you want to know why Ike hits you?" Danny asked.

"I know why! He enjoys it!" Spike snarled.

"I said the same thing about you. Did you enjoy abusing me?!" Danny snapped.

Spike looked skyward, then sighed. "I just want to get this over with, so we can catch homers and I can tell Ike, *ciao*."

"Then see the Pickett Ranch," Danny said through gritted teeth.

As they raced along the undulating road, Spike talked about the west Texas ranch. How the slaughterhouse and crimson barn with the Marlboro advertisement sat close to the road. Cows, chickens and a turkey wandered about the grounds, hunting for weeds or grain. Eating whatever it could find, a dirty-white billy goat stood in the yard of the ranch house. Since Waylon Pickett was a vet, Old Glory always hung from the flagpole next to the front gate. Under the eaves of the front porch, two large swings rocked in the wind. In the corner near the front door, in the shadows, a broom and an axe handle waited for angry hands.

Ike had always been big for his age, awkwardly so, his jaw already square and his beady eyes set deep and dark. As a youth, his hair had been cut militarily short, giving his head the appearance of a jar. The main difference between now and then came from Ike's face, mostly unlined and still touched by the innocence of youth.

With the roar of charging lions, the bright flare engulfed them. They raced ahead through the churning mists, then shot onto the rainbow tunnel. Although the time passage appeared worn, it seemed brand new when compared to earlier, when the barriers were crumbling. The gaps in the walls remained; but they appeared stable, no longer threatening to collapse.

"Do you find this scary?" Spike asked, the howling wind tugging at his words.

"Not any more," Danny replied. "Keep your mind on eight-year-old Ike and the Pickett ranch. Young Ike is walking from the house to the barn." Danny pictured a typical summer day.

The howling wind faded with the brightness, leaving them coasting along a two-lane road cutting through flat fields and pastures filled with Brahma bulls and cattle. The trees swayed, then thrashed as a dust devil crossed the road. The dirty whirlwind bounced several times before racing into the distance.

"Never thought I'd come back here. Still don't want to," Spike murmured, then shivered as if catching a chill. "Hmm. The place looks freshly painted. A new flag, too. And different benches. Hey, who's that by the road? A kid?" Spike asked. "He looks younger than us."

Danny remained silent as they rolled to a stop near the kid. For an eight-year-old, he had long outgrown his overalls, standing tall with long,lanky limbs and big feet like a puppy ready to grow. His ears looked funny, sticking out like handles on a milk bucket. When the boy looked at the bicycle, his eyes danced wildly. He dropped his bucket and ran closer. "Howdy! Great bike! Are you kids new? I'm Ike!" His smile was broad and infectious.

Spike's jaw dropped, pulling him down with it. Danny thought Spike might collapse. After a moment, Spike shook his head. "Did you really say Ike? Ike Pickett?"

"Yeah, what's your names? And kitties! You ride with kitties? What are their names? Can I pet them?"

"I'm Danny. This is Murgitroyd and Krindee. If they allow it, you may pet them."

"Amazing," Krindee projected. "In some ways, Ike reminds me of Comet."

"Not very bright, eh?" Murg replied.

"I was talking about innocence."

"I- I'm Spike," the bully finally managed.

"Spike! Ike, we are a lot alike!" the boy laughed. Spike's face flashed white as if he'd seen a ghost. "What kind of bicycle is it?" young Ike asked as he pet the cats.

"A special one. It's a modified . . . Spacelander." Danny glanced at Spike. He appeared to be in shock, staring vacantly at Ike. "Have you always lived here?"

"Yeah. Grandpa Warren and his grandpa before that lived here," Ike replied. "My grandpa still lives here, but he's sick. I think mom said my great-great grandpa built this ranch."

"That's why it feels like this," Spike muttered. "Probably built on beatings."

Danny wasn't sure what he was talking about; and yet, he felt uncomfortable. The heat swarmed. The stillness bespoke of dire expectations. Danny expected a farm to be lively, but despite seeing livestock, it felt subdued. Worn down. Beaten.

"A bike," Ike sighed. "I've always wanted one, but dad won't let me have one. Doesn't help me get any work done, he says, just out joy-riding, letting my mind wander." He looked at his big hands. "With hands this size, gotta keep them busy, he says."

"Want to go for a ride?" Danny asked. "One of us will give you our seat."

"What???" Spike asked.

"Really?" Ike looked around conspiratorially. "Yeah howdy!"

Danny suddenly felt an air of growing menace as if a storm gathered. Shadows tensed as if ready to flee. "Do . . . do you feel that?"

"This is what I remember," Spike whispered. Sweat poured from him. "I've been inside the barn. I-It's an evil place, full of darkness." His eyes darted everywhere, staying away from the crimson barn.

Ike looked longingly at the bike, his expression hangdog. "I'd love to, but I'd get in big trouble."

"Chase, come on," Spike said. "Let's leave. He's gonna get in trouble."

"IKE!" came a harsh call from the barn. "Ike Waylon Pickett!"

Ike and Spike cringed. "Let's go!" Spike began to pedal.

Danny shivered, then grabbed Spike's wrist, copying Krindee's aikido hold. Spike squawked but sat still. "We watch," Danny said through clenched teeth.

"All right! You don't have to twist my arm."

"Yes I do." Danny let go of Spike.

"Why are you doing this?"

"I'm turning your eyes to the truth. The heart of the matter. What has shaped you," Danny replied. He didn't want to stay, but felt he had no other choice. He wasn't rewriting history. If . . . this was happening, it had already happened in some way. But if they stopped it . . . Spike wouldn't be Spike. Wouldn't that be a good thing? Well, good for him anyway. It would make his life easier.

"Don't think like that," Murg projected. "Remember, you best affect things in the present. It behooves us to make changes in our time, in our lives, not in other times. We are to learn from the past, not poke and prod dog-eared events to do our bidding."

"Yeah, I know. If I didn't change things to save Mom and Sarah, I'm not going to change things to help Spike and me."

"IKE!"

Ike grabbed the bucket and sprinted toward the barn. Just before he reached the open doors, a tall, disjointed man of ropy sinews and protruding bones stepped from the shadows. Sweat from matted hair left clean streaks in the oil, dirt and straw-flecked grime covering Waylon Pickett's harsh face. Both arms sported tattoos, one scrolling all the way to a big clenched fist. "Whatcha doing, boy?" The 'Frankenstein' rancher spat something dark.

"Bringing you the bucket! See!" Ike held up the bucket.

"I can't watch this," Krindee said.

"Cor-ror-o'lans could learn much from cats."

"Coldheartedness."

"At one time, this was not considered bad. Spare the rod, spoil the child."

As his dark gaze sucked the life from everything it touched, Waylon's hands unclenched, then clenched again, bone white under the grime. "I see. I see we have company. I see that if you had *really* been bringing me the bucket, I'd already have it." Waylon Pickett looked at his massive hands, then spat again, leaving a tobacco stain.

"You boys there on your girly bicycle, get out of here. We're a hard-working family. No time for this kind of foolishness." He lurched forward, one foot dragging.

"But . . . ." Spike began.

"At home, don't they teach you to respect your elders?" Waylon snapped. "Get outta here before I have to teach you for them. Ike!" His hand shot out, snatching the boy's ear.

"Daddy! I . . . ." Ike pleaded.

"Don't talk back to me! Embarrass me in front of other people!" He lashed out, slapping Ike. The boy collapsed. Waylon Pickett grabbed Ike by the collar, yanking him to his feet. "Come on! That's just a tap, but there's gonna be more where that came from if you don't mind me!"

"I don't want to go!"

The Frankenstein rancher stared at Ike, then at the boys and cats on the tandem. "You can leave, anytime, but the sooner the better. You're less likely to get hurt."

Spike started to climb off the tandem. Danny grabbed him. "What are you doing? This is Ike? Ike?! Remember Ike! Ike who beat you?!"

Spike blinked, taken aback. "Yeah. Yeah! You're right! He deserves this. Glad you stopped me," Spike muttered, sounding confused.

"Come on. Let's go."

"Where we going?" Spike asked.

"Backward, thirty or so years," Danny said, trying to ignore the slapping and the crying.

"Uh-uh. No more. I'm done with this!"

"Not yet. We'll travel back to the 1930's and visit Waylon when he was young."

"No way! Your help ain't worth this."

"Then I'll do it without you." Just as before, Danny sent them back in time without ever pedaling. He pictured this place, somewhat different, older, but feeling the same. Waylon would be here, carrying a milk bucket.

Moving at high speed, Waylon let go of Ike, who walked backwards to the house. Time sped, things blurred, day becoming morning then night, the sun setting in the east. Time raced, days and night flickering, mingling in a celestial dance.

"Hey! What's going on here?"

Danny tried to hurry. Things changed, yet stayed the same generation after generation. The new barn was dismantled, then ruins of the burned one appeared. The dark husk flared, burning up brightly, then unburned to stand strong. The ranch house shrank, several rooms unbuilt from the foundation. Flags grew nicer, then were replaced by ragged ones. Horses, buggies and carts replaced cars and trucks traveling the road, which returned to gravel, then rutted dirt.

Spike grabbed him. "Stop! What are you doing?!"

A cloud of dust drifted by, sweeping toward the house. Behind it, the sun peeked over the horizon, silhouetting the trees. The shadows gathered, reluctantly huddling from the coming day.

Danny glanced beyond Spike."Look who's coming."

Spike whirled about. "Oh no!"

The young boy walking toward them carried a bucket in each large hand. He appeared to be nearly ten, with short-cropped hair, a square face and a lantern jaw. By his expression, Waylon daydreamed, wishing he played elsewhere. His face brightened, his dark eyes coming alive when he spotted them. "How-dee! Wow! Never heard of a bike two people and cats could ride on. Mighty impressive," he stammered over the big word as if he'd recently heard it, now testing it. "My name's Waylon Pickett. What's yours?" Danny introduced them, since Spike couldn't speak. Waylon looked at Spike and said, "That's a funny name. Does your dad work for the railroad?"

Spike grimaced. "You milking cows?" Waylon nodded. "Then you better get along before your daddy hits you."

Waylon glanced toward the red barn. It seemed larger than before and breathing like a crimson dragon coming to life. "You know?"

"I can tell," Spike muttered.

"Don't matter none what I do. He'll hit me anyway. He's having a bad day, so I get hit a lot. Gotta take it out on me. Better me than little Edna. He's already put Kenneth in the hospital. Said he got kicked by a cow. But I'm tough, tougher than Kenneth, and when the time comes, Dad's going to get his. You'll see. Momma said what goes around comes around, or when she's talking the Bible, what you sow, you reap."

"WAYLON MAVERICK PICKETT! WHERE ARE YOU!? GET YOUR BUTT RIGHT HERE! RIGHT NOW!"

Cringing, Waylon whirled toward the barn.

Spike looked to Danny, pleading. "It's Warren Pickett. I heard he was a really mean . . . ."

"WAYLON!"

"Don't make me stay this time," Spike pleaded.

"Okay, but only if you'll come with me to one more place without bellyaching."

"Deal."

As they rode away, Warren Pickett grabbed the buckets from his son. Spike and Danny heard a whimpering plea, then a dull, sickening *crack* before time's roar overwhelmed them.

THIRTY-FIVE

Future Tense

As they rode away from the ranch, Spike's face paled, becoming ghostly. He appeared old again, his eyes haunted, peering within as much as without. "What now, Chase?!" Spike snapped. "Haven't you tortured me enough?! We just sat and watched as Warren got his beating! Are we gonna go back a couple more generations, keep going back until I cry?!"

"No. We're going forward now."

"What are you, Chase, the ghosts of Christmas Past, Present and Future all rolled into one? I . . . I don't want your pity."

"You don't have it. Last trip, I promise."

"Why should I trust you?" Spike asked.

"I haven't lied to you, and I showed you how to heal yourself by using the bicycle's magic."

"Then you dragged me back into the past for a beat-a-thon. I know plenty about getting beaten. I'm an expert. I don't need to know any more. So what if beating on their kids is a Pickett tradition? Are you trying to say I'll be like them? Well, I won't be."

Murg yawned.

"You already are," Danny replied as he looked into the distance. "I've seen you hit your brother. Boss him around if he doesn't do what you want."

"I'm different, Wimp."

"It's a start. It's what you know best, Spike."

"I'm Spike. I can handle it. Soon, I'll be out of the house, then nobody and nothing will be able to touch me. I'll have money and won't care."

"Whatever happened to Ernest?"

"DON'T CALL ME ERNEST!"

"Okay! Okay! Have you ever hugged your brothers or your sister?"

"What? Hug? Hugging is for sissies and losers," Spike spat, then grew quiet for a time before asking, "Will there be more beatings in the future where we're going?"

"I think that's up to you," Danny replied. "Picture yourself in ten years."

"We're going to meet the future me? The me after I've cashed in the baseballs?" Spike asked. Danny nodded. "Yee-haw. I'll see a stud! A king! Not a loser like you! Heck, think what you could do with the alien bicycle. You have a teenie-tiny mind and no imagination."

"I don't think this is a good idea," Murg projected. "We should deal with this in the now—the present. Besides, there are theories that hypothesize that bringing two of the same beings together from different times can create serious problems."

"Fine. How would you deal with this in the present?" Krindee asked.

"I told you. Rewrite *The Alien Bicycle*."

"If you don't have a better idea than that, then let's give Danny our support."

"And if there is a disaster? We have wreaked havoc across time."

"Is Danny the first?"

"No, but . . . ."

"If there is a disaster, Danny shall avert it as he has already done several times before."

"I worry because he doesn't have nine lives."

"Well, do you want to see yourself?" Danny asked. "Surely, you won't be disappointed."

"Me in ten years," Spike said with a lazy smile, then laughed and rubbed his hands together. "I'll be bigger, rich, and smiling because Ike's outta my life. I won't need to work, but I'm probably a professional football or baseball player. A superstar. An MVP even. A lean, mean promoting machine. I'll be in lots of ads: Be like Spike! I'll have my own place to live. It'll be huge! Rocky, Raymond and Tabitha can live there with me, as long as they don't get in my way; but Ike won't touch 'em any more. They'll be safe. Yeah, it'll be like old times—good times—when Dad still lived with us; but even better. I'll be the man of the house, like it should be. Maybe Mom will wise up. We'll be one big happy family."

Danny wondered what ten years in the future would be like. A space station? Light sabers? Androids that helped around the yard and house? Cloned athletes and artists? Faster than light travel? The government admitting the truth about UFOs? Cor-ror-o'lans living on earth and people living on Cor-ror-o'lan?

"That is a nice vision," Krindee thought back.

"Spike, keep picturing yourself," Danny said.

"Babes will be hanging all over me," Spike continued. "I can play two sports like Deion! Heck, baseball and NFL MVP!"

The wind heightened, then seemed to be sucked toward them as if they'd taken a giant breath. The white sun appeared, then swallowed them. They raced from the swirling mist, rocketing through the rainbow time tunnel. The walls stood solid and complete, arcing over their heads. The rainbow rode smoothly and shone dazzlingly as if leading to a pot of glittering gold. Danny suddenly wondered if this was a good idea. What if bringing the Spikes together created some sort of strange paradox? Or a rift in time? Or an explosion?! He tried to keep a grip on his wild imagination, which seemed to be outracing the magic bicycle.

"Man! This is so different but the same." Spike looked puzzled.

"A true intellect and master of the spoken language," Murg projected.

"It doesn't look worn or anything. And the winds are warm. I guess the future looks bright, so bright I gotta wear shades!" Spike roared.

Kalyde II and its four riders flew onto the brilliant exit ramp, blasting to brightness, then rolling to a stop before a magnificent, five-story mansion of white brick, pillars, and arched windows darkly tinted to keep out prying eyes and the sun. The lawns and gardens along the long, circular driveway appeared healthy and immaculately groomed. The marble fountain of a bucking bronco glistened in the sunlight, water dancing high before falling. To Danny's ears, the water falling onto the marble sounded like slapping. Again, he wasn't sure this was such a good idea.

"Wow. Look at my house! And my car! Sweet! A Rolls Royce with gold wheels and chrome! Yee-haw! I must be a superstar. I'm in the money." Spike clapped, then rubbed his hands together greedily. "With money, you can do anything because you can buy anything!"

"I have yet to change my opinion," Murg projected.

They rolled to a stop next to the long, black stretch-limo. The big man waxing it, turned and said, "Hey! What are you kids doing here? How'd you get past security at the front gate?!" He tossed the rag onto the ground, freeing his sledgehammer hands.

"I'd like to see Spike Blocker."

Danny tried to relax. Would two Spike Blockers make a

right? Or just create serious problems? He could almost hear an echoing boom as time collapsed upon itself.

"Nobody sees Mr. Blocker." The man strode toward them. "This is private property. You're not supposed to be here!"

"It seems Spike hasn't changed," Murg projected.

Spike climbed off the tandem, prepared to fight. Danny stayed astride the magic bicycle, ready to dodge.

Atop the steps and past the pillars, the front door opened.

"Richard. Richard, let them be."

The large man glanced up, then stepped back. "Yes, Mr. Blocker."

Danny tensed, waiting for the worst to happen when the two Spikes met.

Walking between two large, square-shouldered body guards wearing dark clothing and sunglasses, twenty-five-year-old and flabbily obese Ernest Blocker waddled down the marble steps. Hiding his overlapping bulk, Mr. Blocker 'dressed to impress' in a fine, pin-striped suit, lily-white shirt and black and gold tie. His shoes flashed with every step down. His cane sparkled gaudily as it spun, the gems catching the sunlight. The future Spike stopped at the base of the steps and surveyed his visitors. His eyes hid within folds of pasty-white flesh that draped into long jowls and a triple chin that concealed his neck. Sweat trickled down his face. He sounded winded from his descent, leaning heavily on his cane.

"I'm fat!" Spike whispered, stunned. "A blimp. I . . . I guess I'm not a two -sports superstar."

The guards stood as still as stone statues. Danny sensed something familiar about them.

"If only clothes truly made the man," Krindee thought.

"Still, nice threads," young Spike murmured. "Really stylin'. Hey, with enough money, I can create my own brand! Spikers? Or Blockers for the big and tall!"

Spike's enthusiasm sounded forced to Danny. This isn't what he'd pictured, either.

"There you go. Such grand ideas! Greetings, my younger

self." Mr. Blocker spread his arms wide, encompassing the estate, then looked to Spike. "Do you like what you see, Spike? You imagined it. Made it come true. Made me come true."

"I like this place a lot; but are you really me? You're . . . you're so big." Spike ran his hands down his body. "You waddle when you walk. Fat isn't cool."

"Yes, I am you and you are me in about a dozen years. We are not fat, we are richly appointed. Being large in Roman times was a sign of wealth." Mr. Blocker appeared annoyed, then to change the subject, he waved to his home. "This house is new. Just moved in this month. It took them two years to build it to my specifications. This place is what you pictured, isn't it?" Mr. Blocker asked.

Spike nodded. "It has lots of rooms?"

"Of course," Mr. Blocker nodded. "Room for all those lovely ladies. They come and go, a different babe every night. Once we had money, we finally could get a date."

"Cool! They don't care that you're . . . big?"

"Money will buy whatever we want."

"Really? Cool! So what happened? You caught the baseballs, traveled to the present, sold the balls and moved out?" Spike asked.

Mr. Blocker nodded. Danny sensed he avoided telling them something. "So, what happened to Ike?" Danny asked.

"You know, each day, hundreds, even thousands of people die in the comfort of their own homes. Statistics say that's where most accidents take place. You see, poor ole Ike, well, he kinda fell down the stairs."

"Fell down the stairs?" Danny asked, not believing. He was glad there hadn't been an explosion. Maybe this would turn out okay, except Spike was seeing how rich he would be.

"Spike, Ike would've stolen your money, somehow, some way. He could always make things that were wrong work out for him. Wish I could've squashed him like a bug." With a crunching, Mr. Blocker ground a Wingtipped toe into the concrete. "Reggie,

Page and Vargas helped me . . . get through the grieving period."
His smile didn't reach his nearly flesh-hidden eyes. "In fact, my
friends still work for me." Spike motioned to the man on the
right. His hair was dark red. "This is Vargas toned down a bit."
"Where's his face metal?" Spike asked. "It was righteous."
"Not appropriate attire for one of high finance. Clothes
do make the man, or add the finishing touch, anyway. This," Mr.
Blocker gestured to his right, "is Page. This thousand dollar suit
conceals his tattoos. I've put my associates through security
training and bodyguard instruction. Reggie, poor boy, died
tragically during a shooting exercise." He tsked and shook his
head but appeared unmoved. He checked his watch. "Been two
years now. A good two years. I don't like to be told what to do."
Danny thought he saw Page's cheek twitch.
"So the whole family lives here now?" Spike asked.
"Well, not exactly, but it's better that way. Mom, can you
believe it, died from grief shortly after Ike went to Hell." Mr.
Blocker's expression feigned sadness; what little they could see
of his eyes did not. They were cold and hard.
"I never understood how she could love him," Spike said,
"but I wouldn't expect her to die of a broken heart." The future
Spike shrugged, as if saying no big deal.
"What about Rocky?" Spike asked.
"Don't know. I haven't seen him in several years. He
blamed me for Mother's death. Tabitha's, too. I grew sick of him
saying it was because I broke up the family, so I had him thrown
out a window. He's never returned. Good riddance. I don't need
him. He was a loser. All my family, except me, of course, were
big time losers. Just like Chase, here. L-O-S-E-R." With one pudgy
hand he reached into his jacket, removing a cigarette case. He
then took out a cigarette, inserting it into a golden holder.
Lightning fast, Vargas produced a lighter and lit Mr. Blocker's
cigarette.
"I smoke, too?" Spike asked, stunned and disgusted.
"Ike and Spike, a lot alike," Danny said.

Spike scowled at him. "You said Tabitha's dead? How'd she die?"

After a deep puff and extended exhale, he said, "After Mother died, Tabitha became withdrawn from the world. Then, when she reached fourteen, she ran wild. Made me look tame. Anyway, she O.D.'ed."

"She died of a drug overdose?!" Spike's eyes were wide.

"Tragic. We tried to warn her, but she quit listening a long time ago. She wanted to die. Been there, done that. We got over it. Tabitha didn't. She was never as strong as us."

"Do you deal drugs?" Danny asked, suspecting the worse.

"No, nothing so underhanded or illegal."

"What do you do?" Spike asked.

"We," Mr. Blocker stressed, "are arms and munitions manufacturers and international exporters."

"You're a gun pusher? So it's not the size of the fist, but the size of the gun?" Danny asked.

"Or missile, to be more precise," Mr. Blocker replied. He spun the cane in one hand, watching it sparkle in the sun. After a billowing exhale, he said, "We make millions every year. We attended UT, graduating with a business degree. While in Austin, I met a young man whose father owned Strokers Manufacturing in Houston. I bought in and became a partner. In the last two years, we've experienced unprecedented growth, thanks to those helpful conflicts in the Middle East and Central Europe. One thing history taught me, people are always going to be killing each other, and the easier and more effective you can make it, the more money you make."

As if vomiting a hairball, Krindee gagged. Murg looked at her and blinked slowly.

"Spike, you'll be pleased to know that Raymond works with me. He lives here, when he's not in Houston." Mr. Blocker checked his watch. "Right now, he should be just about finished negotiating a deal with some peace loving Turks."

"Nice to see Spike has evolved."

"So Ike, Mom and Tabitha are dead, and Rocky is gone," Spike said, sounding hollow.

"Just as you wished."

"I never wished that!" Spike snapped. "And I don't want to be fat! I wanted to play sports! Prove I was a winner! Be somebody!"

Mr. Blocker spread his hands wide. "Sure you wished it, because it happened. I am proof. After Ike and Mom died, you felt free. Free from loser parents. You'll find that Tabitha and Rocky become heavy iron balls and chains. Total wet blankets. Losers. Your future lies ahead of you, Spike, seize it, just as I did when I was you."

"What did you do?" Spike asked.

"Got rid of your conscience," he began, looking at Danny, who shivered. "Then I laid claim to the magic bicycle. Today, it's a magnificent motorcycle, the replica of a classic—an Indian motorbike. It makes getting to meetings very easy. And it's environmentally friendly." He blew a cloud of smoke.

"What'd you do, kill the Wimp, too?" Spike asked.

"Kill, as is murder, is such an ugly word." Mr. Blocker smiled. "Rather I should say I left him in the past where no one could identify him. Back then though, the loser didn't carry a sword. I doubt he knows how to use it. He'd probably . . . fall on it and hurt himself."

Danny didn't like where this was headed. Coming here might have been a very bad mistake. He pulled the force field tight, like a glove around him and his friends.

"When you returned to the present, did you ever tell anyone about Ike beating you?" Spike asked.

"Never. Telling Reggie, Page and Vargas was hard enough, don't you remember? We didn't want anyone else to know. If we'd told, it might have ended up in the paper, then everyone would know. Besides, who would've supported my accusations? Certainly not Mother. Love is blind. Take it from me, when you fall in love, you give up your freedom. Never fall in love. Rocky thought about speaking up, but he didn't have the guts. Tabitha and Raymond were far too young to be taken seriously."

"Jason and I would've supported you," Danny told them.

"Ha! You maybe, since you're a chump, but Jason, never!"

"He's my friend. He'd understand," Danny replied.

"He might've, I guess, but he's too busy being wrapped up in self pity." Mr. Blocker tried to look sad, but his narrow black eyes danced gleefully.

"What did you do to him?!" Danny cried.

"Another tragic accident left him without both legs. Now he's half-metal, half-man, and all depressed." Mr. Blocker blew a smoke ring. "Now Christina, there was a fine looking girl. She had such a marvelous voice. That girl could sing. Now, well after experiencing my grandeur, she's recovering in a mental hospital."

Red rage overwhelming him, Danny drew the sword. "Danny! Easy!"

Guns appeared in the bodyguards' hands, aimed at Danny.

"Maybe you are not the same wimp I knew. Interesting. But if you try to kill me, you'll surely die." Mr. Blocker flicked an ash.

"Danny, put down the sword," Murg projected. "This is not the way. Remember what happened last time you wielded the sword."

With an angry hiss of metal, Danny slid the sword back into its sheath. He still quivered, needing to lash out.

"Fear not, Spike. You will see the light. It is inevitable. It has already happened, as you can plainly see. Do you like?" Mr. Blocker asked. Spike appeared stunned. "There are tennis courts, stables and a heated pool out back. Would you like a tour?" With the cane, he gestured to the house.

"Almost like the House of Blue Lights," Danny replied. "Soulless ghosts and ghouls live here."

Spike glanced at him.

"Yes, my walk through that 'haunted house' so long ago, following your path, surprisingly enough, inspired me," Mr. Blocker said.

"Chase inspired you? This loser inspired you?!" Spike asked incredulously. What he didn't say seemed to hang in the air: then how can you be me?

"Yes, quite a surprise, I guess, but it shouldn't be. Look who has inspired us all these years. Ike and Daniel Chase. Both people we hate. Both losers. Both inspired and drove me to be a winner. Come Spike, I'll show you around the Ernest Blocker estate." Mr. Blocker put his hefty arm around Spike's shoulder and guided him away.

"You call yourself Ernest? I hate that name."

"Spike didn't sound very businesslike."

After a couple of steps, Spike pulled free. "You know, I'm not so sure you're me."

"What do you mean?" Mr. Blocker asked, appearing annoyed.

"You're a blimp, and Ike and Chase never, ever inspired me. I didn't want to be anything like them."

"Ike inspired you to leave home. To make something better of yourself. To be a winner."

"That was . . . is desperation," Spike replied.

"In many ways, the same thing. You simply bandy semantics. Danny inspired you because he beat you in a different way, winning races, being popular, and having a beautiful girlfriend. Come now."

Spike grimaced. "I don't find Chase inspirational. I just wanted his cool alien bike. You know, I can't believe you didn't help Rocky and Tabitha. They're just kids. They didn't know any better."

"They didn't want my help! They blamed me for trying to escape. For not being happy with being a loser."

"I wanted to play football or baseball. Did you ever do that?" Spike asked.

"There was no need. We have money! We can pay people to hit somebody. Why should I soil my hands?"

"I enjoy playing sports. I wanted a college scholarship. Show people I'm a winner."

"You don't need to play sports to prove you're a winner. We're rich!"

"A soulless fat cat named Ernest." Spike stared for a minute, then said, "You aren't me and I'm not you. Let's go, Chase." Spike climbed onto the front seat.

"One day, you'll see the light!" Mr. Blocker yelled. "And when you do, seize the moment! The future is what you make it!"

"So is the present," Murg whispered. "That went well."

As they disappeared, backpedaling into the past, neither boy said anything; but Danny wondered, just idly wondered, what it would be like to meet an older Danny Chase. What might he tell himself? That this had all been a terrible mistake?

THIRTY-SIX

Dirty Deeds

Coasting almost soundlessly, a trio of motorbikes rolled down an embankment to stop near a hole in the chainlink fence. The dark-clad riders dismounted and steered their bikes through the gap, then into the darkening woods. The sun was falling fast and would set any minute, allowing the chill and darkness to deepen.

"Nobody'll see them here," Reggie said as he pulled off his helmet. "Good job, Page." His words and breathing steamed in the winter air.

The tattooed boy removed his brainbucket, then shook his hair out. "I found it yesterday."

"We Headbangers are going to hit Chase the air thief where it hurts," Reggie said. He leaned the bike against a tree.

"Why are we going to take her to Spike?" Vargas asked. He readjusted his eyebrow ring.

"To show him who's boss. You got the rope?"

"Uh-huh." The flame-haired boy held up the cord. A light struck the darkness, then dimmed to a flame. "Page, put that out!" Reggie snapped. "You can't smoke now. Don't you watch war movies? They always see guards smoking cigarettes. Now put that out and come on!" Reggie marched into the woods. Grumbling, Page followed. Vargas looked around to get his bearings, then joined the two Headbangers. Reggie led them across a creek, then through some trees to a fence.

"Be quiet," Reggie whispered harshly.

"Won't Chase be surprised?" Page asked. He knelt next to Reggie.

"Just like that Chang kid. His laptop is state-of-the-art. We can get some bucks for it." Reggie smiled evilly.

"Hey, lucky day!" Vargas said as he fondled the rope. "She's in the back yard."

"Guys, do you see somebody over there in the trees?" Page asked.

"Yeah." Reggie nodded. "Page, go make a ruckus in the woods. When the watcher investigates, we'll make the snatch."

Page nodded, then took off, staying low among the cover.

THIRTY-SEVEN

A GATHERING OF SHADOWS

"Ready to go home?" Danny asked Spike as the oversized boy walked toward him. The sunset cast a ruddy glow across the clouds floating beyond the Boston Braves' stadium.

"I guess so. This was the Babe's last game." Spike hefted three baseballs to examine them. Each was autographed. "I caught his last homers. When he was signing these, I . . . I said good-bye. Gonna say good-bye to two friends today. The Babe and Grand Slam Slugger, here." Spike patted the magic tandem. "That's a lot when you don't have much."

Danny didn't know what to say. Although he too had been friendless, Danny refused to be sympathetic, instead staying wary. He checked the force field protecting him and his feline companions. Spike could turn on him any minute. Kill him as Mr. Blocker said he'd done—promised would do one day.

"He might have been lying," Krindee projected.

"Nothing wrong with being careful," Danny thought back.

"You don't trust me, do you?" Spike slipped the balls into his pack, then shrugged it onto his back.

"No. Why should I?"

"I've trusted you," Spike said as he climbed onto the bike.

"Only because you felt you had to get what you want." Danny was tired of traveling, fed up with Spike, and weary of holding the force field in place. His mind felt ready to explode. "What would you have done if you'd met the future me and he said he'd killed you?"

"Probably died of surprise. Let's go before I change my mind and ask if the Babe if he will adopt me."

"I can't believe he didn't become suspicious," Danny said.

"He did. I just told him I was Eddie, Ernie's nephew. Drop me off behind my house?" Spike asked. Danny bristled. "Hey," Spike snapped, "we can either travel there directly or ride there when we return to our time. I'm too beat to walk home."

"Tough," Danny rubbed his eyes. "I don't want to go anywhere near your house, especially if Ike Pickett is roaming the woods hunting raccoons and armadillos." Danny thought of the homing devices. What would the Shadow Daggers think if they suddenly hopped to another place? He shuddered at the thought. "Besides, we have to return to the same spot from which we left; otherwise, there's going to be big trouble."

"Why?" Spike whirled around, making Danny jump. Spike jabbed a finger as he said, "I have to hide these baseballs somewhere. I can't just walk into the house with them. There'd be too many questions. I can hide them in the woods behind the house."

"Danny, you may not be able to manipulate time as well as before," Murg projected. "I still feel shock waves rippling through time, disrupting things."

"Spike . . . ."

"If someone catches me, Chase, one of the other Headbangers, my dad, maybe the police . . . ."

"Shadow Daggers," Danny thought.

"... or whoever, walking home, they'll wonder about all the baseballs scrawled with Babe Ruth's signature. If the baseballs weren't dated, they might think they were fakes; but since they're marked with the production year . . . ."

What would the Shadow Daggers think? Danny sighed. "Spike trust me. It won't take long to get from the road to the woods behind your house."

Keeping the force field intact around him, Danny pictured the farm road and pedaled. Spike joined him. They picked up speed, racing along the downtown Boston street. They weaved between people crossing the road and stopped cars at an intersection. "Picture arriving right after you left for Boston 1916."

"I'm going to miss this!"

When they felt the shift, since they were now well-practiced, they turned into an alleyway. Kalyde II raced into the expanding ball of sunshine. The white brightness changed to a waterfall of colors, then they burst through swirling clouds to rocket through the rainbow tunnel. The time passage appeared only a little worn with minor gaps and tears along the arching walls. The faces and disembodied eyes seemed fewer and farther between. Dim patches lay scattered along the rainbow bridge; but some stretches flickered like lights along a runway, encouraging them home.

"We're home," Danny said, the last of his words lost in the *whoosh* of their arrival. For a moment, they appeared on a dark road, then just as quickly, they disappeared in a bright flash of light. Danny received the image of a gray rock, its rectangular head and thin protrusion making it look like a war hammer. Two dead trees were nearby. One stood proud, though gnarled and pock-marked. The second tree lay long, the top hollow and the bottom completely pulled free, the roots spread as if petrified fingers splayed wide.

In a rushing *whoosh* of wind that whipped through the dark forest, the time-travelers rolled to a stop. The moon rose, its orange-gold face peering over the tops of the trees. Crisp shadows stretched long, gathering where the light failed to touch.

"Hey! What?! We're near your home! You . . . . Why did you . . . H-hey it's-it's dark," Danny stammered. The woods seemed caught in a silvery-blue haze thick with shadows.

"Yeah. I wonder what time it is?" Spike looked around. "You said we'd return at the same time; but we didn't."

Danny discovered that his hand drifted to the sword. He wouldn't need it. He was protected, right? "Were you picturing the moment after you left?"

"Yeah, I was. Were you? I think you just wanted to get me in trouble." Spike looked around, frowned, then climbed off the tandem. "What day is it?! If I've been gone long, Ike might've . . . . built up a head of steam."

When was now? Danny wondered. Had damaging the rainbow caused them to overshoot? If so, not only did the homing devices suddenly change locations, but they'd been missing for several hours, only to suddenly reappear elsewhere. What did the Shadow Daggers think now? This kind of thinking caused his stomach to ache and his head to throb.

"It is the same day you left, January 7th," Murg projected. "Some three hours later, about eight o'clock."

"A stitch in time," Krindee thought.

"You know because you're an alien master of time, right?" Danny thought back. "You know about time vortexes and multiple gates and such."

"Time master, yes, as are all cats to varying degrees," Murg replied.

"I'm surprised the Shadow Daggers haven't kidnapped and tested felines."

"They have already tried. We are too smart for them," Murg replied. "Now stay alert."

"It's about eight, same day," Danny told Spike.

"Really? How do you know?"

"I get a sense of it from the bicycle," Danny replied.

"Oh. I see." Spike clearly didn't; but he wasn't going to ask.

"Spike, I'm outta here. My dad'll be wondering where I am. Probably thinks I'm hiding until I can come up with a better story than being shot at by the Headbangers. If he didn't believe that happened, he certainly won't believe that an ancient sorceress from Camelot tried to kill me and steal my bicycle."

"Yeah. I can see that. Hey. Thanks," Spike said gruffly as he held out his hand. Danny looked at it, then Spike. "Still think I'm going to kill you, don't you?"

"You, the future you, didn't say it happened right after we got back. Good luck, Spike. I'm not you, but I'd . . . ."

"You're right. You're not me."

"Thank your lucky stars," Murg thought.

" . . . hide the baseballs, contact an agent, let him handle the sales anonymously for you—that means without divulging your name, then . . . ."

"That sounds good. Yeah, I like that. Thanks."

" . . . talk with your brothers and sister, Tabitha. Maybe if you all speak with your mom about Ike abusing you . . . ."

"You don't know nothin' about nothin'."

" . . . if your mom doesn't believe you, there are numbers you can call—help lines. Or talk to the school counselor. They'll protect you and your brothers and sister."

"You think you're so smart, don't you?" Spike snarled.

"No, just trying to be creative and stay alive. Spike, in the future, we saw that the only family you will have is Raymond. You're rich, cold-blooded, fat and friendless."

"Yeah. So?" Spike snapped, scowling.

"You didn't like that, did you?"

"I can't believe I'm going to be that fat and lazy—a slug. And I wouldn't throw Rocky out a window. That's something Ike would do."

"Spike, until this moment, have you ever seriously considered gathering Rocky, Raymond and Tabitha and seeking help, talking to people and seeking protection?" Danny asked.

"Hell no! No one would believe us!" Spike snarled. "I'll bet no one ever believed Ike, Waylon or Warren . . . ."

"I've been told times change. Remember, Ernest Blocker never considered this seriously either. Even if Jason won't be a witness, I will. I promise. Believe me, they won't think I'm in on something with you. Everyone knows I don't like you."

"That's true," Spike replied thoughtfully. "Why would you? Hey, why *are* you helping me?"

"I care for Jason and Christina, very much."

"Maybe the Headbangers will go away after I'm gone, huh?" Spike asked.

"Something like that."

"Good, I wouldn't want you to be helping me . . . just to be helping me."

"Heaven forbid."

"Spike, if I thought changing Kalyde II into an cattle prod and zapping you until you spasmed the rest of your life away was the right thing to do, I'd do it. But that wouldn't make me feel better in the long run nor solve my problems. Most of which are caused by you!"

"A conscience can be a problem, buddy boy. Whatta ya gonna do with that sword?" Spike pointed. "I'd bet it'd bring some bucks if you sold it to a collector or the right kind of shop."

"Maybe if I keep it on Kalyde II, it'll keep away Reggie and the Headbangers."

"If it comes down to it, it doesn't stop bullets."

"I've outrun them before," Danny replied.

"Sooner or later, that'll give away your secret."

"If they learn about Kalyde II, they'll learn about the baseballs." It galled Danny to think his enemy knew his secret; but his closest friends did not. "If that happens, it'll be Ike and Spike, a lotta like. Heck, fatso Spike might make Ike look like a kindly old grandpa."

Spike growled.

Before he could speak, Danny said, "Who knows? The future is certainly not set in stone. According to the future you, I wasn't carrying a sword last time. Now I am. Things change. Time changes. Somebody even said people change."

Something *snapped* in the dark woods behind them. Danny turned, still wary of Spike.

"What's that?" Spike asked, moving closer.

Danny turned. "What?"

"That?" Spike pointed beyond him.

Remembering the oldest trick in *The Sneaky and Underhanded Handbook,* Danny cautiously rolled away from Spike and looked into the woods. A bouncing light pierced the darkness, casting long shadows before it as though bloodhounds. Kicking up sticks, leaves and dirt, a chill wind blew toward them carrying an acrid stench.

"Oh no!" Danny drew the sword. It cleared the scabbard with a metallic ringing.

"What?" Spike gasped.

Wasn't Morgan Le Fay dead and gone? And if not, could the sorceress find him anywhere, Danny wondered? Would this never end? He readied himself for a fight. He'd run long enough.

Danny suddenly realized he didn't feel Morgan Le Fay's foul presence. Danny looked more closely, noticing the lack of emerald radiance. Was that a flashlight?

"I hear voices. And smell familiar scents," Murg projected.

"I'm jumping at shadows. Maybe it's just . . . Oh, great. It's the Headbangers," Danny whispered.

"The dudes are here?" Spike stuffed his bag inside the fallen hollow log.

Danny mentally checked his protective shield, then gently altered the magic tandem. It squealed quietly as it shifted into his normal-looking bicycle. He sheathed the sword and put a foot on a pedal, ready to go. "I'm out of here."

"Danny, I smell a friend of yours. You can't leave," Murg projected.

"They've kidnapped somebody? Christina?" The light shined on them, blinding Danny.

"Hey, Reggie, it's Spike! What's he doing out here?" Vargas asked.

"And Chase! Spike's with Chase!" Page said.

"Too perfect," Reggie chuckled. "Feels like Christmas all over again."

"Won't he be surprised to see her with us," Page laughed.

"Vargas, you idiot, I keep telling you, it's a he," Reggie snapped. "Spike, I see you finally caught Chase. About flamin' time."

"Yeah, finally," Spike grunted.

Danny looked to the felines. They were gone, the cats having hopped off and snuck away. "Murg? Murg? Krindee?"

"Watching with great interest."

"Got a surprise for you, Chase," Reggie said. A gun hammer click-cocked. "Vargas, haul it into the light so he can see!"

After some scuffling and a yelp, Vargas dragged a black shadow into the flashbeam. The light seemed to catch the white star on the retriever's forehead.

"Comet!" Danny cried.

"Now, Chase, you're going to tell us how you escaped us the last few times. How did you get out of that house?"

"Reggie . . . ."

"Shut up, Spike! I lead the Headbangers now, *not you!* Two more have joined because of *my* leadership." Reggie gestured to the right and the left. Two figures stepped from the woods, one thin and bony and the other the size of a mature tree trunk.

"Now, what do you have to say for yourself, Chase? You gonna tell us how you escaped, or do we shoot your mutt?" The silhouette of the gun's nose slid into the flashbeam.

"You wouldn't believe my bicycle is enchanted by Merlin, would you?" Danny asked. Silence. "Or that I got it from an alien? That it's metal from the heart of a star and does whatever your mind imagines?"

"Shoot the mutt! He's suckin' up good air, too!" Reggie snarled.

"Wait! You're being watched, too!"

"Say what?!" Reggie snapped. The gun barrel shifted to Danny.

"You're being watched by government agents," Danny said. In a few minutes, Danny expected the Shadow Daggers to arrive; but did he have a few minutes? "Can you gals help?"

"We don't need instructions. Concentrate on what's happening to you."

"Shoot the mutt!"

"Wait! Give me a minute to explain!" Danny cried. Reggie nodded. "I work with my dad, who works for the Air Force. They're testing a new product. Black box stuff. Hush hush, ya know." Danny suddenly had an idea.

"Sh . . . ."

"Reggie!" Page squawked. "Remember, somebody was watching Chase's house when we swiped the mutt."

"Hmmm." Reggie was thoughtful.

Danny shivered. Somebody watching his house? That didn't matter now. He could deal with it later. For now, saving Comet and getting away from the hoodlums were his first priorities.

"I have two devices on my bicycle," Danny began. "One is a tracking device so the powers-that-be can find me. The other turns my bicycle invisible and silent by warping light and sound waves. I'll show you."

"Fine, but don't touch that sword or you won't be stealin' my air any longer," Reggie snapped.

"Dude, that's a bad lookin' blade."

"Page, don't get close to him, you idiot! Don't move! Chase, show us or the mutt's history!" Reggie snarled.

"I'm reaching for something." Danny slowly pulled a red metal box from under the frame. Still connected to the bicycle, wires trailed from the device. It was the best he could imagine under the circumstances. "Now watch!" Danny started to reconnect the device.

"Wait!" The darkness behind the flashlight shifted. "Page, take some rope and tie it to the bicycle."

"We don't . . . ."

"Take it off the mutt," Reggie snapped.

After a whine and a few moments, Page cautiously approached. The rope dangled in the dirt behind him. His gaze still on Danny, Page looped the rope around Danny's leg, then through the spokes of a wheel.

"That's good, Page, now get back here!"

Page grabbed the sword and yanked as he moved away. The sword never moved, so he stumbled, landing on his behind.

"Page! Leave that cleaver alone! Get back here!" Reggie barked, then loosed a string of curses. "Chase, get on with it!"

Danny imagined fading away to nothingness. It didn't matter whether they were transparent or that the protective field deflected and rearranged light, making him invisible.

"Hey! Where'd he go?" Vargas gasped.

"The ropes float in the air," Page replied.

"It's still attached to the little air thief!" Reggie snapped.

"See, I spoke the truth about the government," Danny began. "The Men in Black, actually there's a woman too, are watching to make sure this device doesn't fall into enemy hands." He watched in amusement as they searched the woods; all but Reggie shifted nervously.

"Chase, show yourself, or we start shooting. I mean it. We can drop you where you stand. Chase! Come on, or we're blasting away!"

A shotgun chucked ready, followed by a harsh voice in the darkness. "If there's going to be any shooting, I'll be doing it, boys!"

THIRTY-EIGHT

Nick of Time

"Funny how life works, sometimes, ya know." Massive and gnarled, Mr. Pickett looked at home among the twisted trees, stumps, and shadows. His dark eyes caught the moonlight, glinting madly as though he were Dr. Frankenstein instead of his monster. White, hammer fists gripped a shotgun. Its barrel gleamed silvery, excited at the prospect of violence. "Out hunting 'coons and 'dillos and what kind of infestation do I find? Weasels." He spat a dark stream of tobacco juice.

Danny wasn't glad to see Mr. Pickett; but he intended to use the diversion. "Murg? Krindee?"

"'Ice and dust particles flying through space is safe'," Murg mindspoke.

"Huh? Oh! Thanks for taking Comet to safety."

"I'm sure I will regret this moment for the rest of my nine lives."

"I'm gonna leave. They've forgotten about me. They can settle this among themselves."

"You're really going to let them kill each other?" Krindee asked, a shrill edge to her thoughts,

"I don't think it will come to that," Danny replied. "I'm betting the Shadow Daggers will come looking for me, now that the homing devices are operating in this time again. I expect them to arrive any second."

"Not if you leave. They will follow you," Krindee thought.

"I'll drop one transmitter and keep the other. We should go home now, to my normal bicycle. I have to put the second device on it and stash Kalyde II."

"Our lucky night, Headbangers. A two for one bonus on air thieves tonight." Reggie aimed his gun at Pickett.

"There's only five of you." Mr. Pickett smiled, flashing crossed and crooked teeth. "Ernest, where you been, boy?"

Spike scowled. "Don't call . . . ."

"Ernest?" Page laughed. "Ernest Blocker?! As in 'Frank and Ernest'?" Vargas and Reggie grinned.

Spike glared, sobering Page and Vargas.

One fist holding the shotgun like a blunt spear, the other swinging like a hammer, Ike Pickett lumbered toward Spike. "You know what happens when you're late, Ernest." Mr. Pickett shotgun-whipped Spike, catching him flush with the barrel. As Spike dropped to his knees, Mr. Pickett snapped the shotgun around, aiming at one Headbanger after another.

Gun hammers cocked loudly. Fingers turned white, tightening on triggers.

"You got a lotta nerve, old man," Reggie snapped

"More than you'll ever have, sonny boy," Mr. Pickett responded.

Reggie glared at Spike as he rose groggily to his feet. "Spike, I wouldn't let anybody do that to me! But you're one of us—a Headbanger—and Headbangers stick together."

"You're part of a gang, are you, Ernest? Not a smart idea! You're part of the Pickett family now." Mr. Pickett drove the butt toward Spike.

Spike caught it in both hands. Yelling at the top of his lungs, Spike twisted with all his might. "No more, do you hear?! No more!"

Danny nearly yelled encouragement. Then he remembered it was Spike.

"That a way, Spike!" Page yelled.

"Get him, Spike!" Vargas cried.

Mr. Pickett kneed Spike, dropping him to all fours.

Reggie fired once, then twice, his gun spitting twin forks of fire.

Startling Danny, bullets ricocheted off the invisible force field. Sparks flew, then the slugs ripped through the trees.

Mr. Pickett whirled. The shotgun roared, unleashing a blast.

Caught in the crossfire, Danny prepared to bolt, even if he made lots of noise. Then Danny saw Reggie grab his chest. His mouth hanging slack, his eyes rolled back, as he collapsed. Danny stopped, stunned by the death. He'd seen people "die" on TV. It had never been like this.

As the guns roared on, one of the boys in the shadows screamed. Mr. Pickett cursed as he grabbed his leg, then turned loose another explosion of shrapnel. Vargas and Page cried out in shock and pain, then silence.

Spike slammed both fists across Ike Pickett's back. Pickett staggered forward, then whirled as he drew a knife. Spike jumped back.

"They're killing each other!" Krindee telepathically screamed.

"Murg, I gotta do something! This could be why Spike became the amoral Mr. Blocker of the future. Who would've thought Spike could get any worse?" Danny glanced at the sword. That wouldn't help. Violence led to violence; Spike was a perfect example. Danny felt infected; otherwise, why use the sword?

Einstein's words returned to Danny. Knowledge and imagination were power. He could manipulate time. He knew what was going to happen. He could prevent it by going back in time. Then maybe as Plato said, gazes could be shifted. Danny decided to change his role, as Shakespeare had suggested.

Danny thought about the copse of trees just down the road from his house. His ordinary ten-speed leaned locked against the tree. The slanting rays of the setting sun cut through the branches, mingling shadows and bright red streaks along the bike.

"Danny . . . ."

"Gonna cut you bad, boy!" Ike Pickett roared.

"Do your worst! I ain't takin' this . . ." Spike rattled off a string of profanity, ". . . anymore. You hear, me, Sir?!"

"Murg, I won't change time much!" The world disappeared in a bright flash, then Danny catapulted backward through colorful mists. They swirled in his wake as he sped rear reflector first onto the rainbow tunnel. Almost before he could blink, Danny reappeared in the dark gathering of trees. He slammed on the mental brakes and squeezed the handbrakes, stopping inches from his plain ole bicycle. Darkness cloaked the two-wheeler.

It wasn't supposed to be dark! He'd aimed for five o'clock, which would have given him plenty of time.

Through the trees ahead, headlights played among the trunks. Danny peered at his watch, watching the glowing hands spin. After a few seconds, they finally settled, resting on seven-fifteen. In about forty-five minutes shots would be fired! How had this happened?! He'd been aiming for daylight, planning on riding home to make an anonymous phone call to the sheriff about the gunfight!

Danny snapped his fingers. The ripple in time must still be affecting time travel! Should he try again? Danny was sorely tempted; but he wasn't sure where he might end up. Another time trip might make things worse! He'd have to race home and call the sheriff. Surely he could do that in forty-five minutes.

What had been the name on the mailbox next store to the Pickett's? Something weird. Without it, the dispatcher might not believe him.

The name hadn't been weird, not exactly, but a strange hero's name. Something Mexican. It started with a Z.

Danny paused at the edge of trees near the street, waiting for another car to pass. He wished Murg were here. With her feline memory, she would've recalled the name. Something to do with swords. ZORRO! That was it! J. Zorran!

As Danny rode from the woods, a paranoid thought struck. What would the Shadow Daggers think? Would they come looking for him? Worse, the Shadow Daggers might be waiting for him?! He couldn't ride Kalyde II home! They might confiscate the magic bicycle! And what would they say about Joan of Arc's sword?!

Danny rolled Kalyde II back into the woods. He glanced at his watch. He didn't want to make the magic bicycle into a watch. He might be searched; if so, he didn't want to be caught with two identical timepieces.

Danny closed his eyes and concentrated, thinking about silver and silence. As Kalyde suddenly shrank, a flash of light bleached the woods. The transformation finished almost without a sound, the squeaking mimicking upset chipmunks. Darkness and quiet returned as a silver wristband settled in Danny's hand.

I'm getting better, Danny thought as he slipped on the silver band. He'd made less noise than ever. Now he needed to work on muting the bright flash.

Danny examined the silver wristlet. It made his arm appear to be a warrior's, like Conan or Sha-zam, except that he lacked muscles. Danny wished he could be as brave as a warrior and as smart as Aristotle and Einstein.

Danny hid the sword, then ran to his old bicycle. He quickly unlocked his two-wheeler, then coiled the lock under the seat. After switching the homing devices onto his old bicycle, he hopped aboard. A glance at his watch told him time slipped away, leaving less than forty minutes. Danny sped home. What if the Shadow Daggers waited for him? He could tell them what was happening, and they'd tell the sheriff. That'd be even faster!

In a couple of minutes, Danny neared home. He slowed, looking for dark sedans. Nothing appeared out of the ordinary; and yet, the neighborhood seemed strange, a nervousness in the air as if something was going to happen. Could they have found him by satellite?

Danny pulled into his driveway. The only illumination came from the front porch light. It cast shadows out from the bushes, looking like twin bogeymen. Hopping off his bicycle, Danny sprinted for the door. He pulled the key from his pocket, slid it shakily into the lock, then twisted, hearing a *click*.

A huge hand fell on his shoulder. "What's your hurry, son?"

THIRTY-NINE

The Long Arm of the Law

"You nervous?" A deep voice asked as the strong hand jerked him around. "Where's the fire?"

Danny swallowed heavily and stared, trying to regain his breath and composure. He'd jumped at least a foot. Had this . . . guy stepped from the shadows?

A shadow with the pale stare of Death, the man loomed in all black, from his hat, along his face, down his coat all the way to his pitch gloves and dark shoes. The Shadow Dagger stood relaxed, but Danny sensed the Black-Ops agent coiled to act.

Danny started to reply, felt he would stammer and stopped. After a deep breath, he recognized the man as one of Colonel Hawker's men—the unnamed stranger who'd stopped outside his closet. "Where's my father?" Danny asked. "I must speak to him! Dad! Dad!"

"Calm down! He's working late. Now, I asked you a question. What's your hurry?"

"Somebody's going to die! I have to call the sheriff!" Danny whirled around and opened the door.

The Shadow Dagger spun him around, bringing Danny eye to eye. "Explain yourself," the kneeling man in black demanded. His voice stung like barbs on a lashing whip.

Danny sucked in a deep breath, thought, then said, "After school, I followed Spike home. He'd stolen my bicycle seat and I wanted it back!"

"I see it here." The agent nodded toward the two-wheeler.

Danny nodded. "I got it back! That's when the trouble started!"

"Go on." As if he could read the truth, the Shadow Dagger's glare pierced Danny.

"Spike's gang, the Headbangers, showed up. They're a bunch of thugs! Reggie Tuckett is part of them, along with a tattooed kid and one with bright orange hair. There were two others there, too, new guys, I don't know their names. While I was arguing with Spike, they just suddenly appeared out of the woods. They had guns!

"They were going to shoot me, but Spike's stepdad, Mr. Pickett, showed up carrying a shotgun. He blew his top when he learned Spike had been stealing and was part of a gang. He hit Spike, then they fought! I grabbed the seat and raced home! I gotta tell somebody! They'll kill each other!"

As Danny tried to turn back to the door, the black man held him fast. "Where have you been since school?"

"I told you! Following Spike! Who are you? Are you one of Colonel Hawker's men?" Danny asked. The man in black nodded. "Good! Then you can call the sheriff faster than I can! Don't you have a cellphone?" Danny decided to let his imagination run amok. "Or a wristwatch communicator? A lapel button you can talk into? I heard those replaced the headsets."

"I am not calling the sheriff," the man said coolly. "I don't believe you. Now, tell me the truth." His gaze seized Danny, making it hard to breathe.

Danny suddenly realized this man had simply watched while the Headbangers had stolen Comet. Danny started to shake. "You're not going to call? You don't care, do you? One of Colonel Hawker's men would care. I know they would. Or a-are you an alien? A Durlen?"

"What?! I heard you mention them before. Some kind of shapechangers and an enemy of the Cor-ror-o'lan, right?"

Danny's eyes widened as he stared past the man in black. "Oh no! There's two of you!"

As the man in black spun around, he drew a gun. Just as quickly, he whirled back to Danny. "There's no one there. Now listen to me . . . ." He screamed as the bright flash from the wristlet blinded him. As the man's hands went to his eyes, Danny slipped free, shoving the door open and darting inside.

He locked the door and ran to the phone. He had to call before it was too late. The Shadow Dagger didn't care about anything or anyone but aliens.

The front door suddenly slammed open.

Like a deer caught in headlights, Danny hesitated. Should he rush into a room? Lock the door and call the sheriff? Or better yet, teleport?! The magic bicycle was free of tracking devices! But the Shadow Daggers would wonder what happened to him! That might lead to a more extensive investigation. And what about the time stream?! Where might teleporting take him? Right now, time-jumping was unpredictable.

Danny spun, racing out the back door. Hearing pounding footsteps behind him, he sprinted across the yard, jumped the fence, then dove into the dark woods. As he rose to his feet, he heard the creaking of the fence.

Danny bolted into the trees, weaving in between them. Leaves *crunched* and sticks *snapped* behind him, growing louder and closer. He felt hands reaching. Closing. Grasping.

Danny threw himself headlong, leaping off a stump and flying across the creek. With a gasp of surprise, the man of shadows stumbled and *splashed* into the creek.

With frantic exhilaration, Danny rushed up the embankment, then scampered up the fence. It shook as he reached the top and dropped. Hands snagged his sweatshirt, leaving him hanging.

"You're not going anywhere until you tell me the truth." Inch by inch, the man in black hauled Danny upward.

He couldn't be caught! Lives were at stake! Throwing his arms over his head, Danny slipped free of his sweatshirt and dropped to the ground.

"HEY!"

A truck rumbled down the road toward him. Danny leapt into the road, waving his hands. "Help! He's after me!"

Brakes squealed as a truck came to a stop. "What's going on?!" the young woman driver asked.

"That man!" Danny pointed. "He's trying to kill me! Take me to the sheriff, please!" Danny hopped into the back of the truck.

With squealing tires, the pickup roared away. "You did say the sheriff, right?" the woman asked through the rear window.

"Yes!"

"Are you hurt?" She was pretty with dark eyes.

"No, but somebody else is in danger. They might already be dead!"

"Hang on!" Tires squealing, the truck surged forward, racing toward town.

Despite its nearness, getting to the county office seemed to take forever. The cars they passed became sands dropping into the bottom of the hourglass. Seconds grew to minutes. A minute to hours, then eternity—worse than waiting for the end of the day for the school bell to ring. People and Comet were in danger.

The sudden stop and the squealing of brakes jerked Danny from his swirl of worries. He looked around, noticing the white and gray concrete two story building. They were here! He glanced at his watch. Twenty minutes left!

Danny hopped out of the truck. "Thanks!"

As he ran toward the steps, Danny spotted a dark blue sedan. The windows were tinted, making it impossible to see the driver. Were the Shadow Daggers already here? Waiting for him? Thinking he was made of lightning, Danny surged up the steps and burst through the door.

Ahead, a sign on the door read SHERIFF'S OFFICE. Danny looked around. Nobody wearing black waited for him. The only person in sight was a stern-looking woman in a tan uniform sitting at the admittance desk.

Unless, Danny suddenly realized, Shadow Daggers could turn themselves invisible or blend with the shadows. Maybe that's why he couldn't see the man of shadows. He could definitely feel the presence of the government agents; the sensation reminded him of being near Morgan Le Fay.

Danny hesitated. What choice did he have?

"Excuse me," Danny asked as he calmly approached the admittance desk. Well, he hoped he looked calm, instead of a boy with secrets bulging from his pockets.

"How can I help you, young man?" The woman's hard voice and the fatigue lines on her face spoke of the daily grind. Her eyes reminded Danny of his father, and what he wasn't able to tell him. If caught, his father might disown him. Maybe the Cor-ror-o'lans would adopt him. "I said, can I help you?"

"Yes, ma'am. I'm here to file a complaint. I was shot at the other day by a gang near Red Stone. Tonight the Headbangers are going after a gang member's father . . . ."

"Whoa! Slow down, young man! What's your name?"

"Daniel Chase."

She looked at her log book. "Daniel Chase. Do you live at 115 Oak Ridge?"

"Yes, ma'am." Danny asked, stammering just a bit. How did she know where he lived? The Shadow Daggers! Had they initiated a covert all-points bulletin?

"That was fast. Your mom just left."

"My mom?!" Danny stood stunned.

"Are you all right, Daniel? What's wrong?"

"Uh. Um," Danny stammered. "You see, my mom's been dead since June."

"Oh! I'm sorry. I just thought . . . ." The woman flushed, looking guilt-stricken. "A woman already filed the complaint for you. I thought you were here because Sheriff Fernandez had called you. I'm . . . Why don't you speak to Sheriff Fernandez? I'll ring him."

Danny nodded numbly and watched. What woman had been here? The ghost of his mom? Well, if anyone could do it, she could. Danny shook himself. He was tired and thinking crazily. But then, people thought the same thing about traveling time. And Shadow Daggers who could blend with the darkness and were half human and part computer. Could it have been the woman agent, Ms. Torque, who'd filed the complaint? But why would she do that?

Get a grip, Chase! Danny glanced at his watch. Seconds raced, chasing after minutes toward death. Before his heart jumped into overdrive, he tried to imitate Murg—cool, calm and collected.

The woman officer spoke on the phone. "Certainly, sir. Yes, sir."

When she was off the phone, Danny asked, "What did this woman look like?"

"Sheriff Fernandez can tell you." She ushered Danny in the door. "Third office on the left. Daniel, I'm sorry about your mom. I . . . ."

"I understand." Danny nodded and raced inside. He had to go through with this. Tell someone! Get someone to listen!

A clock on the wall read fifteen until eight. Underneath the sound of the radio dispatcher handling calls, a bustling *buzz* filled the offices. Beyond an open area full of desks with officers talking on the phones, reading files and interviewing people, a Hispanic sheriff stood in an office doorway halfway down the hall. He smiled and waved at Danny. "This way, young man. You are Daniel Chase, correct?" One dark eyebrow rose in question.

"Yes, sir." Danny looked around. Cameras peered from everywhere. Were Mr. Hawker's Shadow Daggers watching? "Come in and have a seat," Sheriff Fernandez said. He gestured inside. The upper half of the walls held glass, allowing everyone to see in all the offices. The sheriff's desk sat neatly, only a few files lay open on a writing pad. The nameplate on the desk read Thomas Castin.

Danny felt watched, gazes of ill intent resting heavily upon him. Who was this man and why was he in somebody else's office?

"Okay if I stand?" Danny asked, ready to bolt.

"Sure. Have you come to follow up on the report filed by . . ." He picked up a file, flipped it open and read, ". . . a Ms. Mayfair? She filed it for you against Reggie Tuckett and some teenagers called the Headbangers."

"Ms. Mayfair?" Danny asked, stunned again.

"Sheriff Castin is driving to the Red Stone development to confirm that it's the same place where the builder filed a complaint of bullet holes and vandalism."

"Ms. Mayfair? She came here?"

"Yes. She said your father didn't believe you about being shot at. Is that correct?" Sheriff Fernandez asked. Danny nodded. "Well, I guess Ms. Mayfair checked out your story. Said she found bullet holes in some boards.This is not our first complaint on the Headbangers. Want to tell me what happened?"

Danny stood stunned. Ms. Mayfair had believed him? Well, not exactly, he modified; but she'd checked out his story. More than his dad had done.

"It doesn't matter, Sheriff Fernandez. I'll take it from here," Major Torque said as she strode into the office. "As of this moment, this is a federal matter."

"I knew it! I knew you'd be here!" Danny cried.

FORTY

The Stand Off

"Major Torque!" Danny took a step back. His eyes darted about. Nowhere to run.

Standing in front of the only exit, the dark-haired woman's stare locked on him—locking on target. In the hall behind the Shadow Dagger, two men in dark suits watched stiffly alert.

"You may go, Sheriff Fernandez." Major Torque handed the sheriff a piece of paper. "As I said, this is now a federal matter."

"I am so glad to see you!" Danny cried. "You can help me! They're going to kill each other! I swear I heard gunfire! Can you get somebody there fast, super-stealthy, ya know?!"

Dark eyes angry, Major Torque demanded, "Sheriff Fernandez, please?" She motioned toward the open door.

The sheriff looked to Danny, who kept talking. "It might already be too late. You have to stop the Headbangers from killing Mr. Pickett!"

"Danny!" Major Torque stepped forward, seeming to grow larger and looming. "Calm down."

"The Headbangers and guns. Hmm," Sheriff Fernandez said quizzically, his interest piqued.

"Sheriff, this young man has quite an imagination . . . ."

"She thinks I . . . ." Danny couldn't say broke the law or made a mistake, because he hadn't, ". . . betrayed my country. So she doesn't believe me. Reggie Tuckett and the Headbangers. . . ."

"You are a student at Eagle Valley, correct?" the sheriff asked. Danny nodded. Sheriff Fernandez looked at Major Torque. "If this is the same gang that attacked Jimmy Chang, a student at Eagle Valley, and stole his laptop, then there's a warrant out for their arrest. If this young man can lead me to them, then we may save lives. Major Torque, you have yet to show me how this young man," the sheriff glanced at the sheet and frowned, "compromises national security."

Major Torque said nothing.

"I don't have time to explain everything," Danny blurted, "but Spike stole part of my bicycle, so I followed him home. While we were arguing, some of the Headbangers—Reggie Tuckett and a couple of other guys—showed up. They had guns and my dog!" Danny's hands pleaded.

"Your dog?" Major Torque and Sheriff Fernandez asked as one.

"Yeah! Comet! They kidnapped my dog! They were gonna shoot us when Mr. Pickett showed up. He had a shotgun, and he *hates* kids. Well," Danny finally breathed, "Mr. Pickett was furious when he learned that Spike is a member of the gang, so he smacked him with his shotgun. Spike fought back! I grabbed my bicycle seat, racing home as fast as I could. I was going to call from my house, but a man dressed in black tried to stop me, so I came here. It hasn't been very long! Help me, please! They're crazy! They have my dog!"

Sheriff Fernandez and Major Torque exchanged glances. "This I have to see," the woman said coldly, her left eyebrow raised in disdain. "Sheriff. Daniel. Follow me. I have a very fast car at my disposal. Mr. Johnson," she nodded to a square-jawed man dressed in black. "Call Mr. Zeck immediately. Send him to the woods behind the Pickett household on . . .Whippoorwill Road?" she asked Danny.

He nodded. "How did you know?" Danny asked.

"We know many things." Major Torque replied.

"Whippoorwill Road. Yes, sir." Johnson left as swiftly as a breeze.

The other lanky agent stepped close to Danny, escorting him as they walked behind Major Torque. The sheriff gave orders, then followed.

The Shadow Daggers led them through an underground garage to a black sedan parked out back. As the foursome neared, the Shadowmobile's engine started and the doors sprang open. A gangly, unnamed Shadow Dagger guided Danny into the back.

The backseat area spread wide with two leather bench seats facing each other. Above a radio and television, curtains cut in half the interior of the sedan. All the tinted windows seemed to have one way glass. The doors didn't appear to be locked; but they looked bomb-proof solid.

"You too, Sheriff Fernandez. According to Daniel Chase, time is of the essence." She waved him inside. Reluctantly, the sheriff climbed in the back, looking wonderingly at Danny.

He glanced at his watch. It was almost eight. "Hurry! Please!"

As Major Torque stepped inside, the sedan raced away. "You'd better be telling the truth, Daniel."

Danny remained silent. A glance at his watch revealed time passing as quickly as minutes on the last day of summer vacation. Danny looked outside, but in the darkness he couldn't gauge their progress. How far away were they? He glanced at his watch, again. A minute until eight! "Can we hurry, please?"

"We are of no use to ourselves or anyone else if we are injured in an accident," Major Torque said. "And we certainly don't wish to injure anyone, either." Her lips pressed together, her stare still digging at him.

Danny watched the second hand fly around the face of his watch. Seconds ripped past as though lightning. The minute hand surged toward eight o'clock. Zero hour. The second hand flashed by, running to catch up.

Danny groaned. He prayed Comet would be all right. He was just an innocent puppy.

"Something wrong, Daniel?" Sheriff Fernandez asked.

"I'm worried about Comet. I don't feel very good."

"Are you scared?" the sheriff asked. Danny nodded. "That might be making you sick."

Again, Danny nodded. He hoped against hope. Murg had said it was *about* eight o'clock. Danny had never glanced at his watch to check the exact time. There had to be at least a few minutes until the Headbangers and Mr. Pickett arrived, didn't there? Danny remembered arguing with Spike. Then the gang had arrived. How long had they confronted Mr. Pickett? Minutes? It had seemed long enough, all those guns poised to fire.

The doors sprang open. "We stopped? We're here?" Danny asked, surprised. He'd felt nothing.

A *whirring* sounded and the curtains parted. "Major Torque, Mr. Zeck is waiting."

"Thank you, Mr. Danvers. Mr. Steele, watch Daniel Chase. Come with me, sheriff." Major Torque climbed from the car. The sheriff followed, extending his hand in greeting to the dark man. He ignored it, looking to Major Torque.

"See anything, Mr. Zeck?" she asked.

"No, sir. I haven't seen anyone, except Mr. Pickett. He appears to be hunting something."

"How long ago was this?" Major Torque asked.

"Maybe two minutes."

Danny breathed a sigh of relief, then a surge of panic struck. He hadn't arrived yet. What if they went searching and he and Spike just suddenly appeared? Danny could imagine himself looking over at himself. What would happen then, two Danny Chases in one spot?

"I found one of our tracking devices on the ground," Mr. Zeck said.

"Interesting. Daniel, step outside," Major Torque told him. Danny reluctantly crawled from the cavernous back seat. Time, who could figure it? One minute it zipped by, the next it inched at a snail's pace.

"Mr. Zeck here hasn't seen anything," she asked.

Danny looked at the black man in black who before now didn't have a name. The Shadow Dagger was the closet investigator and sentinel at his house. "Did you see my dog, Comet?" Without a word, Mr. Zeck shook his head. "Any—any blood?" Danny asked, wincing. The man simply stared.

"Now that you've taken us on this wild goose chase, Daniel . . . ." Major Torque began.

"Did you see that?" Sheriff Fernandez cried.

"What did you see?"

"A bright light."

"I saw it. Heard something, too." Mr. Zeck scrutinized the moonlit woods. "And look, over there!" He pointed into the trees. Even in the full moonlight, a long beam of light played along the trunks and across the ground. "Somebody else is here."

"It could be Durlens," Danny said, sticking with his made-up story of the Cor-ror-o'lans' alien enemies.

"Mr. Danvers! Watch Daniel. Lead the way, Mr. Zeck."

"I'm coming, too!" Sheriff Fernandez stepped up to join them. Major Torque hesitated, then nodded. The three black suits slid into the shadows, followed by the stout officer in brown.

Danny watched restlessly, pacing. Again time dragged, molasses running up hill. Why did he have to wait here?

"Stop pacing," the Shadow Dagger driver said.

"I can't. I'm worried about my dog! Murg! Murg! I'm over here! I brought help." Danny waited for a reply. And waited. And waited. Discovering he held his breath, Danny finally breathed.

The moon continued to rise, the shadows shifting ever so slightly. The wind puffed, rustling the woods, but nothing else moved.

Danny strained to listen. He imagined the magic wristlet amplifying sounds. "SHOOT THE MUTT!"

"NO!" Danny bolted. He remembered this. In less than a minute, the shooting and killing would start.

Before he could take three steps, the Shadow Dagger driver grabbed Danny. Imagining he was coated with ice, Danny twisted and turned, slipping free and sprinting away.

"HEY! Hey! Come back here!"

"They want to shoot my dog!" Danny kept running, full speed ahead.

An anguished cry cut the night. Was that Spike?

Danny hopped over a fallen log, then raced headlong through flickering shadows and swaths of silvery light. Less than a minute. Faster! Run faster! As though running an obstacle course, he bounded, bobbed and weaved through the woods. He wished he could just teleport; but he didn't dare.

How far was it? Danny saw light ahead. He hoped he'd turned invisible by now. He should've. He didn't really want to see himself coming and going.

A dog barked, then its voice suddenly cut short. Comet! "Don't hurt my dog!" Danny yelled.

"You're part of a gang, are you, Ernest?" Mr. Pickett asked. "Not a smart idea! You're part of the Pickett family now." Danny remembered Ike Pickett striking at Spike with the rifle's stock. Spike would catch it, and they'd struggle. Danny tried to put on a burst of speed. Ahead, shadows moved. Halogen beams splayed through the trees.

"No more, do you hear?! No more!" Spike cried.

"That a way, Spike!" Page yelled.

A shot fired, echoing through the night.

"I said, drop the guns!" Danny didn't recognize the voice. The sheriff?

"Murg?!"

"Welcome back."

Danny rushed to the light, sliding to a stop just before being grabbed by Major Torque.

"Easy, Daniel! This is a dangerous place." She held a revolver that glinted strangely. At a second glance, it didn't look right, less pistol and more of a flowing metal sculpture.

"Murg! Krindee! Wherever you are, be careful. The Shadow Daggers are here."

"No worries. We'll stay in the shadows. Comet is with us and doing just fine—for a dog anyway."

Sheriff Fernandez stood near a tree, ready to seek cover, and yet also ready to fight. A white fist held his still-smoking .38.

"I think you're a little outnumbered, man," Reggie laughed. He held his gun tight, knuckles white, and steady, trained on Sheriff Fernandez. Vargas also aimed at the sheriff, but Page and the others still faced Mr. Pickett.

"I repeat, drop your weapons," the sheriff demanded. Reggie laughed.

"Go away, sheriff!" Ike Pickett yelled. "This is a private matter!"

Danny and Spike exchanged glances. Having seen Danny leave just moments ago, Spike appeared confused and angry.

"Hey, Chase! Who's the babe?" Reggie asked. "Slick. Is she one of those Feds watching you? Wee-who! She can watch me anytime!" Reggie grabbed his crotch.

Major Torque bristled. Her finger tightened on the trigger.

"You are under arrest . . . ." the sheriff began.

"You are history, man," Reggie snapped. His finger tightened.

Ike Pickett's knuckles whitened.

Holding the strange looking guns in each hand, Mr. Zeck and Mr. Steele stepped from the shadows.

"I believe," Major Torque announced, "that the numbers have evened just a bit."

Reggie suddenly trained his gun on Spike. "Make a move, and Ernest Blocker is a dead boy!"

Spike's eyes widened, then his expression grew grim, his gaze flattening like that of a snake's. "Now I see how Headbangers stick together!"

"Thank you, boy! You can make my life easier with just a squeeze," Ike said.

"R-Reggie," Page stammered. His eyes were wild.

"Shut up!" Reggie's trigger finger twitched.

Danny wondered if he could extend his force field to protect Spike. Protect Spike! What was he thinking?! The future Spike was going to kill him! But he couldn't let these people shoot each other! What else could he do? Plug the gun? Then it would explode in Reggie's face.

"I want you to drop your weapons!" Reggie commanded. "Then get on outta here. You're breathing my air."

Air? Danny thought. That gave him an idea. Closing his eyes, he formed the force field. As a thin tendril of thought energy, it invisibly snaked down Danny's body, then across the ground, heading for Reggie. The field reached Reggie's feet, then slowly oozed up his body. •

Reggie brushed at himself, then snapped alert, re-aiming his gun at Spike, who'd moved. "Now don't get any stupid ideas. Hey! I don't see anyone dropping their guns! Drop them now!" Reggie scratched at his chest. The force field continued to rise, becoming a globe encircling Reggie's head. With a thought, Danny solidified the field, making it air tight.

"Son, we can work this out," Sheriff Fernandez said. Major Torque stood next to him now, her stare burning towards Reggie Tuckett.

"Sure we can, if you drop your guns and leave!" Reggie's voice sounded muffled. He tugged at his collar.

"There's no where to run!" Ike said. "Put up or shut up."

Reggie laughed, then choked before saying, "Sure t-there is. T-Texas is a big place."

Danny watched carefully. Reggie's eyes didn't look quite right. Reggie began to speak, then blinked. Suddenly, his eyes rolled back, then he collapsed, passed out. Danny dismissed the thought, so the force field faded.

Page and Vargas jerked as if shocked, their hair standing straight up, then they crumpled to the ground. The smell of ozone drifted through the woods.

"Drop the guns! Put your hands on your head!" Mr. Zeck yelled, his gun leveled at the other Headbangers.

"Do what he says!" the sheriff yelled. The new Headbangers dropped their guns as if they were red hot, then placed their hands atop their heads.

"What's going on?!" the sheriff rushed in, kneeling next to Page. He checked for a pulse. "Shocked? Did you use tazers?" He moved to Vargas, then Reggie

"The boys will be fine, Sheriff, if a bit disoriented when they awaken," Major Torque replied. "They will suffer no permanent damage. Good shooting, Mr. Zeck. Mr. Steele."

Danny was stunned. He hadn't seen anyone shoot. Or heard anything either.

"Just following your example, sir," Mr. Zeck stepped in to retrieve the dropped weapons.

Major Torque appeared puzzled. "I never fired at the Tuckett boy."

"You didn't, then . . . ."

"I don't know what you did, honey, but I like that trick!" Ike Pickett grabbed Spike by the ear and twisted. "Now, you explain this, boy!"

"Mr. Pickett, I'd advise you to let go of the boy," Major Torque said, her tone flat.

"Butt out, honey. This is family business. I know how to discipline my boy."

"I will question him. We will learn what transpired." Her shoulders were squared and her jaw tight as she steeled herself.

"And you'd better not lie again." Mr. Pickett cuffed Spike, then shoved him toward Major Torque. With a cry, Spike collapsed, obviously exhausted. Mr. Pickett moved closer, hand raised to strike. "You hear me, boy!"

Danny was sure he saw Major Torque pull the trigger, but whatever happened was soundless. Mr. Pickett suddenly jumped, his eyes wide. As his hair stood on end, he dropped his gun, then jerked about as though a crazed puppet. He finally collapsed, twitching now and then.

"You make me ill, Mr. Pickett," Major Torque said coldly as she looked down on the big man. "Sheriff Fernandez, where are your men?"

"They should be here any minute," he replied.

A black blur suddenly slammed into Danny. Wet, sloppy kisses covered him. "Comet! You're all right, boy!" Danny hugged him. "Murg! Thank you for rescuing Comet."

"As I said, in the shadows, we don't want to make a scene. And you are welcome. If not predictable, cats are certainly dependable."

"Thanks, Murg, you are the best!"

In the shadow of the woods, the calico simply nodded.

Spike looked around, taking it all in. After a moment, he walked over to Danny. "You know, Chase, you're not such a wimp after all. In fact, you're pretty damn tough. And while we'll never be buds, if you ever need my help, you can count on me." Spike leaned close. Danny tensed as the bully whispered, "And I promise not to kill you."

"Thanks, Spike. Just keep riding your imagination." Danny shook Spike's hand. The wristlet suddenly felt warm. "Hey, was that a pulse?"

"What did you say?" Murg asked.

"I get the impression Kalyde II is . . . happy?"

"Really?"

"Could it have been helping Spike all along? You know, helping him use its magic?"

"That is possible, I guess."

"Maybe the star metal is sentient! Who'd ever believe this?"

"I would," Krindee projected, still hiding in the woods. "I believe I have plenty of amazing discoveries to tell the Cor-ror-o'lan elder council. Danny, I must go."

"Slip silently away while the slipping is good?"

"Yes, but I will be back soon. Your actions speak a convincing argument, and I must pass them on. Thank you so much, my friend. Keep being the best you can be. Farewell. It's been fun and educational!" The disguised Cor-ror-o'lan disappeared into the dark woods.

FORTY-ONE

Helping Hands

After the deputies arrived, taking the groggy Headbangers and angry Ike Pickett into custody, the Shadow Daggers whisked Danny and Comet into the black sedan. Just before Danny left, he heard Sheriff Fernandez promise to look into Spike's claims of parental abuse.

"Where are we going?" Danny asked.

"To a more private place where you can be questioned." Major Torque sat flanked by Mr. Zeck and Mr. Steele, similarly clad bookends of ebony and ivory.

"About what?" Danny asked.

"The Durlens. Mr. Zeck told me you saw one." Her stare cut as a scalpel.

"I just said that so I could distract him," Danny replied. Mr. Zeck stared straight ahead as if an android. "He didn't believe me, and he wasn't going to help me, so I had to do something! Comet's life was at stake!" Danny stroked the dog. "He didn't believe me then, so why would you believe me now?"

"I don't know what to believe, Daniel." Her tone was flat.

"I told you the truth about the Headbangers, Mr. Pickett and Spike."

"Yes, you did. But there is a matter of the silent homing devices."

"Homing devices?" Danny asked, acting surprised. It was important to Earth and Cor-ror-o'lan that the Shadow Daggers learn nothing of Kri-neee-dee. "You mean you were tracking me? Then you *know* I followed Spike after school? He gave me the slip at first, but I caught up with him north of here along one of the farm roads."

"Yes, that is where we lost the signal for nearly three hours and when the signal returned, it had moved. How do you explain that?"

"Three hours passed? I can't stand still?" Danny shrugged. "I'm not good at math or with electronics." Danny sighed. "Did you track me by satellite?"

"No, but I wish we had. There is something you're not telling me."

"Well, why don't you use one of your superduper truth verifying machines, sort of like the device you use to identify aliens?" Danny asked.

"Because they are not wholly reliable as of yet," she replied. "My instincts are better. I still don't understand why Reggie Tuckett collapsed."

"Well, if I'd had one of those things, I would've zapped Reggie," Danny told her. Comet barked in agreement.

Major Torque appeared annoyed, the left corner of her thin lips twitching.

"Are these agents," Danny motioned to the Shadow Daggers in the car, "robots, androids, or cyborgs? You know, half-human and half-machine."

"I have read *The Alien Bicycle*. It makes for very interesting reading."

"Just interesting?" Danny deflated. "I guess I need to keep practicing. What was wrong with it?"

"Wrong with it?"

A rear door opened. Again Danny hadn't felt the sedan stop.

Mr. Danvers stood stiffly at the curb. Behind the Shadow Dagger driver waited two people—Ms. Mayfair and Captain Chase.

"Dad!" Danny jumped out of the car and into a hug.

"Son! I'm so glad to see you! Please, please don't scare us like that." Captain Chase squeezed Danny tightly. "Are you in trouble again?"

"I don't think so," Danny replied with wishful thinking.

"Major Torque, what's going on?" Captain Chase asked. "Why's Danny in your custody?"

"He came to us seeking help," Major Torque said, then explained about Spike, Ike and the Headbangers.

Danny reached out to Ms. Mayfair. The lovely blond-haired lady smiled and took his hand. "Thanks for believing in me. Otherwise, Comet might be dead."

"You're very welcome, Danny. Friends help each other. We are friends, aren't we?"

"I'll give it a shot," Danny replied.

"But there are still things left unexplained," Major Torque continued. "Like the silent homing devices . . . ."

"You bugged my son?" Captain Chase asked.

"It's a matter of national security."

"Is my house bugged?" his father asked.

Danny froze. He hadn't thought of that?! I am an idiot! But . . . if they weren't bugged before they might be bugged now. He had to be really, really careful.

"That's a matter of national security."

Danny's father did not appear pleased. Danny could feel a storm building.

"Have you given any thought to the simplest answer, that your bugs malfunctioned?" Captain Chase asked, an edge to his voice.

"We are checking into it," Major Torque replied coolly.

"And you'll let me know?" Danny's father asked. "No, wait, don't tell me, it's a matter of national security."

Major Torque frowned. As Mr. Zeck returned from the Chase's front porch, he said, "I have it, sir."

"Does it appear damaged?" Captain Chase asked.

Mr. Zeck said nothing as he climbed into the black sedan.

"Do you have any further questions you haven't asked Danny?" Captain Chase asked.

"No, but we may."

"Then I believe that'll give me my answer about your homing devices, won't it? Come on, Danny." His father guided him toward the house. "Let's go inside. Good night, Major Torque."

"Good night, Captain Chase. Be wary. Your son is smarter than you think."

"In some ways, he takes after his mother," Danny's father replied.

As they strolled toward the house, Danny asked, "Is my bicycle okay? Did they do anything to it?"

"Let's take it inside and see," Ms. Mayfair suggested.

Murg lay on the porch, her eyes closed.

"Well, I see Murg is excited—as always—to see you," Danny's father nodded to the calico.

Murg didn't move, comfortably sprawled. "Danny didn't run all the way home and damage the tracking device attached to your old bicycle."

"You are the best, Murg," Danny thought back.

"Certainly. I am a cat, therefore created that way."

"What about Krindee?"

"She returned to report to the elder council. She said she'll come back once the uproar has diminished. Before you look sad, she left me with two quotes. 'A friend may well be reckoned the masterpiece of nature.' Emerson. 'Friendships multiply joys and divide grief.' Fuller."

Danny smiled, then sighed. "I'll miss her."

"She'll be back. This would have all been easier if you'd just re-written *The Alien Bicycle*."

"In a way, I did. But if I'd done as you suggested, Spike would still be a pain in the butt. And he may still be, I guess." Danny sighed. "At least Dad is getting better. Maybe one day I can tell him about the magic bicycle."

"When he's retired, maybe. Time will tell."

FORTY-TWO

Secret Trust

On a surprisingly beautiful and unusually pleasant winter day, Danny rode into Christina's driveway and eased to a stop. Murg sat apparently asleep, basking in the warm sunshine atop her palanquin on the back of the magic tandem.

"Are you sure you want to do this?" Murg asked.

"Yes," Danny thought back as he climbed off the bicycle. "Since Spike knows, Christina and Jason should know about Kalyde II. I want to be honest with them. What if the secret gets out, and they learn that Spike knew but they didn't? That would be horrible. I trust Christina and Jason. Along with you, Kalyde, Krindee and Gretchen, they're my best friends."

"Quite a list you've compiled."

Danny smiled. "We survived Gretchen and Spike knowing. How could it be any worse?" Danny set the kickstand.

Murg stretched full-feline, claws extended. "Don't even think about it, let alone imagine it," the calico replied. "Now get to it before you chicken out."

"This is worse than walking through the haunted house," Danny thought as he approached the door of the river stone house. Danny's palms perspired. His stomach shifted unsteadily. After a deep breath, he pressed the doorbell.

A minute later, the door opened. "Oh, hi Danny," Christina said, looking put out. "To what do I owe this honor?"

Had she missed him? He'd missed her. "An explanation of things," Danny replied.

"Hmmm." She appeared skeptical, blue eyes distrusting. One hand toyed with her blond locks.

"Mysteries and secrets to be revealed!" Danny announced.

"Really? Such as?"

"To really, really understand, you need to come riding with me," Danny replied.

"Hmmm. I don't know. I have . . . ."

"I promise you won't be disappointed. We'll have fun!"

"All right but don't let me down, again. You've pressed your luck twice. The third time is not a charm."

"You are in lots of trouble," Murg projected. Danny pretended not to notice.

"I'll be right back. I need to grab my sunglasses and jacket and tell my mom." With a growing smile, Christina closed the door.

Danny returned to Kalyde II. "She's coming along for the ride."

"Of her life."

After a few minutes, Christina bounded down the sidewalk. She wore an Eagle Valley jacket, her braid hanging over one shoulder. "Good! You left me the front seat. Thank you. Hello, Murg. You look quite content." She stroked the calico, then climbed onto the tandem. "Where to?" she asked as Danny pushed off.

"If you could go anywhere in the world, where would you go?" Danny asked.

"This time of the year, HAWAII!"

Hawaii made Danny think of his friend Happy; he had drowned and chosen not to be saved during Danny and Murg's first time-traveling adventures. Danny felt mixed emotions of profound sadness and calm joy. Happy had accepted things— accepted dying because he'd saved somebody. Heroic, but sad in Danny's eyes. It would be nice to add another pleasant moment to his Hawaiian memories, show a friend where his best friend had reveled in life.

"Hawaii's warm and balmy. I could sprawl on the beach." Christina threw her arms out. "Stare out over the water. Listen to the waves. Sketch some landscapes. Draw some fish. Eat some fish!" She hugged herself. "Ah, I get warm just thinking about it, although it's nice out today. I'd love to see something besides school, cars, houses and fields." She sighed. "But, that's wishful thinking. I thought you were going to explain things to me, great mysteries and secrets so dark and deep you'd have to kill me, if we weren't friends, of course."

"Do you remember my story, *The Alien Bicycle?*" Danny asked.

"Of course! It's one of my favorite stories. I wish you had an alien bicycle, then you could take me to Hawaii like you did Heidi in the story!" She cocked her head. "Is the Heidi character Gretchen?"

"Yes." Danny smiled. "Murg, where would you like to go?"

The calico yawned. "Hawaii is fine. I love fresh fish. Mahi-mahi is smooth tasting and has fewer bones than many fish."

"Hawaii it is!" Danny laughed as they left the neighborhood.

"Danny, what's going on?"

"A lot, let me start at the beginning," Danny said. "To start with, *The Alien Bicycle* is based on a true story."

"A true story! Danny you need help!" Christina cried.

"Wait, hear me out!"

"Danny, you're delusional. You need help."

"I'm . . . ."

"Take me home! Take me home now!"

"Christina, calm down, you're acting like a five-year-old."

"Danny . . ."

"I didn't say anything!" Danny replied.

"You . . . Danny. . . ." Christina whirled, a finger pointed at Danny.

"Please listen to the boy," Murg said. The calico clung to Danny's back, leaning over his shoulder. "Your friendship means a lot to him." Danny nodded.

"M-Murg?! MURG CAN TALK?!"

Danny nodded again. While Christina sat stunned, Danny turned at a light and raced along a frontage road. For a Saturday morning, few cars cruised the highway.

Danny focused on Hawaii. He'd lived there, so he easily pictured Surfer's Beach. Happy had taught him to surf along a stretch of white sand nestled among the palm trees, gray rocks and black coral. When the green waters lay calm, he could hear the highway but not see it. Usually the waves roared into the rocks, clashing, splashing and throwing water high into the air. A set of rocks formed a blow hole. On windy days or before a storm, water shot high as though from the back of a whale.

"D-Danny we're going very fast! Danny? D-Danny, slow down, you're scaring me. We can't be going this fast."

Fence posts rushed together. Telephones poles flipped past. Green and brown blurred as the white center stripe flickered, threatening to become one long line.

"You're safe, Christina," Danny told her. "Think how fast we are going."

She closed her eyes. "I don't want to!"

Danny gently smiled. "Think about *The Alien Bicycle.*"

A bright flash erupted, bleaching everything white. The sound of a thousand lions roaring swallowed Christina's scream. They blasted through the mists to emerge gliding across the rainbow highway. Brilliant colors as though inlaid gemstones catching the sun stretched below, far above the earth. In the dark sky, the stars twinkled mischievously as if knowing something secret.

"Danny, this is . . . is amazing! Incredible! It's feels so . . . I can't describe it." Christina twisted around to look at him, her blue eyes aglow.

"You feel free?"

"Yes! I'm soaring! *The Alien Bicycle* is real, isn't it? Really real?!"

"As Danny was trying to tell you." Murg stood proud, the wind ruffling her halloween-patched fur.

"And you can talk! So this tandem is Kalyde II, from Kahlaye-dee! It's made of star metal. So incredibly cool!"

Another sunburst carried them atop the water. For a moment, Danny couldn't see anything. Night still reigned over the Pacific, the waning moon cast a faint golden light across the ocean. Kalyde II rolled from swell to swell, heading toward the pale predawn light along the horizon.

"Danny, I think I understand things a little better now. You didn't tell me because of Gretchen letting your secret slip, right? You're afraid I might do the same thing?" Christina asked.

Danny nodded. "Funny how a change in perspective—like riding across water, which I'd thought was impossible—can make things clear." She looked around, eyes wide. "Are we going to fly?!"

"Of course!"

"Danny, I promise I won't ever betray your secret. No matter what happens! Say, have you told Jason, yet?"

"I wanted to tell you first."

Christina hugged him, then kissed Danny on the cheek. "Wonderful! I can tease him about being the last to know! He'll be upset, until you take him riding. But why have you been so busy, have you just been riding around?" She frowned, thoughtful.

"Oh, does he have a story to tell," Murg said. With one eye warily watching the water for fish, the calico sat, paws tucked underneath.

"And it happened several times," Danny said. "It took a

while for me to get things right, ending up with Spike and his family seeing a counselor and you riding the magic bicycle with me. I think Spike and I swapped sneakers for a while."

Christina appeared confused.

"Well, you see, it all started when Spike and the Headbangers were chasing Jason and me . . . ."

EXCITING SELECTIONS FROM: THE MAGIC BICYCLE

First Ride

As the bicycle raced faster and faster, the world around them blurred into a whirlwind of colors. Denny felt lighter and was sure the bicycle had lost contact with the road. But he still felt safe.

A roaring sound like a thousand charging lions was followed by a tremendous clap of thunder. Bright, almost blinding, sparks surrounded them, then the world went white for a moment, then turned into a hazy grayness as if they were riding through engulfing clouds. Danny suddenly noticed it was quiet. Where was the sound of the wind.

Clouds parted. They were riding atop a gleaming rainbow. Below were brilliant streaks of red, orange, yellow, green and blue. Forming walls along each side of them was an electric purple. It was so bright that when Danny looked at himself, everything he wore, even his skin, glowed brilliant violet.

Murg meowed loud and long. Danny looked over his shoulder. The calico was standing on his shoulder staring skyward. Danny followed Murg's gaze and found sparkling stars in the darkness above. They were riding across the sky to South Carolina!!

The world suddenly went white, then flashed brightly as if they rode directly into a star. The lions roared once more and the thunder cracked as if a giant hole was being ripped in the sky. Danny was disoriented for a moment, then he realized they had done it! In less than a minute, they had ridden from Texas to the east coast near Myrtle Beach, South Carolina.

Alien Encounter

Danny tumbled head over heels as he crashed down the stairs, each step biting into him as he bounced. He covered his head as best he could and hoped he survived. His feet rebounded off the bannister and sent him cartwheeling over the edge of the stairway.

Danny landed on an old tattered mattress that cushioned his impact. Something warm brushed against him leg. "I'll live, Murg," Danny groaned. He opened his eyes and was shocked to be staring at himself. Crimson and azure light flashed through the boarded windows of the basement and splayed about the room, illuminating his double.

Jumping to his feet to flee, Danny conked his head on the edge of the steps. Stars seemed to fill his vision, falling across his double's face. Its expression had changed from imitating his surprise to capturing his pain. "Who . . . what are you?" Danny whispered.

Words sounded inside Danny's head, "Greetings, I am Kah-laye-dee, a stranger to your planet." Danny was amazed. Not a word had touched his ears and the alien's lips had never moved.

Danny watched slack-jawed as the wondrous transformation took place before his eyes. His double's features changed, no longer mimicking Danny. The shapeshifter's form shrunk, becoming thinner, although its head stayed the same size. Its flaming red curls disappeared, now replaced by short blue hair that stood straight up, reminding Danny of a classmate. Its skin had lost its fleshy color and now gleamed with a bronzed hue. The stranger's nose had lengthened, flattened and spread wide. Its - or maybe - his eyes were still blue, but now glowed from deep within the tall, recessed sockets of his elongated face. Thin lips curled as the skinny being smiled, then reached out to touch him.

THE VAMPIRE HUNTERS

Excerpts

The Initiation

"Ahhh.." the barn door opened slowly, allowing a faint light to be cast across the barn yard. Scooter jumped at least a foot and almost screamed, barely managing to swallow.

Chandler's shadow was crisp, his form distinctly outlined against the light. With a bottle in each hand, he stepped outside and began to guzzle from one bottle, then the other.

Shakily raising the camera, Scooter tried to get a good look at Marcus Chandler. Even the darkness couldn't totally conceal his pale complexion. It seemed to have a gleaming quality that reminded Scooter of the house's eerie luminescence.

Scooter took a breath, crossed his fingers, then jumped in front of the author. With quivering hands, he snapped picture after picture, the flash illuminating the night as though flickering lightning.

"AWWW!" Chandler screamed. He dropped the bottles, clenching his empty hands. In the flashing white light, Scooter could see Chandler's gaunt face. It had been transformed into something horrible, contorted and twisted as if he were in sheer agony. His flesh appeared to take on an unholy illumination. His eyes were amazingly bright, blazing embers within black holes.

Chandler suddenly stepped forward and swung at Scooter, who stumbled backwards to avoid the blow. Almost dropping the camera, Scooter turned and ran toward the Armadillos. The pale man blindly pursued.

Kristie and Paul looked at each other, their thoughts the same: Run! Straining at his collar, Flash barked. As Scooter raced past them, not even pausing as he tossed Kelly the camera, the golden Lab jerked free and joined his friend in flight. Paul and Kristie bolted together, following in Scooter's wake.

"The bicycles. . ." Bobby Joe said. Holding their bats, the brothers fled. TJ was just a few slower steps behind.

Kelly looked at the camera, then at Chandler. As Kelly watched the author stumble through the grass, unerringly heading toward them as if he were guided by radar, he felt Racquel's fingers digging into his arm.

Kelly's sneer was fleeting. His expression slowly becoming doubtful. He wasn't afraid of anything. . .unless this guy was really a vampire. Come on Racquel, Kelly breathed, scared for the first time in a long time. As Chandler hurdled the fence, Kelly grabbed Racquel and ran, pretending he had wings.

"Please! So help me, I'll never do this again!" Paul gasped as he ran, holding his arms in front of his face for protection from the ripping branches. He could barely see Scooter and Flash ahead of him, darting in and out of the trees with surprising agility.

Despite his awkwardness, nobody could outrun the Scooter. He would get to the bicycles first. But what about the rest of them? The slowest one was always caught first. At least TJ was with them: he was the slowest. Paul was mortified by his cowardly thought, but he ran as if slavering Dobermans were hot on his heels.

Huffing and grunting, TJ ran as fast as he could, rumbling through the woods. He wanted to be far away from here. TJ liked to believe he was like his brothers, a tough hombre. But now, all he wanted was to cruise the backyards on his Harley, the wind in his face blowing away the fear and sweat. He suddenly felt something grab at his feet, and he stumbled. Unable to recover, TJ was struck by something as he fell forward into the darkness.

CALIFORNIA GHOSTING
Selection from Chapter One
"Ghostly Hitchhikers:

Blasing didn't respond. He recognized when simply saying anything could provoke a confrontation. Blasing saw something out of the corner of his eye. "LOOK OUT!"

Angela looked back to the road and slammed on the brakes. An old man and his mule were in the road! Angela cringed, awaiting the bone-crushing thump and the sight of bodies flying.

Instead, the pack animal and its master passed through the hood, then the windshield. The ethereal prospector smiled a toothless grin and doffed his dusty cap as he sliced through the interior of the 4-Runner. The ghostly mule was less accepting, its eyes wide with panic. Suddenly, the rank smells of old sweat, dust and unwashed mule overwhelmed them.

After the 4-Runner squealed to a stop, Blasing whirled around, eyes popping wide. "What the hell was that?" He pointed at the grayed and somewhat translucent miner dressed in worn clothing. As if desert mirages, distorted background shapes could be seen through the spirit. The ghost was obviously angry, cursing and tugging on his mule's bit, trying to convince it to move. The pale beast was amazingly overloaded with transparent boxes and bags bound together as if caught in a large spider's web.

"Is that a ghost?" Blasing whispered incredulously. "Ms. Starborne, I . . . ." His lips worked silently.

Angela watched Blasing struggle with the concept of wandering spirits, his handsome face a mast of stunned confusion and his eyes unsettled. He ran a hand through his hair, then his dark gaze met her unwavering stare; he seemed to have composed himself quickly. "I don't believe in ghosts." He didn't sound convinced.

"You will," Angela said cryptically, no longer looking at

Blasing but feeling the weight of his stare. "Maybe he's . . . wandered away." According to Peter, this wasn't supposed to happen.

"Wandered away? From where?"

"I'll ask," Angela said, trying to sound casual as she began rolling down her window. Her heart was pounding, her palms were damp, and the urge for a cigarette was strong.

"Isn't that dangerous?" Blasing asked. The near accident was not a big deal, but she was acting as if this were an ordinary, everyday experience.

"It might be."

The ghost spat, wiped his mouth "Lillybell! Dang it ya floppy-eared varmint. If I had my stick ya wouldn't be actin' like this!" The mule appeared offended, setting its ears back in preparation for the forthcoming struggle.

Angela cleared her throat, starting to speak, but was stopped by the ghostly prospector. "This is your fault, purdy lady. Why I oughtta . . . ." He began stalking toward the car.

The mule snorted, then nosed its master, almost knocking him off his feet. The miner staggered, then whirled quickly, yanking off his hat and slapping his unruly companion. "Think you're cute, do ya?" Lillybell bared her teeth, then began hee-hawing and rocking back and forth. Madder than a hornet, the prospector threw down his hat and began hopping back and forth.

"You know, I've never heard of a ghost being this far away from the resort," Angela said tightly. Then she realized she'd let important information slip.

"You mean the Ghostal Shores Resort really is haunted?" Blasing asked. "Not just a gimmick like Disneyland?"

"This makes no sense at all" Angela continued uneasily, trying to ignore Blasing's hot stare. "Spirits are supposed to be tied to a person or a place, not wandering around looking for food and lodging."

"Ghostly hitchhikers. Right."

"Believe it," Angela replied.

WIZARD SWORD
COMING SOON—EXCERPTS

Brin took a deep breath, then grabbed the knob just as the burning house erupted, exploding the door into millions of fiery shards. The deafening blast jerked him off his feet, hurling him across the ice-crusted and snow-covered courtyard.He landed in a twisted heap next to a frozen fountain.

Brin tried to scream but was breathless. He felt shredded, every inch of his body painfully raw. I'm about to die, Brin thought with surprising clarity.The snow's embrace eased his pains a little, making it easy for himto slide deep into quiet unconsciousness.

A brightness flared. "BRIN, FIGHT TO LIVE!"

Whatever—whoever—seized him, dragging him back to consciousness. Pain surged over him as he gasped for breath. The sharp air embedded burning needles deeper and deeper into his body. He tried to recall something—anything.Who. . . who was he? Brin . . .who?

A quick glance revealed why he remembered so little. He appeared to have been mauled by a hoard of fiery tigers. His clothing and skin were blackened, burned, and shredded.

Why had . . . guardian spirit brought him back to this?

A low moan came from Brin's right. A badly injured man lay buried in a nearby snowdrift. Noticing the skinny young man's red-streaked aura, Brin knew he wasn't dead, yet; but he would be soon if he didn't received a healer's attention.

Jumbled memories sprang free. Thom? Lane? Juliana? What had happened to them?

"I must've been ambushed!" Brin reached for the sword, finding neither Mageblade, nor its scabbard. Had he dropped his sword? Where? If there'd been an ambush, his family and friends needed him! Fighting through the agony, the stabbing blades and searing knives, Brin struggled to his feet. Halfway to standing, he gasped, then crumpled to his knees.

Angry black clouds rolled in to cast an all-consuming shadow. The bustling alpine meadow grew quiet, then dead calm. Not a whisper stirred the lush glades.The rabbits, woodland mice, and big-eared mountain *coyitts* quivered as they cowed beneath teal-leaved bushes.

The storm's chilling air slunk forward, creeping into the Palisadian Mountains. Mule deer stood frozen for a moment, then fled, bounding across the slopes. Flying squirrels darted to hide high among the *everblues and bluspens*, their azure leaves sagged as if ill. Johnny jump-ups and dragon-tongues, just moments ago looking vibrant, shrunk back, their red and gold petals wilting.

A lone, hungry howl interrupted the strained silence, rushing through the valleys and racing up toward the towering peaks. Before the lone canine wail died, other hounds joined the hunting call.

The baying grew louder as the pack drew closer to the meadow. Just outside the clearing a burst of fire gushed skyward, singeing branches and leaves. A second, then a half dozen, gouts of flame shot through the woods. A tall stand of oak trees caught fire, screaming silently as they desperately fought to shed their leaves and limbs.

A pulsing tongue of fire clearing their way, the hellhounds suddenly burst into the meadow, chains clanking and clanging. Long tendrils of flame gushed from the Dydokk'ns twisted maws, streaming over spiked collars and streaking along chains and blackened flesh to become fiery comet tails. Awkwardly long legs, hurtled them faster and faster, long claws ripping up the ground. Crimson eyes never deviated, staring somewhere far ahead where the hunting pack senses their prey.

Six beasts disappeared into the woods again, their baying grew defiant.

In the hellhounds' wake, snatches of flame banded

together. The fires raced along the grass and jumped from *bluspen* to *everblue*, creating gigantic torches guttering in the sudden winds.

Moments later, a sextet of dark knights cantered their black stallions into the burning meadow. Each warrior wore a red tobard adorned with the symbol of an ebony sword. Their great black helms and faceplates covered their heads entirely, making them appear faceless. In the lead rode two tall men— a pale, withered wizard in blood-splattered robes adorned with bleached skulls and a black dragon-helmed lord locked in armor covered by spiked greaves.

"Silent screams. Music to soothe the savage beast," the dark knight mused, his baritone voice echoing from the dragon helm as though from the belly of the beast. The master of the hunt motioned to the others to stop, then reigned in his iron stallion. With a dying hiss, the dark stallion slowed to statue stillness. Steam chuffed from its nostrils, adding to the smoky haze. "That's good, Steelwind." When the dark knight patted his beast, his gauntlet rang metal on metal.

A low moaning arose eerily to drown out the echo.

OTTER CREEK PRESS, INC.
3154 NAUTILUS ROAD
MIDDLEBURG, FL 32068-6607

TELEPHONE: (904) 264-0465
TOLL FREE: (800) 378-8163
Email: otterpress@aol.com
http//:www.otterpress.com
www. fantasyhill.com

YOU MAY ORDER

Retail price: $14.95 (U.S.); $18.95 (Canada)SC
Retail price: $22.95 (U.S.); $26.95 (Canada) HC

Please include $4.00 per copy for tax, shipping & handling

Copies: _____   Amount Enclosed _____

Name of Book _____

Name _____

Address _____

City_____State_____Zip_____

Otter Creek Press, Inc., accepts money orders and checks.

ABOUT THE AUTHOR

William Hill is a native of Indianapolis, Indiana and learned to read first through comic books, then adventure and science fiction novels. As a youth, "Bill" spent many late weekend night's watching Nightmare Theater and Science Fiction Theater.

Although not a military brat like Danny Chase of *The Magic Bicycle*, Bill has lived in Kansas City, Nashville and Bristol, TN—setting of *Dawn of the Vampire*, and Texas—setting of *Vampire's Kiss* and The *Vampire Hunters*. Bill has "serious" degrees from Vanderbilt University in economics and an MBA from the University of North Texas. He thinks a good education fuels imagination and creativity.

Since realizing that writing was his best talent and a gift, Bill escaped the drudgery of the corporate world to craft his tales. Bill has been *employed* as an "alchemist" in South Lake Tahoe and a ski patroller at a North Lake Tahoe resort.

Although his first writing love is magic-oriented fantasy, Hill's first and second novels—*Dawn of the Vampire and Vampire's Kiss*—are supernatural thrillers. *The Magic Bicycle* , Chasing Time—The Magic Bicycle 2, and *The Vampire Hunters* are crafted for young adults. *The Vampire Hunters* was inspired by bicycling along, boating on, and spending creepy and stormy nights along the shores of Cedar Creek Lake, Texas.

Bill, his new son—Brin—and his lovely and supportive wife, Kat, currently reside in Lake Tahoe. Bill intends to write imaginative fiction and fantasy until dirt is shoveled upon his coffin.